PENGUIN BOOKS

SHADOW PLAY

Shashi Deshpande is the author of nine novels, and several short stories, which have been included in various collections and anthologies. She has also written numerous essays, some of which have been included in anthologies such as *Writings from the Margin* and *Subversion*. She has recently written her memoir *Listen to Me*.

Her novel *That Long Silence* received the Sahitya Akademi Award in 1990. Deshpande received the Padma Shri in 2009.

Shadow Play

Shashi
Deshpande

PENGUIN BOOKS
An imprint of Penguin Random House

PENGUIN BOOKS

USA | Canada | UK | Ireland | Australia
New Zealand | India | South Africa | China | Singapore

Penguin Books is part of the Penguin Random House group of companies whose addresses can be found at global.penguinrandomhouse.com

Published by Penguin Random House India Pvt. Ltd
4th Floor, Capital Tower 1, MG Road,
Gurugram 122 002, Haryana, India

Penguin Random House India

First published by Aleph Book Company 2013
Published in Penguin Books by Penguin Random House India 2024

10 9 8 7 6 5 4 3 2 1

This is a work of fiction. Names, characters, places and incidents are either the product of the author's imagination or are used fictitiously, and any resemblance to any actual person, living or dead, events or locales is entirely coincidental.

ISBN 9780143463986

Typeset by Digiultrabooks Pvt. Ltd

www.penguin.co.in

The Wedding

'Here is Sita, my daughter,
She will walk the path of Dharma with you,
Accept her, she is auspicious,
Take her hand in yours.'

—King Janaka to Shri Rama in the *Ramayana*

Traditionally, a wedding comes at the end of a story, a story with a happy ending, that is; in fact, the wedding *is* the happy ending. However it is not the end but the beginning: the beginning of a new life for the couple, the creation of a new family—in fact, the beginning of life itself. Which is why, perhaps, the whole world loves a wedding; why it looks upon it with the same fond indulgence with which it looks upon babies and lovers.

This is a rather unusual wedding, a quiet and modest affair taking place not in a lavish wedding hall, but at home. The young banana plants on both sides of the rickety gate, (a gate that has been hastily and badly painted as dribbles of paint and large blobs show) as well as the festoon of mango leaves and marigolds strung above it, tell the world an auspicious event is taking place within. But it could as well be a baby's naming ceremony, a sixtieth birthday celebration, or a satyanarayan puja; though, in fact, even these are celebrated with a greater flamboyance. Here, even though it is the morning of the wedding, there is none of the frenzy of activity a wedding seems to call for—no silk-clad women rustling up and down with plates heaped with flowers and puja articles. The house is quiet. A few guests arrive at lunch time, but they are immediately swallowed up by the house and all is silent and peaceful once again.

The pace quickens by late afternoon. This is an evening wedding, a rare godhuli muhurta has been chosen. The bride's grandmother was delighted by this. Such a beautiful time of the day, she said, such a beautiful word. Cow dust a beautiful word?

Well, not the word itself, she tried to explain, but what it evokes: the serenity of the evening, the time of the day when the cows come slowly back home, their bells ringing clear and sweet, the last rays of the setting sun tinting the dust turned up by the cows' hooves into a golden and orange haze. But for the family, the timing had caused some anxious moments, because today, as the bride's sister pointed out, it is not cows but cars that come home; evening means peak hour traffic. Would people be able to come on rime? Ultimately, though, they are lucky and all those invited—and unlike most weddings the guests are few—do get there on time.

It has been a beautiful day, the kind of day only this city can provide. It has drizzled a little during the night and the day is cool, lazily drifting clouds alternating with brief spells of bright sunshine. But suddenly, by late afternoon, it turns windy. The sides of the shamiana billow in and out rhythmically, as if a giant bellows is at work. Once, the top rises to an alarming height and becomes a giant bubble before gently and reluctantly subsiding. Faces look up fearfully—is it going to rain? If it does, it's a disaster, because they have given no thought to the possibility of rain, made no alternative arrangements. Later they will wonder how they could have been so . . . so . . . So what? Foolhardy? Feckless? Optimistic? Whatever it is, luck is with them; it does not rain.

As evening approaches, there is a sudden spurt of activity. People can be seen moving from the house to the shamiana at the back. Cars, two-wheelers and autorickshaws disgorge guests. There is a sudden buzz, not of excitement, but of consternation, when the bridegroom steps out of a car, followed by his mother, an uncle and an aunt. A delegation from the bride's family has gone to their house to escort them. What happened to them? Where are they? There is a sudden babble of talk, a flurry of questions, a medley of overlapping voices. This is the one moment of excitement, the single moment of drama that every wedding must have. A few hurried phone calls are made before they realize all is well. The delegation is on its way back with the bridegroom's father, brother and sister.

'He wouldn't let us wait, he made us hurry,' the bridegroom's mother tells them with a smile, referring to her son. The smile spreads to other faces, jokes are made about the groom's impatience, there is some laughter. The groom says nothing, he stands in silent composure until the women come to them with the aarti plates to give him and his mother a ceremonial welcome. There is some awkwardness when they get to the house; the hosts don't know what to do with this advance party. Bridegrooms are, strangely, often figures of fun, but a small twitch of this man's lips indicates that it is he who finds this, the unpreparedness of the bride's family, slightly amusing. Finally, they are taken into the house. Chairs and sofas are hurriedly cleared of stuff piled on them so that the small group can sit down.

Someone, in deference to the bridegroom's arrival, switches on the fairy lights that are strung along the walls and hanging down the sides of the house. The building suddenly takes on a look of dignified beauty. With the lights outlining it, the shamiana, hidden until now by the house, becomes suddenly visible. In a short while the groom and his immediate family are taken to the wedding pandal. He is made to wait inside the flower decorated mandap, where the rituals will take place, with the priests, his mother and other women from his family clustering around him. He cuts a striking figure as he stands in his spotless white dhoti and kurta among the women in their colourful saris. There is a subdued whispering among the women as they wait for the bride to arrive.

The bride enters, escorted, not as is traditionally done by her mother's brother, but by her mother's sister. There is a sudden hush. Even the chirping of birds, settling down noisily for the night in the trees above them, is stilled, as if the birds know that their territory has been invaded. The bride comes preceded by the fragrance of the pink-stemmed chameli bunched at the nape of her neck. To the bridegroom, this fragrance will forever be associated with desire and delight.

There is a dignity, a composure about the bride and the groom as they stand facing each other, waiting for the rituals to begin, a turmeric-daubed sheet held between them by the priests. This is a good moment to describe the two. They are both rather serious young people. But in the groom's face, in his eyes, there is a hint of humour, as if he *sees* something which, if he wanted to, would make him smile. The bride on the other hand is more solemn, a grave-faced young woman. But when she laughs, lines ripple and scatter across her face, her eyes narrow, and her mouth opens wide in whole-hearted laughter. Her laughter is spontaneous, infectious. Brides are the cynosure of all eyes in a wedding, their looks, or the lack of them, are eagerly taken note of. This bride is good looking, though not startlingly so. She is not very tall, though her slim figure and erect posture make her seem so. She is wearing a traditional Kanjivaram silk, a red and gold sari echoing the colours of the chrysanthemum and the marigold, blooms of the season. Unlike most brides, it is clear that she has not gone to a beauty parlour. She is made-up, but the make-up has been so skillfully applied that it scarcely shows. Her hair is in one long plait, as usual—the only concession to the day being the flowers she is wearing in it. She looks, in fact, like herself, not like a glamorous stranger, which is what a beautician would have made of her. Even her jewellery is minimal, which is why the magnificent diamonds in her ears stand out, rays of white and blue light shooting out from the diamonds each time they catch the light.

Unusually, there are three priests standing by the bride and groom, two on the bride's side, one by the bridegroom. The oldest of the three, (perhaps it will obviate confusion if we call him Guruji, the way he is addressed by the bride's family) starts chanting the mantras, beginning in the traditional way with Ganesha's name. *Svasti Shri Gananayakam Gajamukham Moreshwaram Siddhitam*—the sonorous chant fills the pandal. The guests relax, enjoying the rhythmic rise and fall of the lines, the stately beauty of the Sanskrit words. The groom, who has waited a long time for this day, this moment, smiles at some thought of his own, whereas the bride listens in composure to the priest's chanting. In a while, Guruji stops and the bridegroom's priest takes over. The two priests take turns, moving from one to the other with such precision, it is as if they have rehearsed this earlier. Suddenly there is a change. Guruji looks meaningfully at the third priest, a young man who now begins singing some verses. The young voice, rich and deep, is singing the mangalashtaka, verses composed in honour of the bride and groom and their families, the names of the couple skillfully woven into the verses. Most guests are unfamiliar with this custom, a tradition in the bride's family, and since the verses are in Marathi, they don't understand the words, either. But the young man's voice catches their attention; it is a voice that has the clarity and the resonance of a temple bell. His beautiful rendering makes this an unforgettable moment for everyone present. For years they will remember the enchantment of the young man's voice, the way his music dyed the simple and austere occasion with a deep and rich colour. When he comes to an end, Guruji looks at his watch, continues hurriedly with the mantras, says the final words, Shubha mangala savadhan, and, bringing down his hand like the starter at the beginning of a race, whisks away the cloth held between the couple.

Whoever first thought of this ritual had a wonderful sense of drama. This young couple have known each other for years; nevertheless, when they look at one another now, it is as though they are seeing different persons. The garlands are handed to them by the priests and they garland each other. Immediately after which, the guests and the priests shower the couple with the akshada, the rice grains making a gentle patter and looking like tiny stars on the bride's dark hair. There is a sudden release of tension, a collective exhaling of breath and the women wipe the tears that this ceremony invariably seems to bring on. A babble of sound fills the pandal as the guests settle down to talk among themselves and the rest of the rituals get under way. The smokers go out for a smoke and women move around with plates of haldi, kumkum and flowers. In a few moments the major rituals will begin. But it's not going to be a long drawn-out affair, the couple have decided that only the minimum essential rituals will be done.

The groom's father had been aghast at the decision. Actually, nothing in the wedding arrangements had fitted into his idea of his family's grandeur and importance. But he had protested loudest at this shortening of the wedding rituals. 'My father's wedding was celebrated for five days, mine went on for three days. And now my son's, my *eldest* son's wedding is going to be a half-day affair? I won't allow this.'

'It's too late to change, Appa.'

'It can never be too late.' He would talk, he said, to the bride's father.

'He's not in charge. You know his wife is dead and so . . .'

'Who's doing the kanyadaan?'

'His nephew.'

'Give me his number, I'll talk to him.'

The nephew, however, is a busy cardiologist, and it's almost impossible to get him. (Or perhaps the groom is careful not to ring him at the right time?)

'Let me talk to her grandmother then.'

She's very ill, his son tells him, with a slightly accusing air. Surely he knows that? Wasn't that why they decided to have a simple wedding?

The father gave up after this, wresting, however, two concessions from his son. There would be a satyanarayan puja in their house the day after the wedding followed by a lunch. And he, yes, *he* the groom's father, would host a dinner that night for their family and friends.

Except for these two things, all the decisions about their wedding have been taken by the couple themselves. They are not puppets or pawns to be moved about; these are young people who know their own minds. Time, therefore, to stop calling them bride and groom, (though this is better than calling them 'boy' and 'girl') and to give them their names; after all, they have very important roles to play in this story. And so their names: she is Aru, short for Arundhati and he is Rohit.

Aru will organize her own wedding: this had been a family joke, first made by her father and then brought out every time Aru, impatient with her family's slapdash ways, took things into her own hands, each time she tried to impose order on their casual way of doing things. But now, there is a conspiracy to keep Aru firmly in her bride's place, at least on the day of the wedding. A bride, she has been firmly told, is not supposed to do anything on her wedding day but *be* a bride. And so her aunts, her sisters, even her father, are watchful, making sure that Aru does not get up to do anything herself. Her younger sister Seema sits a little behind her throughout the rituals, attending to her every need. But they need not have worried; Aru, once the rituals begin, concentrates on what is happening, on what the priests are saying, on what they are telling the couple to do, scrupulously repeating what she is told to say, doing what is needed. In fact, the three priests and the couple form a tight closed group of their own, heads close together, concentrating on the rituals, oblivious to people outside the mandap. Once or twice there is some laughter, which comes from the mixture of languages they are using. The groom's priest speaks to them in Kannada, Guruji, knowing that the couple knows no Marathi, speaks in Hindi, which his grandson, a stunningly handsome boy in spite of his shaven head, as Aru and Rohit now notice, translates into English—perhaps to show off. He was the one who sang so wonderfully earlier. 'By the time this boy takes my place, I am sure the whole ceremony will be in English,' his grandfather says. There is laughter at this, but the boy gives his grandfather a level, consciously adult look, as if sharing some secret with him.

When the rituals are done and the priest gives them permission to get up, Aru is on her feet in a moment and is moving away when she is stopped with a jerk. She has forgotten that her sari pallu has been tied to Rohit's upper garment. 'Wait,' the priest stops her. 'Don't forget you and your husband are now tied together,' he jokes. He calls for Seema, who unties the knot to the accompaniment of some mantras from the priest. Aru, after a few words to Rohit, goes swiftly out of the marriage pandal and into the house. The lights are on in all the rooms except the one Aru enters, in which only a small night light is burning. Her grandmother, Kalyani, is sleeping. Goda, Kalyani's sister, sitting by her side, puts her finger to her lips. Aru stands irresolute in the doorway and then enters, trying to make no sound. When she nears the bed, Kalyani immediately opens her eyes.

'Not sleeping, Amma?'

'No, I was waiting for you. I knew you would come. Is it over?'

'Yes.'

'I was there until the garlanding.'

'I know. I saw you leave. You and Godaajji.'

'Let me see you. Switch on the light, Aru, and come and stand here. I want to see you as a bride. I never saw my Sumi's wedding, she and Gopal had a registered wedding. And Premi's . . .' Goda and she look at each other, then Kalyani says, 'Let it go . . . Where's Rohit?' she asks. 'Go and call him.'

When he comes, Kalyani says, 'Come, Rohit, stand by Aru. Let me fill my eyes with the sight of the two of you together.'

She struggles to get up and, with Goda's help, sits at the edge of the bed. Surprisingly, she is dry-eyed; instead, it is Goda who wipes her tears. Aru and Rohit stand before her for a moment, then, with a look at each other, they bend down and touch her feet. She puts her two hands on their bowed heads and murmurs something, a blessing, they guess, and lies down again.

'Go, now,' she tells them.

Charu, Aru's sister, enters carrying a plastic bag in her hands. 'Aru, you have to change into this.'

'What's that?'

'A sari. Rohit's mother says you have to wear this and then go round taking the blessings of all the elders—from both the families, mind you. It'll take you at least an hour. I told you, you should have eloped.'

'Silly girl,' Kalyani chides her.

'Let me see the sari,' Goda says. The two older women look at it, they touch the sari with gentle fingers and smile at each other. They are pleased, thinking not of the sari, but of Aru getting married, of Aru being a bride.

Charu is getting impatient. 'Come on, Aru,' she says. 'Seema is waiting to help you.'

'I'm coming.'

But Aru does not follow Charu. She goes back to Kalyani and sits by her looking at her in silence. Kalyani takes her hand and strokes it. Strangely, it is Aru who asks her grandmother, 'Are you happy, Amma?'

'Yes, child. Very happy.'

'Go to sleep now. I'll come and see you after dinner.'

'Don't worry about me, Goda is with me.'

'And,' Aru goes on, 'if you're sleeping, I won't disturb you, but you will know I had come.'

'Yes, Aru. Now, will you go?'

'And I'll come to you tomorrow morning as early as possible.'

'I said don't worry about me. Goda is with me,' Kalyani repeats, as if the name is a talisman. Goda is actually Kalyani's cousin, but both women would reject the English word. In fact, Kalyani does not call her a sister; she is, Kalyani always says, more-than-a-sister-to-me.

Aru suddenly thinks of something. 'But Godaajji, when will

you have your dinner?'

'Aru, Aru, don't worry. It's all arranged. Devi and Premi are taking turns. And the nurse will come at nine. Rohit—where's Rohit? Will you take your wife away from here?'

Wife? Rohit and Aru look at each other, a little startled. Then Rohit smiles and says, 'Come, Aru, you have to change. We can't keep people waiting for too long. My appa must be already throwing a tantrum.'

'Yes, yes, you better go, Aru.'

'Are you okay?' Rohit asks her when they are out of the room.

She nods and goes into her room where her sisters are waiting. Charu is brisk and businesslike, clearly enjoying her role.

'What were you doing, Aru? I told you to hurry up. Here, take off that sari. Do you want to have a wash before changing?' She looks at her sister's face, suddenly stops and asks, 'Aru . . . what is it, Aru? What's wrong? Aru, don't, don't do this, Aru, don't, stop it . . .' But Aru, who has controlled herself all this while, is sobbing, something she does so rarely that her sisters are frightened. Charu goes to her and holds her, she, too, is crying now.

Gopal, who has come to check on Kalyani, hears his daughters' voices and looks into the room. He sees the two sisters holding each other and sobbing, while Seema sits on the bed, her shoulders hunched, her face resolutely turned away from her sisters.

Gopal closes the door and goes out. He knows why they are crying, he knows too that he has no right to intrude on their grief for their dying grandmother and for their dead mother, his wife. He quietly walks away.

Gopal

When I saw my daughters in tears, I knew why they were weeping, I knew whom they were grieving for. Sumi has been everywhere, in everyone's thoughts, all the time in this wedding—her absence a large cloud looming over us, something we can never lose sight of. There were many people trying to fill Sumi's place, trying not to let Aru feel her mother's absence— Aru's aunts Premi and Devaki, my nephew Ramesh, and of course Kalyani and Goda. Everyone had tried to plug the gaps, not only of those who had gone, but even of those who had never been. For Premi's son, Nikhil, to take on the role of Aru's brother, since Aru has no brother, was easily and naturally done. But for Premi to take on the role of Aru's maternal uncle was rather unusual. In fact, I can't think of any wedding where such a thing had been done. The idea had been mine. Aru, I remember, had looked at me with approval for the first time in—how long? I can't remember. But Premi had demurred; Guruji may not like it, she said. She was mistaken. The idea of an aunt escorting Aru to the mandap instead of an uncle had seemed to please him, rather than otherwise. I must confess that I was a little surprised by this until I saw the old man's grandson, who assisted his grandfather in the ceremony. He came in jeans, a T-shirt and a baseball cap worn back to front. And there he was during the wedding in a dhoti, sacred thread prominent on bare chest and a shaven head which had been concealed by the cap. But why was I surprised? Don't all of us have many selves concealed within us?

As for me, Aru's wedding, in which I had no role to play, made me realize that I had lost my place in the family. Ever since I came back, I had seen the way my daughters had managed their lives without Sumi and me, I had seen the way the women supported one another. At times, I asked myself: why did I come? Was it for this, to know that I no longer had a place in my daughters' lives? And if I had truly lost my place, did I have any right to complain? Perhaps this humiliation is part of the atonement I knew I had to make. Paschatap and prayaschitta: remorse and atonement, they go together, one follows the other. I have never believed that remorse can right a wrong. But perhaps remorse and atonement together can mean something, maybe they are two faces of the same coin; neither is complete without the other. Atonement, however, is not punishment; and will Aru, with her strong sense of justice, be satisfied unless I suffer punishment as well? I remember her indignation when, as a child, she thought she was being unfairly punished. 'But, Papa, that's not fair,' she would cry out. Always protective of her younger sister, she nevertheless refused to take the blame for anything Charu had done. When I told her that she had to take on the burden of being the older sister, she would say—a reply that was astonishingly reasonable for a child—'I don't mind if you punish me instead of her, but you must say it's not my fault, you must say it's her fault.' Yes, Aru will believe that I should be punished, that this sense of being unwanted is not enough, there has to be more visible punishment.

Yet she has not been hostile to me since I came back. There is some change in her. All my daughters have changed. Charu, so open and impetuous, seems to have changed the least. But I see a wariness in her, as if life has taught her to be careful, not to trust it completely—a loss of trust which spells the end of her girlhood. Seema has changed the most physically. Long-legged and elegant, she is a poised person; the blankness in her has been transformed into composure. And yet, I still sense that emptiness in her, something which had worried Sumi and me. Besides, there's now a dependence on Aru, which worries me just as much. Aru, who was always active, is restless, constantly moving, afraid, perhaps, that if she is still, something will go wrong. But she no longer flares up as easily as she used to do. She has realized, perhaps, that being in charge, being responsible, forces you to be kind; you cannot be harsh to those over whom you have power. I can't say that she is softer or more mellow; she is only more circumspect. The flashing sword she had come to me with when she visited me after I left them, has gone back into its sheath. I know, however, that it is still with her, that it will be drawn out whenever it is needed.

It was Premi's letter which first informed me about Kalyani's condition, after which there was a letter from Ramesh telling me about their fears for her. I thought then that I should go back; nevertheless, for some reason, I hesitated. And then Kalyani wrote asking me to return. As if I had been waiting for this, I made up my mind and within hours was out of the place in which I had lived for nearly three years. I had few belongings to pack, fewer to leave behind and agonize over.

I had gone away from home (Home? No, it was not my home, it was Sumi's parental home) after Sumi's death, my wounds raw and bleeding. When we returned after the funeral, we were mute, unable even to think of our sorrow. Two deaths, two funerals, two people, a father and daughter, who had left home well and active, dead a few minutes later—it was hard to accept. I also realized I could not stay in that house. There was no room for me in Sumi's family home where they were mourning a daughter and a mother, grieving over the death of a man who had never known how to be a husband and a father. I seemed to see myself in him. I saw with a blinding clarity what I had done. I walked out of the house. I did not know where I was going, there was no place in the city that I felt was mine. Finally I went back to the room in which I had lived for the last few months. I sat up all night in the dark, the smell of death, of the crematorium, clinging to my unbathed body and unwashed clothes. I thought of Sumi and of our life together, I went over and over through the moments of our last meeting. I kept wondering whether there was anything I could have said and done which could have averted her death. I was suffering the guilt of the survivor, a guilt much greater than what most people have to bear, because I *had* done my wife wrong. The knowledge that she had died before I had had a chance to make reparation made my grief harder to bear.

It was still dark when I bathed, pouring cold water over myself, and set out to go back to Sumi's home, back to our three daughters and to Kalyani, Sumi's mother. I walked all the way, as if it was a mortification I needed to undergo. Auto drivers, who had just begun their day, slowed down when they passed by, hoping I would get in, that I would be their first passenger. I waved them on and kept walking. When I got there, it was bright, the day had begun. No one spoke of my absence during the night, no one greeted my presence either. Death and grief had left no room for curiosity and questions. I stayed on until the ceremonies were over, I took on my share of the tasks that had to be done, performed the few rituals that we owe our dead. I thought then of how little we speak of these things and yet, when the time comes, we go through them as if we are familiar with the morbid rituals. For me, there was a distant memory of performing these rituals as a child, of doing them for my dead parents. My sister Sudha had been against making me perform the funeral rituals—he's only a child, she had said. She had even offered to do it herself, which for her, a very traditional woman, was earthshaking. But her husband, P.K. had said, 'He will never be free of his parents if he does not do this for them; it is something he owes his parents'. Even if this is true, it did not happen to me; I was not free of my parents in spite of performing their last rites. There was a time when I kept wondering about them, when I tried to recover their features through Sudha's face, or by looking at my own in the mirror. Curiosity died, however, when I married Sumi. I was no longer interested in the past. I was preoccupied with the present, the now, with Sumi and my children. I thought often of the future, Sumi's and mine and of the future of our children. I am not yet free of Sumi, either. Perhaps, for those who believe in rituals there is some healing. For me there was none.

Somehow we got through those days of intense grief. Ramesh, my nephew, Sudha's son, was with me throughout. I survived those days because of him. He had disapproved of what I had done, of the way I had abandoned my family; but his affection and support for me never flagged. I have not forgotten that; I never will.

And then it was over. I went back to the house after the thirteenth day. Only Kalyani and Aru were at home. It suited me, because I wanted to talk only to the two of them. I told them that I could no longer stay there, I had to go away. I gave them the excuse, which was also a reason, but only part of the reason for my going—that I wanted to immerse Sumi's ashes in the Alakananda. Sumi had come to me night after night after her death, a joyous Sumi frolicking in the river which had so delighted her when we had gone with Sudha and P.K. to Badri. For Sudha and P.K. it was a pilgrimage, but for Sumi and me it was a holiday; we went to give them company and for the adventure of going to the Himalayas. Sumi was the youngest among us and her happiness, her love of the mountains and the river had delighted the three of us, me specially. I had fallen in love with her all over again.

I did not say these things to Sumi's mother and to our daughter. I could not. I was brief and businesslike. They listened in silence to what little I could tell them. Then Kalyani said, 'Go,

Gopala, go. Let my daughter find her final rest in the Ganga.'

Aru came out of her somber silence just before I left them. 'Go, Papa,' she said, repeating Kalyani's words. 'Go, don't worry about us, we'll be all right.'

I had thought then that she had forgiven me. I know now that she had only declared a temporary truce. Her gentleness was part of the first stage of grief, of sorrowing for the dead, a time when we are filled with tenderness for the world, and more so for our co-mourners. But this doesn't last long. After a while it changes into anger, resentment; the grudges against the dead (how could you go away, leaving me to bear all this?) as well as against the living come back to us. I had seen my sister Sudha go through all this after her husband's death.

Aru showed no emotion when I returned. It was an opportune homecoming for me. The crisis of Kalyani's surgery ruled out questions and awkwardness, my presence was easily accepted and no questions were asked. Premi had told me that the biopsy had confirmed their worst fears. The disease was far advanced, there were already secondaries. When I saw Premi weeping after the surgery, I knew there was no hope. The surgeons had done their best, but Kalyani would not live beyond a few months. Ramesh, also a doctor like Premi, was, however, more sanguine. We can never predict how an individual responds to the treatment, he said. Kalyani's age was against her, he said, but it was possible she could go on for some more time.

In the event, Kalyani proved Ramesh right. She surprised us and lived nearly a year and a half after her surgery. When she came home from the hospital, we evolved a new routine. I found that I could be of use, since Aru and Charu were at crucial points in their studies. Premi came as often as she could from Bombay to be with her mother, but it was I who spent the most time with Kalyani.

We sat in the side veranda, which the girls called 'Amma's drawing room', in the afternoons. It was a good time of the day for Kalyani. She would be rested and fresh after her afternoon nap, though exhaustion would soon overtake her. Always a small woman, Kalyani seemed even tinier after the surgery, more so after the chemotherapy. The large comfortable chair Rohit had brought for her nearly swallowed her up. But her face was unchanged, even the kumkum on her forehead was intact. I had been surprised to see her that way; a woman of her generation would have done away with the kumkum after her husband's death. I thought it was Aru who had prevailed on her to retain this sign of wifehood, but Premi told me that it had been Kalyani's own decision. 'I lived like a widow even when your father was alive, why should I change anything now?' she asked. A surprising woman, Kalyani.

I had thought it strange that no one had spoken of my absence, that they had not asked me about my life in the three years I was away. But Kalyani did. She wanted to know about my stay in the mountains, she was interested in hearing about my life there. So I told her how I embarked on my Char Dham pilgrimage, of the accident which happened just when I was about to return home. I told her about my friend, the doctor, who helped me and who induced me to stay on in the ashram where I found work to do. Kalyani listened to my account in silence. I could see she was really interested. And then she asked me a question—one I had not expected. Actually it was a tentative question, as if it was something she knew she should not ask. She asked me, I remember this vividly, 'You were happy there, Gopala?' I had hesitated. What could I say? Would she like to be told that I was happy after her daughter's, my wife's, death? I thought for a moment, then told her the truth—that I found some kind of peace during my stay in Uttarkashi. She smiled and said nothing more. Apart from this, we rarely, almost never spoke of the past, of the tragedy which had sent me away. Only once, she said, 'I always liked you, Gopala. You have been more like a son than a son-in-law to me. And now we have something in common. You lost your Sumi and I lost my. . .' she hesitated. She didn't know what word to use, she could not say the word 'husband' for the man who had denied her wifehood, so she changed track and said, 'You lost your Sumi the same day Sumi's father died.'

Most of the time, we spoke of my daughters. Ramesh and Premi had given me some news about them in their occasional letters, though Ramesh's letters, like any man's, had been factual and brief. It was Premi who had written about Charu and Hrishi's greater involvement. 'They seem to have come to some definite decision,' she wrote, 'but Devaki is not happy about it.' Premi also told me of Aru's steady friendship with a classmate of hers, but when I returned there was no one, except Rohit.

Kalyani, like all patients who go through this deadly illness, had her good days and bad days. On one of her bad days—this was after the chemotherapy—she said, 'I don't know how long I can go on, Gopala. Sometimes I want to say, stop all this, stop these medicines, stop this treatment and let me go, I can't go through this any more. But I can't let go, not as yet. I want to live until Aru's marriage, I want to see her married. Then I don't mind letting this monster have its way.'

Strangely, the monster allowed her to live until Aru's wedding. It was not just Aru's marriage that Kalyani longed for, it was her marriage to Rohit which was her hope, her dream. I was with her the day Rohit and Aru told her they were getting married. I remember how happy she was. When they went out, she said, 'Now I can die in peace. Though,' here she had a mischievous smile on her face, 'you never know; I may want to see Charu married, then I will want to see Aru's child, then Seema's marriage . . . No, it never ends. How we hate to give up! But I won't be greedy, I will say enough! when Aru is married. She will have Rohit with her. Charu, I know, will have Hrishi, and you will be there for Seema, for all your daughters. I won't ask for more. I will be able to go easily.'

There was only one thing she asked of me. It was unexpected and painful, the intensity with which she spoke to me one day,

'Promise me one thing, Gopala. Promise me you will be with your girls, promise me you won't go away.'

'I will be here as long as they need me, Amma.'

'But you will go back some time. I know you want to go back to the mountains.'

Yes, I was often homesick for the place. How did she guess that?

'My Sumi went away without telling me. She was always like that. Don't go out without telling me first, I used to scold her. After that she always told me when she was going out. But she would only say, "Amma, I'm going" and rush off. She never told me where she was going, or how long she would be out. Finally, she went away without a word. She had her way, she always had her way. But you, Gopala, you have to be here for your children.'

'What can I do for them, Amma? What can I do for Aru? I didn't even dare to give her my blessing when she told us she was getting married.'

'That is not right, Gopala. That is the one thing we can always do for our children: we can put our hand on their heads and say "be happy, be good". Do you know the words with which Kashyapa Rishi blessed Shakuntala when she was leaving her home? My father used to tease Goda and me saying he would bless us with the same words when the time came.'

Yes, I knew the words. And I had always thought it a very strange blessing. 'May you be cherished by your husband as Sharmishta was cherished by Yayati.' Why Sharmishta, who was Yayati's second wife, the woman he married in secret, the woman whose marriage was not validated for years? But perhaps the secret lies in the next words, 'May you have a son like Puru.' Yes, Sharmishta had that wonderful son Puru; that perhaps, is what marriage is really about. I wonder how often Kalyani's father thought of the words later and grieved for his daughter who was neither cherished by her husband like Sharmishta nor had a son like Puru. No, I could not say these words to Kalyani.

'I knew them, but now I don't remember the words,' I lied to her.

'Never mind. But remember, Gopala, if you go away, your daughters will be orphans.'

I thought no, Amma, they can never be orphans as long as you are with them. Even afterwards, when you have gone, they will have each other, they will have Premi, Devaki, Ramesh . . .

'You must be here for Aru's sake. She took us on, her sisters and me, after Sumi died. She has been carrying this burden since then. Now I want her to be free to enjoy her life with Rohit. I want Rohit to have his wife's company, not to share her with others. They must be completely free for each other. Aru can have that freedom only if she knows you are with Seema. Nobody else can do this for her.'

I promised Kalyani I would stay with Seema. I said I would be with my daughters as long as they wanted me (yes, I said *wanted,* not *needed).* Kalyani relaxed after that. We never spoke on this subject again.

Now Aru's wedding is over and I can see the change in Kalyani. She has let go. I know she will not last long. Aru keeps moving between her new home and her old one. She is very practical, she shows no emotions, but I can see that she knows as well as I do that a great sorrow is waiting for her, for all of us. For my daughters, Kalyani's death will be like losing their mother all over again and Aru will lose her greatest pillar of support. Yes, a great sorrow is coming our way. I have to be here with my daughters when it comes.

The Home

'The present, like a note in music, is nothing but as it appertains to what is past and what is to come.'

Aesop to Rhodope in *Aesop and Rhodope—Imaginary Conversations* by Walter Savage Landor

Sometime after Sumi moved back into her parents' house, she enlisted the help of an estate agent to find a place of her own. Nagaraj, the agent, had at first found her a difficult client—hard to please, unable to tell him what exactly it was she wanted. And exasperatingly honest, even when it worked against her. Yet something in her plight—he soon guessed she was a single mother with three daughters—went past his hard-headed businessman's defences. But his ideas about her really changed when he saw the house she was living in.

'When you have *this,*' he had waved his hand, the gesture taking in the large house as well as the ample space around it, 'to live in, why are you looking for a rented place?' he had asked her bluntly.

'This is not mine, it's my father's.'

'Yours eventually'—the thought had travelled from his mind to hers and Sumi had been horrified that she had allowed herself to think it. Am I waiting for my father's death? she asked herself.

In the event, Sumi and her father died together, and the house became Kalyani's. Now Kalyani too has gone, the house has been demolished and in its place stands a new one, built, according to Kalyani's desire, for Sumi's three daughters. A new life for these children, she had said. They must forget the past.

There had been much debate about naming the new house. (For some reason they had been convinced it must have a name, not just a number.) Why not 'Kalyani', someone had suggested. But Premi and Aru had vetoed the suggestion. Kalyani would have considered it presumptuous, they said, to have the house named after her. It was Kalyani's father, Vithalrao, who had built the house. 'Vithalrao', then? The idea of naming a house Vithalrao, or even Vithal, had evoked much laughter. There had been many other suggestions, from 'Madhav Mahal' (Premi's suggestion, in honour of Madhavrao Peshwa, the short-lived warrior ruler who had brought the family down South) to the clichéd 'Smriti' and 'Matoshri'. The last two were Charu's idea and she had been mortified when she had been laughed at for being so sentimental. It's just right, she said, it will include both Kalyani and Sumi, she had protested, but no one had taken her seriously.

Ultimately the thought had occurred to them: why not go back to the original name, 'Vishwas'? What was wrong with it? Nothing. In fact, it ensured continuity. And, this was Rohit's thought—they could use the same stone on which the name Vishwas had been so beautifully etched in both Devanagari and Kannada.

So Vishwas it is. A new home, but the same name yet again. A name that, in the minds of this generation, is not connected to their ancestor Vishwasrao after whom the house had been originally named. This time, at least for Rohit, the architect of the new house, the name stands for trust. Vithalrao had built the house with the faith that it would endure for generations, that his children, his children's children, and their children would live in it. Rohit, a man of his time, built it for his wife (and therefore Hrishi's cheeky suggestion that they name it 'Taj Mahal'!) and for himself. A home in which, he trusted, they would live in harmony and happiness; in which their children would be born and grow up, from which the children would eventually go away, but to which they would return again and yet again. Yes, in a way Rohit had, like Vithalrao, built this house with the children to come in mind. And, therefore, he had built it around an open courtyard, creating an enclosed space in which toddlers could safely play watched over by their parents from either of the verandas that flanked the courtyard. Where the children could leave their toys, their tricycles and little cars overnight, and no one would have to worry about picking up these things when their day's play was done.

Rohit had breathed and lived the house for two years. He had loved the old house from the day he saw it; it was the day he first saw Aru, as well. He still has a distinct memory of the girl coming towards him, a puzzled, who-are-you? look on her face, her helmet still on her head. And then, he remembers, she removed the helmet and shook her head, so that her long plait, which she had tied into a loose knot, came free and flew about her face. This image had accompanied him through the months when he sketched, drew the plans and watched the house come up. And at some time, just as the girl and the house had come together in his mind, the old house had gradually segued into the new one.

There had been a time when Sumi had been desperate to get away from her parents' home and have a place of her own. So desperate, that in her idle hours she had begun sketching the plans of a house where she and her daughters would live, dependent on no one. She knew it would never happen, she knew it was only a dream, for where would the money come from? Yet it gave her comfort and the idea of the house that would never be took possession of her. Strangely, each time she began a sketch, the old house showed up, superimposing its lines on her sketch. Perhaps the same thing happened to Rohit as well, because even now, even after the old house is gone, it comes to the minds of those who had known it; to see the new house is like seeing a reflection of the old one in a misty mirror at dusk. It lingers like a family trait, or the physical resemblance of a child to a parent. There is a sense of continuity, not only in the name, but in the symmetry and proportions, in the verandas and the broad window sills. Above all, the old idol of Ganesha, installed by Sumi's grandfather, Vithalrao, is still with them, placed this time not inside but outside, in the courtyard. Brought into the open it seems somehow diminished, divested of the mystique Kalyani had invested it with. Seen this way, at eye level, Ganesha no longer seems fearful, but a benign presence. Aru cleans the idol now, something which had not been possible when it had been placed at a great height in the hall. It had been Bora's job then, Bora, Kalyani's gardener and all-Jobs-outside-the-house-man. He would clean the Ganesha, standing precariously on the top rung of a ladder, while Kalyani shouted out instructions interspersed with 'be careful, Bora' warnings from below. It was Bora, too, who did a kind of puja, applying kumkum to the idol's forehead and feet, and placing some flowers in the curve of the trunk and between the god's feet, flowers which would stay there, dried to a crisp fragility until the next cleaning.

Now Nagi, Kalyani's loyal maid, who continues to work with Aru, does the puja, scrupulously following Kalyani's methods. Aru considers her job is complete with the cleaning, which she does rather casually and whenever she finds time. Yet Aru's feelings towards the Ganesha have changed. She, who had taken on the job of cleaning the idol as a duty, has now begun admiring it. When it is freshly cleaned and gleaming in the sun, she gets a glimpse of the old story of the mysterious sculptor whom Vithalrao had come across on the outskirts of a village, a sculptor working on a flawless piece of stone. That perfection can still be seen in the gloss of the stone, in the proportions and in the benign expression of the idol, which speak, not only of the sculptor's skill, but of his love for what he was creating.

Unlike the house, which carries a hint of its past, the garden is a complete change from the earlier one. The desolate front yard, the wilderness at the side and the patchy overgrown-with-weeds kitchen garden have given way to a carefully and lovingly planned order. Knowing the difficulty of getting a mali, and that they themselves will have little time to work in the garden, Aru and Rohit have gone for the functional. No seasonal flowers, no hedges that need to be trimmed, no beds that have to be constantly weeded. Instead there are larger plants: the frangipani, raat-rani, parijaat, a throng of mallige bushes. The garden is not a blaze of colours, for most of the flowers are white, but a riot of fragrances. Aru's one failure is the curry-leaf tree. Kalyani's lovingly tended trees had had to be sacrificed during the construction of the house and Aru planted new ones as soon as the house was complete. She looks after them the way Kalyani did, assiduously anointing the tree trunks with hing and watering them with buttermilk, something which she and Charu had laughed at earlier. 'Feeding the curry-leaf trees,' they had called it. Now, in spite of Aru doing the same, they never seem to achieve the lushness, the luxuriance of Kalyani's trees.

Since Rohit and Aru moved into the new house, it has become a meeting place for their friends and family. Closed, shuttered and quiet from Monday to Saturday afternoon with no one except Nagi going about her work, it comes alive on Saturday evenings and on Sundays. At such times, the two-levelled living room which connects to the dining area and the veranda on one side and the cosy nook—Aru's favourite place for relaxing—on the other, seems to fulfill the purpose for which it was meant.

Today the house is full once again, but this time it is only family. It is a special occasion. Charu and Hrishi have come for a brief holiday from the U.S., their first visit since their son was born. It is Hrishi's birthday and the young people have gathered in Aru and Rohit's house in the evening. Rajiv, Rohit's younger brother, has unexpectedly turned up with his estranged wife Uma. They separated a few months back, but have recently begun seeing each other again, to the bewilderment of Rajiv's parents. Are they getting back together? But why, then, are they so casual with each other, giving no indication of being anything more than just friends? Their reconciliation, if it is that, is as much a mystery to Rajiv's parents as their separation had been, for there had been no quarrels, absolutely no sign of hostility between the two. Even now they leave early—and together. Two of Charu's old friends had dropped in earlier to see the baby, but they left early, too. So it's just the three sisters, Rohit and Hrishi and Nikhil, their aunt Premi's son.

Nikhil is studying Engineering in a college on the outskirts of the city and is a regular visitor to Aru's home. He often stays over during weekends. Tonight, however, he will go back because his girlfriend is with him. She and Leo, Seema's friend, are the only two who are not family. Leo, a clean-shaven Sikh, is a photographer and the only one of Seema's friends the family has met, the first one to find his way to their home.

It is now ten years since Sumi's death. A long time in the life of the very young; adolescents become adults and children suddenly become baffling strangers to their parents. Nikhil, however, made the leap to adulthood so comfortably that they have been treating him as an adult since he was fifteen. The youngest in the family now is Pavan, Hrishi and Charu's son, a toddler a little over a year old. He is the centre of attraction as he moves about the room with the tottery gait of an infant who's just learned to walk, the weight of his diaper-padded behind, which looks comically like one half of a parenthesis, making him even more unsteady. He's constantly on the move, searching for something with the patient tenacity of an explorer. There are alarmed cries and shouts of laughter when he falls, cries of triumph when someone manages to hold him. But he wriggles out of their grasp and continues on his mysterious journey, clutching at knees and chairs, intent on his search, looking for something which no one, not even he, perhaps, knows.

There is an ease about the group, the intimacy of people who have grown up together. Resemblances flit across the room, lighting on a face, picking up a smile, the shape of a nose, a laugh, a gesture, linking not only the three sisters and their cousin Nikhil, but also Hrishi, Charu's husband, for he too is family, the son of Sumi's cousin Devaki. It would seem to a casual observer that being together has revived their old selves; but this is an illusion. They have changed, all of them, and Hrishi the most altered of them all. He is changed by having to make his own way in a foreign country without his father's position and money and his mother's pampering to make life easy for him. Changed, too, by his father's close brush with death and his mother's total breakdown during that time. Changed, of course, by fatherhood. But Hrishi was changed, above all, by what happened to the country he went to with such optimism and hope. The two planes that sliced through the twin towers have sliced the country, indeed the world, into two, leaving Charu and Hrishi asking themselves: where do we belong? We don't belong to the faith that the terrorists claim they belong to, but the colour of our skin, our country, the part of the world we come from, mark us and make people—some of them at least—look at us with suspicion. Is this where we want to live the rest of our lives? Is this where we want our son to grow up, they ask themselves. Hrishi never speaks of his fears when his parents are around, knowing very well that his mother will immediately ask: why, then, do you live there? Who don't you come home? A question that always fills him with confusion and guilt. But when he listens to the talk about what has happened, what is happening, even here at home, the horror of it, the vileness of the deeds done, he wonders whether there's any place in the world safe from hatred and fear. If this is how it is, Hrishi thinks, then why not live *there* instead of *here?* Charu, however, thinks exactly the other way round: if this is how it is, why don't we stay here, at home, rather than there, in a strange country?

This, however, is not the time for talking of such things. They have gone through these subjects at the family lunch in Hrishi's parents' home—about Bush and Iraq and Afghanistan, and the paranoia and the xenophobia showing up in the United States. Now, with no parents around, Hrishi reverts to his old clowning self. Nikhil joins him and they are like two comedians, egging each other on.

Charu has been telling them that Hrishi has now officially changed his name to Rishi, dropping the 'H'. 'And this is the fellow who used to insist on being called Hrishi. Remember, Aru, how he used to say, "My name is *H*rishi, I say, not Rishi?"'

'Oh well, those guys have enough trouble with our names, why make it harder for them?'

'Don't apologise, Hrishidada, you're right. It's sensible to simplify your name. Hru,' Nikhil rolls the syllable on his tongue, emphasizng the *h* and the *r* sound, 'is hard enough even for me to say. Look at Leo, how sensibly he's accepted Leo instead of Manvinder Singh. And talking of difficult names, I know one woman, a lawyer, who calls herself Shakuntala Sahasrabuddhe-Swaminathan.'

'You must be joking.'

'No, I swear it's true. She thought she was making a point. Saying I am myself. And there she was, using two male names, her father's and her husband's! And there's Aru's boss, the lawyer Surekha Shanti. What kind of a name is that?'

Aru, used to being a butt of jokes because of her ideas of feminism, has been silent so far, her face deadpan, not a muscle on her face quivering. But at this, she suddenly exclaims, 'What's wrong with it? Shanti is her mother's name.'

'Then why aren't you Arundhati Sumi, sorry Sumitra? What kind of a feminist are you, Arutai? You use your father's name, Arundhati Joshi. You should have a hyphenated name like the triple-S woman. Arundhati Joshi-Kashyap. Don't you feel left out, Rohitdada?'

'Whatever she calls herself, she's still my wife.'

'But Rohitdada . . .'

Nikhil had been a delightful child, happy to be with his grandmother Kalyani, his aunt Sumi and his cousins. He had adored Sumi, a feeling which he seems to have transferred to

Aru after Sumi's death. Aru, whenever she is exasperated by him, thinks of him as he was, a child in white pyjamas and kurta, sparkling clean after his bath, his hair slicked down in the endearing way of little boys, his palms and soles pink and a little puffy after a hot bath, the fragrance of talcum powder surrounding him like an aura. She remembers him joining them to watch a TV programme, his dinner plate on his knees, eager to share their enjoyment of whatever they were watching, earnestly watching them so that he could laugh when they did.

While Charu and Nikhil spar, Rohit listens silently to their conversation, entranced by the way it flows, by their easy comfortable intimacy, by the way affection holds them almost visibly together. They are a traumatized family, Rohit thinks, traumatized by Gopal's leaving, most of all by the sudden deaths of Sumi and her father. Rohit still remembers the day of Sumi and her father's deaths, he can almost see the two bodies on the floor, the deathly silence in the room, as if everyone had stopped breathing. He remembers Aru's stoic silence and Charu standing with her face to the wall, her body heaving with suppressed sobs. But they have come out of it, he thinks, not damaged, but intact. My family has suffered no such crisis, there have been no such devastating moments, but we can never get together in this way, never feel such joy in one another. In fact, all of us, except Rajiv, escaped from home as soon as we could.

Conversation slows down after a while, becomes softer and more serious. Aru listens in silence. It has been a long day for her; she looks tired, her head leaning against the wall, her body sagging with fatigue. At some time, she has captured Pavan. After some initial squirming he now lies quietly in Aru's lap while she pats him gently on his chest, her eyes fixed on his face with a look that makes Rohit uneasy. Mother and child, Rohit thinks as he looks at her, a picture that has fascinated humanity, providing, perhaps, an atavistic sense of security. Mother and child. But

Aru is not the baby's mother. Rohit suddenly gets up and asks, 'Another drink, anyone? Hrishi? A final birthday drink?'

It is Charu who starts unwinding the evening, saying, 'No, Rohit, it's time for Pavan's bottle. And Aru is tired. Look at her, she's almost sleeping.'

'Oh, well, I know when I'm being thrown out. Come on, Swati, let's go.'

'Nikhil, don't you dare! You have to help clear up all this. Get up, Hrishi.'

'That's right, Hrishidada, get on with it. And what the hell are you doing, Swati, just standing about? Go and help Rohitdada and Leo.'

The girl instantly gets up and, despite Rohit telling her to relax, joins him and Leo in collecting the debris of the evening. They are all amazed at the way Swati jumps up to obey Nikhil, like an eager puppy. She makes no secret of the fact that she adores Nikhil. True, Nikhil can be very charming when he wants to. And he's an extremely good-looking boy—beautiful, if a man can be called that; there's a flyaway look about him, as if he's standing on tiptoe like a ballet dancer. Nevertheless, Swati irritates Aru; has she no pride, she thinks. She is an intelligent girl, she's enjoyed all the privileges that a young person can get. Yet she allows Nikhil to walk all over her. Aru is almost sure she and Nikhil are sleeping together. It doesn't bother her too much (though she knows she will never tell Premi about it!) yet at times she thinks, but they're such infants! What really worries her, however, is the girl's mindless adoration of Nikhil, her absolute obedience and Nikhil's casual treatment of her, which almost borders on cruelty at times. Like now, when after having ordered her to help, he suddenly yells, 'Swaati!' When he is shushed, he asks 'What?' and shouts 'Swaati!' again, a little louder. 'I'm leaving. If you want to come with me, hurry up.'

And he's out of the house and in his car in a moment, honking impatiently for Swati, who flings herself in her seat just before

Nikhil starts the car. Seema and Leo are the last to leave; they part without a word to each other, Seema going upstairs to her flat and Leo to his motorbike. Rohit and Aru, after locking up and putting everything away, finally go to bed.

'Do you have everything you want?' Aru calls out to Charu.

'Yes, we're okay. Go to sleep, Aru. You don't have to worry about us.'

In a while the lights are switched off and there is silence.

After the deaths of Sumi and her father, the family home wore a melancholy look, grief and loss hanging over it like a miasma. But the violence of grief does not last forever. Aru and Charu were, at the time, at crucial points of their careers—Charu trying to get into a medical college and Aru in the process of moving from her humanities course to law. There were entrance exams to be prepared for, forms to be filled, certificates to be collected. Life had to move on. It was good for Aru to have these practical matters to deal with, for if she had had time to think she would have realized that she was trying to fill the vast space left by Sumi's death—something so impossible that she would have been overwhelmed by despair. Aru, at the age of eighteen, had suddenly lost the innocence of imagining a happy future, of thinking that there would come a time when all would be well, that you could live 'happily ever after'. She had been suddenly jolted out of her idea of the world and its order. Was this, the sudden death of her mother, she asked herself at times, something she had to accept as part of the normal order of things? And if that was the way it was, how was she to live her life always apprehensive of disaster, forever fearful that something was waiting round the corner to trip her up?

Thankfully, she had no time to brood. Charu, who had sunk into bouts of painful weeping, had to be brought out of it. With Hrishi's help Aru prodded and urged Charu to start preparing for her medical entrance exams. And there was Seema . . .

It was not easy to put that dreadful year, when everything went to pieces, behind them. But it helped that Charu got admission into a local medical college. They had reluctantly prepared themselves for her going away from home. To know that they would still be together lifted their spirits. They could not bear any more parting or separation; healing lay in being together. Sumi's death remained a constant ache in their hearts but after some time they were able to look back at the year just before her death as a piece of perfection—despite all the turmoil, bitterness and heartache that had been their lot during that year. Each one of Sumi's three daughters has her own special memory of her mother in that year, a memory to be treasured for all of her life.

For Kalyani, the first few days of shock were succeeded by an intense and painful grief. She became a confused and bewildered woman, suddenly losing words, getting names mixed up, calling her three granddaughters by one another's names, sometimes even as Premi, and worse, at times as Sumi. But once the girls went back to school and college, Kalyani, with a courage which Aru realized only later, pulled herself out of her mourning and resumed her place in the house. Grief, however, returned at night to haunt her. Sorrow for her daughter's untimely death, for her husband's shattered hopes, for the way he had been coerced into an unwanted marriage, for his loveless life and her own share in his unhappiness—these things came back to her at night. There were also fearful dreams of the man who had been her husband, dreams in which he was still the angry, silent man he had been. She dreamt of Sumi too, Sumi as a young girl, once again the daughter who had always baffled her with her elusiveness and her willfulness. Kalyani found great comfort, however, in a new bonding with her younger daughter, Premi. They now met on common ground, both of them survivors of a war that finally ended with the death of Shripati, Kalyani's husband and Premi's father. Premi came home often to be with her mother and her sister's daughters; fortuitously, she was with them when Kalyani died, something that was a great comfort to Premi.

They did not mourn Kalyani for too long. Her death was expected, her suffering in her last days had been so great that her death was almost welcome. Besides, there were many memories for them to share, to talk about, to laugh over. And to admire. They realized how Kalyani had made it possible for them to get over mourning their mother and grandfather. To a great extent it was because of her that in time the home became a cheerful place. (It was a dreadful thought, but impossible to escape, that without their grandfather's presence looming over the house, happiness and enjoyment became possible.) Soon, like any house in which there are young people, there was much activity, a coming and going of friends, constant phone calls and voices calling out to one another. And, of course, with two attractive young women in the house, there were the 'bees', as Kalyani called them.

'Bees?'

'Yes, bees. Those insects which visit flowers for the honey.'

'What are you talking about, Amma?'

'She means your boyfriends, stupid! You're such a tubelight, Charu.'

'My boyfriends? I beg your pardon, Aru, I don't have any boyfriends. Who has the time for boy friends?'

It was true that Charu, like all medical students, was extremely busy, but being an open friendly person, she had many friends, both male and female. Nevertheless, there were no 'boyfriends' in the sense in which Aru had used the phrase. Though Kalyani and Aru were just beginning to realize that, for Charu, Hrishi was becoming something more than a cousin, more than just a good friend. It was Aru, who, in spite of being more reserved, or, perhaps because of it, had more admirers. She always managed to shrug them off, though there was one persistent young man who ignored all the negative signals that Aru sent out and continued to ring up and to call on Aru on all kinds of pretexts. The young man eventually became a family joke, until Aru took pity on him and told him, so clearly that there was no possibility of his misunderstanding her, that she was not interested in him.

Kalyani, surprisingly for a woman of her generation, welcomed all their friends—boys as well as girls. Perhaps she remembered the days of her girlhood when boys and girls were kept strictly apart. Remembered too, possibly, how her own life had changed because an unknown boy had written her a love letter. It was an innocent and childish letter, completely harmless. But Kalyani's mother had panicked, taken her daughter out of school and rushed her into marriage with her own brother, as if she could not trust any other male. So now Kalyani took messages from the girls' friends, she chatted with them when they called, she even sympathized with Aru's rejected 'boyfriend' when he came home. Kalyani had no fears that her granddaughters would get into unsuitable relationships. Apart from the fact that they were too focused on their future careers, she had a strong feeling that their fates were linked to the two young men who were not only constant visitors, but almost part of the family. Hrishi *was* family, he was Goda's grandson, and Devaki's son. Since Sumi and Devaki had been very close, he had grown up with Sumi's daughters. Charu and he had a contentious relationship, they were constantly bickering, constantly arguing; yet the strong bond between them was unmistakable. It would clearly, in time, move into marriage. The two belonged together.

Rohit was different. A regular visitor who did not conceal his interest in Aru, he nevertheless kept his distance and never gave her the feeling of being pursued. Aru seemed indifferent and, at times, not hostile, but thorny. He met her indifference with blandness, her thorniness with wariness. It worried Kalyani. She hoped he would not be discouraged and go away. At one time it did seem that he had given up, for he disappeared for a while; they learnt later that he had gone abroad. But he returned and this time he made no secret of his intentions. Aru had to take note of his presence, of the fact that he was serious about her and that he wanted to marry her.

Sumi's two daughters are now married to the men who had set their hearts on them. But the marriages were not entirely welcome to Hrishi's and Rohit's families. Lalita, Rohit's mother, was distantly connected to Kalyani's family, she knew the family history. She had heard the story of Shripati and Kalyani's doomed marriage and she also knew that Gopal had walked out on Sumi and their daughters. Not a very desirable history, she thought, for her son's wife. But she saw the way Aru coped with the situation after her mother's and grandfather's death, the courage and the tenderness with which she looked after her grandmother and sisters. Above all, she knew her son, she had gauged the strength of his feelings for Aru and she knew there was no way he would give her up. And so she accepted Aru.

For Rohit, his mother's acceptance was enough. His father's protests and objections meant nothing to him. He had never got on with his father. He had left home early, unable to tolerate his father's drinking, his infidelities, and contemptuous of his father's idea of the family's past glory. 'My grandfather was an advisor to the Maharaja, my father was an accountant with a British firm in Calcutta, I was sent to England when I was only twenty Rohit had heard enough of these things. Now he had to hear his father's complaints about Aru: 'Who is the girl's father? A university professor who was kicked out of his job!' Lalita persuaded Rohit to pay no attention to his father, she asked him to leave it to her to deal with him. Which Rohit did, knowing that Lalita, in the strange way of suppressed wives, now had the upper hand.

Charu's case was a little different. Devaki, watching Charu's closeness with her son, Hrishi, had been a little uneasy. At first, like Sumi once had, Devaki thought, they're like two friends of the same sex. She had consoled herself with the thought—when they go to different colleges their friendship will peter out like so many friendships of the young. They will forget each other, they will make new friends, she told herself. It did not happen. Aru had been more on the spot, she had predicted that Charu would marry Hrishi. 'You'll go on and do all the things you want to do,' she had said to Charu once. 'You'll become a doctor, boss your patients and staff, make money, get married to Hrishi. . .'

'Help!' Charu had exclaimed.

But Aru had not been deceived. It was impossible for anyone not to notice that Charu and Hrishi, in spite of being in different professional colleges, in spite of the heavy load of their studies, were on the phone with each other at least once a day. And so, when Hrishi, after his graduation, told his parents that he was going abroad, Devaki was torn between not wanting him to go and being glad he was going, because it would distance him from Charu. It was a big blow when Hrishi told her, just before he left, that Charu and he had decided they would get married immediately after she completed her internship and that she would join him in the US soon after. He said this very matter-of-factly, leaving no room for arguments. She realized he was *telling* her, not *asking* her. Sensibly, she accepted the fact. She seemed enthusiastic enough during the wedding but the resentment remained and came out in the open when they came home with the baby.

During this visit, knowing how possessive Devaki is about the baby, Charu has been constantly shuttling between the two houses, careful not to spend too much time with her sisters. She has noticed, however, that Devaki is not happy even with this. One night, when they return home late after an evening with their friends, there is an explosion. Devaki is furious. She accuses them of thoughtlessness, of being uncaring of the baby, of not trusting her ('I'd asked you to leave him with me, I'd have looked after him'), of not thinking of her, Devaki, sitting up, anxiously waiting for them. And so on and on. They listen in silence, but when they go into their room, Charu bursts into tears. Hrishi, who would otherwise have joked her out of it, watches her helplessly, unable to say anything even faintly comforting.

'The worst thing,' Charu tells Aru when she meets her the next day, 'is that when she's angry she takes it out on Hrishi. It's so unfair. I'm the one she's really angry with. And I don't even know what I've done wrong, where I've gone wrong. I wish she would let me call her Devimavshi like I used to. I'm sure both of us will be more comfortable. But no, I have to call her Amma, so that we both remember that she is my mother-in-law and I am her daughter-in-law, and not Charu, Sumi's daughter.'

'It's okay, Charu, you know Devimavshi had a bad time after Murthykaka's bypass surgery.'

'But why take it out on me?' Charu wails. 'You won't believe this, but the other day she went on and on about Pavan's toilet training, and how I must start training him soon and how wrong it is to have him in diapers all day and how she had trained Hrishi, putting him on the potty every hour and hissing like a snake, going ssssss. . .'

'Wait till I tell Devimavshi this!' Aru says, trying not to laugh.

'You wouldn't dare! You wouldn't! You wouldn't, would you?'

The appeal in the last words makes Aru smile. Reverting to the language of their childhood, she says, 'As if!'

'I knew you were only funning

'But maybe, I'll tell Hrishi.'

Charu grins and retorts, 'Tell.' Then, suddenly, she becomes serious and says, 'But it's not really funny, Aru. I just don't understand why she does this to me. I always knew Devimavshi liked you better, but she was never like this to me. I can't do anything right, I get it all wrong. I mean, even her son used to piss better than mine. Stop laughing, Aru, I'm serious.'

Aru's laughter and Charu's indignant voice are suddenly interrupted by a shriek—an outraged yell from the baby. Charu has been changing Pavan's diapers as she talks and now, perhaps, she pricks him, for the baby lets out a loud indignant howl.

'Now don't you start, you little pest. What's wrong with you?'

'You must have pricked him, Charu. Let me see. Oh, the poor little thing.'

'Poor little nothing. Stop howling.' In response to her angry tone and her fierce glare he goes into a major bout of sobbing. She shakes him. 'Stop it, Pavan, stop it at once.'

He stops for a moment, then, looking at her face, begins to sob again, louder than before. She shakes him again.

'Charu, what are you doing? Stop this nonsense. Charu, stop it!'

The two sisters look at each other, both of them equally amazed.

'How dare you shake him! Don't you know how dangerous that is? And you call yourself a doctor. Don't ever do it again.'

'I wasn't shaking him,' Charu says finally, in a small voice. And then suddenly she thrusts the baby at Aru, saying, 'Take him, keep him with you. I'm a bad mother, I don't deserve him. I know you'll look after him much better than me.' She is sobbing in earnest now.

The baby, who had momentarily stopped crying, looks from his mother's face to his aunt's with a bewilderment that is almost comical—what are they doing, passing him about like a parcel? He begins howling all over again.

'Look, we've scared him. All right, baby, go to your Amma, she's not angry with you. Here, Charu hold him. And for god's sake, be gentle with him.'

'Yes, ma'am,' Charu says, kissing the baby, who soon hiccups himself into silence.

'And don't do such a thing again. What a stupid thing to do, scaring him like that!'

'But I meant it, Aru. I mean it. You'll be a much better mother. And I can soon have another child, you know.'

'Another child! As if you can replace one baby with another! This is Pavan, stupid. Not just any baby.'

The two sisters, with less than two years between them, have always been very close. Their mother's death and their father's long absence had brought them even closer. Aru is used to sharing most of her thoughts with Charu, whose occasional cheekiness, though irritating at times, can bring Aru out of her bad or low moods. But now she is unable to talk to Charu about the thought which haunts her the most—her terrible sense of deprivation, her aching need for a child. She seems to have surrounded herself with an invisible barricade and makes it impossible for Charu to cross it and reach her.

Charu, however, pursues the thought and comes back to Aru later with a proposal. She says it in a swift rush of words, as if she has primed herself before speaking to Aru.

'Aru, I've been thinking, I mean I've got an idea, don't say no, just listen to me first.'

'I'm listening.'

'I have a plan. I'll have a child for you, your own child, yours and Rohit's. I'll only bear the child.'

'A surrogate mother.'

'Yes, that's right.'

'Charu, have you gone crazy?'

'But listen, Aru, just listen. It's the best, it's the most sensible thing to do, you've got to admit that. And it's no problem for me, I get pregnant so . . .' she falters, then stops.

'And what if you don't want to give up the baby?'

'As if I would do that! But if you want to be sure, we'll sign a document

'Yes, and if you don't keep your word, I'll take you to court! This is really crazy.'

'But, Aru, listen, I'll be doing this just for you. It will never be my baby, it will be yours. Why would I not give the baby to you?'

'That's not the point, you fool. It's . . . it's . . . oh it's absolutely impossible. And what about Hrishi? You think he'll agree?

'Oh, he'll be fine.'

'Charu, don't speak of this to him. I'm sure he'll be furious.'

Charu, in her ardent desire to do something for Aru, ignores this warning. But Aru is right. Hrishi, when Charu speaks to him, is aghast. 'What! Let my wife bear another man's child!'

'Don't be stupid. It's not another man's child. It will be Aru's . . .'

'Virgin birth, eh? No male involved?'

'Why can't you understand? This is surrogacy.'

'Call it anything, it's still the stupidest idea I've ever heard.'

'But Hrishi, look at Aru, it's so cruel. When I see her with Pavan . . . Don't you care at all about Aru?'

'I care for her. You know that.'

'Then why can't you help her? You know how much she did for me and Pavan, for all of us, when Pavan was born. She came to us the moment she knew Devimavshi, sorry Amma, had to go back home.'

'I know, you don't need to remind me.'

'She did everything Sumi would have done for me, maybe she did even more.'

'You don't have to sing Aru's praises to me, Charu.'

'Then why?'

'Because I think your idea can be a total disaster. No, no again and finally no! Got it? And don't bring up this subject again.'

Charu in her distress talks to Rohit.

'How did you ever think Hrishi would agree, Charu? I'm with him. It's too complicated, emotionally, I mean. I don't want Aru and you to risk your relationship. And we don't need to go to such desperate measures.'

'It's not desperate, it's sensible.'

'No, Charu, adoption is the sensible thing. It's the right thing for us to do. But Aru says no.'

'Why, Rohit?'

'Ask her yourself. She may tell you. Perhaps Aru feels that to agree to adoption is to give up all hopes of having our own child.

Maybe she thinks that to adopt is to deprive a mother of her child. Aru has a client, an unmarried mother, she has seen the girl's determination not to give up her child for adoption. To tell you the truth, I don't really know, Charu. Sometimes I wish her condition had ruled out conception totally. But when doctors say there is a small chance. . .'

'No, Rohit, let her have her hopes. And even if you adopt, it doesn't mean you can't have your own child. You must convince her.'

'Have you tried talking to her?'

'I have, but she changes the subject immediately.'

'Exactly. I've realized I have to leave it to her to take her decision.'

Charu lingers as if she wants to say something more, but desists and moves away. It's hard on Rohit, she realizes. She thinks of her relationship with Hrishi, of how there is nothing they can't say to each other, how they don't mind hurting each other, either, because they know it can always be put right. Rohit's careful handling of Aru saddens her. There is too much of family with Aru, she thinks, too much of Aru's family between Rohit and her. Thank god, I'm not here. But there's Nikhil. And there's Seema . . .

***

If there are three sisters in a fairy tale, (and so often there are) it is invariably the youngest who is the most beautiful, the most virtuous, she is always the heroine of the story. But Seema flouted all the rules of these old stories. Actually, all the three sisters are good looking, though none of Sumi's daughters have that special quality which made Sumi what she was, none of them have Sumi's look of aloofness, a distancing, which gave her, at times, the look of an old sepia picture. Her daughters do show flashes of beauty during certain moments, Charu most often, Aru only when she is relaxed. At such times she has, not Sumi's passive look, but one of quiescence, though always with a hint of alertness lying under it.

Seema had always been thought the least attractive of the sisters. Her face has an unfinished look, like a child who is yet to grow into adulthood; it does not match either her age or her body. It is her body that has the assurance her face lacks. It is her body that finally gave her a career, one which changed her life entirely and has given her more money than both her sisters.

That the two elder sisters achieved their goals did not surprise anyone. It was Seema who was the surprise in the pack. As the youngest in the family, she should have been the most favoured, the pampered one. But by the time she came into the family, certain relationships had been established. Gopal and Aru had, after Charu's birth, forged a bond between them and Aru became Gopal's responsibility, while Charu remained her mother's baby. Seema was different. She was an unplanned, unexpected baby—both the pregnancy and the delivery had been difficult. After Seema's birth, Sumi had gone into depression; she was unable to feed Seema, or do anything for her. Gopal had taken charge of Seema, as he had of Aru after Charu's birth. But there was a difference; this time there was no joy in it. There was too much anxiety about Sumi, too much pity for the baby who was so strangely quiet, rarely crying even when she was hungry. But with Kalyani's help he coped, he managed Seema until Sumi was better and could look after her. Later, Gopal often wondered whether her mother's inability to look after her immediately after birth had marked her for life. There was always something waif-like about Seema; to Gopal, she never seemed to be entirely at home in this world.

Seema continued to remain the odd one out in the family. Aru and Charu were friends as well as sisters. They shared everything, even, initially, their friends. Seema, much younger than the two of them, was never part of their activities. And surprisingly, unlike most younger children, Seema did not clamour to be included either. She was content, it seemed, to be left out, to be left to herself. But there were sudden inexplicable fits of rage and bouts of tears which worried them. In spite of this, they only thought of her as different, never as a child with a problem. After Sumi's death she sank into muteness and apathy. Frightened, knowing Seema needed professional help, Aru, on Premi's advice, took her to a psychiatrist. It seemed a miracle when Seema came out of the state she had got into. There was nothing very wrong with her, the doctor said, except that she was fragile and vulnerable, she would always find any kind of stressful situation hard to deal with. She was persuaded to go back to school, a different school this time, and it seemed that her life would go back on track.

The real change in Seema came about after she started running. The doctor had advised them to let her get more involved in physical activities and soon Seema, with Aru for company, began running every morning in the park. They went out early, when it was still dark, because Seema did not want to meet people and socialize. She liked the fact that, as if there was an unspoken covenant between the early-morning walkers, they ignored one another. Aru ran one lap, then sat on a bench waiting for Seema to finish her rounds. Almost no words were exchanged during the entire period of their run; but this time together, this exercise, was important to both of them. They came home content, energised, ready to start the day.

This was the beginning of Seema's preoccupation with her body. It was not a narcissistic indulgence; rather, she treated her body as if it was something separate from her, like a child she loved, but was determined not to pamper. She made rules for herself, regulating her food and her activities. Her sisters and grandmother watched this a little anxiously, hoping it was a passing phase, but relieved that she had come out of the terrible state she had been in, that she was able to take interest in the world, even though her world was limited to herself, her sisters and Kalyani, Premi and Nikhil. Along with her fitness obsession came a great interest in appearance—her own as well as her sisters'. It was she who had dressed and made up Aru on her wedding day. Charu had been horrified. 'How can you leave it to her, Aru? What if she makes a mess of you?' But Aru had no desire to do what had become the norm for brides—to go to a beautician and be dressed and made up by a professional, as if, she said, 'my wedding is a drama I'm acting in.' Besides, she had faith in Seema, a faith which was justified, because in the end, even Charu had to admit that Aru looked both beautiful and herself. Since then, Seema has taken charge of Aru's clothes; she buys them for her, she has them tailored; in fact, she has turned Aru into a well-dressed woman.

All this should have prepared Aru for what was to come. But she was totally surprised, stupefied almost, at Seema's career, which began almost by chance during her last year of school. Devaki had run a sari boutique for years. She had a genuine feel for textiles and colours and a knowledge about, as well as a love for, saris from different parts of the country. This, along with her connection with weavers, especially in the south, helped her to have some of the most original one-of-a-kind saris in her shop. The prices were prohibitive, but even this became an asset, for Devaki managed to collect an exclusive clientele. Her reputation spread rapidly by word of mouth and her boutique became a place for women to shop at leisure, to meet and enjoy the filter coffee she offered while they looked at the saris. Devaki brought out a calendar each year—a promotional gift given to special customers. It carried pictures of a model showing off some of Devaki's best saris, one for each month. That year, she decided to have Seema as the model.

'Why did you choose Seema, Devimavshi?' Aru asked her later. 'Was it because of her height?'

'That, too. But mainly because I saw at your wedding how good she looked in a sari.'

Devaki, who was, according to her son Hrishi, on a one-woman 'Save the Sari' crusade, had gifted not only Aru with a beautiful wedding sari, she'd given saris to Charu and Seema as well. 'To wear during the wedding,' she'd admonished them sternly. 'There's no need to wear ghagras and lehngas and look as if you're part of a Hindi movie wedding scene.'

Charu, her future daughter-in-law, had complied with some almost audible groans; but Seema had worn her sari with positive pleasure. And Devaki was right. Seema had looked wonderful, elegant and stately. Seema, it is now obvious to everyone, has the model's gift of looking good in whatever she wears, whether it's a sari, trousers, skirts or shorts. Even a business suit, which looks terrible on most Indian girls, looks right on her.

Devaki was pleased with the calendar. 'It's one of my best calendars,' she said. Aru still didn't take it seriously; this was a one-off thing as far as she was concerned. The one good thing that came out of it, she thought, was that Seema had found a friend in Leo, the photographer.

And then one Sunday morning, Seema told Aru, 'Come with me.' She would not tell her where they were going. When they came near the park, Seema stopped outside the gates and said, 'Look!' It was a large hoarding put up at a very strategic spot, a place where three main roads converged. And placed at such a great height that it loomed over them. The hoarding was advertising a newly established sari shop. 'Look,' Seema said and Aru looked at the picture of a model in a sari, a bride, clearly, from the way she was dressed and the jewels she wore.

'But Seema, what . . .?'

And then it hit her; the model was Seema, a totally unrecognizable Seema, a Seema who had been completely recreated. Her hair was drawn severely back from her face and tied into a small chignon at the nape of her neck. And since it was a bridal sari shop being advertised, Seema was wearing heavy bridal jewellery—stone-studded armbands on her slim arms, an array of bangles on her wrist, necklaces and a chain that came almost to her waist—all these subordinated to her sari, a heavy gold and red traditional silk. Seema wore it with assurance, the pleats falling in a waterfall effect to her feet. She was sitting in a low chair, her hands demurely folded in her lap, her brief choli accentuating her tiny waist clasped by a gold waist-band.

When they were clearing the house before its demolition, Aru had come across pictures of Kalyani and of Kalyani's mother, Manorama, as brides. Manorama, a tall rather statuesque girl (even sitting in a chair she gave the impression that she would be taller than her bridegroom) looking straight into the camera with a 'I'm not scared' look of bravado on her face. And Kalyani, a frightened child, weighed down by her heavy sari and jewellery, looking as if something dark and forbidding was awaiting her. And now Seema, who looked more of a bride than her grandmother and great-grandmother did, looking the way a bride was supposed to be—shy, demure, entirely sufficient to herself, giving herself up to be admired.

'Seema, this is you!'

Seema smiled her rare smile, that seemed to vanish the moment it appeared.

'You recognized me.'

'Of course. And you're wearing Amma's diamonds.'

Seema was indeed wearing Kalyani's diamond earrings, earrings given to her by Kalyani just before she went into surgery. They had seen the diamonds everyday on Kalyani's ears and scarcely taken notice of them. Here, in the picture, they seemed to blaze out at the viewer, drawing everyone's eyes towards them and towards Seema's face. Aru was jolted by the fact that Seema, so private a person, who almost refused to participate in the world, had agreed to be on display in such a public place, wholly open to public gaze. But in time Aru realized that Seema was not violating her own privacy, that she was not presenting herself to the world. She was, in fact, concealing herself behind the woman the world could see. Later, when she saw ads that showed Seema as a young girl showing off her glowing skin to the world, (thanks to a special cream) Seema as the young woman who swung her mane of shining hair around her face, (a shampoo made this miracle possible) she knew that neither the girl nor the woman was Seema. And the young woman modeling a sari, wearing a very short choli, the sari worn low on her hips, exposing both her slender waist and the gentle curve of her hips, an enigmatically enticing smile on her face was not Seema, either. It sometimes seemed to Aru that the peculiar blankness on Seema's face, which had made her so different from most people, was, in fact, meant for this purpose: to be occupied by the expressions and emotions that the photographer wanted from her. And she is, what matters most in her career, not only tall and slim with narrow hips and a flat behind, but photogenic; in her pictures she gives the impression, if not of beauty, at least of a kind of perfection.

Initially, they thought of this as a phase. But Seema got more offers and she decided to give up her studies. She had never enjoyed school very much, so the family was not much perturbed by her decision. And in fact, she did not opt out of school so that she could take on more work; it was more an indication of the change of direction in her life. Seema was not very ambitious.

The fact that she soon became a very popular model was due to Leo, who became a sort of agent for her (though it was never so spelt out) and to Seema's own professionalism. The truth is that Seema is lucky to be living in an age in which beauty and fitness are equally valued, for she has both. But Aru, pleased though she is that Seema has found her niche, has often worried about Seema's profession, which is associated in her mind with a Bohemian lifestyle. She has had anxious moments, doubts about late-night parties, drinks, drugs, sex and promiscuity. But Aru need not have worried; Seema's dedication to her body has kept her away from anything that can harm her body. Even if her routine is erratic, she imposes her own order on it. The two sisters still run every morning, besides which Seema goes to a gym to work out and does yoga. And there are regular visits to the beauty parlour for her beauty treatments.

But there are other niggling doubts in Aru, because this is so clearly a profession which exploits women's bodies. In her younger days, Aru had joined a feminist group. She had participated in their activities, standing on roadsides in protest demonstrations, attending meetings and distributing pamphlets in the cause of women's issues. Many of her friends who had earlier shared her beliefs have now moved on. Absorbed in their careers and families, they regard their earlier ideas about women as obsolete, feminism as an outdated issue. Aru can't blame them, she thinks it is a backlash which was bound to come, the result of persistently making victims and martyrs of women, of ascribing everything that happens to them to the 'evils of patriarchy'. If Aru herself has not put away her beliefs and principles, it is because she has seen so much injustice towards women in the course of her work, that she has more questions in her mind than before, questions that have to do with justice. Her convictions about the exploitation of women remains. She has always hated the falseness, the tall claims of ads, the seducing of women into having an unreal image of themselves which the advertising world promotes. Tolerance has been, and still is, to Aru, another word for abetment; but she has learnt to be tolerant, to put her judgement aside where Seema's work is concerned. She won't question something which has brought Seema out of the strange dark place she had inhabited for years. She will say nothing against the work which has enabled Seema to find a place for herself in this world..

And yet, some fears cannot be entirely dismissed. She cannot but think that Seema has entered a profession in which Time is the greatest enemy. Seema has put her entire faith in something as impermanent, as evanescent as the body. A body which ages each day, so many cells dying each minute. And the things that occupy Seema so completely now, her hair, her skin, they will continue to deteriorate day by day, however much care she takes of them. What will Seema do when her body begins yielding diminishing returns? But for Seema, it is only the *now,* the *today* that matters. And in this today Seema is earning good money. It has made little difference to her lifestyle, though it shows in her bedroom, a room with two full-length mirrors and wardrobes built along the entire length of a wall, her dressing table and her bathroom shelves both crowded with bottles and tubes. Seema had worked with Rohit on the interiors of her home and unlike most of his clients, she knew exactly what she wanted. He was surprised by her quick grasp of measurements and costs. He had revealed his surprise, rather tactlessly he now thinks, to Seema, who had said, 'I like numbers. They are so definite, so unshakeable, you can't push them around.' It was a touch of whimsy, which, in Seema, was totally unexpected.

One of the first things Seema had done when she began earning money had been to buy a car. Nowhere is the new Seema more visible than when she sits at the wheel of her car. She enjoys driving and is a confident driver, quite unfazed by the chaotic traffic. Unlike Aru, who loses her temper, Seema is able to keep her cool even when she is in the midst of rule-defying drivers. She is one of those rare women who love their cars; she does not see her car merely as a means of conveying her from one point to another. Yes, Seema is now a confident, independent young woman. Nevertheless, Aru remains protective. Charu has noticed during this visit that if Seema begins her day with Aru, she ends it with her as well. She comes to Aru every night before going to bed; she sits for a while with her, often Aru brushes her hair which seems to soothe Seema. Not much is said, but Seema seems to need the reassurance of Aru's presence. Rohit is never part of their companionship.

It's not right, Charu thinks. Aru has to let go of Seema, only then will she give Rohit what he needs. Which will happen only if Aru has her own child, or if Seema goes away.

Gopal

Could I ever have imagined, when I left home after Sumi's death, that I would be back here one day and living with my daughters? If I am here, it is because of Kalyani. When I first met Kalyani, I had thought her a crushed and defeated woman with no will of her own. And yet, at the end of her life, she was able to control not only her own life, but ours as well; she made sure that my daughters and I lived together. It has worked out well so far, much better than I thought it would. I guess it is because we are independent of one another. Seema and I share a house, fairly companionably I must say, without getting in each other's way. And Aru—well, we don't meet much, which is the way she wants it, I suppose. I still have no sense of permanence here, I feel like a man who knows he has to move out some time. But it is no longer the kind of restlessness, the gnawing, as if something was devouring me from inside, that had sent me away after Sumi's death and kept me constantly on the move.

Initially, my only purpose had been to immerse Sumi's ashes in the Alakananda. It was the first thing I did after leaving Hardwar. I chose a spot where the river was so shallow that I could easily paddle my way to a rock. I sat there for a while. It was one of those moments of utter silence, as if the universe had come to a standstill—a hush so great that it was not an absence of sound, but something positive. I opened the little copper urn . and holding it over the river, shook it a little. The ashes fell out, came together and formed a lump, a few grey bubbles forming on the surface, and then swiftly floated away. Something more solid fell out too—I did not want to see what it was—and plummeted to the depths in a moment. Nothing remained but the few flowers I had placed on the urn, flowers, which, too, the river carried away from me. I closed my eyes and all of Sumi's and my life together seemed to be condensed in that one moment. I felt a rending inside me as if something was being torn out of me and for the first time since Sumi's death I wept, my body heaving and shuddering with sobs. I realized then the wisdom that made it the duty of children to perform the last rites of the dead. Though Sumi was much younger than me, our lives ran on parallel lines; she would always be with me, travelling along with me. Whereas, however much Sumi's children loved her, at some time she would become their past. Easier for the children to let go. I understood then the great grief of people who lose those younger than themselves; it seems like a huge injustice that death commits against time.

With the immersion of Sumi's ashes, I had done what I had come for. There was nothing left for me to do; I felt empty and spent. The same evening I was befriended by a family; seeing, perhaps, my forlorn state, they took pity on me and spoke to me. I had noticed them, they were a large cheerful group. In the course of our conversation—the man spoke to me softly and compassionately, as if he had guessed that I had come here on a painful duty—I came to know that he and his family (his wife, two children, his mother, sister and her two children) were on a pilgrimage of the Char Dham. His mother had a great desire to do this pilgrimage before she became too old and so he, his wife and his sister decided that they would fulfill her wish. The children joined them; for them it was an adventure. They were enjoying it hugely, he said. His wife, entering our conversation, asked me what I was there for. Where was I going? Nowhere, I said. What were my plans? I had none, I said. In that case, why didn't I join them? And so my pilgrimage began.

People come back from pilgrimages with Gangajal, rudraksha beads, polished stones from the river, holy ash, kumkum and all kinds of copper articles. What I brought back was a revelation, one which came to me from the pilgrims. It is no longer only the most pious and the bravest who venture on this pilgrimage. Now that it's easier and more organized, hordes descend on these places in the season. They come from different parts of the country, from varied backgrounds and professions. I met accountants, doctors, lawyers, shopkeepers, bureaucrats, groups of older women on their own. There were the young, middle-aged and the old, the rich in their Nike shoes and warm clothes, as well as the poor in socks sagging to their ankles and worn-out sandals, with threadbare shawls and ill-fitting sweaters. Why were they there? For many of them, the yatra was something that had to be done at some time in their lives; it was a tradition they believed in. For some it was an adventure. There were yet others who came to perform their duties towards their dead. And maybe, there were some like me, who did not know what they were there for and who, again like me, had a sense that what we see is not all that there is. If it is, why do we have moments of deep yearning for what we do not know, a sense of missing something, of loss, even in the midst of a full and crowded life?

What amazed me was the astounding faith of some of the pilgrims. Looking at them, I got an inkling of what faith is: a magic mantra, an open sesame which unlocks the door, if not to understanding the world, at least to accepting and absorbing it. One old woman, I remember, walked barefoot for much of the way—this was her penance, I was told. Another had a dip in the icy cold river without hesitation and came out without shivering. When we reached Gangotri, I heard joyous shouts of Jai Ganga Mayi. I saw tears in some eyes, many stood with closed eyes and hands folded for so long it seemed they had gone into a trance. Their exaltation when they saw what they thought was the origin of the great river (it is not, but that is another matter) their faith that had brought them so far and made them endure everything without a murmur of a complaint—to me, these were astonishing. And the fellow feeling among the pilgrims, the sharing, seemed like a miracle, as well. My family, for example, never let me eat by myself. Perhaps, when they got home, they would resume their normal selfish selves. But to realize that there is a better self inside us, that the need to love is an intrinsic part of us so that we can care even about strangers—I had to go a long way to see this miracle of our humanity, to understand that an invisible umbilical cord connects us to all of humanity. We are never separate unless we cut the cord ourselves; then, indeed, we are truly alone.

To believe in miracles is to believe in life. When Charu rang me up from the hospital to give me the news of her son's birth, she was tearful yet laughing, she seemed elated, exalted almost about the birth of her baby. She spoke of the baby as if he was a miracle. And she a doctor! But in truth the baby was as much a miracle as a spring of water gushing out of a rock—both are pure, pristine. Seema's conception, I remember, had taken us by surprise; she was born after I had a vasectomy. That Sumi could get pregnant, that a child could be conceived even after we had ensured it should not happen, made me aware of the miracle of life, of its persistence, its stubbornness, its whimsicality, its infinite variations.

I was with 'my family' until we returned from Gangotri. They had completed the Char Dham, but I still had the Yamunotri to visit. It was the most difficult of the four pilgrimages with a long and hard trek at the end. I decided to take it easy for a while and to spend some time on my own before going on. My family and I separated at Uttarkashi. I got off the bus to their cheerful farewells, promises to correspond, to meet again; their voices floated back to me from the bus. I would miss them, but I must confess it also felt good to be on my own, not to have to constantly respond to their goodwill and good nature.

Things had gone well until then. Then came the accident. It happened when I was returning from a hike. It was evening, but it was still bright when I fell. There was a moment of such acute pain that I blanked out for a moment. When I came to, I realized I was in the middle of the road, that I could be run over; vehicles would not see me because I was just round a curve in the road. I tried to stand up, but could not. Ignoring the pain and putting aside the fear that I had suffered a fracture, I dragged myself to the side of the road. But this meant that I was not visible—two vehicles went past without seeing me. Twilight fell and I began to worry for the first time about having to be there all night. I could not move at all now and with the cold rapidly increasing, I was glad to stay in the shelter of the rock. I sat with my back to it. The sharp edges cut into my back, but the greater pain in my foot made me oblivious to these small pricks. In a while the pain settled down to a steady hurting throb. I could feel my foot swelling with each throb. I removed my shoe and wrapped my scarf around the foot. Now nothing mattered but the cold. I huddled into my inadequate windcheater, meant more for the rains than for the cold, and tried to keep awake, alert to every sound. I think I must have dropped off to sleep now and then, for I remember moments of waking up, confused and disoriented. At times I must have had hallucinations. I thought Ramesh was with me, saying he would take me to the hospital, asking me to wait, he would bring his car to me. Each time the pain pulled me out of the dreams and back into the reality of my injury.

Finally, I felt someone shaking me. This was real. A man was leaning over me, his face anxious and concerned. It was bright. The night was over. 'Kya hua?' the man kept asking me, while I tried to pull myself together. I pointed to my foot. He removed the scarf, looked at the foot, nodded and walked away. For some reason I was not afraid he would leave me and go away; I knew he would be back. And he came—with a kettle and two mugs in his hand. He poured out tea for both of us. Later, I understood the wisdom which made him join me in drinking the tea; I felt safe and secure, I had not been abandoned, he was with me. The tea was hot and sweet, it tasted like nectar and brought me back to life. In a while, another man came with a plastic chair. They lifted me into it after first helping me to stand and relieve the pressure on my bladder. They carried me to a wayside tea stall, one of the many that dot the roads and took me to a little shed behind the stall. There was a bed inside, grimy and smelly, but when they put me on it, I was filled with relief. I could even smile at them. 'The doctor will come,' the first man said and they went out. The doctor did come in what was perhaps a short while, but which seemed a long wait to me. I don't know what I had expected, but the bearded plump cheerful man seemed competent enough.

'I don't think there is any fracture,' he said after examining me. 'Only a ligament tear. Give it good rest and you'll be fine. You just need a proper bandage.' He saw my face and said, 'Oh *yes*, I'm a real doctor. Not a surgeon, but a proper MBBS.'

'Where do you live?' he asked when he had done the bandaging.

'Nowhere.'

'That's yours?' he nodded at my backpack which the men had put by me.

'Yes.'

'Stay here for now. You have enough money? Good. Bahadur will look after you. I'll drop in as often as I can.' He gave me some painkillers and left.

That was the beginning of a new existence for me, of living in a place I had never seen, of being looked after by total strangers. Their kindness did me good, but their complete ignorance of who I was and of my past life did me even more good. The doctor came every evening, more to chat with me, I think, than to look after my foot, which was healing well. He needed the conversation, he told me frankly; though what he really needed was to talk, what he wanted was a listener. And I was, still am, a good listener. In a few days the doctor got me a pair of crutches and I was able to go out to the tea stall and join the men there. By this time, people had heard about me and my plight. They greeted me with smiles, asking no questions except for the inevitable 'How are you?' to which I had only to nod. They went on with their talk then, with their tea drinking, leaving me alone which, too, did me much good.

It was there, in that rackety little shed and the tea stall, that I slowly came back to life. Not in one epiphanic moment, but a little each day, through the small pleasures of daily life. The sight of the mountains when I woke up in the morning. My morning cup of tea, the smoke rising from its surface like a benediction. Distant sounds of peoples conversation. Men at the tea stall laughing and talking, embracing me into intimacy without my having to say a word. Children with early-morning shining faces waving to me as they rushed off to school. The happy excited cries of children while they played. The sound of a woman's laughter. The sight of a woman's face, of her body. It was at this time that I began to understand that you have no place on this earth if you are not connected to anyone, to anything. Only saints can soar over their own physicality and attain a bodiless existence which severs you from everything in life.

At the end of three weeks, the doctor asked me what I wanted to do. 'I don't know,' I said. 'You can come and stay in the ashram until you make up your mind,' he said. He had told me he was living in an ashram. 'But I'm not a proper ashramite,' he said with a smile. 'The swamiji has given me the freedom to live the way I want. You can stay with me, you can be of some use,' he said.

And so began my two-year stay in the ashram. Like the doctor I lived in it, but was not part of it. Certain rules had to be observed, of course, but it was not a problem for me. And I became useful, as the doctor had predicted. I helped him. I worked in the ashram garden. I taught in the little school the swamiji had established in the ashram premises. 'My Hindi is not very good,' I told the swamiji. 'Never mind,' he said. 'Children want to learn English now. You teach them English, they will teach you Hindi.' I began to help Bahadur. When he went out once a month to buy provisions, I worked in the stall. His wife Kunti made the tea while I served the customers. Kunti was pleased that my presence kept Bahadur from going off on his drunken binges. The abstinence, unfortunately, didn't last long. Once he got over his awe—I was 'Professor saab'—he went back to his old ways. I helped in the stall during the days of his reckless drinking as well.

I went out on long walks and slept soundly at night as I had not done for years. The doctor and I became friends. His name was Gandhi, but 'I'm completely unlike my famous namesake,' he said the first time he told me his name. 'I'm a sinner. I drink, I eat meat, I have no self-control at all.' I realized what that meant when I heard the sound of a woman's voice, of a woman's laughter, in his rooms. But he was a good man. There was healing for me in his companionship, in my relationship with Bahadur, Kunti and their children and my time with the children in school. Healing also came in the letters that arrived for me from Ramesh, from Premi, from Kalyani and even, occasionally, from Charu, after I had written to Ramesh telling him where I was.

When Kalyani's letter came asking me to go back, I was full of trepidation, but I knew I had to return, I had no choice in the matter. Actually it was not just Kalyani's illness, nor her appeal to me to return that made me come back. There was the promise I had made to Seema, even before Sumi's death.

'So you will come back?' she had asked me.

I had hesitated and said, 'Yes, if you need me. When you need me.'

When I returned Seema met me as if I had gone away on work, or on a holiday; there was no rancour in her at all. I don't know what I expected (or feared) but the one thing I never expected was she would be earning as much money as she does. Sumi, too, had worried a great deal about Seema, she had felt that her inability to look after Seema after her birth was responsible for her difference from her sisters. Now, what pleases me most is that Seema lets me share in the household expenses equally, never letting me realize that she earns much more money than I do. We share the household chores as well; Nagi does the cleaning and washing up, we do all the rest. Seema's rages, her bouts of tears, her tantrums, have gone, though she still has moods when she withdraws from everyone. And there is Leo, a young man who has found a place in Seema's life, in all our lives, in fact. It does not seem like a romantic involvement, but why, then, is he always with Seema? I don't understand, I have given up trying to understand things that I can't decipher—like why do Aru and Rohit not adopt a child? I ask my daughters no questions, I leave these things alone.

The most unexpected thing in my life is that I have found work to do. I have gone back to my subject. An ex-colleague got me this work. I am part of an ambitious and gigantic project of an encyclopedia of Indian history. I am supposed to edit and check all the entries on the Peshwas. I also have to work on a few entries on the era myself. I earn some money from this and some more from reading academic books for a publisher. During the weekends I work with a group of young people who help educate street children.

Yes, I am busy. And reasonably content. There's this too, that for company I have my neighbours—Rao and Kasturi. Rao is an urbane well-read man and a great conversationalist. I enjoy his language—languages, rather; both his Kannada and English are equally elegant. (Kasturi says he is the only man who speaks Kannada with an English accent!) I enjoy his erudition and sense of humour. He offers his jokes in a rather solemn manner, waiting for you to appreciate the humour, expecting your smile, your laughter. 'At my age,' he told me soon after we met, 'there is not much I can contribute to the world. But there is one thing

I can do—I will not burden the world with another unnecessary memoir, though I realize I am expected to write one about my experiences. But I will not. Too many people write. Or try to write.'

I presumed he was referring to the time when he, only a journalist then, not yet an editor, had been jailed during the Emergency. Kasturi told me that he rarely speaks of that time, or of what he had done to be jailed.

I said that I thought his story could be interesting, it would, perhaps, add a little more to our knowledge of that time.

'Spoken like a historian. But, no, I have too great a respect for writing to do something as trivial or meaningless as writing about myself. I believe,' he said, 'that writers are the only people who can stand up against that greatest force in the world— Time. Even if the tidal wave of Time finally destroys them, as it destroys everything, they will have taken a stand, they will have made that one act of resistance which matters.'

'All writers? All writing?' I asked with a smile.

'No, of course not. There is writing and writing.' And he spoke to me of Kasturi's writing, the serials she wrote for TV and the contempt she had for her own work. 'In any case, writing is taken too casually. Everyone thinks that he or she has a story to tell the world.' Then he went back to his own experience and said, 'Too much is made of the Emergency. It is such a minute dot in our history. Mrs Gandhi lost her head, she was stupid, I think. But so are most tyrants. They forget that slaves will rebel, that people will rise against them at some time. Statues are desecrated, they are razed to the ground, bodies dug out of graves and hung at crossroads; but each dictator thinks—such a thing won't happen to me. And none of them have any sense of remorse, either. When their end comes, they still think they did right.'

I reminded him then of Aurangzeb's remorse, of his words:

> My years have gone by profitless. God has been in my heart,
> yet my darkened eyes have not recognized his light.

'Did he really say that? Remarkable. And this is the man who gouged out his father's eyes, imprisoned him and killed his own brothers. Dr Jekyll and Mr Hyde, eh?'

An interesting man, Rao. And Kasturi? I don't know what the relations between them are, but I see that they lead separate lives.

He has his own routine. 'I read,' he told me, 'I play bridge, solve crosswords, go for music programmes—not Hindustani, I enjoy Carnatic music, though it's becoming too gimmicky for my taste.'

Kasturi and he rarely go out together. She never uses his car, she always travels in an auto. In fact, that is how she and I met. I had been interested in her mainly because she talks so much like my sister Sudha. If I close my eyes, it seems to me it could be Sudha talking. Not only the voice, but the words and expressions she uses, the bluntness of her speech. Kasturi, I guessed from her Kannada, comes from the north of the state, as I do. I asked her once where she was from.

'Jogipura,' she said.

'Why, I know Jogipura,' I said. 'In fact, I went to school in a place close to it.' She looked inquiringly at me. 'Shivpur,' I told her.

'I went to school in Shivpur, too.'

We discovered that while I had been in the government school, she had gone to the convent school. 'My father wanted me to learn English and become an IAS officer,' she said. The self-mockery was not harsh, it was as if she was laughing at herself. 'I never managed to do that, but at least my brother did. My father had that satisfaction.'

I knew by then who she was, or rather, whose daughter she was. Her father had been a politician, a Congressman who had wielded huge influence in the state's politics for years. He had been the president of the State Congress for a long time. But she rarely speaks of him, or indeed of her personal life. I have no idea whether she is, or was, married, whether she is a spinster, a divorcee, or a widow. Rao told me she had been a journalist, that she had joined his paper as a novice. 'I don't know why she opted for an English paper, she was a complete misfit. I told her it was a mistake, that she should be working in a Kannada daily. She left and did just that after some time. And then she went into television.'

Now she writes scripts for serials. 'I thought I could make a difference,' she said once, 'that I would write something sensible, meaningful. But no, it's impossible. You can't move away from the formula. The great god of TV—the TRP—is watching.'

She and I met the day I was waiting for a bus, and she, going past me in a rickshaw, offered me a lift. I hesitated and then got in. When we reached home, she opened her purse to pay.

'Let me pay,' I said.

She gave me a stern look then turned to the auto driver. 'What do we do now, Raju? This sir doesn't want me to pay and I don't want him to pay for me. So what do we do?'

'Make it fifty-fifty,' the man said.

So fifty-fifty it was. The driver drove off with a grin. I laughed and she gave me a friendly smile. That was the beginning.

Kasturi's presence in Aru's family home can be explained by Kalyani's will, a document that deserves to be spoken of in detail and at length. At this time, it's enough to say that Kalyani herself had wanted the family home to be demolished. That she, who was so devoted to her home, should express such a wish had caused much astonishment. Kalyani, however, had her own reasons which she stated in her will. In its place she wanted a home to be built for Premi and her three granddaughters. She also clearly specified that the architect of the house should be her granddaughter Aru's husband, Rohit Kashyap. But Premi, to everyone's surprise, did not want a home for herself. Nothing could make her change her mind. 'Why do I need a separate home?' she asked. 'I will stay with Aru when I'm here,' she said. 'Aru's home will be my home.' When pressed hard, she had agreed to have a bit of land at the back where she could build a house for herself if, at any time, she felt the need for it. And so the land was divided into two parts, the new house being built on the larger portion, and the smaller portion at the back left bare until Gopal decided to convert it into a kind of fruit garden, growing bananas, chikoos, guavas and other easy-growing fruit trees. This didn't solve Rohit's problem of having to build three apartments without making it a three-level building. Ultimately, he invested his own money in the house and made the entire ground floor into a home for Aru and himself, with two apartments on the first floor, one each for Charu and Seema.

Now Seema and Gopal occupy Seema's home and Charu, living abroad for she doesn't know how long, decided to rent out her apartment. That is how Kasturi enters this story and Aru's life—as Charu's tenant.

She seemed to be an ideal tenant, a middle-aged woman living on her own. 'But she's okay, you don't have to worry about her, madam,' the agent who had managed the deal had told Aru. As if, Aru thought indignantly, a woman living on her own had to be vouched for as being 'okay'.

Aru takes her beliefs about women and their place in the world seriously. She is earnest about not saying anything that smells even faintly of prejudice, careful never to run down women, at least women in general. Which is why she had, in response to the agent's remarks, said a little sharply, 'It's none of my business what she is or does, as long as she pays the rent regularly.'

Oh, there would be no problem about that, the man assured her. The woman had a very successful career in TV. 'You must have seen her, she is quite famous, she did many interviews with film stars and politicians. She wrote the script for one film. It was a hit, it ran for a very long time, it also got many awards.'

Though Aru is not a movie person, she had heard of this one because it had been a mammoth hit. Not that this fact impressed her. In any case, she told herself, it doesn't matter, we won't have anything to do with one another.

However, soon after Kasturi came to live in the apartment, Aru had stumbled into a gaffe which had embarrassed her more than it had annoyed Kasturi. The family had noticed that Kasturi, when she moved in, was not alone, that a man had moved in with her and now lived in the house—not as guest, but a resident, for his car was parked in the parking lot. There had been some curiosity about who he was. Even Aru, though she told herself sternly that it was none of her business, was curious. Was he her husband? No, he seemed too old for her. Besides, the lease had been signed by Kasturi and it was her name—Kasturi Patil—that was spelt out on the nameplate at her door. Her brother, then? Apart from the unlikely possibility of a brother staying with his sister in *her* house, once again the man looked too old to be her brother. Lover? Same problem, though, of course, a great difference in ages was possible in such a relationship. Forced to speak to Kasturi one day about their driver having parked the car so awkwardly that Aru could not get her own out, she had said, playing it safe, 'Your father's car is blocking my car. Could you tell the driver

'He's not my father,' Kasturi had said bluntly. She had, what Aru thought, was a supercilious smile on her face. (The smile was actually for what Rao would say when she told him that this girl had thought he was her father!) Kasturi had added, to make it clear, 'His name is Mr Rao. He's staying with me for a few months.'

Aru had flushed in embarrassment, angry with herself for making assumptions, annoyed because she felt she had been shown to have made a mistake. But Aru, opinionated though she is, is always willing to be corrected if she is wrong. This humility is what saves her from priggishness, it is what Rohit finds endearing. 'Bossy, bossy,' Rohit had once heard her muttering to herself, rapping herself hard on her head with her knuckles. 'What's that about?' he had asked her in amazement.

'Charu says I'm bossy. I try to warn myself each time I feel I'm becoming bossy, specially when I hear that tone—you know, a kind of brassy tone of authority in my voice.'

In this matter with Kasturi, Aru knew she was wrong. She admitted to herself and to Rohit that she was wrong; but the sense of discomfort, which Kasturi made no attempt to do away with, remains. The two women rarely meet and when they do, it's usually on the stairs. Aru gives her an unsmiling nod and Kasturi has only the faint beginnings of a smile as they pass each other.

'She doesn't like me,' Kasturi tells her friend Mira.

'What an unreasonable expectation! Why should your landlady like you?'

'She's not my landlady, she's my landlady's sister. And why is it unreasonable to want to be liked? It feels good when people like you. Don't you want to be liked by everyone?'

'Not me, thanks. I don't care about being liked. Liked! It's such a wishy-washy word. I want the people I love to love me. I want my husband, my daughter, my mother and sisters and you to love me.'

'You know we all do.'

'Yes, but tell me what makes you think she dislikes you?'

'Not dislike, perhaps. I think she disapproves of me. She's disapproved of me since I told her Rao is not my father.'

In this Kasturi is wronging Aru, something she will not know until much later.

'I told you, Sonu, I knew you'd have problems because of your old man, sorry, I mean Mr Rao. You shouldn't have agreed to take him into your house.'

'How could I have refused, Mira? After all that he's done for me?'

'He got his reward for that, didn't he?'

'Don't be vulgar, it doesn't suit you. Anyway, it's only for a year at the most. His daughter will be back in a few months and he'll go back home. And do I really care what that girl thinks of me?'

'Girl? Or woman? What is she?'

'Whatever she is, she's very self-absorbed. Sure of herself. She's . . . what do you call it? Haughty? High and mighty?'

'You should know which word you want to use. What is she exactly? Haughty? Or high and mighty?'

Kasturi hesitates, she fumbles for words and wishes that, like Mira's family, she could compare the woman to a character in a book. For them, this comparison is like a code word, providing an immediate understanding of the person. Later, when Mira comes to know Aru, she will try to place her and will think first of Dorothea Brooke. But she will soon reject the comparison, for Aru is a woman of today, she does not need a Casaubon, she is able to work out her ideals on her own. When Mira understands Aru better, she will see that, unlike Dorothea, Aru is striving not for goodness, but for justice. Ultimately, Mira will settle for Margaret Hale, Mrs Gaskell's wonderful heroine, thinking that Aru has the same dignity and sense of responsibility. Kasturi, however, has read neither *Middlemarch,* nor *North and South. Middlemarch* had been offered to her, pressed on her is more like it, by Belinda, Mira's mother. Kasturi had kept the book for a week, then returned it, admitting she hadn't read it.

'How will you learn good English, child, if you don't read good books?' Belinda had asked.

Long before young people realized that their future lay in English, Kasturi had decided to arm herself with the language. Her father had begun the process when he had taken her out of the Jogipura school where they were taught only Kannada and where, often, there was one teacher for three classes, and sent her to a 'convent school' in Shivpur. He was ambitious for his daughter. So it was generally considered. Only much later did his other, perhaps his real purpose in sending his (daughter and wife away from Jogipura, come to light. He even set up another home in Shivpur where Kasturi and her brother lived with their mother. Fresh from her village school where, because of being her father's daughter and because of her own quickness she had been able to queen it over all the other students, Kasturi was miserable in her new school where she was a nobody. Her first few days in school were a nightmare; she was confused by the English language, wretched at being ignored and friendless. She, who had always been the first, often the only one to put up her hand when a question was asked, was now afraid to open her mouth. When she was forced to speak, she fumbled for the words and ultimately broke into Kannada, at which the entire class burst into laughter, as if the language was comic. Her mother was incapable of helping her; she was disinterested in her children's problems and her only job, as she saw it, was to cook and feed them, to comb Kasturi's hair, wash it once a week, and see to her clothes. Kasturi's brother, to whom she could have spoken, had become distant. He was, Kasturi thought unfairly, furious with her since it was because of her that he was deprived of the opportunity to live independently in a hostel as he would otherwise have done.

It was Mira who saved Kasturi. They shared a bench for the odd reason that they were of the same height. An inch more or an inch less, they often told each other later, and we would never have been friends. But that was impossible, they were meant to be friends. Mira helped Kasturi with her English and stood up for her against the girls who made fun of her because she had come from a village. Soon they were 'fast' friends and remained that way all through school and college; in fact, all their lives except for a brief while when they lost touch. Once Kasturi had said to Mira, 'Thank god, Miri, this gay business was not so much around when we were girls. I'm sure they'd have called us lesbians.'

'And how do you know they didn't?' At the look of consternation on Kasturi's face, Mira had laughed and said, 'Come on! No one could think that of you. You made it amply clear that you love males.'

'And you don't?'

'I will love only one male,' Mira said primly.

Everything about Mira was a discovery for Kasturi. She had not known any Christians until then, there were no Christians in Jogipura. She had never heard about Anglo-Indians, either, which Mira had told her she was on the very first day, as if to make something clear. Soon they were visiting each other's homes and met each other's families. Kasturi was utterly fascinated by Mira's family, especially by Belinda, Mira's mother. Belinda had been an eye-opener for Kasturi. Getting to know her had been like seeing another world, one where women didn't have to live the way her mother did—frightened of her husband, afraid to open her mouth. Belinda not only talked back to her husband, she ordered him about. 'Ma's the boss,' Mira said. 'Even the hens obey her, they lay at least three eggs every day for the three of us.' And when Belinda spoke to Mira's father, he would say, 'Yes, ma'am, yes, I hear you loud and clear.' And the way Belinda looked in her skirts and white blouses with lace-edged collars and sleeves, a belt clasped about her slim waist. She had short hair, used lipstick and wore shoes (even inside the house) that went clickety-clack clickety-clack as she walked briskly about doing her chores. She was constantly walking, up and down, to and fro; she walked even when she was taking a class, so that her students had to keep swiveling their heads, like spectators at a tennis match. Belinda talked all the time, constantly quoting from her favourite authors, mixing her own words with theirs, so that often her children were never sure whether the words were her own, or whether she was quoting someone.

'Remember, Mira, god could not make Antonio Stradivarus's violin without Antonio,' she said sternly to Mira once, chiding her for something done sloppily. But Kasturi was baffled. Antonio? Stradi . . .? Violin? What was that all about?

'Shakespeare,' Mira mouthed to Kasturi.

'Mira, dear, don't open your mouth if you're only going to exhibit your ignorance. That's not Shakespeare, that's George Eliot.'

'God,' Mira said, once again soundlessly.

'I heard you, Miranda, you're being very cheeky. And I'll forget your rudeness if you remember what I'm trying to tell you—unless *you* do things right, no one else, not even god, can do it for you.'

Above all, Belinda worked, she taught English in a local college. Kasturi learnt later that the names of her daughters came from Shakespeare; each got her name from the play Belinda was teaching at the time she got pregnant. So there was Olivia who became Livvy, Cordelia who became Delia and Mira who had been named Miranda. There had been a daughter between Delia and Mira who had been named Ophelia. 'And can you believe it?' Mira asked, 'She drowned.' What was odd about it? It was years before Kasturi found the connection between the name and the manner of her death. Belinda abandoned Shakespearean names after Ophelia's death and chose names from George Eliot instead, George Eliot, who, according to Mira, stood third in the hierarchy of Belinda's greats—first God, then Shakespeare and then George Eliot. So Livvy's twins became Seth and Adam, (these were their Christian names; to Belinda's consternation they were also given Muslim names). Delia's children were Tom and Maggie and Mira's daughter was Ramola, Molly for short.

To Kasturi, Belinda was perfect. She was shocked when she heard Belinda's daughters criticize her. 'Must you show off, Ma?' Delia often asked.

'Ma, will you please stop talking? I am working.' That was Livvy, who was always studying.

'Ma, must you use so much perfume? And why must you use it even at home?' This was Mira.

Belinda took up the challenge of teaching Kasturi English. She made her read books, she insisted Kasturi speak to them only in English and she gave her three words a day to find the meanings of and then use in sentences of her own. Kasturi would scratch her head over the words. Plenitude? What was that? Apostasy? Equivocate? Execrable? When she got the meaning, she wrote the sentence: *English is an execrable language.* Ma will be furious, Mira had said, but Belinda had laughed. 'You're a clever girl, you'll soon get the hang of it,' she said.

Kasturi never did. She worked hard, she struggled with the language, at times she despaired. I will never learn this language, she thought. She had always considered herself a reasonably intelligent girl, but the language seemed to defeat her with its quirkiness, its inconsistencies, its strange rules of pronunciation, the irrational rules of grammar, the articles which she never seemed to get right and the prepositions which were a thorn in her flesh. She did learn enough to get respectable marks in her examinations and to converse without disgracing Belinda. But she never graduated to reading the novels Belinda told her to read, let alone attempting Shakespeare. And finally, in spite of her father's ambition for her, it was not English, but her own language that gave her a livelihood. She worked for a Kannada TV channel, first as a news reader, then as an interviewer, an anchor and finally as a script writer for serials.

Now this work was beginning to pall on her. 'I don't know whether I'm fickle, I just don't seem to be able to stick to any work. Whatever I do, I keep thinking my real work is elsewhere.'

'I'll tell you what your problem is. What you're doing is not work at all.'

'It's writing.'

'You call this, what you do, writing?'

Mira is Belinda's daughter. To her, like to Belinda, there is something sacred about writing, something blessed about writers. And writing meant poetry, it meant fiction, writers meant Keats and Browning, Yeats and T.S. Eliot, it meant George Eliot and Jane Austen, Dickens and Hardy. Inevitable, therefore, that Mira should see Kasturi's writing as not writing at all. She's happy that Kasturi, who got into script writing only to earn money, will soon be giving it up. Kasturi's brother, who had been fighting a case in the courts to get back their lands and other property from their father's mistress, had recently won the case and magnanimously given Kasturi a half-share in everything. 'He's trying to make me forget what he did to me. As if I will ever forget!' Kasturi had said darkly when she told Mira about it.

'Have you thought about what you'll do when you stop working on this serial, Sonu?'

'I don't know. I mean, I'm not sure. I keep thinking of Jogipura. Remember how it was during election times? You came home with me once, remember?

Yes, Mira remembered. If Mira's family had been a revelation to Kasturi, Jogipura had been one for Mira. The house was large, with huge rooms but scarcely any furniture. There was only one bed in the house, which was for Kasturi's father; all the others slept on mattresses that were laid on the floor at night and rolled up into a pile during the day. The front and back doors of the house were so perfectly aligned that you could look from the front door into the backyard. Both doors were kept open all day. On her very first day, Mira saw, in total amazement, a cow march in majestically through the front door, as purposeful as if she knew her way, as if this *was* her way, and exit through the back. Mira was even more amazed that no one raised an eyebrow, as if it was normal to have a cow walk into and out of your house. Eventually, within a few days, she got used to things, she found even the smell of cattle dung in the backyard not very unpleasant. It had been election time and bikes and vans were all over the place, clusters of men standing all day in the front yard. Cups of tea were served continuously and food was cooked in the open in the backyard to feed volunteers and party workers. She remembered the campaign posters and banners, the party flags strewn all about and the air of excitement which always quickened when Kasturi's father joined the crowd of workers. The two girls had gone with him on one of his election campaigns, rattling on the bad roads in a jeep, surrounded by a haze of dust. Seeing the way he was greeted, the way his authority was recognized, Mira saw the culture of political power for the first time. She realized that her friend's father was a very important man. No, she was never to forget that visit, because it was there that, for the first time, she had a sense of where she really belonged. After that visit, she decided to shed the 'Anglo' and keep only the 'Indian' part of her identity. So she was ready for Ranjan when, years later, he came along.

'You want to go back to Jogipura?'

'Maybe.'

'And do what?'

'I don't know, Mira. Maybe just stay there for a while. Maybe I'll travel about in the district and meet people. Write about it. You know Vasant and Shalini have moved back to Jogipura. Shalini wants us to go back to my father's times, I think. She's getting ambitious. But Vasant refuses to do anything to help, he won't lift a finger, she complains. I've worked hard, now I'm going to take it easy—that's his line. Retired bureaucrats are of no use at all, Shalini says. And so she picked me to help her.'

'To do what?'

'I don't know. Maybe try to get elected in the next elections. She thinks that because I'm known, I will be more accepted. I was on TV, you know.'

'Yes, madam, I know you are famous.'

'Was.'

'Not *was,* Sonu, you *were* famous.' Then Mira suddenly says, using Belinda's words and in her tone, 'Come on, come on, no more dawdling, let's get to work.'

Mira and Kasturi have 'brainstorming sessions' ('Does anyone need brains for writing this?') during which Kasturi tries to work out some kind of a sensible episode for the serial. It has become a habit for Kasturi to consult Mira about her serial, specially when she is stuck, as she is now. It is a 'mega serial', which means it goes on and on, almost, it seems, forever. It doesn't matter how illogical and incredible the story becomes in the process, what tortuous bizarre paths it takes as it winds its long way towards no discernible end. Characters come and go, people die and come miraculously 'alive' again, actors leave and other actors play their roles and the story often branches off into vague areas, many times getting lost there.

Kasturi is in charge, so to say, of the 'good sister' in the story. (It was a revelation for Mira that the serial has not one, but a team of writers. What about creativity then, she asked Kasturi. Creativity? What's that?) This good sister continues to be good in spite of being wronged and cheated, so good that she even gives up the man she loves, because her sister, the bad one, wants to marry him. Kasturi dislikes the good sister, she irritates her enormously. Now Kasturi has to make her fall prey to the villain's machinations yet again and have her come out of his villainous coils, pure and unscathed.

'To tell you the truth, Mira, I want to kill the silly girl off, but they won't let me.'

'Of course you can't. How can they have the ultimate triumph of good if she dies?'

'Actually, I think they may not mind her dying. If they kill her they can bring her back to life a little later. It creates suspense and makes the viewers sit up, I am told. Oh god!' Kasturi makes a vomiting sound. 'And stop laughing, Mira, give me some ideas.'

'Well, let's see what we can do without killing her. Where are you now?'

They talk, they discuss, they argue, Kasturi makes notes. They have just finished when Ranjan enters. As soon as Ranjan joins them, the friends' conversation ceases and Kasturi prepares to respond to either of the two sentences he always greets her with. Mira is a little defensive when her husband and friend come together. She is aware of the edge of hostility between them. The hostility has been slightly blunted since Mira's surgery; in fact, it was to Kasturi that Ranjan had come when he got the news that the tumour in Mira's breast was malignant; it was Kasturi before whom he had sobbed, Kasturi who had helped him to get through those terrible days. Mira, however, is still apprehensive. Today she is relieved when Ranjan does not ask about the serial Kasturi is writing. Kasturi hates her own work, but she resents the condescending way in which he talks about it. It's not fair, Kasturi thinks. I know it's trash, but I work hard at it, I earn a living from it. She never says these things aloud because of Mira. Today, fortunately, he asks the question she can comfortably deal with: 'And how's your old man?'

'My old man? He's not mine! I don't believe in possessing people.'

'Well, you may not, but I do, Sonu. *My* husband, *my* friend, *my* sisters, *my* mother, *my* . . .' Mira falters, she does not go on.

Mira and Ranjan's is a happy marriage, they are a rare couple, happy to be together. And yet there is this deep chasm between them.

'Why don't you ask Molly to come for a visit?' Kasturi has asked Mira. 'Ignore Ranjan.'

'I can't. I can't bear to see them saying hurtful things to each other.'

Mira is spoilt. She has always lived among people who love one another, she doesn't know about people who can hurt savagely, who can torture and draw blood and still call it a marriage.

'Molly insists that if she comes, it will be with Ian. And she's not going to pretend they are married.'

'But, Mira . . .'

'Oh, let it go, Sonu. Both she and Ranjan want to be unreasonable. Let them. And if I die without seeing Molly . . .'

'Don't talk rubbish. If you really want to see her so much . . .'

'I said, let it go, Sonu.'

'Your friend thinks she owns me, eh?' Ranjan now says. 'You women make a big fuss about being treated as objects, you can't own us, you say and then my wife says she possesses me. Well, Kasturi, how do you explain that?'

'You know, Ranjan, there are two kinds of men, even among the decent sort. There are men who like women but can't take anything they say or do seriously. And the other kind are men who don't hear what they are saying. Of course there's a third kind, but let's not waste our time talking about them.'

'Which type am I?'

'The first, of course.'

And so they go into a light kind of bantering which Kasturi knows makes Mira happy. She hates any kind of conflict. It makes me really ill, she says. Which is why they rarely talk of Mira's daughter, why they move away from all uncomfortable subjects. Easier to talk of things we don't much care about. But why, then, converse at all?

Like so many choices we make in life, Aru's choice of a career came out of her own life—from her mother's experience of being abandoned by her husband and from her grandmother's story, which came to Aru in driblets over the years. And there were Surekha's words which Aru had heard in a lecture, words Aru knew she would never forget: 'Some of the greatest cruelties in life are inflicted within families. These are the worst, because they so often remain shrouded in silence. More voices are silenced by families than by the State.'

The words had seemed to go straight into her; it was as if she had been waiting to hear them. She knows, Aru had thought, she will understand. And so Aru had gone to meet Surekha in the hope of getting justice for her mother. Surely, she had thought, a lawyer would help her? If not, what were lawyers for, what were the law courts for? But Surekha had been blunt. 'I can't do anything for you or for your mother, Arundhati,' she had said. And when Aru spoke of justice, she had replied, 'That blindfolded woman holding the scales in her hand has no place in the courts. These are courts of law, not courts of justice.' Finally she had told her, 'I will give you some advice. Free. Don't do anything. Just get on with your lives, as your mother is so sensibly already doing.'

This unfavourable reply had put an end to Aru's quest for justice for her mother, but it did not end her association with Surekha. She knew after meeting Surekha that she would become a lawyer and would work with her. So, while her classmates scrambled for places in the corporate world and joined large law firms, Aru entered Surekha's office immediately after graduation.

She was often told, in fact, she knew it herself, that litigation was not rewarding and that it took years to make a mark in that world, decades to make good money. But Aru had no doubts; she wanted to work for clients, she wanted to get them justice as far as it was possible to obtain.

Since Aru joined her, Surekha's stature, her reputation and her work have grown. She is now more involved with constitutional cases, with corporate contracts and negotiations and arbitration cases, (this office needs to make some money, she says) leaving Aru and Nagma to deal with the personal cases in the family courts. Jaisimha, Surekha's husband, calls the office 'the harem'. But Surekha had not planned on making it an all-women office; it just so happened that her male juniors left after brief stints with her, whereas Nagma and Aru have stayed on. Apart from the lawyers and an occasional intern who helps with the research, there is Mangala who runs errands and cleans the office and Tressa their office assistant. Tressa it is who deals with phone calls, with correspondence, keeps the records, makes appointments for clients, talks to clients when they first come and most important of all, she keeps track of the dates of filing of cases, of hearings and adjournments. 'Our woman Friday,' Surekha called her once when Tressa had tracked down a missing document. Tressa does not know what a 'woman Friday' is, but she knew it was meant as a compliment and was pleased. But when any one of the three lawyers says, 'What would we do without you, Tressa?' she demurs. On the contrary, she thinks that she is lucky to be working in such an office, to be working with such women. Through them, she has glimpsed a better world, one in which girls will be educated in the same way and to the same extent that boys are, in which women will not be punished for not bringing dowry into a marriage, a world in which they will not have to silently endure all the cruelty of a bad marriage. Tressa comes from a community in which women are valued according to the dowry they bring with them. Like many others, she left her village as a girl to work and save money for her dowry. When she came to Surekha, she was a frightened girl who did not know a word of Kannada, while her English was impossible to understand, overlaid as it was by her thick Malayali accent. She was also overawed by the competent women she was working among. Now she is, miraculously it seems to her, one of them. But it is no miracle, for, if Tressa has changed immensely, it is because she worked hard; she drove herself into learning to work on the computer, she has even learnt to speak almost idiomatic Kannada, though her accent is a dead giveaway.

Tressa, bright, cheerful, quick to learn and eager to work, is indeed a treasure. Soon after she started working for Surekha, she met Ramu who wanted her, not a dowry, and they got married against the wishes of both the families. How could they marry, she a Kerala Christian girl, a Roman Catholic, and he a Tamil Brahmin boy, an Iyer? Aru calls them Romeo and Juliet. Tressa knows what *this* means. She blushes and says, 'What, Aru ma'am, you are making fun of me!' But they did get married and now they have a daughter, Gracy, who comes with her mother to the office when she has school holidays. Sometimes Nagma brings her daughter Shabnam along too, and the two girls go out to play. While the women battle against human wickedness, human frailty and human idiocy, the girls' voices, as they laugh and shout, come to them from outside, reminding them that there is still hope for the world, that innocence and happiness still survive in their midst.

Nagma and Aru need this hope. Aru remembers her bewilderment when she first entered the family court, the chaos and the crowds a total contrast to the orderly court scenes that she had imagined, her idea coming mostly from movies, TV serials and novels. She had thought then of the way marriages were celebrated—in flower-decorated halls with perfumed and silk-sari clad women rushing about, the air redolent with the smell of flowers and attar. And this was where they ended—in a dingy room that smelt of sweaty unwashed bodies, rooms that reeked with the odour of failure, frustration and anger. Disappointed love, disappointed hopes, hate, fury, despair—all the emotions so carefully kept out by the lawyers and judges—seemed to hang in the air, suffocating them. Aru remembers even today a mother-daughter pair she saw once, both doggedly following the daughter's lawyer, a blank inscrutable look on the young woman's face, as if following her lawyer was the only and the entire business of her life, and this, the ending of her marriage, but one more chore she had to go through. It was the mother's face which was full of grief and hopelessness, as if she had taken on herself the burden of her daughter's failed marriage.

For Aru, justice has been the one thing that makes sense of a seemingly chaotic and senseless world. But she has since realized that there is no such thing as absolute justice; her work in the family courts has destroyed that idea, it has given her a picture of family life, of marriage, of the relationship between men and women, between parents and children that makes her marvel that there still are people in this world who can have good relationships with one another. Human relationships, she is now convinced, are so complex, the variations in human behaviour so myriad, humans so skilful in devising new forms of cruelty, that it is impossible for statutes to provide for every single contingency. She now understands why judges so often quote a sentence from an early English judgement: 'The categories of cruelty can never be closed.'

Before Aru joined Surekha, she had bought a book which contained all the laws concerning women. On the cover of the book there was a picture of a woman's profile, tears rolling down the one visible cheek. She had wondered at this picture: who could have thought of such a fanciful, almost dramatic picture, as the cover for a drab law book? She lost the book at some time; it did not matter because the office library had all the books she needed. But it seemed to her, in the early days of her work, that the grief-stricken woman had walked out from the cover of her law book and was sitting in the chair opposite her. She has never forgotten the older woman who had come to them, not because she wanted a divorce, but because her husband was insisting on it. He had been having an affair with a woman for some years, he had promised to marry her after his daughter's marriage. Now the girl was married and the other woman wanted marriage, she wanted the man's name, she wanted to live with him openly as his wife in his home. Her client told Aru this story haltingly, reluctantly.

Aru listened in silence. Finally, when she was done, Aru told her that divorce by mutual consent was possible only if she, the wife, agreed. 'If you don't want a divorce, tell him so. He can't throw you out of your home. Tell him *you* will divorce him for adultery. Then you will get a better deal. You . . .'

'If he leaves me I don't want anything. What's the use of anything if I'm left alone? I don't mind if he marries her, I don't mind his having another wife, but I don't want a divorce, I don't want to leave my home.'

Aru finally realized that she wanted Aru to negotiate with her husband and make sure that she would not lose her status of a wife and her home. Aru tried to convince her that this was no solution. The woman listened in silence and at the end of Aru's arguments, as if she had heard nothing of what Aru had been saying, she said, 'My home . . . She . . . she wants. . .'

The woman had then put her head on the table and begun sobbing. 'I can't,' she had said over and over again between her sobs, banging her head on the table with each 'I can't'. Aru's heart had begun pounding so loud it was as if it was echoing the woman's 'I can't, I can't', as if it was beating to the rhythm of the banging of her head on the table. And then anger had taken over. She had waited silently for the woman to control herself and advised her about her rights. She told her to go home, to think it over, and come back with a decision. 'We will do the best we can for you. But if you want to let him marry her, you don't need us.'

The woman never came back. She burnt herself in her home the home she did not want to be deprived of. She had, in the time-honoured way of women in India, doused herself with kerosene and then lit a match.

It had taken Aru a long time to get over this. The day they got the news, Surekha sat with her for a long time, saying nothing, merely giving her the comfort of her presence. She listened silently to Aru as she poured out her guilt. 'I could have talked to her husband, to his lawyer, I should not have sent her away, I should have negotiated, I should have got her some time . . .

'Don't be too hard on yourself, Aru. You did what you could. You can't take these things personally. And people who want to kill themselves will do so anyway. She would have done this at some time, you can be sure of that.'

Aru has been lucky that at the end of the day she is so tired that the moment her head touches the pillow she plunges into a deep dreamless sleep. Occasionally, very rarely, there are dreams, vague and formless, but when she wakes up she has no clue to what the dream was about. After this client's death sleep evaded her for weeks. She could not get away from the memory of the woman banging her head on the table, of her saying, 'I can't, I can't'. She kept thinking of the flames enveloping her, heard her anguished cries as the flames touched her, she could almost smell the singeing flesh. She could have been Sumi, the thought had come to her at one terrible moment. But Sumi did not lose her place in the world without Gopal. Aru found herself full of a new respect for her mother and contrition at the way she had badgered her to 'do something'. I wronged Sumi, I thought she was weak, I kept prodding her to fight, when what I really wanted was to punish Papa . . .

In time Aru learnt to distance herself to some extent from her clients. She now cloaks herself in a professional composure and detachment. But this fails her when it comes to custodial cases, parents fighting over children, making a bitter battle of it, revealing their selfishness, exhibiting the worst of themselves. She has *seen* that there is often a greater desire to hurt the wife, or the husband, than a concern for the child. I can see your child's confusion and grief, she has often wanted to say to the parents. Why can't you? Now Aru knows that revenge is yet another form of a desire for justice, but a desire for justice gone wild. She has learnt slowly, and with surprise, that the line between the exploiter and the exploited, between men and women, is not as clear a one as she had thought; it is shifting, fluid.

Nagma, who works in the mediation centre, has her own stories of couples who are illogical, stubborn, more intent on punishing the other, on flogging grievances than on ending the marriage and getting freedom. Aru and Nagma have laughed over Nagma's story of the wife who, even as Nagma was trying to find common ground on which the couple could meet and talk, had flung her heavy purse at the man and walked out of the room. Funny, *yes,* especially the look on the man's face, as Nagma described him. (And yet, perhaps, not so funny after all.) Reconciliation is far from the minds of the couple, negotiation almost impossible. But occasionally, rarely, they decide to come back together, to give their marriage another try, providing the happy ending, which rarely has a place in the courts. There are also those who agree to part amicably, both desirous of moving on, there are parents who agree to give custody to the other parent, making the happiness and comfort of the child the only consideration. Aru has been able to go on because of these things. And because of Surekha; Surekha it is who has saved Aru from both despair and cynicism.

Both Aru and Nagma, though they are earning more than before, much more than they expected, are dismayed by their rapidly increasing work load in the family courts. It frightens Aru, the number of divorce cases they have to deal with, from couples married for just a few months to couples married for decades. It is not just the number of cases, it's the stories that the couples tell their lawyers, from stories of silly trivial disagreements to those of enormous cruelty. She has often asked herself, 'Would I have gotten married if I had known how difficult it is to stay in marriage, how fragile this relationship is?' Dealing with couples who have decided to part, Aru has seen so much anger, so much hate, so much grief and anguish, that she thinks this brief time of the ending of their marriage will mark the couples forever. She thinks fearfully at such times of how little time Rohit and she spend together. But there is no problem between us, she reassures herself, no major differences, it just so happens that this is the time of our lives when work occupies us most.

On the face of it, Aru and Rohit, married for nearly seven years now, are on the whole content. No, content is too weak a word. Happy, then? Yes, there have been, and still are, times of happiness. They have got through the first difficult stage of getting used to living together. The sharp edges of strangeness, of irritating habits, have been blunted by the years, absorbed by familiarity. Some irritants, coming out of their very different personalities, still remain. Rohit can't understand, nor can he appreciate Aru's austerity, her habit of not making herself comfortable, of putting up uncomplainingly with discomfort. For years she went rattling about in autorickshaws, until Rohit, without telling her, bought her a car. It is a small Maruti with no extra fixtures. 'No A/C. And you have to roll the window glasses up and down manually,' Rohit had said. Aru had grinned, pleased, both with the car and his understanding of her needs.

Aru's thriftiness, which she had imbibed in childhood from both her parents, is less concerned with saving money and more about making do only with what is necessary. (Though she is slowly learning how elastic the word 'necessity' can be!) She disapproves of Rohit's carelessness with money, his habit of rarely switching off the lights and fans when he leaves a room, of wanting all the lights to be switched on in the house in the evening. Rohit has other extravagant habits which horrify Aru. Like when he came home with a tall table on which to place the exorbitantly expensive vase he had bought earlier.

'This is like the story of the man who got a cat to kill a mouse, then bought a cow to provide milk for the cat and . . . but you know the story.'

'I do.'

'If you hadn't bought the vase, we wouldn't have needed the table.'

'On the other hand, because I bought the vase we now have this beautiful table.'

The first time Rohit had seen her against the background of her grandparents' house, she had seemed to him like a princess in a story. Now he knows she is a woman with faults and foibles; nevertheless he continues to find her as enchanting as when he first saw her. She is still slim enough to look younger than her age and is better looking now than she was as a girl. There are moments even now when Rohit gets glimpses of her old flashing eagerness, like the time she came rushing home, shedding her slippers at the door, dropping her keys with a clang into the metal bowl, letting down her hair as she went inside to wash. As soon as she came out, her face scrubbed and glowing, she switched on the TV. 'What is it?' Rohit asked. For answer she held out her hand to him, patting the seat by her side. He sat by her and they watched a minister apologise for a crude remark he had made about a raped woman.

'Do you think he means it?' Rohit had asked when Aru switched off the TV.

'Of course he doesn't. But I wanted to see him humble himself.'

'My fierce wife,' he had said and, putting his arm round her, had drawn her closer. She had laughed and nestled in his arms. He had then felt again like the young man who had fallen so instantly and deeply in love, he had thought what have I done to be so lucky to have this girl as part of my life?

Rohit's habit of spending too much money is not a major issue for Aru; what she finds hard to put up with is his habit of retreating into himself when he is troubled or angry, his refusal to speak to her, or to anyone, when this happens. Generally an even-tempered man, he becomes a blank-faced stranger at such times. Aru, who believes in being open, in saying what's on her mind, who wants to clear the air even with a quarrel if necessary, finds his behaviour infuriating. But she has now learnt what his mother Lalita could have told her much earlier—that she has to leave him alone at such times. She also knows a little more about what drives Rohit into such moods. It happens if she does not let him know she will be late coming home, it happens if she shows her ignorance about some activity of his of which he had spoken to her, if she lets the entire working day pass without ringing him up on the rare days when he does not ring her himself.

Rohit has tried to rationalize himself out of such moods, to tell himself: hers is a more demanding profession. I am, to some extent, more in control of my day, of my time, than she is. But the pang remains. And the fear—I haven't been able to reach her as yet.

The truth is Rohit knows, he *knew* when he married Aru, that he cared for her more than she cared for him. (How do you quantify love, Aru will argue if he were to tell her this.) It was a risk he had taken. Throughout his courtship Rohit had veered between two states. There were times when his love brought about a surge of adrenalin in him, a rush of energy, when everything seemed possible: miracles could happen, she would love him as much as he loved her, and yes, he would make this happen. At other times, he felt fragile, vulnerable, he wanted to cry out to Aru, 'Careful, you can hurt me.' Once she agreed to marry him, he had thought: she would never have agreed if she hadn't had feelings for me, if she hadn't wanted to live her life with me. That she had responded to his restrained caresses before marriage had assured him she liked him physically.

And yet, the evening before their wedding, he had suddenly lost his nerve, he had abandoned all his self-comforting arguments which suddenly seemed hollow and futile. He had gone to Aru on an impulse. The large front door of the house was open and he could hear a babble of female voices inside. Yes, of course, they were having the mehndi ceremony, something the family and Aru's friends had coaxed her into having. 'For our sakes, Aru, if not for yours,' had been the general cry. Rohit stood at the entrance, hesitant, when Charu ran into the hall. She saw him and exclaimed, startled, 'Rohit! What are you doing here?'

'I want to see Aru.'

'What do you mean you want to see Aru! You can't.'

'Why can't I?'

'Because you're the bridegroom. You shouldn't be here, you're not supposed to be here. Shoo shoo,' she said, as if to a cat.

He laughed. 'Go and tell Aru I'm here. I'll wait until she comes.'

His face told her he would not go without seeing Aru. Charu capitulated. 'Yes, boss,' she said and went in.

Aru came out swiftly, a puzzled, slightly alarmed look on her face. She was dressed in an old salwar kameez, nothing of the bride about her except for her mehndi-decorated palms.

'Rohit, what is it?

'Charu says I shouldn't be here.'

'Charu?' she laughed. 'Fat lot she knows about any rules. Come in.'

'No, let's talk out here.'

They moved to a side of the house where the shamiana had already been put up. Long strings of tiny bulbs lay about, waiting to festoon the house and the shamiana. Something kept them from entering the place where they were to get married the next day. Rohit got two chairs from the pile stacked inside. Only when they were seated did he lean towards her to ask his question.

'Aru, tell me, honestly, do you want to marry me? Do you want to be my wife? Do you want to live the rest of your life with me?'

Aru let out a relieved sigh. 'And that's it? You scared me, Rohit.'

'Aru, please answer my question.'

'And if I say no, what will you do?"

'Call off the wedding.'

'And all this?' Aru asked, opening her decorated palms and then waving her hands at the shamiana, the bulbs lying about, the chairs piled up, the sounds of pots and pans at the back where the cooks were making their preparations.

'These things can be dismantled.'

'And the people who've come—your family, my family? What about them?'

'They can go home.'

'And Amma? And your mother?'

'I can make my mother understand. And your grandmother wants you to be happy, Aru, not just to get married.'

He then expressed one of his fears—that Aru had agreed to marry him to make Kalyani's last days happy. She gave him her full attention then; she realized he was serious.

'Have you been worrying about this?'

'Yes.'

'Rohit,' she said, 'I want to marry you, I want to be your wife, I want to live the rest of my life with you. I know our marriage has made Amma happy, but that's a by-the-way. I would never marry just for that, I could not be so dishonest, I would never cheat any man, least of all you. Believe me, Rohit.'

He did, he told her he did.

'And never doubt me again.'

He would not, he promised.

Rohit had first visited Kalyani's house because Murthy, Hrishi's father, knowing his interest in old houses, had told him to go and see this place which belonged to his mother-in-law Goda's family. Rohit had seen Aru then and fallen in love with her in an instant. He became a constant visitor to the family after that. He was lucky that his mother had discovered some kind of a connection between her family and Kalyani's; it meant that his visits were accepted without questions. Kalyani grew very fond of him, but Aru stayed away from him. She sensed his feelings, though she never knew how strong they were. He kept his feelings under tight control, he had no desire to push things at this stage; she was too young and, besides, his own career was just beginning.

And then came the terrible day. Murthy rang him up to tell him about the accident and the two deaths. Rohit was there on the day of the funeral. He has never forgotten the sight of Aru as she stood on the steps, erect, silent, tearless, watching her mother and grandfather leave the house forever.

He continued to visit the stricken family, but spent more time with Kalyani. Aru was rarely at home, she had too much to do. 'Amma, I'm your son, I'm your daughter,' she had cried out to Kalyani after Sumi's death. She remained steadfast to that promise. She took on the entire responsibility of the home, of her grandmother and sisters. Her grandfather had been a secretive man, they knew nothing of his affairs; his financial matters were a mystery to them. Patiently, with Premi's and Ramesh's sporadic help, Aru went through his papers and bank books, sorting out matters. Apart from this, she was also preparing herself for her new career.

Knowing all this, Rohit did not press his presence on her. He had the wisdom, rare for his age, but which came with the kind of love he had for Aru, to realize that trying to get close to her at this stage would not serve his purpose. Yet he remained as unswerving to his purpose, as true to his desire of making Aru his wife as Aru was to the promise she had made her grandmother. To the world, he looked a confident young man, but inside him hope was shriveling, especially when he came to know of Aru's friendship with a young man in her class. He came to Kalyani one day to tell her he was going away. He was going abroad for a year, possibly more, he said.

'You'll come back?' Kalyani had asked him with an intent look, as if trying to look into him. He promised her he would.

Aru parted from him casually. She had much to do, both at home and outside. Yet every morning when she woke up, she was conscious of a certain blank space in her day, she woke up to the knowledge of something missing in her life, a feeling which, however, dissolved like the mist the moment she got out of bed and started her routine. It was only after Rohit returned that she realized that sense of blankness had been connected to his absence.

Rohit did not communicate with her the entire time he was away. He had gone, despairing of ever being able to touch her. Yet he knew he would go back; the tug of his feelings for her was too strong, so strong that he had wondered she had not felt it. At the time he left, Aru's grief had been raw. When he returned, she seemed to have absorbed the grief, though there were times when she remained silent, her eyes darkened as if she was looking inwards at the dark moments of her life. On the whole, however, she was easier with herself and with others. Rohit made his feelings for Aru very clear this time. He took her out to movies, for dinner, for long walks on Sunday mornings in the park, ending with a breakfast of masala dosas in a much-frequented little place. He took her to see the houses he was building, only two or three then, but in which she could see he had invested much of himself. Kalyani was delighted. When she was diagnosed with uterine cancer, she told Rohit about her wish to see them married.

'I'm ready this minute, Amma, but Aru . . .? No, I have to wait.'

Waiting was hard for Rohit, especially when he saw the easy relationship, the casual physical intimacy between Charu and Hrishi, now clearly in love. He could not help but notice how Hrishi's arm went around Charu's waist when she was near him, how unselfconsciously Charu rubbed her cheek against his and how comfortably they held hands. Rohit envied them their uncomplicated relationship, one in which everything lay out in the open. But Kalyani's condition and her surgery drove out all other thoughts. The family came together, even Gopal returned and Rohit took his place among them. Aru was stoical through the surgery and the post-operative period, but when Kalyani was brought home, she wept in Rohit's presence. He had never seen her this way and was torn with love and compassion for her.

'Would you like to take a break? Go away somewhere with me?'

Aru wiped her tears, composed herself and looked at him. 'You mean overnight?'

'Of course. You can't call it getting away if you have to rush back in the evening.'

'And do you want . . . I mean, do you intend us to sleep together?'

'It's up to you. Only if you want to. All I want is to give you a break.'

She seemed to consider it seriously, then shook her head. 'I'd like to wait until we get married. There will be more dignity in it then.'

Rohit couldn't speak for a moment. Then he said, 'Did I hear you right? Did you say *I'd like to wait until we get married*?'

'Yes.'

'But I haven't asked you to marry me!'

'Ask me now.'

'Aru, will you marry me? Sorry, do I have to kneel before you?'

'No, Rohit, you don't have to kneel. And yes, Rohit, I will marry you.'

***

This, then, is the history of their relationship. On the whole, things have worked out well since their marriage. Rohit, after years of waiting, of dreaming and imagining a life with Aru, could have found the reality disappointing. On the contrary, it was a happy discovery of a new Aru. She was no bashful ignorant bride. She was a woman who had been aware for some time of her need to extend the boundaries of love beyond her own family, of her desire for male companionship. She was very much aware of the demands of her body as well. Rohit, on his part, wanted to give his beloved pleasure, he wanted to share his joy in sex with her. This made him apprehensive, too, though. It was an apprehension that came out of his great love for Aru; he had more to lose if things went wrong. Their anxiety was not just about the sex, but about the total physical intimacy that sex calls for—an intimacy stretched beyond anything either of them has ever known. It was, Aru had thought, like jumping off a precipice, this leap into the closest intimacy that two humans can achieve. On the whole, however, they were lucky; both of them looked forward to their times of love-making.

Sex is a brief flare, a flame that dies at the moment of its greatest intensity. When it is done and the urgency, the madness is over, and the world suddenly stops spinning and begins to move again at snail's pace, a couple can be confronted by a sudden abyss between them. Only tenderness can bridge the gap, only humour can save the couple from mortification, only love can make them rise above the physical awkwardness of two bodies with nothing between them. Rohit and Aru found all these.

'Did you get the dignity you wanted?' Rohit asked her, holding her close.

'What? Dignity? Oh yes, dignity.'

She realized then that it was not dignity she had wanted; it was love. If there is love everything, including dignity, follows, everything seems natural. She did not say these things to Rohit, she began to laugh at herself instead, laughter in which he joined.

Rohit, to his great joy, found Aru a passionate woman, generous and uninhibited in her love-making. They decided not to have children right away, wanting to stabilize their careers before thinking of a child. Aru now remembers with an angry grief that she was on the pill those days. But they knew they would not wait too long. Rohit gave up smoking even before their marriage, saying, 'I might find it difficult to give it up when the kids come. I can't give up overnight.'

When their new home was ready and they moved in, Aru suddenly said, 'Let's have a baby.'

'You mean it?'

'Yes.'

'Then let's start right now. Why wait?'

There was a sense of release from their plans, from their careful calculations. If there was less urgency now in their love-making, there was more tenderness, more passion. Such passion, Aru thought, has to result in a child. How could such a coming together, such a union, not result in new life? She was both apprehensive and eager about pregnancy. But nothing happened. Charu had told Aru that quite often after stopping the pill there is a rebound effect. Nothing happened.

They waited a whole year before approaching Premi. She took them to Bombay and the diagnosis was made—Aru suffered from endometriosis. It did not seem hopeless, because conception was not wholly ruled out, it was just that the chances were fewer. Aru underwent surgery. Let's hope it helps, Premi said. Still nothing happened. They thought of IVF, then the doctors decided against it. At times Aru thought she could have coped better with a diagnosis that ruled out conception totally. Anything was better than this cycle of hope and disappointment. Each month when she went through her painful periods, Aru thought that this pain had been given to her in lieu of the agony of giving birth.

Aru has lived with the idea of childlessness for over three years now. She has learnt what it means—continuing despair, continuing grief, always accompanied by the shadow of hope. Rohit and she have become conscious of a blank space between them. There has been no waning in their affection for each other, only a sense of bewilderment, an inability to grasp the huge gap in their life, and to understand that it is final. When she went to help Charu during Pavan's birth, Aru saw how a child occupies the entire space in a couple's life. Actually, it was when she was with Charu and Pavan that the real torment began. At first, it was enough to delight in the baby. As the time came for her to leave, she thought, he's not mine, I have to leave him and go. The thought settled in her heavily, like a stone. She tried to get away from the longing, but she could not. When she went to the park she saw children playing, toddlers on a leash being held back from rushing away, mothers with babies strapped to them, babies in strollers. She watched them almost furtively, like a voyeur, and she thought that the complete, total dependence of infants on parents, their complete faith in them, was the most beautiful thing in the world. And the most fearful thing as well. How do parents live with it, she wondered. We are such frail vessels, all of us, so flawed, so unsuited to carrying the load of such immense trust. But her childlessness kept her out of the whole world of parents and children. I am an exile from that world, she thought.

There was no place where she could get away from children. She went to an art museum once, sent out by Hrishi and Charu to see something of the city. There was a room full of paintings of mother and child, of infants on their mothers' laps, of babies being adored by the mother, by other women. It was a special show of paintings by Mary Cassatt, an American painter. At any other time, a few years earlier, or perhaps even a few years later, Aru would have been intrigued by this painter, described as the first professional woman painter in America, she would have been fascinated by the fact that she painted women and children over and over again. So many variations on the single theme of motherhood. But at that moment, seeing the array of mother and child paintings, she was overcome by a sudden onrush of grief, so great that she had to rush to the restroom. She got there just in time before the tears came. She was still sobbing when the door opened and someone walked in. Aru turned her face to the wall and stood there until she heard the sound of water flushing, of footsteps briskly walking to the door. Then they stopped and a woman's voice asked her, 'Are you okay?' Aru turned round at last and faced the woman who could see the marks of tears on her face. 'I'm better now, thank you,' she said.

The woman still hesitated and then said, 'Forgive me for being banal, but it's true that nothing is as bad as it seems at the moment.' And then she was gone.

Aru wondered, like so many of us do, why the kindness of strangers is so effective. She felt better and was able to go home and show Charu and Hrishi an almost composed face. But she put away the postcards of Mary Cassatt's paintings she had bought, not showing them to Charu, or even to Rohit. She could not bear to look at them herself, either. Once again, she regretted that she had no time to read. I could have found comfort in books, she thought, I would have read about women I could identify with, I would have been able to feel reassured that there are others like me, that my feelings are only natural. None of these consoling factors were available to her as a lawyer.

Back home, she tried to involve herself in her work. But something had changed between her and Rohit. Her inability to bear a child seemed to make a mockery of the sexual act. What was it for? Only pleasure in the act itself? In time that would become just a habit, a release of sexual tension. She could feel herself withdrawing from Rohit when she sensed his desire. Rohit, conscious of her reluctance, became wary of approaching her. And the doubt she had repudiated so emphatically before marriage now came between them in a different form. Doubt, that great destroyer of the erotic mood, the great detumescencer for a man, lay like a sword between them, like a blade of grass. There were still rare times when they could come together, when Aru went back to being a passionate woman. On one of those days, she said to him after they had moved apart, 'Nothing changes, does it?'

He knew what she was talking about. 'No,' he said, 'nothing changes. But this . . . this loving still matters.'

Aru had silently absorbed the words. She was sitting up in bed, her arms round her knees, and after a pause said, 'I guess it does. I guess you're right.'

Rohit, torn with pity for her, thought, You are enough for me, my darling, why am I not enough for you?

After Rohit had fallen asleep, Aru, unable to sleep, thought, it's the unchangingness that I can't bear, it's the unchangingness which frightens me. Charu has gone, soon Seema will go away as well, Leo keeps saying she should go to Bombay, he says this is too small a place for her. And then it will be just Rohit and me. Just the two of us, only the two of us always, only the two of us forever.

She often remembers Kalyani's words: you marry to have someone to share your life with, you marry to have children, you marry so that you can bring up your children together. Amma was right. Two is not enough, two is never enough, two is not a family. She remembers her childhood, the three of them in bed, Seema asleep, Charu and she talking in whispers, then Charu too falling asleep and she listening to Sumi's and Gopal's voices conversing companionably, and she, the unseen listener, finding immense comfort in their voices. Later, Sumi, just before going to bed herself, would come in to see if they were asleep, to cover them if their blankets had slipped off.

Rohit cannot but sense her despair. It hurts him to see childlessness slowly snuffing out the flame in her; but there's little he can do. He knows he can't deal with her silent secreted grief. And how can he comfort her, anyway? To say that this, their childlessness, does not matter, is to belittle her grief, it is to insult her. To tell her that he is grieving as well will not help, it will make it worse, for it will add to her grief and guilt, make her realize, all over again, that it is she who is depriving Rohit of a child. It is true that he wants a child, too. I want to make my wife pregnant, he thinks, not only because I want a child, but because I want *our* child, Aru's and mine. I want the two of us to become parents of a child, I want to experience fatherhood, to become the kind of father my own father had never been. And yet, if it does not happen, I can live all my life with just Aru. I will also be happy to adopt a child. But he can say none of these things to Aru. It hurts him deeply that she refuses to consider adoption, but he has decided to let her come to it in her own way, in her own time. In the meantime, time is passing them by. Aru's biological clock is not the issue, she is still young; what Rohit resents is losing moments of possible happiness.

Kalyani comes often to his mind these days. He was the first person she had chosen to speak to about her plans to demolish the old house and build a new one for the family.

'Demolish the house!' he had exclaimed, for he knew how she loved the house her father had built. He had sensed her feelings the first time he had come to see the place, from the way she had spoken of it, touched the walls and doors, he had seen her intimacy with the house when, without looking down, she raised her feet to exactly the height required by the thresholds.

But Kalyani had her own reasons, which she did not speak to him about. She had only said, 'I want you to build a new house in its place, a home for all of you, so you can be close together and yet independent.' And then she had added, 'This is the only way to get rid of the shadow which has been hanging over this house for so long.'

Rohit had come to know later, a little through Aru and some of it from Premi, about the child, Shripati and Kalyani's only son, a mentally challenged child, who had been lost at a railway station. He learnt too of the aftermath of that loss—the lifelong silence which Shripati had inflicted as a punishment on Kalyani. Now Rohit wonders whether the shadow had been patiently waiting all this while, waiting to reenter the house and make its presence felt all over again. Not the shadow of a lost child this time, but the shadow of a child who is not yet born, who will, perhaps, never be born.

Premi has arrived on one of her frequent unannounced visits. Earlier, her visits had been both rare and short, Nikhil's school and her own work being her excuse. But after her sister's and father's deaths, she came more often, torn with pity for Sumi's daughters and for her mother. With Kalyani's illness and surgery, Premi's visits became more frequent, she came almost every alternate weekend. When Kalyani died, her visits once again became few and far between, one of the reasons being that the house was gone; Aru and Rohit were living in a rented home, Gopal and Seema in another. Nikhil, too, was in the crucial last years of school at the time. Now that Nikhil has joined an engineering college in the city, Premi comes both to see him and because she enjoys being with the family, specially with Aru.

'However did you manage, Premimavshi?' Aru asks. Premi has gone through the whole exercise of working in a stressful job, (what can be more stressful than being an obstetrician?) with frequent spells of night duty in the early days—all this with a baby, a difficult mother-in-law and a not-very-cooperative husband at home.

Premi answers a little cursorily, her mind obviously elsewhere. 'I managed somehow, like we all do. But it was hard, especially when Nikhil was a baby and when there were emergencies.' To Aru's surprise, she gives credit to her mother-in-law. 'Thank god, Aai was at home. She was a terrible mother-in-law, but I knew I could trust her with Nikhil. That made up for everything else. That's the only thing that can help, to have someone you can trust your baby with.'

'Oh, well, that's one problem I don't have to worry about.'

Premi begins to say something, but looking at Aru's face she suddenly changes the subject, going back to what she had been obviously brooding over. 'You know, Aru, I've begun wondering why I come at all. The moment Nikhil sees me he has that why-has-she-come-again? look on his face. I'm such a fool, Aru, I don't seem to understand that he's quite happy not to see me.'

Aru knows that Nikhil was not very pleased to give up his weekend plans because his mother was coming. 'I've got my own plans,' he had grumbled.

'Well, change them.'

'Easy for you to say. I owe something to my friends.'

'You owe much more to your mother.'

'Oh come on, granny, don't start on that now.'

'Honestly, Nikhil, you shouldn't grudge your mother two days in a month.'

'I know what those two days will be like. She'll ask questions, you'd think they are innocent questions about my studies, my friends and all that. But I know that all the time she's probing, she thinks I smoke, I drink, I do drugs. She's crazy!'

'And are you?'

'What? Crazy? No!'

'Smoking, drinking, doing drugs?'

'Arutai, you too! Et tu, Brute?'

'What!'

'Stunned you, didn't I? I know the next line too, if you think this is a fluke.' Dramatically he goes on, 'Then fall Ceasar.' He reverts to his own tone and says, a little reproachfully, 'And you think I'm an ignorant idiot, that I know nothing.'

'I never think that of you, Nikhil. And I know you had *Julius Ceasar* as a text in school.'

'Still, I surprised you, didn't I? Admit it, Arutai.'

'You always surprise me, Nikhil. You continue to surprise me.'

'Don't be sarcastic, Arutai, please don't be sarcastic. It doesn't suit you. It's not you, this nasty snideness.'

'I give up.'

'Come on Arutai, you know I was only kidding. Of course, I'll be here when your dearest Premimavshi arrives.'

Nikhil takes nothing seriously; he's always light, flippant, skimming on the surface of things. But Aru knows that he holds this flippancy like a barrier, a barbed-wire fence between him and the world. There's an edge, a brittleness to his sparkle; he's like a shard of glass, a sharp piece that can hurt, especially when he's speaking to his mother. There's a world of resentment in him, a struggle to get out of the complex web of his mother's obsessive love, of his father's high expectations. And there's the burden of belonging to a family which boasts of scholars, eminent lawyers, judges, freedom fighters. Nikhil, the only child, the only son of an only son, is expected to live up to this family tradition.

'They send me to a school where you hear nothing but English and then they expect me to speak excellent Marathi. They keep throwing the names of the family Sanskrit pandits at me—Gangadhar Rao, Sarvottam Rao, Purushottam Rao . . . Shit! The names are enough to crush me. Whatever I do, they have a name to bash me with. What about me, guys, I want to say. I'm me. I'm Nikhil, I'm not your Gangadhar Rao or any other Rao. But does anyone care?'

Aru asked him sympathetically, 'Why don't you say this to your father some time?'

'What?'

'That you're Nikhil, that you can't be those people.'

'Say that to my father! Are you crazy?'

But he has his own ways of getting back. Subtler ways. He scrupulously follows the family rule of addressing family members by their kinship terms. It's always Aru*tai,* Charu*tai*, Rohit*dada,* Hrishi*dada* and so on. But there seems to be an undertone of mockery in the way he says the names, as if he's sneering at the custom even while following it.

Nikhil had been very much cosseted as a child. He was not just the only child in his father's home, he was the only grandson in his mother's home as well. He had a genuine affection for his aunt Sumi's family. Aru remembers Nikhil as a child, eager and enthusiastic, ready to join in anything they were doing, to go any place with them. He's trapped now into doing what he's not interested in doing. Worse, he doesn't seem to know what he wants to do. In spite of his desire to get away from his parents, he had been desperately unhappy for the first month or two when he came away from home. Aru and Rohit's home had been his escape from loneliness, his refuge at that time. Now he is well settled, he has enough friends, in fact he is very popular. Nevertheless, he has not stopped his visits to his cousins' home; very clearly it's a place where he comes to with pleasure. Except, it seems, when his mother is visiting.

This time, he does come to see his mother, as he had promised Aru; but it's a careful, scrupulously polite Nikhil, answering his mother's questions, otherwiset remaining aloof and silent. Premi has always been a little jealous of Nikhil's open display of affection for Sumi and now for Aru. 'How do you make him obey you?' she had asked Aru, her voice brittle, the first time she heard Aru setting the rules for Nikhil.

'You have to put your clothes in the washing machine. And, mind you, no smelly socks, no underwear in the wash.'

'Yes, ma'am.'

'Tidy your room before you leave. No wet towels lying about. And the bathroom must be clean.'

'Absolutely, boss.'

'How do you make him obey you, Aru?' Premi asked. 'If I gave him so many orders . . .'

'But I'm not his mother, Premimavshi, that's why I can get away with it.'

Nevertheless, Aru, guessing at Premi's feelings, generally takes care to stay away when he comes to see his mother, for he then becomes even more friendly and intimate with Aru, showing off their closeness, manipulating his mother. Today, however, he's playing a different game; he seems indifferent to Aru as well, scarcely addressing a word to her. It's only when Premi goes out to take a phone call that he suddenly becomes himself and whispers, 'When is it coming?'

'What?'

'The lecture: Remember who your father is, remember he's a judge. At one time it was: Remember he has a good chance of becoming a judge, so be careful, don't make him ashamed of you. Once the lecture is over I can go to bed.'

'Oh stop it, Nikhil,' she says crossly.

But he goes on, seemingly immune to snubs. 'And what about your cross-examination? Is that over?'

'*My* cross-examination? By whom?'

'My Aai, of course. She asks you all about me, doesn't she? You have to give her a report on me when she's here.'

'Listen, Nikhil,' Aru says, clearly showing her anger, 'I never speak to your mother about you, I never tell tales. If there's something, I'll speak to you first. Got it?'

'Yes, Arutai, got it. And I'm sorry I said that, I shouldn't have.'

Then he does a strange thing. He picks up her hand, takes it to his face and presses his lips on her palm. He's perfectly serious when he does this, there's no 'kidding' (his favourite word) about it. Aru is startled, it makes her uncomfortable. For a moment she is tempted to snatch her hand away, but then tells herself, he's only a kid. (But the pressure of his lips? Nothing childlike about that!) Nikhil smiles at her, a curiously adult smile. And, letting go of her hand, like he is giving it back to her, he pats it, as if he has read her thoughts and is reassuring her.

Premi enters the room at that moment and Nikhil immediately gets up, declaring his intention of going to bed.

'Where do I sleep, Arutai?'

'Upstairs, with Papa and Seema. As you always do when Premimavshi is here. As if you don't know that!'

'I was hoping there's room for me here.'

'No, there isn't. Sorry.'

'Oh well.' He sighs heavily and goes out with a martyred air. Aru wants to laugh, but restrains herself and calls him back. 'I've left your sheets on the bed, Nikhil. Make your bed, don't sleep on the covers.'

He waves an impatient hand at her as he goes out. Premi, who has listened silently, says, 'I think I better go to bed myself.' But she lingers, as if reluctant to go to her room. When Aru comes back a little later, she finds Premi still in her chair.

'Brooding over Nikhil, Premimavshi?'

Premi comes out of her thoughts. 'No, actually I was thinking of Amma, I was remembering what a bad daughter I was.'

'Bad daughter? Why do you say that, Premimavshi? You came almost every weekend when Amma was ill.'

'Yes, I know I did, but my mind was always with Nikhil. I was always counting the hours, no, the minutes, until I could go back. Thank god I was with her when she died.'

Knowing that the end was near, they were constantly with Kalyani; but that afternoon, Premi was, for some reason, the only one with her. Kalyani lay with her eyes closed; she was sedated most of the time because of the pain. But she had suddenly opened her eyes and looked at Premi, her eyes no longer pain-filled, but clear and unclouded.

'Goda?' she had asked. How did she know Goda had been with her until a few minutes back?

'She's gone home for a short while. She'll be back soon.'

Kalyani closed her eyes again. In a while her hand began moving restlessly on the bed, her fingers seeming to be searching for something. Premi took Kalyani's hand in hers and said, 'Amma.'

'Sumi?'

'No, Amma, I'm Premi.'

She held on to Premi's hand then. In a while the hand became limp. Premi thought she was sleeping; in fact, she had slipped into the coma from which she moved imperceptibly into death.

'When she went into a coma, I remember thinking, "How long will this go on?" You can never tell, it can go on for days, sometimes weeks. And I kept thinking, shall I go away and come back later? Luckily Amma died the next day; she spared me that terrible choice. But I can still remember how I kept wanting to go back because of Nikhil. I'm so ashamed of myself, Aru, when I think of it. Not that Nikhil needed me, either, no, he didn't. Children! Why do we have children, Aru? And never never have an only child . . . Oh god, what am I saying, Aru? I'm sorry, I'm really sorry.'

'That's okay, Premimavshi. I've got used to it.'

Premi has been with Aru through the early days of doubts and investigations, the diagnosis and the treatment. Until suddenly one day Aru had said, 'Enough, I'm not going to do anything more.'

She refused even to talk of it, which hurt Premi. They have always been as much friends as aunt and niece. But Aru was never one to let anyone see her wounds. Premi remembers Aru after her mother's and grandfather's deaths, tearless, going through her tasks stoically, fending off all sympathy and offers of help. She remembers Aru washing her mother's and grandfather's clothes the day after their deaths, steadily refusing Nagi's offer to wash them. She had washed the clothes, put them out to dry and in the evening folded them and put them away in their usual places, as if for her dead mother and grandfather to wear the next day.

'Look at her face, Premakka, look at her eyes, she has not shed a tear.' Nagi herself had been sobbing when she said that and Premi had hastily walked away, afraid of breaking down.

Nikhil leaves early next morning. To his surprise and Aru's, Premi asks him no questions, she says nothing about meeting him again. And to Aru's greater surprise, she makes her own plans for the day. 'I want to take all of you out for lunch,' she tells Gopal. 'Seema can tell us what's a good place to go to.'

During lunch, she does not bring up Nikhil's name even once. 'Let's have a good time,' she says and they do. Gopal, who does not often join them in their outings, has come because Premi made it impossible for him to refuse. Premi and Gopal are old friends. He has known her since she was a child, a gawky thin girl, carefully keeping out of everyone's way. She has put on weight in the last few years. There's a kind of certainty about her now; she's lost the diffidence, the slight air of hesitation that had been part of her charm for Gopal. He had, perhaps, been a little in love with her, the way a man can often be with his wife's sister, the likeness between the two pleasing, the difference intriguing. Since Sumi's death, Premi was no longer Sumi's sister, but herself, Premi, and it had made for a better, easier relationship between her and Gopal.

That night, Premi who has given Aru the feeling that there is something she wants to say but is holding back, speaks to her about Gopal. 'Do you know,' she asks her hesitantly, 'that Gopal has been—I mean he has—okay, I'll say it plainly. Devi tells me she has seen Gopal and that woman, whatshername, Charu's tenant. . .'

'Kasturi,' Aru says mechanically.

'. . . that she has been seeing them together often and in different places?'

'What places?'

'She saw them in the park quite a few times, once or twice in the coffee place around the corner . . .'

'So?'

'What do you mean so? Devi was shocked. You know how she is about Sumi. She's sure that woman will take Sumi's place . . .'

'Take Sumi's place? Impossible.'

'That's what I said to Devi. No one can take Sumi's place.'

Both Premi and Devaki had been witnesses to Gopal and Sumi's love affair. When Sumi and Gopal walked out to get married in the best traditions of romantic movies, the girls had thought it an ideal romance. Later, when Gopal walked out on Sumi, they couldn't believe it, they couldn't understand Gopal, couldn't understand how Sumi could take it the way she had, accepting what Gopal had done without demur. And now Gopal with another woman?

'Impossible!' Premi repeats Aru's word, as if trying to convince herself. And then, seeing Aru's face, she adds, 'Now, Aru, don't take this seriously. I didn't want to tell you actually. But I thought you should know.'

***

Aru has known about it for some time. She has watched her father's and Kasturi's increasing intimacy with many misgivings. She sees them each morning behind the house, where Premi's bit of land is slowly becoming a fruit orchard. It seems to have become a habit for them to walk among the growing trees and the just-planted saplings. Sometimes they stop, their heads come together and they laugh; she can hear the laughter from her room, laughter which brings back memories of the Gopal of her childhood. So had he laughed in those days with Sumi and the three of them, so had he laughed with Sumi at them. Aru is ashamed of herself, of her furtive watching. Ashamed, too, of her resentment at Gopal's pleasure in being with the woman, of her disapproval of the fact that they look like two people who have been friends for years. Ashamed that she is unhappy at his coming alive. Yet she can't help herself. Gopal's laughter seems a betrayal of Sumi and their daughters, an act of treachery against the life they had lived together as a family.

But Aru, being Aru, tries to be fair. She knows it is wrong of her to feel this way. Sumi is dead. And they, his daughters, are now grown women leading their own lives. He is no longer the most important person in their lives. So why do I grudge him this companionship? I'm small-minded, I'm mean, I'm selfish, she chastises herself. I must stop this. And yet when she sees them together, she gets prickly.

She doesn't like the woman, that is the truth. She's too loud; everything about her, from her saris to her large bindi and her behaviour is meant to draw attention to herself. Aru doesn't like her free and easy ways, either. She often sees her chatting with Lokesh in the mornings, joking with him. Once she had seen Lokesh's assistant singing, and Kasturi singing along with him, Aru could see her body swaying to the tune, while Lokesh himself, car duster in hand, kept the beat, a big grin on his face. There was a day when Aru saw her get off a rickshaw outside the gate and then stand there for nearly fifteen minutes talking to the driver. Aru is not class conscious, that's what she tells herself, anyway, but she wonders what Kasturi and the rickshaw driver have in common. Aru chides herself: her behaviour has nothing to do with me, it's none of my business. What she hates is the idea of Gopal getting friendly with such a woman. After Sumi how can he? And then she tells herself that she has no right to judge him. I've kept him out of my life, I should keep out of his.

And yet. . .

Aru is not so young as to think that people of Gopal's and Kasturi's age cannot have romantic feelings for one another. But when it's your own father, a father who abandoned his wife . . .

She speaks to Charu about it. Aru is sure her sister will understand her feelings; they are almost always on the same side. But this time, Charu is unsympathetic and brusque with her.

'So what, Aru? If Papa's found a friend you should be glad for him. Poor Papa, he's had a bad time.'

'*Poor* Papa! *He's* had a bad time? *He?*'

'I'm sure he didn't enjoy going away from us. Something happened to him, he was so unhappy, remember? And then Sumi died. Think what that must have done to him. And he must be lonely. It's more than ten years since Sumi died.'

'And more than eleven years since he left us,' Aru adds bitterly.

'Well, all the more reason to leave him to himself.'

'What if he marries her, Charu?'

'Rubbish!'

'You should see them together.'

'I wish I could. Send me a picture.'

'You're hopeless.'

'Right, then, let's suppose he marries her. How does it affect your life? Or mine?'

'What about Seema?'

'I'm hundred per cent sure he won't do anything without thinking of Seema.'

'You'll be sorry when you have a stepmother.'

'Then tell me what you think we should do? Go to him and say you've got to stop seeing that woman? We, your daughters, forbid it. Or do you want us to say, Hindi-fillum style, "Yeh shaadi nahi hogi?"'

'Ha ha. Very funny.'

'Relax, Aru, nothing will happen. And if it does, you should, I mean, you have to accept it. Seriously, I think you should be glad for Papa and stop worrying about something that may never happen.'

Aru feels humbled by Charu's attitude. Why can't I be generous like Charu? Has having a child and becoming a mother given Charu this two-way vision, so that she can look both ahead, at Pavan, and back at Papa, with an understanding I cannot get because I have no child? She remembers Charu holding her baby after his birth, saying through her sobs, 'Sumi should have been here, Sumi should have seen my baby, why isn't she here, oh Sumi Sumi. . .'

And then immediately she had said, 'I want to talk to Papa, I have to tell Papa myself, I want to ring him up.'

Aru remembers her crying out, weeping and laughing at the same time, 'Papa, I have a son, I have a son.' But when she had finished talking to Gopal, there were no more tears; her face was calmer, serene, as if talking to her father had taken away some of the sorrow of her mother's absence.

Why can't I be like Charu, Aru thinks, why can't I let my father go? Am I like my grandfather, then, who never spoke to his wife all his life? Have I inherited this inability to forgive from him? And am I not doing my father an injustice by clinging on to such an old grievance? I thought. . . I used to think, I wanted justice for Sumi. Now Sumi is gone. So why am I still hostile to him? Is this a desire for justice, or is it merely a desire to hurt him, to punish him?

And then she thinks of Kalyani's will, a document which has been for Aru a magic potion, a secret weapon to be brought out in times of distress.

Kalyani's parents had given their entire property, not to their only daughter, but to her husband, for reasons which were never spelt out. This meant that all her life Kalyani had to depend on a man who for decades had not only not spoken to her, but had lived as if she did not exist. He allowed her some money every month to run the house, a sum so small that life was a constant struggle for her. When, after his death, Aru had to transfer his bank accounts to Kalyani's name, she had been shocked at the amount of money there was in his account. She had raged at the injustice which had made Kalyani scrimp and save when her grandfather could have, when he *should* have, made Kalyani's life easier by giving her more money. But, perhaps, that was the point; he did not want to make her life easier. He was punishing her, decades after it happened, for the loss of his only son. And yet, in his will he left everything he possessed to 'Kalyani, daughter of Vithalrao and Manoramabai'.

Property matters: Aru has learnt the truth of this most important fact, one that every lawyer knows only too well. When love is gone, affections displaced and even hate becomes a distant memory, property remains. And it was through property, through her own will, that Kalyani, who had unquestioningly accepted her parents' disposal of their property, had sent the boulder of injustice rolling with a gigantic heave.

She made a will before she went in for surgery. Surekha had drafted the will; none of them knew its contents. When they got to read the will after Kalyani's death, they realized that it was more than a legal document disposing of her property. It was a testament of faith, both in the past and the future. She, who had been written out of her father's will, had herself made a will which was a proclamation of faith in her daughters and granddaughters. At the time she made her will, Kalyani knew that death was near. She was in that rare position that proximity to death brings, occupying a small sliver of time, detached from the past, knowing there is no future for her and the present only a transitory ephemeral period. She could see her whole life with a detachment which is never possible for a person in the midst of life.

Kalyani had lived under the tyranny of silence almost all her married life, she had so absorbed it into herself that even those she lived with never realized the yoke of cruelty she was carrying. Except Goda; and even she didn't know all of it. Her story remained untold and unknown—until the will was read. It was, Aru realized, meant to right the wrong done to her; to put an end to injustice. It was like a triumphant ending to her story. Mistress of all the property, she had distributed it between her 'surviving daughter Premalata and the three daughters of my deceased daughter Sumitra—Arundhati, Charulata, Seema'. The will was a recital of a litany of female names: her daughter and granddaughters, her more-than-a-sister Goda and Devaki, Goda's daughter, who 'has been like my own daughter', each name mentioned with great love. Nikhil, the only grandson, got only her blessings 'because I know that everything that his mother has will be his one day.'

To Surekha, who had patiently listened to Kalyani's story and then drafted a legal document, the will is a triumphant flaunting of the female line, a document to set things right, to erase the injustice of the past. To change, as much as is possible for one person to change the ways of the world.

But Aru, who has often seen flashes of her grandmother's mischievous spirit, knows what Kalyani was really doing when she wrote her will: she was standing everything that had shaped her life on its head, she was cocking a snook at all the beliefs which had made her life what it had been.

Gopal

However much we think otherwise, the truth is that none of us are indispensable. I saw this in Aru's wedding when she had three couples willing to act as her parents—Premi and Anil, Devaki and Murthy, Ramesh and Chitra. It was Kalyani who finally decided that Ramesh and Chitra would do the kanyadaan. In the end, it was a ceremony in which nothing seemed to be missing, so beautifully had Kalyani, Premi, Devaki and the others put it together.

Ramesh was pleased, inordinately pleased, I think, to take on the responsibility of being the bride's father. So was Chitra. They had had a difficult relationship some years earlier. Chitra's concentration on her twin sons, her great ambition to make them tennis prodigies, must have left Ramesh lonely and bitter. I remember once I rang him up and whoever picked up the phone put it down without a word, not even a 'hello'; obviously so disturbed, that she or he forgot to disconnect it. I could hear angry voices, loud recriminations. I had quickly disconnected the phone myself, feeling chilled at the rage I had sensed in the room. How could they live with such anger between them?

Things are better now. So I guess. And hope. The twins are out of the house, they are constantly travelling from tournament to tournament and have become doubles players to be reckoned with. When they come home, it's only for a few days. Chitra and Ramesh seem more comfortable now with each other; at times

I think, a little cynically I must confess, that Ramesh's increased prosperity—he's now an intervention cardiologist—has helped. However, to do Chitra justice, she was as serious and committed as Ramesh was to doing everything right in Aru's wedding.

Actually, Ramesh wanted to pay for the entire wedding. I told him she was my daughter, it was my duty, I wanted to pay for the wedding myself. Finally, I was allowed to host the lunch on the wedding day for the family and the children's friends. I asked Aru's permission, of course.

'Why do you ask, Papa?'

'I want to be sure you don't mind.'

'I'm happy you want to be part of my wedding.'

It was not very comforting, but I had to make do with it. No, Aru had not forgiven me. During the lunch when I had to act the host, I felt something of a fraud; but Charu was with me, so were Ramesh and Premi. And I got through it somehow.

The evening of the wedding I was dazed, confused by the number of people present. It was, as a matter of fact, a small gathering by normal wedding standards, but I had lost the habit of being in the midst of a crowd. So many seemed strangers, but were not, whereas others, whom I thought I knew, turned out to be strangers. I felt like Rip Van Winkle. Even my daughters had become young women with a certainty about themselves which seemed remarkable to me especially since I had not seen the process of their gradual evolution into adults.

The one person I recognized in that crowd was Surekha, the lawyer with whom Aru was working, with whom she still works. She too knew me immediately. 'Aru's father,' she said. It was a statement rather than a question. She looked exactly the way she had when we had met in the park before Sumi's death. She was now wearing a silk sari in deference to the occasion, but her hair was still a little untidy, straggling down her neck and escaping from its confines in just the same way. Aru had set up our first meeting. She was thinking, Sumi had told me, of taking legal action against me. I had expected Surekha to talk of laws and lawsuits, but she had spoken instead of her younger days and her ardent desire to change the world.

I reminded her of it at Aru's wedding. 'You told me you had wanted to change the world,' I said.

'Oh, I gave up that dream long ago. We all have our dreams when we are young. Look at Aru,' she said.

Both of us looked at her, young and beautiful. Most women look beautiful on their wedding day, but the sight of Aru brought a lump to my throat.

'My husband and I thought Communism was the answer. We were influenced by Professor Srinivasan, do you remember him? No? Before your time at the university, I guess. Anyway, we thought Communism was the answer to all of humanity's problems. We were soon disillusioned. We learnt that people don't change because they subscribe to an "ism". And so I became a lawyer and Jai a bureaucrat. We thought that we could be of some use in these jobs, do more good, perhaps, from within the establishment.'

'And?'

'I'm not sure that we've done any good.'

'You've done my daughter a lot of good, though. When I first met you, I thought of you as Aru's wise counselor. I knew you would do Aru good.'

We looked again at Aru. Surekha smiled and said, 'She's done me much good, anyway. She's brought back some of my early enthusiasm. Your daughter refuses to give up hope. Nagma and she keep my hopes alive. I'm very grateful to them.'

We parted then and I thought of what she had said to me at our first meeting. 'Why are you here, then?' I had asked her finally, when she told me that she had advised Aru not to take any legal action.

'I wanted to see the man who could walk out on a daughter like Aru.'

It had been totally unexpected, like a blow to my chest, making me breathless. I wanted to bend over, as if I was suffering actual physical pain. I have never forgotten those words. Never forgotten, either, something else she said that day. 'There are no second chances,' she said. 'You will have to live with the thought that there are no second chances.'

No second chances! The words had sounded like a knell in my ears. We can live with ourselves, with our mistakes and our sins, because we are certain that we will be given a chance at some time to correct our wrongs, to do things better, to set them right. We desperately need to believe in this. We have stretched this hope, this belief, into imagining that we will have more lives given to us to do all that we've left undone in this life. But what, the thought often occurs to me, if the new life is lived in exactly the same way as the old one? Isn't this a possibility we need to take account of? For, if it is the same self, the soul or the atman or whatever we call it, that takes rebirth, it means that we cannot escape our selves. It seems like a nightmare to me, the thought of going through this whole exercise we call life over and over again. And if all these lives are the rungs of a ladder leading us to moksha, how shall we ever climb the rungs if we are chained to ourselves?

It amazes me that we put our faith in life after death, that we believe in Paradise and Heaven. I have to admire the human imagination which has created these, the optimism that promises happiness even after life is over. But, of course, the future is always malleable; we can shape it to our desires and our dreams. If, however, we look at our past record, (and what else can a historian do but look at the past?) we can't help being cynical. 'History says, Don't hope on this side of the grave,' Rao quoted to me in his gravelly voice. I think it is the most bleak statement I have ever heard. So, possibly, poets are even greater cynics than historians. In any case, I am quite certain that, given a second chance, there is a strong possibility that we will fritter it away in exactly the same way, all over again.

Yet there was Kalyani. Talking to me about her daughters, this was some time after her surgery, she said one day, suddenly, as if she was following a train of her own thoughts, 'I was a bad mother.' It was a statement of fact. She was not asking for reassurance, she did not want me to refute her statement. She was telling me a fact: 'I was a bad mother.' She confessed to me that when her daughters were children, she had been angry, anguished, confused. 'So I took out my temper on my girls. Sumi escaped, she always managed to escape.' She paused and I knew what she was thinking of. Then she went on. 'But Premi, my poor Premi, she got it badly from me, both from my tongue and my hands. Yes, Gopal, I was a bad mother.'

If she was (and I believe that she was telling me the truth) she redeemed herself at the end of her life. She gave Sumi refuge and support when she needed it. And Premi too, after Sumi's death came closer to her mother. It strikes me now that Kalyani got the second chance Aru's lawyer told me we never get. She not only reconciled with Premi, she became a mother to her granddaughters. If Seema improved, it is because of Kalyani. And maybe, I now think, Kalyani called me back home to give me a second chance. That would have been like her, very much like her. That I am here, living with my daughters, being a part of their lives, even if only marginally so, is because of Kalyani.

'Aru should live her married life without worrying about Seema,' she said. 'I want her to enjoy her life with Rohit.'

How strange that, despite her own experience, Kalyani's faith in marriage remained unshaken. A man and a woman living together, the two of them having children and bringing them up together: this remained the ideal of life for her. An atavistic instinct, I suppose, for all of us. But such a family life is brief, it is evanescent. It fills me with compassion when I see young parents with their children, the children trusting their parents, regarding them as the centre of their existence, feeling safe and secure, the world kept at a distance by the love of their parents. But this is a very small period in our lives, it passes quickly, in a flash, it's just a twitch, a blink of an eye. And yet, brief though this period is, it remains the core of our lives, the reason, it sometimes seems, for our entire existence.

I think one of the things which makes Kasturi different, and which makes me curious about her, is that this part of her life seems a blank. Not only does she never refer to marriage, husband, or children, she gives the impression that none of these things exist, or ever existed in her life. The only time I saw faint shadows on the seemingly blank slate of her life was when she was speaking to me of her work and her impatience with the stupidity of serial makers who refused to budge from the formula.

'Look at the villains! The women have too much make-up, thin high eyebrows . . .' she made an exaggerated arc with her finger, 'they wear sleeveless blouses and lots of horrible jewellery. And the men—they leer, they twirl their moustaches and laugh wickedly. I tried to tell the director that villains look like everybody else, that they wear masks, which is why they're really dangerous. They wear the masks of friends, lovers, saviors, husbands—and suddenly they tear off their masks and show you who they are. That's what is really frightening.'

Something told me that this came out of some place within her, that she was speaking out of her own experiences. But I said nothing. And she never spoke of these things again.

She does speak of her father at times now. Whatever her problems with him were—and I am sure there were some—she speaks of him with admiration. 'My father was a farmer,' she told me, when I first found her walking through Premi's garden, peering at the saplings. 'Can you believe it, he grew grapes? In those days! Everyone laughed at him. Now everyone grows grapes and they call it a vineyard.'

He was a very progressive farmer, she said, who believed in improvement, innovation, and using new ideas. It was the time of the green revolution, when ideas about agriculture were changing. He brought irrigation to their region. He wanted change, she said, he wanted people to be able to live better lives. 'He himself, first of all, of course,' she added cynically. 'He was not a Gandhian, though he named me Kasturi,' she said.

Kasturi? Oh yes, of course, from Kasturba, Bapu's wife.

'He didn't believe in poverty, he thought everyone should be able to make money and lead a comfortable life. I think he was far ahead of his times. He should have been in today's world where making money is not a crime. Or in America, where becoming a millionaire is the goal of all normal men. He was more a Nehru man,' she told me, 'than a Gandhian, though his real hero was Indira Gandhi.'

He had been the state party president in Indira's time and had had much to do with her. He had such complete faith in her that he even believed that the Emergency was necessary. When she called for elections, he was sure she would be re-elected, and the Emergency would be vindicated. Her defeat was a greater shock to him than his own. He never recovered from it.

Kasturi and I have moved beyond our Shivpur connection. We meet more often now, almost everyday, either in Premi's garden, or in the park. I'm comfortable with her, she's easy to talk to. An interesting woman.

Why do I keep calling her an interesting woman? It is such a dry word, with no sap in it; it's like a dried leaf. Am I trying to tone down my feelings about her, to conceal the fact that I enjoy her company? If that's all that she means to me, why do I wake up in the morning with anticipation, knowing that I will meet her? Why do I have a kind of blank feeling on the days I don't meet her? And why have I begun dreaming of women again? It's as if I have gone back to the days of my adolescence when I had dreams which frightened me. I now realize that, for my age, I was a very ignorant boy. I was confused and bewildered by what was happening to me, unable to deal with the urges of my body. I thought I was abnormal, disgusting, a pervert. I thought I was the only one to have such feelings, to do such horrible things to myself. I looked at Ramesh, sleeping peacefully and innocently, with envy. I could not understand the conflict between my body and my mind. There was no one I could talk to about it either. P.K., my substitute father, was, in my mind, far removed from such gross matters. I never heard him use a coarse word, never saw him touch Sudha, or even his daughters after they grew up.

Suddenly a memory rushes out at me, a conversation between Sudha and P.K. She was telling him about a name she had thought of for their baby who was soon to be born. She wanted a girl, she thought if they spoke of the baby as a girl, they would get their daughter. And so it was a girl's name.

'No,' P.K. said abruptly. 'Not that name. No names of flowers.'

'But why? That was my mother's favourite flower.'

'No,' he said again. And reluctantly added, 'Only *those women* have names of flowers.'

'*Those* women?' Sudha asked. Then she laughed, in sudden comprehension, I now realize, laughter that brightens up this memory I have unearthed from the distant past. 'How do *you* know that?' she asked.

'It says so in the Natyashastra.'

And Sudha laughed again. Children are very unobservant, very self-centred. They never take much notice of what others, specially adults, say. But now, when I go back to that moment, I imagine that Sudha must have laughed at his squeamishness, at the scholar in him who got even this forbidden information from a scholarly treatise.

I also imagine, when I remember the look of embarrassment on his face, that perhaps even a scholar like P.K. had to drag the burden of his libido behind him all his life. Nature has been unkind to the male, I think, saddling him with this yoke for almost his entire life. Whereas women . . .? I don't know women, I only knew Sumi.

Anyway, I could not talk to P.K. And yet Sudha and he had three children. How I could reconcile this to my idea of him as a man above sexual feelings, to my idea of my sister's chasteness, I don't know. P.K. was nearly sixteen years older than Sudha. After he died, I was able to make out, through Sudha's disconnected grief-stricken ramblings, that he had married her, not, as I had thought, because he wanted to help his teacher's suddenly-orphaned children, but because he passionately loved her. I had tried to dismiss Sudha's words from my thoughts. I was reluctant to imagine him and my sister having a sexual relationship, to think of him as a passionate man. And yet, Ramesh had once told me that his father had been addicted to Hollywood movies, that he saw each new movie which came to town. 'You didn't know?' he had asked me, with a rather suggestive grin. No, I didn't. I would never have associated P.K. with those movies and their passionate love scenes, the long wet kisses. What did he do when the lovers locked lips on the screen, when they began to strip off their clothes? Did he close his eyes? Or did he go to the movies only to see these things? I remember I found a copy of the *Gita Govinda* in his room, a Kannada translation. I read it in an erotic daze. 'Paint my breasts, oh Krishna'—would a woman really say this to a man? Would he do it to her?

I have to laugh at myself now. It took me a long time to realize that most of us go through these feelings. It is a miracle that so many of us emerge unscathed from that maelstrom of ignorance and guilt. Young people are, perhaps, better off today, though I have to wonder whether the openness of this age has, in fact, cushioned the pangs of ignorance, or whether it has made things worse. To know so clearly the things you cannot easily have is terrible.

Marriage resolves the issue to some extent, it puts this hideously troubling matter of sex in its place. It is no longer a major torment, no, not even a minor torment. When Sumi and I were married, I told her about my desire to read the *Gita*

Govinda to her. She laughed at me and said, 'Read it to me. Now.' I did, and as I was reading, she stopped me and pulling down her nightdress she offered me her beautiful breasts. The greatest act of love, the most generous one I have ever known. Her eyes were luminous as she said the line that had haunted me for years, 'Paint my breasts,' she said, but instead of 'Krishna', she said my name. 'Paint my breasts, Gopala.' I put my hands on her firm soft breasts, then put my lips to them. And they came together then, the erotic that had so excited and frightened me and my love for Sumi. In the outpouring of my love, I realized that the erotic was but one half of a whole.

In the early days of our marriage, thoughts of Sumi possessed me all day; I can remember my feverish excitement to get back to her, to hold her in my arms, to put my lips on hers, to mingle my body with hers. This can happen only once in a lifetime. The need for sex remains, but this madness can never happen again. At our ages, Kasturi's and mine, there can no longer be thunder and lightning, no more a rush of blood to the head, no sudden savage arousal. And yet I have a sense of excitement when I am with Kasturi. She has awakened something in me. I like to be with her, I like to see her smile, I want to put my finger in that little pit in her cheek, feel the skin of her cheek against my palm. She knows my feelings; no woman can be unaware of a man's interest in her. But neither of us allows this interest to make itself obvious. I have my reasons, and so, I am sure, has she.

Strangely, (or, perhaps, not so strangely, because these two people are travelling on the same road) Kasturi has been thinking of Gopal too, having the same thought that, in spite of their spending time together, she knows very little of his personal life. All she knows is that he was a university professor, and that he resigned from this job, she does not know why, and that he is a widower with three daughters and a grandson they all dote on. She has come to know a little more about the family from Nagi, though. Nagi and she have become friends. Sometimes, when Nagi is free, she visits Kasturi, has a cup of tea with her, chats a little. She talks about the family with whom she began working when she was a girl. She has told her of the accident in which Gopal's wife and her father died and refers vaguely to a time when Gopalanna 'was not here'. She does not say where he was, nor does Kasturi ever ask, uneasy about gossiping with Nagi about her employers. But she gets a sense of something wrong, something she can't put her finger on. Gopal never speaks of his dead wife either, not even a passing reference. But why should he talk of her to me, Kasturi thinks. We don't want to talk of the dead, we don't want them to intrude on our daily lives. They come to us when we lie awake in the middle of the night, they haunt us in our dreams. My father never spoke of my mother after she died.

There's a picture of Gopal's wife in the living room of their home. It's unlike the usual picture of a dead person. For one thing, it's a very small picture, and, placed on a table where it is dwarfed by a much larger one of the three sisters. This was taken, obviously, during a wedding. The three of them are wearing silk saris—Seema, sitting erect and regal in a chair, is the centre of the picture, with her sisters on either side. It is a posed and formal picture, unlike Sumi's, which is more casual. Sumi obviously does not know that she is being photographed. She is looking, not at the camera, but elsewhere, not a vague look, but a sharply focused one. The picture must have been taken to capture that moment, that look on Sumi's face and to put it on record—perhaps. Whoever took that picture was making some kind of a statement about her, saying something about his (if the photographer is a man, that is, and Kasturi thinks it must be Gopal) feelings about her.

To Kasturi, Gopal is something of an enigma. But she is content to leave it that way for the present; she has no desire to join the dotted lines.

'I like your friend Gopal,' Rao says to her. 'He thinks a little too much,' he nods vigorously and says, 'otherwise he's worth spending time with. I like him.'

The fact that he speaks to her of Gopal, that he calls him her friend so emphatically, makes her wonder whether he is implying something. Putting her on her guard, perhaps? But that's not like Rao, he's never intrusive, never judgmental. He finished with all that in the early days when they were boss and employee. He took to her mainly because, she soon realized, he was physically attracted to her. He had taken full charge of her, helped her to recreate herself from the small-town girl that she had been. He had taught her how to dress, how not to be imitative, but to be herself. Nothing escaped his notice—from the size of her bindi to her footwear. He took charge of her languages as well, smoothened the roughness of her rustic Kannada and was merciless in correcting her English. (Belinda all over again, Kasturi had thought with resignation.) By the time he was done with her, or rather by the time they were done with each other, she was the old Kasturi again, the self-confident and cheerful woman she had been. That crazed desperate woman who had repeatedly banged her head against the wall until there was a bleeding gash on her forehead was gone. Rao had distanced her from her and from the woman who had stood in the middle of the road, waiting for a vehicle to run over her.

Her failed suicide attempt not only changed her life, but brought her back into it, because it led to her meeting Raju. Kasturi often wonders what her life would have been without Raju, whose rickshaw almost ran over her. She had seen a bus approaching and decided to stand in the middle of the road, to let it run over her. Instead, Raju's autorickshaw reached her first. At the last minute, when he realized she was not moving, he had swerved and the rickshaw had toppled over. The driver had emerged, thankfully unharmed, but furious. He had raged and yelled at her, calling her a mad woman. Later, he told her he had just got his license. 'What would have happened to me if the police had made a case against me? Tell me that.' At that moment, however, he had looked at her face, stopped yelling and said, 'Get in. Where do you want to go? I'll take you.' When she was still silent, her face blank, he had taken her to his home, to his wife and mother who looked after her until she came out of the blankness and knew what she wanted to do.

Raju, Chandru, Rao—Kasturi knows she has been lucky that she met men like them when she walked out of her home, leaving everything behind her. But the greatest luck in life has been having Mira as a friend. She can't imagine life without Mira—soul sister, mother confessor, guardian angel. And her sternest judge. Kasturi has a vivid memory of how harsh and angry Mira had been with her about what she called her pointless and stupid affair with Ranganath, the movie director. How can you, Mira had raged. And are you surprised that people say you slept with him so that he would give you work in his film? What about his wife and kids? What about your theories of sisterhood?

Mira had been wrong in thinking his wife cared, or that what Kasturi was doing hurt her. His wife didn't give a damn about their affair, she didn't want him. (This, in itself, should have alerted Kasturi.) She used the affair to dump him. But that didn't justify what she had done, Mira sternly told Kasturi.

'You can't expect everyone to be like you, Miri,' Kasturi had said. 'You know they called you the Ice Princess in college.'

'I had to be strict,' Mira had told Kasturi once. 'Everyone expected an Anglo-Indian girl to be easy to get, we were supposed to be *loose women*' Mira said the words *loose women* with disdain, both for the words themselves and what they were supposed to mean. But Mira thawed when she met Ranjan. To Kasturi, it is one of the mysteries of the laws of attraction that Mira should have finally succumbed to Ranjan, a rather plump army officer with a small Charlie Chaplin moustache. She has never spoken to Mira about her feelings about Ranjan, so ordinary a man for a girl like Mira! Except for this, Mira knows almost everything about her. She knows what 'that woman', her father's mistress, had done to Kasturi's family, she knows about Kasturi's rift with her brother, she was her confidante during Kasturi's affair with Neel. There's only one period of her life that Mira knows nothing about. Kasturi has often been tempted to tell her about it, but has restrained herself, afraid that by opening the gates, her defences will go down and she will be left open and vulnerable again. She can't afford to let that happen.

And now there is Gopal. She has not spoken about him to Mira, not as yet. Is it because I am afraid he will become important the moment I speak to Mira about him? Or am I just too confused to know what to say? She has no answers to these questions.

Today she is here to share Shalini's plans with Mira. Shalini, Kasturi's brother's wife, has gotten in touch with her after years and is eager to renew their relationship. Mira advises her to respond, to take the hand she's offering.

'I know, but she's after something else. Shalini wants me to go to Jogipura for the Panchayat elections. She wants to get involved and she wants me to be there as well. After all, she says, we are both daughters of politicians, aren't we? I've begun to think I should go. I can still remember how it used to be during election time. Remember, Mira, you had come home once during an election campaign? Remember the two of us had gone with my father on one of his campaigning tours? Do you remember one day when . . .'

Mira watches Kasturi as she talks of those times, her face animated and happy. Suddenly she interrupts her, saying, 'Promise me, Sonu, promise me you won't go away, promise me you won't go back to Jogipura for good.'

'Why, Mira, what's this?'

'I know how you love the place. And now Vasant is back and Shalini wants you, I know once you go there, you won't want to come back

'You stupid woman, what's got into you?'

'I'm afraid, Sonu, I'm afraid you'll go away. You keep saying there's no need for you to work any more. It makes me think that you're planning to go back to Jogipura. Promise me you won't go away, at least for some more time.'

'You silly girl, I was talking of a visit. You know I finished with Jogipura once I left it. And who was it telling me just now to take the hand Shalini is holding out?'

They laugh, but they are both uncomfortably aware that something has been said which they don't want to spell out. 'Fear and hope, fear and hope,' Mira had said to Kasturi, 'that's what this disease means. Even after you go through the treatment and the doctors say you're fine, go home and forget about it, even then you know that the disease has not let go of you. It's still waiting for you, you never know when or where it will strike. I keep prodding myself every day, thinking is this a lump? Or is it only muscle and fat? And what about this?'

Recently however, Mira had stopped talking about it which Kasturi felt was a good sign. And suddenly she says 'don't go.'

Surprisingly, Belinda, Mira's mother, says almost the same thing to Kasturi. Belinda has come on one of her biannual visits, her second daughter Delia accompanying her. Now that Delia has retired and handed over her advertising agency to her daughter Maggie, Delia says she can, unlike other times, stay a little longer. Not for too long though, she says; she wants to go back to her grandchildren, her son Tom's two little ones. 'That's all I want now, to be with the little darlings.'

The day Kasturi visits them, Belinda is talking of going on a holiday, 'Delia, you and I. Somewhere abroad. London, maybe? And Sonu, why don't you join us?'

'What about my poor Ranjan?'

'Sure, let's take your poor Ranjan with us. After all, we need a man to look after the practical details so that we can have fun.'

'When did you ever need a man to look after you, Ma?'

'I'm old now, darling.'

'You! Old!'

'You girls will never realize that your mother's old.'

'Girl! And me with grandchildren!'

Kasturi, as always, listens to them with great pleasure. This is a game they play, mother and daughters, since Belinda's husband's death. When Belinda realized she could no longer live alone, she gave in to her daughters. She sold her house in Shivpur, left the place she had lived in since she got married and moved to Bombay to live with Delia. Determined to start afresh, she reinvented herself and cast herself in the mould of a character: an interesting, gutsy, funny old woman taking pleasure in making outrageous statements. Her daughters realize what she is doing and go along with her. They play up to her and give her the chance to say things they can protest against, allowing her to make even more audacious statements which they enjoy enormously.

'I married your daddy because he was so handsome. Like an Adonis. What a beautiful body he had!' she had said once.

'Ma, don't!'

'Grow up, girl. Your parents are also human. What do you think I married him for? He had no money, or very little of it, his education was negligible, and he lived in that godforsaken place, Shivpur. So, why did I marry him? For his conversation? You know he didn't have much of that, either. The original strong silent man, my Denny.'

'Ma, you had enough conversation for both of you,' Mira, her father's pet, had said.

Belinda ignored her and went on, 'My family was furious with me, but I knew I had to marry that gorgeous creature.'

'Ma,' Delia said, 'you married Daddy because you knew he was the only man in the world who would let you live the way you want. And let you talk as much as you want.'

Kasturi's greatest pleasure when she listens to their badinage, the quick repartee, their arguments, is to feel herself back in Mira's home, Mira and she doing their homework, listening with one ear to Belinda arguing with Delia. In the intervals of their argument, Belinda chivvies Mira and Kasturi, saying, 'Come on, girls, hurry up, dinner is ready. Mira, your daddy will be home soon. And Sonu, that man of yours, whatever his name is, has been waiting for you for hours. Your mother must be anxious. Get on with it, girls.'

Kasturi would collect her books, Mira and she lingering with their last minute talk at the door, until Belinda's 'Mira!' drives her back in. Kasturi would then give her books to Basappa, who has been squatting outside the house for so long that there was a semicircle of bidi stubs before him. Often, when they got to the main road, Kasturi would suddenly start running, leaving Basappa behind, flying almost, because she is so full of happiness, Basappa stumbling after her, calling out 'Sonakka, Sonakka, wait, don't run, wait.'

But things are not the same. They are all changed by what life has done to them. Delia lost her Alan soon after Tom was born and when Maggie was only six. She struggled alone with the advertising agency she and Alan had started, brought up her children on her own. The struggle shows on her face, on her thickened figure. There's Mira, fighting for her life, constantly grieving over the absence of her beloved Molly. She had said to Kasturi, 'You have to get close to death to see how stupid things like worrying about living together without marriage are. But for Ranjan, it's what will his Ma say and what will his sister say and what will his uncle and aunt say when they know that Molly is living with a man without marriage. But I can't change him and I can't change Molly, so I have to put up with it.'

Yes, Mira has changed too, she thinks. But the affection between the mother and daughters has remained constant. So when Belinda says she is old, Delia replies, 'No, Ma, you can never be old.' Belinda, a small-sized woman, has always looked younger than her age. However, now in her seventies, her age shows.

'Age-defying Belinda, eh? Come on, sweetie, we can't help aging. It's not in our hands. We're pushing the boundaries further and further back, but it's got to stop at some time and then it will have a rebound effect. Remember the miracle of the four-minute mile? I forget who broke the barrier, it was an Englishman . . . '

'Roger Bannister.'

'When he did it, it seemed such a huge achievement. But after that, it suddenly became possible for so many more runners to do it. And yet, how far can they go? Can they run the mile in one minute? Now they're trying to make us ageless with pills and hormones and whatnots. But you can't stop time, you can't push it back, it's time that keeps pushing you forwards. Until it stops. And so do you,' Belinda ends dramatically.

'Ma, you would have been fine if it wasn't for your drinking and smoking.'

'Listen to this child! My drinking! What drinking? Am I an alcoholic? With my one glass of wine a day? What about your Ranjan's whisky?'

'But why must you smoke so much?'

'I have a right to live the way I want to. Whether I smoke like a chimney or drink like a sponge is my choice.'

'Cliches, Ma dearest, cliches. And you the one who warned us against them!'

'I've worked hard, I've earned my own money, I have the right to enjoy what I can,' Belinda says grandly.

'Carpe diem, our mother's motto. Remember gather ye rosebuds while ye may, Sonu?'

Kasturi does. For some reason the words 'carpe diem', which Belinda used when she read the poem had sent the two of them into fits of giggles. It had nothing to do with the meaning; the mere words were enough to set them off, in the manner of schoolgirls. 'What's so funny about what I'm saying?' Belinda would ask them in exasperation.

Now, refusing to be sidetracked, Belinda goes on, 'I've brought up three daughters, never depended on anyone, never cheated on my husband

'Spare us the gory details of your marriage, Ma.'

'What gory details? I said I never cheated. I had my temptations, let me tell you. When people say to me, Belinda you haven't changed, I get furious. I want to tell them, I beg your pardon, I wasn't always an old hag like this. I may not have been beautiful, but I looked good. Nice figure, good legs, and a tummy as flat as a drum, as my Denny used to say. Yes, yes, laugh if you want to, but . . . Now what was I going to say? You girls have made me forget what it was.'

'That you didn't cheat on our poor Daddy.'

'That's right. And I brought up my girls to be good women, though one of them married a Hindu

'Don't you start on Ranjan now.'

'Well, he's better than that other one, Livvy's husband, that Pakistani son-in-law of mine. Did I ever imagine that one of my daughters would become a Mrs Bannerji and another would marry a Pakistani and become Mrs Khan?'

'Did you?'

'Of course I didn't. Didn't I just say so? That was rhetoric, if you can remember what that means. Marrying a Muslim was bad enough. But a Pakistani I cannot stomach.'

'Ma, you can't say such things! It's not right.'

'Why can't I? My father was in the '65 war, my brother died in the '71 war, my grandnephew fought in Kargil—I have every right to say these things.'

Belinda comes from an army family, she's very clear about who the enemy is. 'My father,' she told them once, 'said all this bhai-bhai stuff is for the politicians. For us, he said, the only question is—friend or foe?' Which is why, when Olivia married Imran, a Pakistani, Belinda was furious. Her silence and noncommunication travelled across oceans and continents and Livvy's letters remained unanswered. But when Livvy had twin boys, Belinda immediately decided to visit her.

'Off goes St. Belinda to fight the Crusades,' Mira had joked. 'Only, travelling in the wrong direction this time, going West instead of East.'

Belinda had felt she had to go and stop Imran and his mother from 'doing that barbarous thing to the poor little tots, cutting off the tips of their little thingies,' as Belinda called it. Mira and Delia had been in fits of laughter, but Belinda was serious.

'It's supposed to be good, Ma, it prevents them from getting cancer later,' Mira had argued.

'You don't see the men who have their thingies intact dropping dead, do you?'

Thankfully, for both Livvy and Imran, (and their marriage!) when Belinda went to them, she found Imran such a gentle creature, even gentler and quieter than Livvy, that all her belligerence vanished. Belinda had come back chastened.

For all Belinda's air of bravado, she's conscious of the depredations of age. She has scoliosis and leans slightly to one side, she has osteoporosis (no one told her to take calcium, or enough exercise) her eyes are less sharp, her hearing a little duller. And the sound of her heels as she walks is no longer a brisk tip-tap tip-tap, but a slower tattoo, an ek taal. Her mind, though, is still lively, able to turn somersaults, lithe and swift enough to swing on a trapeze and change ropes in midair. She has disciplined her mind to accept the inroads of time on her body, she tells Kasturi, when they are by themselves; what she really fears is an assault on her mind. She's terrified of Alzheimer's, she panics at the thought of senile dementia. 'I don't want to be like my mother, drooling and in diapers, like a baby. But babies are fresh and wholesome, they smell sweet. Old people have a sour stale smell, like something that's been kept too long.'

Delia was to stay a fortnight, but she left after a week. There's a big campaign coming up and Maggie has suddenly got cold feet, she needs me there.'

Mira rings up Kasturi after Delia has left. 'Ranjan and I are going out for dinner. Can you come and stay with Ma until we return?'

Belinda is apologetic about having made Kasturi give up her evening for her.

'I want to go soon, Sonu,' Belinda tells her. 'Look at all the trouble I cause my girls. And look at you, dragged here for my sake, giving up your own plans, god knows what they were.'

Kasturi reassures her, but Belinda can't get away from her thoughts. 'I know Delia will look after me when the time comes, but she's had a hard life, I want her to enjoy her grandchildren, not look after an old woman.'

'They go together, don't they?' Kasturi asks. 'You can't think of enjoying your future unless you take care of your past.'

'Become quite a philosopher, haven't you, Sonu? Who taught you all this?'

'Life.'

'Ah, that's the hardest teacher, even worse than time.' Later she says, 'I can't leave my Mira and go, Sonu. I brought Miranda into this world and I need to be with her when . . . you know what I mean. Who else can help her like I can? But that's cruel. It's hard to see your children go before you, it's the cruelest thing in the world. I know, I lost my Ophelia. You too lost one of your brothers, didn't you, Sonu?'

'Yes.'

'How old was he?'

'Eighteen.'

'Eighteen! My god! Young men are like gods at that age. I remember visiting your mother after it happened. She looked like a lost soul.'

'She never got over it.'

'Mothers never do. We have such dreams, Sonu, so many dreams for our children, we think that they will go on after us, carrying our dreams with them. And then to see it all snuffed out so suddenly . . . But why do I say mothers? Even Denny suffered for Philly's death, yes, until the very end. Poor man, he lived his entire life to make us happy and comfortable. He was always terrified he'd leave me and the girls without money. Then he died without enjoying any of the money he made. And now here we are, the girls and I, all of us with more money than we know what to do with. Life is strange, isn't it? But, Sonu, I want to ask you something, promise me you'll do it. I know it's selfish, you do so much for Mira. . .'

'She does much more for me. You don't have to hesitate.'

Belinda rushes into speech. 'Promise me you will be with Mira. I know you will be with my girl whenever she needs you, but I'm speaking of after I'm gone. Ranjan and Delia will be with her, I know that, but it will be hard on them. They love her too much.'

'And I don't?'

'I didn't mean that, sweetie. But the ties of blood are cruel, child. The cut goes deep, you bleed . . .'

Kasturi reassures her, she says that cancer is no longer like in the old days, people live much longer, they live almost normal lives, the quality of life is much better. Isn't Mira doing good? Belinda listens, she seems calmer, she knows that a promise has been made and will be kept.

'Tell me, Sonu,' she says after a while. 'You're a Hindu, you should know. Do you understand this karma thing? Why did Mira, who's never harmed anyone all her life—she's the gentlest of my three—why should she have to suffer this?'

'I don't know. I don't think about such things. It's hopeless trying to understand why things happen. I think they just happen and we have to accept them. That's all.'

'You think so? I must say it makes sense. But it still makes me angry: why Mira, who has done nothing to deserve this?' She sighs heavily and says, 'Loving can be very exhausting, Sonu.' She *sees* Kasturi's wondering face and goes on in what Mira calls her 'solemn quoting voice': 'And the heart must pause to breathe And love itself have rest. That's Byron,' she adds in her normal voice. 'We read that poem in school.'

'Recite it to me,' Kasturi demands.

'I'm not sure I can remember it. My memory has become treacherous; it works when it wants to, not when I want it to. Memory is always capricious, isn't it? Mine certainly is.' Belinda sees Kasturi looking at her expectantly. 'All right, I'll try to remember, but give me a moment.'

She pauses, as if retrieving the words from the deep well of her memory and then begins, intoning in a singsong manner, the way they had been, perhaps, taught in school:

So we'll go no more a-roving
So late into the night,

Though the heart be still as loving,
And the moon be still as bright.
For the sword outwears its sheath,
And the soul wears out the breast,
And the heart must pause to breathe
And love itself have rest.

She is silent for a moment, then says, 'Poets know how to pierce your heart.'

Kasturi *sees* tears shining in her eyes. She gently puts her hand on Belinda's. Belinda pats her hand, as if it is she who is comforting Kasturi. Kasturi lifts Belinda's hand to her cheek and then puts it down.

'I'm sorry, Sonu dear,' Belinda says. 'I didn't mean to get weepy. But tears come easy these days. As if they're just under the surface.'

After dinner Belinda dozes in her chair. Kasturi watches her with compassion and thinks of her life, rich with love of children and grandchildren. Rich, too, with her work and students, with the books she has loved and which have given her so much joy. What does she dream of? The living? Or the dead? Or is her sleep only a dark uninhabited space?

Belinda suddenly wakes up, looks disoriented for a moment, then becomes aware of her surroundings.

'Haven't they returned?'

'No. Why don't you go to bed? I'll sit with you.'

'No, you don't have to sit up, sweetie. Lie down yourself.'

When Mira comes, Kasturi is fast asleep and Belinda wide awake. 'Not sleeping as yet, Ma?'

'You know me. I fell asleep, woke up and now I'm ready to struggle against sleeplessness the whole night.'

'Take your pill.' They are both whispering. 'I better wake Sonu up.'

'Let her sleep here. She can go home tomorrow morning.'

'No, she has to go. She works at night.'

As Ranjan and Kasturi drive back through the brightly lit streets, which look entirely different without the large crowds and endless vehicles, Kasturi has a sense of disorientation. This is a strange city, it's not the city she knows. When she sees a huge illuminated hoarding which seems to dwarf everything else, she gives a sudden exclamation.

'Did you say something?' Ranjan asks.

'No.'

At home, she looks in on Rao and goes to bed herself. She thinks of Belinda's words: Blood ties are cruel, the cut goes deep.

Yes, Belinda, they do. I know it better than you do. You still grieve over Ophelia, you are afraid for Mira, who herself mourns the absence of her beloved Molly—but I . . . I did it to myself, I cut the umbilical cord myself. A clean cut. No looking back, I told myself. But it seems like my eyes have moved to the back of my head, because I am constantly looking back, always thinking of what I did. I can't ignore it any longer. I have to go to Jogipura, I have to find out where my son is.

The World

'The categories of cruelty are not closed.'

Lord Denning, in *Sheldon v. Sheldon* (1966)

It was during her illness that Gopal had heard Kalyani say to Aru, comforting her, perhaps, 'He looks after us.'

Gopal had immediately understood that Kalyani was referring to the Ganesha in the hall. But Aru had been puzzled until Kalyani had added, 'Our Ganesha, Aru.'

'Oh! He doesn't do a very good job of looking after the women, does he?'

Gopal had felt a pang; he had known that among other things Aru was referring to what had happened to Sumi, to what *he* had done to Sumi. But Kalyani, unfazed, had replied, 'What can even the gods do against our own destinies, Aru?'

Gopal had been intrigued, a little amused as well, at Kalyani's idea of the powerlessness of gods, of their helplessness against individual destinies. What did that make of destiny, then? Was destiny chalked out not by god, but by some other power? Or was it born of itself, self-created, swayambhu, something that stood apart from creation and therefore impossible for anyone to control? Gopal has always believed that it is the human will which shapes human lives. The idea that we come into life carrying our destinies with us, and that everything flows from an unseen power, seems strange to him. He has an aversion to thinking of humans as pawns to be moved on the board by an unseen hand. If this is how it is, why, then, have we been given this great, never-to-come-again opportunity of human life?

But Gopal's belief that we work out our destinies through our own lives, his absolute faith in the human will, has taken some beating over the years. He has accepted the possibility that there are a great number of factors that influence human life—like the times we are born in, the families we are born into, the places we live in. Connected, too, to the lives of others. In fact, he has begun to wonder whether there is such a thing as an individual destiny at all. Human lives are so inextricably tangled together that it is almost impossible to pick one strand out of the skein and say 'this is *my* life'. Our lives criss-cross and often turn us from the paths we had thought we would take. Gopsil remembers how, when he first came to this city, he had found it hopelessly narrow and provincial, its people, not hostile, but indifferent to strangers, to the world outside its borders. I won't stay here long, he had thought. Then he had met Sumi . . .

After Sumi's death, his fragile bond with the city became even more tenuous. What keeps him here now are his daughters—Seema, of course, but Aru as well. He has some unfinished business with Aru that he needs to resolve some day. Aru and Rohit, he knows, will continue to live here. Charu has gone, Seema, too, some instinct tells him, will leave one day. But Aru and Rohit will remain, rooted in the city by birth, by their home and their work.

Rohit, actually, has always had a rather complicated relationship with the city, he has mixed feelings about it. As an adolescent, he had wanted desperately to get away from a place inhabited by people who knew about his father's alcoholism and asked him awkward questions; even worse were those who looked at him with pity. His mother, sensing his unhappiness, had urged him to go away. He was unwilling to leave her to face the situation at home alone. But when he got admission to the college of architecture in Delhi, he went. By the time he graduated, his father was better, frightened off alcohol by a major illness. He knew then that he could go anywhere he wanted. But by then Aru had entered his life. Once he married her, he was anchored to the city by Aru.

Rohit had, by sheer accident, chosen the right time to start his work in the city. Boom time had come to the city, galvanized into a feverish pace of growth by the money flowing into it. Such a great spurt in building activities made it a good time for architects like Rohit. But most of the new constructions were malls, shopping complexes, office and apartment blocks and hospitals; whereas, what Rohit enjoyed was building homes for people. By doing that, he realized, he was translating their dreams about their lives into reality. It was this clear understanding of his own leanings that had propelled Rohit into giving up his job in an architect's firm where most of the work consisted of commercial buildings, and teaming up with a like-minded architect friend. Initially, their struggle was mainly to get work, any work. Then, like a reward, a dream project came into their hands. This is the restoration of an old bungalow, one of the few left in the city and still intact, if slowly getting more and more derelict. For Rohit, working on this bungalow, that has all the classical features of its times, is like a dream come true. He has finally found his place in the city through his work and through Aru; yet it is never his city like it is Aru's.

For Aru, this is *her* city, the one she was born in, where she has lived all her life. It is a part, not only of her life, but of herself as well. For long, she took the city for granted, its very familiarity ruling out curiosity. It was only when she began going about on a scooter that her eyes seemed suddenly to have opened to the city. The scooter allowed her to move through the city with ease, to explore areas she had never seen before. She rode through lanes so narrow that even autorickshaws hesitated to enter them, lanes with so many twists and turns that no rickshaw could negotiate them. She still remembers the fascinating glimpses of people's lives through doors that opened into courtyards: women clustering around a single tap, women cleaning grains, women bargaining with street vendors, school children in gleaming uniforms emerging with their satchels on their backs. She saw large houses standing back to back, with narrow 'conservancy' lanes in between, meant for humans to do the kind of work Aru cannot even imagine today. Once she had seen a beautifully carved wooden door left wide open, the interior, a temple obviously, dark, except for a single light before the idol, a light which shone like a star in the surrounding darkness. She has never forgotten that sight. She can never forget either, the time she had lost her way, and an unknown man on a motorbike had tersely said, 'Follow me'. He had led her through a maze of streets, leading the way with confidence, never looking back even once, but sure, somehow, that she was following him. Never going so fast that she would lose him, or so slow that she could catch up with him. It had been raining at the time, a fine mist-like rain, which scarcely wet the streets. In her dreamlike memory, there had been no one on the streets but the two of them, and a silence so total that she had heard the whisper of the rain on her cheeks.

Then came the day when she had to give up the scooter. Not only because it had been destroyed, ruined beyond redemption, but because of her promise to Kalyani. 'Promise me you won't ever go on a scooter again,' Kalyani had pleaded. Thinking of the mangled bodies of her mother and grandfather, trussed into macabre bloodstained bundles, she had promised. Besides, there was her own guilt. For a long time she carried the thought within her: it was I who taught my mother to ride the scooter. She vividly remembers the moment her mother had taken off on her own, remembers how she had driven out of the gate and on to the road for her first independent ride. Aru had waited for her, anxious, heart in mouth. In a short while, Sumi drove in through the gate, she saw Aru waiting for her and a wide happy grin split her face. She took her hands off the handlebars to raise them in triumph, the scooter wobbled. 'Don't!' Aru cried out and ran towards her, steadying the scooter. Sumi got off and hugged her daughter. Aru had begun laughing as well, sharing her mother's happiness, her triumph. Now the thought dogs her:

if I hadn't taught her to ride the scooter, maybe she would never have died.

Aru was steadfast to the promise she made to Kalyani, though it was not an easy promise to keep, for the city is not kind to commuters. Even after she began working, she moved about in rickshaws until Rohit got her a car. She uses the car very rarely, for it can become a burden; it is *her* responsibility, she has to worry about where she will park it. It also alienates her from the city, for when she is driving she can see nothing but the stream of vehicles before her, on either side of her. When did so many vehicles come into the city? Sleek new cars, large luxury buses, vans with orange and lilac streaks on their sides—everything spells affluence.

Yes, affluence has come to the city. And inevitably, with prosperity comes its Siamese twin, violence. Aru, as a lawyer, has seen her share of what the law calls domestic violence. (As if, Aru often thinks, it is a tame household pet.) It is the same violence that has now spilled over into the streets. (Or is it the other way round?) The underworld made its way to the city and gang warfare, shoot-outs at night and police encounters became part of life in the city. No longer an invisible middle-of-the-night war, but one fought brazenly in broad daylight. A man was dragged out of his car and hacked to death in a street close to where Nagma lived, another kidnapped from a park in the early morning. The twinning of affluence and violence can be most clearly seen in Nagaraj's story to which Aru's family have had a ringside seat.

Nagaraj, the estate agent who had befriended Sumi, ran a small estate agency from a modest room. He had begun visiting Kalyani after Sumi's death. He often brought his two granddaughters with him, Malashree and Vijayashree, (their mother had an unfortunate fascination for the names of movie actresses) especially on festival days. Dressed in zari-bordered lehngas, flowers in their oiled plaits, they would prostate themselves at Kalyani's tiny feet, one after another, when their grandfather said, 'Give them your blessings, ajji.' They lay flat on the ground then, their heads resting on Kalyani's feet, their skinny bodies straight as arrows, their skirts rucked up showing their silver anklets. Kalyani would place her palms on their sleek heads, murmuring words no one ever heard or understood. Nagaraj always said that it was Kalyani's blessing which brought prosperity to the family; but everyone knows that it was his son's association with the underworld which had made the family prosperous. The girls now go to an exclusive girls' college. No more lehngas or oiled plaits for them; they dress in fashionably faded jeans and scruffy, rumpled T-shirts, they have their hair trimmed and shaped, their finger and toe nails manicured, pedicured and painted in flamboyant colours in exclusive salons. Their scooter rides on their grandfather's creaky scooter are now a distant memory; they travel in chauffeur-driven cars, as do Nagaraj and his wife. But, despite the fact that his son goes about with two security guards, Nagaraj is afraid for him and thinks with nostalgia of his little agency. He and his wife have their compensations, though; they live in the kind of comfort they had never dreamt of, they travel abroad and come back loaded with gifts for envious relations. So Nagaraj closes his eyes to what his son is doing, though he never fails to make large offerings to the neighbourhood Ganesha temple, including, one year, a gift (anonymous, as his son insisted, though Nagaraj's wife has broadcast the fact to a large number of people) of a diamond-studded crown for the god. But Nagaraj knows that even Ganesha is helpless against the underworld, and he lives in constant fear.

And then came terrorism. How can a city, which has aligned itself with global prosperity, escape it? The city received its baptism of terror when a lone gunman suddenly appeared at an international science conference. One scientist died because he came in the way of the bullet, one of the many fired at random. The killer escaped, to the discomfiture of the police. Soon, connections with global terror emerged from the city. A family of professionals living quietly in a middle-class neighbourhood was linked to a suicide attack in another country; their son was the suicide bomber, the almost completely burnt body lying in hospital was his. Their home became the sudden focus of attention, TV cameras and reporters converging on the house and laying siege to it until they finally got to interview the mother. Grief-stricken, devastated, she could say nothing but reiterate her belief in her son's innocence; this, despite the fact that another son had identified his brother. The father, grim and silent, refused to speak.

Now terror makes a direct entry into the city, not with a gun this time, but with bombs. Two bombs go off. One, placed in a quiet residential street at the foot of a street lamp, goes off in the afternoon, a time when children are at school and those at home are either taking a nap or watching TV. The few who hear it think it is a firecracker and wonder whether the country has won an important cricket match, or an election result has been declared. Then they forget about it and realize only later, when they hear about the bigger second bomb, that it could, possibly, have been one too. Someone rings up the police who come with a detonator squad and confirm that it was indeed a low-intensity bomb—unlike the other, which goes off in the parking area of a shopping complex. A number of vehicles are destroyed by this one, the parking attendant injured and one woman is killed, a woman who had completed her shopping and was about to leave. She could have driven away, but being an honest woman, she waited for the parking attendant to collect the parking fee for her two-wheeler. Before he could reach her, the bomb went off. He was flung backwards some distance away and stunned; he received only minor injuries and soon recovered. The woman, however, died on the spot.

Swiftly jokes begin to make the rounds in the city, about how the bombs could have been manufactured only by a local person, for who else but people living in this city could have been so amateurish? Newspaper headlines are, however, dramatic. 'Terror comes to the city', they scream the next day. 'Only one dead', some newspapers report. 'One woman dies', another clarifies. She is quickly identified by the cards in her purse. Though most papers call her a housewife, a few discover that she was a working woman and is variously described as teacher, a secretary, or a nurse. Only some newspapers get it right. She was working, they reported, with a prominent lawyer in the city. An intrepid photographer got a shot of the distraught husband, shocked beyond words, his face the face of human grief.

***

It is a Friday. Aru is in the court when she gets the news. She is arguing a maintenance case, exasperated at having to make the same arguments all over again. 'My client has not been paid her maintenance for more than a year, she badly needs the money, she lives with her mother who herself has a very meager income; my client has two small children, she is trying to get some work, but she is not qualified for anything and has not yet found anything suitable . . .'

The husband's lawyer, who has been offering different reasons for evading payment, goes into his usual spiel. The room is crowded, it's hot, everyone is tired, wanting the day to be over, to go home and shed the burden of the week's work. The judge, too, looks tired and irritable and Aru knows that once again her client will not get the money. 'You should file a case under the Criminal Procedure Code,' the judge said to Aru the last time. But Aru didn't want that. The husband was capable of paying much more, whereas under the CrPC she would get just the bare minimum.

This time, the judge comes down heavily on the husband's lawyer when he argues that his client, a fairly well-to-do farmer, cannot pay because he has had a bad year as it has not rained.

'What do you mean it hasn't rained? Is your client starving? The next date he has to be here with the money, or else I will have to take strong measures.'

Aru is pleased with the grilling, but the opposing lawyer makes a face at Aru as they make their way out of the courtroom, as if saying, 'Are you happy now?' Aru has a childish impulse to stick her tongue out at him, but stifles it and walks out in dignified silence, followed by her client.

Aru is trying to explain what was said to her confused client when her phone, which she has automatically switched on, rings. 'Wait a minute,' she tells her client and speaks into the phone. 'Yes, Nagma?'

'Is your case over?'

'Yes. Why?'

'Something terrible has happened.'

Seema, she thinks in sudden fear, Rohit . . .

'It's Tressa.'

'What about her?'

'Tressa is dead.'

'What? I left her just two hours ago

'It was a bomb.'

'Bomb? What bomb?'

'I know, it's hard to believe, but it's true. She was going to pick up Gracy and she stopped near the market when a bomb went off.'

'Nagma, how could it . . .?'

'Aru, we don't know much. Ma'am has gone to the hospital. She told me to ask you to pick up Gracy from her school, she's still there, waiting for Tressa.'

'Oh my god!'

'She doesn't know what's happened. Ma'am says don't tell her. Take her home, don't bring her to the office.'

'Nagma, how can I . . .'

'Go, Aru, go. She'll be waiting.'

'Ramu?'

'I think ma'am's told him. I'll ring you later.'

The child is waiting with a teacher when Aru gets to the school. There is no one else, all the children have left. Gracy jumps up when she sees Aru.

'Aru ma'am, I'm coming with you to your house. My father told me I must go with you.'

Aru exchanges a look with the teacher over Grace's head. The teacher gives an imperceptible shake of her head. No, they have not told her.

'Come, Gracy, let's go.'

'We are going in the car?'

'No, Gracy, I don't have the car. We're taking an auto.'

Fortunately, the child has been to Aru's house earlier, she has met Rohit, Gopal and Seema, so it won't be an entirely strange place to her. But when they get home, she suddenly draws back, Aru can feel her hand tugging at her, as if to pull her back. It's as if she knows that this is not one of those happy visits.

'Come in, Gracy, let's get you a glass of milk and something to eat.'

Nagi, surprised to see Aru home at this time, and with the child, looks questioningly at Aru. But Aru's look seems to warn Nagi not to ask any questions. Instead, she says, 'Nagi, I'll get Gracy's milk, you take her to the bathroom to wash.'

When they go out of the room, Aru rings up Rohit. She tells him what has happened. 'Come home, Rohit, I can't cope with this alone.'

He will come as soon as he can get away, he says, but it may take some time. He is on a site, nearly an hour's distance away. Aru, after a moment's hesitation, rings up Gopal. He listens to her and says, 'I'm at home, I'll be down in a minute.'

He comes almost on the instant. 'Where is the child?' he asks.

'She's having her milk.' She tells him that Gracy does not know yet her mother is dead, Aru will have to tell her that. They look blankly at each other, then go inside. Gracy is drinking her milk, but the biscuits which Aru had foraged for her are untouched. This is not a house for children, Aru thinks. We have nothing which a child would like to eat. Gracy finishes her milk and the moment she is done, she slips off the chair and asks, 'Can I go home now, Aru ma'am? Can you take me in the car?'

'No, Gracy, you have to wait for your father. He'll come as soon as he can, okay?'

'I'll take you out,' Gopal tells her. 'Let's go to the park. Come on, wear your shoes.'

The child hesitates. Aru reassures her that Gopal is her own papa and Seemaakka's papa. 'Remember Seemaakka? You went to her room last time?'

The child thinks it over, finally says 'yes' and goes out with Gopal, holding his hand trustingly. Aru can scarcely bear to look at her, and is grateful to Gopal for taking her away.

By the time Rohit gets home, Aru has had some more details from Nagma. Tressa had stopped at the shopping complex to make some purchases before going to Gracy's school. She was just leaving when there was an explosion in the parking lot—the bomb had been placed in a two-wheeler. Tressa, closest to the vehicle, was blown to pieces. Surekha and Jaisimha were with Ramu at the hospital.

'Ramu is in a very bad state, Aru,' Nagma tells her. 'Ma'am says he is in a state of shock, he still hasn't taken in what has happened. She thinks you better keep Gracy with you tonight.'

When Gopal and Gracy return, the three adults try to keep up a semblance of normality, but the child senses their uneasiness. Surprisingly, she does not talk about her parents, does not ask when she is going home. But when Surekha's driver comes a little later with a plastic bag of Gracy's clothes, she perks up, as if her clothes are a kind of link to her home and her parents. Whoever packed the clothes has done it in a hurry, or else it has been done by someone who knows nothing about her clothes. Things have been haphazardly chosen and shoved into the bag. Gracy's pyjamas are there, but there is no top.

'What to do now, Aru ma'am?' Gracy asks, crossing her arms to cover her skinny chest. 'How can I sleep like this?'

Aru finds a blouse among the clothes and makes her wear it. Gracy giggles, says, 'I look funny, no, Aru ma'am?'

When Aru puts her to bed in the spare room, Gracy asks her, 'Where will you sleep?'

'In my room.'

'You sleep here with me, Aru ma'am. Please,' she adds, remembering her manners.

'All right.'

When she goes to her room to pick up her pillow and blanket, Gracy follows her, as if she is not sure Aru will be back.

'You're taking your Aru ma'am with you?' Rohit asks.

'Yes.'

'What about me, then?'

'You can sleep alone, no, Uncle.'

'But I'm frightened to sleep alone.'

She giggles and says, 'Then you also come to our room.'

'Thank you, Gracy.'

'You're welcome,' she sings out. Aru thinks, Tressa must have taught her to say that. Once in bed, Gracy's brief spell of gaiety deserts her and she lies on her back, looks at Aru and says, 'When my father comes, wake me up.'

'It's late now. He'll be here tomorrow. Okay? Now go to sleep. Uncle and I will come in a little while.'

Aru lies awake for a long time, her eyes wide open, thinking of Tressa dead. Smiling cheerful Tressa who never lost her cool. 'I am so lucky, no, to be working here,' she would often say. Yes, she was proud of working with the three women, she considered herself part of their attempt to build a better world, a world she hoped her Gracy would inhabit; she had said this to Aru once. Her rupture with her family had hurt her deeply, though she showed no sign of it, not to Ramu and Gracy anyway. But they had been happy, they were earning decent money both of them, they had Gracy and . . . Oh god! Aru suddenly remembers that Tressa was four months pregnant. She had told them the news with great joy, promising she would not take much leave. 'As if that is all we care about,' Aru had said reproachfully to her. Tressa was sure it would be a son. Gracy wanted a brother, she had said, so it had to be a son.

Rohit comes in. 'Rohit, she was pregnant,' she says, 'Tressa was pregnant.' She is weeping for the first time since she heard of Tressa's death, she is weeping for Tressa and Ramu, for Gracy and the unborn baby, she is weeping for her own and Rohit's children who will never be born.

Gracy stays with them for two days. Surprisingly she does not speak of going home after the first evening. Aru, with Nagi's help, tries to cope with the child's routine. What about her bath, she wonders the next day. Does she have her own bath, or did Tressa bathe her? At what age do you allow a child to bathe herself? At what age did I bathe myself? But there was a difference; Cham's birth had propelled her into becoming an older sister, Gopal had taught her to become independent early.

'I'll bathe her, don't worry,' Nagi tells Aru.

Gracy refuses indignantly. 'I can have my own bath,' she says. But after Nagi has gone, she says softly, as if not wanting Nagi to hear, 'You can come and put soap on my back, Aru ma'am. Afterwards. I'll call you.'

Aru goes in when Gracy calls out to her. She sees the child on the stool, hunched over, as if concealing her body, offering only her back to Aru. Her mother must have done this for her, Aru thinks and the extent of the child's loss hits her. As she soaps her back, feeling the frail bird-like bones and the knobs of her spine moving under her hand, she tries to control her sobs. When Gracy comes out of the bathroom struggling with the too-large towel around her, Aru is sobbing. She tries to compose herself.

The child looks at her, but says nothing. She quickly gets into her knickers and lets the towel drop, asking Aru, 'Where is the talcum?' Aru gets it and Gracy powders herself, her chest and arms, her underarms, then gives the tin to Aru, saying, 'You put it now for my back.' This is the routine she had with her mother, Aru thinks and now the tears can no longer be suppressed, they flow. Gracy watches her in sombre silence.

Gopal comes to spend time with her in the morning. Watching him teach her to play cards, taking the game as seriously as she is doing, Aru remembers his patience with her, with the three of them, of how he had never seemed to tire of her endless questions.

Why can't I forgive him for what he did? That was an aberration; what he was to me when I was a child has not been wiped out because of what he did later.

Nagma brings Shabnam with her in the afternoon and the two women go with the children to the nearby park. The girls run off to play and Nagma tells Aru about the battle raging over Tressa's dead body. Old resentments and hostilities have surfaced and the families, who had left the couple severely alone all this while, are now claiming Tressa's body. Ramu's mother wants her to be cremated. She's my son's wife, when she married him she became a Hindu, if we don't cremate her, if we don't do all the rituals, how can we face our people, she asks. Tressa's brother, a priest and, therefore, an authority in the family, insists on service in church and a burial in the Christian cemetery. While Nagma talks and Aru listens, they can hear the voices of the two girls. 'See me, Amma, see me, Aru-auntie,' Shabnam calls out. She is sitting on the top of the slide and when she is sure they're looking, she lets herself go with a scream and rushes down. Gracy, now sitting at the top, cries out too, 'See me, Aru ma'am, see me, Nagma ma'am,' and holding her arms out on both sides as if she is flying, her legs held out rigidly straight before her, she flies down and tumbles into a laughing heap like Shabnam.

Finally, Nagma tells Aru, Ramu decided that Tressa would be buried. He told her family they could have the body. Ramu's mother got hysterical, but Ramu was firm. Not only would it give her mother great comfort, Tressa herself would have liked to go back to the Church, he said. And the people she had known for so many years, the people who had loved her, her family, her friends, her neighbours and so many others—she would have liked them to be there. You and I, he told his mother, we have known her for only a short time.

'Thank god, Aru, ma'am and sir were there, they supported Ramu, which is the only reason I think his mother stopped arguing with him. Otherwise, ma'am says, she would have gone on and on. And poor Ramu close to collapsing! At one point Ramu told his mother, what are you fighting for, Amma? There is no more Tressa left, there are only bits and pieces of her, what does it matter whether those bits are burnt or buried? Ma'am told me this, Aru, she told me he said *only bits and pieces.*'

The two women are in tears by now. This is a children's park, parents are too engrossed in their own children to look at anyone else. The walkers, intent on their walk, go past with determined strides, looking neither right nor left. One or two people do look at the two women with curiosity, a burqa-clad woman and the other in jeans, sobbing together.

'Have you told Gracy?' Nagma asks.

'No, I haven't, I can't, I don't know what to say.'

'You must, Aru. Ramu is coming tomorrow morning to pick her up, he is going home with his parents for the ceremonies, his mother is determined to do all the rituals. You must tell Gracy before her father comes.'

'I think she knows.'

'How?'

'I don't know. But she hasn't mentioned Tressa since she came to me, not once, not a word.'

The women get up finally. Nagma calls out to the girls, 'Come, children, we have to go.'

Shabnam comes with a rush to her mother and falls with a practised ease into her open arms, crying out, 'I came first, I came first.' Gracy follows on her heels, comes to Aru, then stops. Aru hesitates as well before she puts out her hand. Gracy holds it, looks up at Aru's face and smiles.

'How do I tell the child her mother is dead, Rohit?' Aru asks him bleakly. Gopal has taken Gracy to his place giving Aru some breathing space. In the event Gracy makes it easy for her.

'Your father is coming tomorrow to take you home,' Aru tells her.

'I'm going home?' There's no joy in her voice, no smile on her face.

'Yes. I mean you are going to your grandparents' house.'

'Where's my mother?'

The question comes at last and Aru, in spite of her preparations to meet this question, has no answer ready. She thinks, Gracy will always remember this moment, for her this will be the moment of her mother's death. She remembers Premi's call which she had taken, Premi's words: 'Aru, she's gone, your mother is no more.' That had been the moment of Sumi's death for her. She remembers how the words had haunted her, kept coming back to her for months. It had been like hearing an echo coming back from a distance. Aru, she's gone, your mother is no more . . .

'She had an accident.'

'She died?'

Again Aru hesitates. Then she says, 'Yes, Gracy.'

The child says no more. Gopal, Aru and Rohit are with her all evening. She is silent, but seems composed. At night she asks Aru, 'Will you sleep in my room, Aru ma'am?'

'Yes, Gracy.'

'And you also, Uncle?'

'Yes, we'll both be with you.'

When her father comes the next day, she says nothing, only holds him in such a tight grasp that he can't move. He bends down, gently loosens her hold and picks her up. He is the one who is weeping.

Aru leaves the room. When she returns, Gracy is sitting on her father's lap, her arms round him. She does not talk to anyone but her father. And she speaks only in Malayalam, as if she knows no other language. When they are ready to leave, Ramu coaxes her into saying 'thank you', which she does. 'Thank you, Aru ma'am, Uncle, thank you Aru ma'am's papa,' she says. None of them can respond. Gopal and Aru stand and watch Rohit drive the father and daughter back to a home which is no longer a home. Gracy, who had always fought to sit in the front seat, now refuses to be separated from her father and sits with him at the back. When the car is out of the gate, both Aru and Gopal turn simultaneously to each other. Then they part wordlessly, going to their own homes.

Aru can't get away from thoughts of Gracy, from what has happened to her. She can still feel the satin smoothness of her skin, the fragrance of the talcum on her body, of her silence since she heard of her mother's death. What does death mean to her? I lost my mother too, but I was so much older, I have so many memories of her. What will this child remember of her mother? She thinks of Gracy in the office, wearing Aru's black coat and her mother's high heels, prancing up and down saying, 'I'm a lawyer.' And Tressa adding, 'Gracy is going to join Surekha ma'am, no, Gracy?'

And Nagma saying, 'Aru, we better look out for other jobs, this mother and daughter pair will leave nothing for us to do.' Tressa smiling broadly then, Gracy not understanding what Nagma meant, nevertheless laughing with delight because her mother was smiling. Aru thinks of Gracy standing on tiptoe and whispering in her mother's ear, Tressa listening intently, nodding, and then saying, 'Okay, okay' and Nagma saying, warningly, mock stern, 'No secrets, Gracy.' She remembers how, when the mother and daughter were speaking in Malayalam, she had sung out, 'I can understand Malayalam.' And Gracy had replied, 'No, you are telling lies, Aru ma'am, you don't understand.' She thinks of Gracy sitting behind Tressa on the scooter, holding her mother round the waist and suddenly butting at her mother with her head, Tressa saying, 'Don't be naughty, Gracy.' And Gracy correcting her, saying, 'Not notty, Amma, you must say nautty.'

Silly jokes, ordinary talk, but converted by Tressa's death into painful memories. Everything to do with Tressa in the past tense now.

But grief is slowly giving place to anger—at the senselessness of Tressa's death, at the huge suffering the death has brought upon Ramu and Gracy; at the void in Gracy's life that will never be filled.

'You know, Aru,' Charu had told her in the days after Pavan's birth, 'ever since Pavan's birth, I'm suddenly afraid of dying. I keep thinking, what if I die and leave him without me?'

Such a strong bond between mother and child, the strongest in the world, but death goes through it with a cleaver, splashing blood everywhere. Tressa has gone, leaving Gracy and Ramu, Ramu, who so loved Tressa that he thought of her mother's grief and love and gave her back Tressa's poor body. Bits and pecies, he had said, bits and pieces. And Tressa's mother, who, Surekha told them, had sat mute while the two families argued over Tressa's body, numbly letting the conflict flow over her and around her. It was only when Ramu finally decided that Tressa would be given back to her family for a Christian burial that she had spoken. Still tearless, she had spoken directly to Ramu. 'She was frightened of the fire, she was always frightened of fire,' she said. Aru will never forget this poor mother agonizing over her dead daughter's fear of fire.

Surprisingly no organizations, none of the acronyms which people have become familiar with, have claimed responsibility for the explosion. Too small an incident, perhaps, not enough deaths to make it worth owning up to. There are stories circulating that this was a trial run, a precursor to a bigger explosion elsewhere. Other cities are put on the alert, and for some days policemen are visible everywhere in this one. Then everything dies down.

Gopal

Aru so rarely rings me up that when I got her call I was startled; for a moment, I almost didn't recognize her voice. When I did, her distress came through so clearly that I was alarmed, I guessed that something had happened. Finally I got the message: Tressa, who worked in her office, was dead. Incredible though it sounded, she had died in a bomb explosion. Aru had brought her little daughter home, and Rohit could not come back immediately. Could I come as soon as possible?

I went down at once. She was sitting, doing nothing, her hands tightly clasped together as if she was trying to control herself. She did not notice me until I put my hand, gently and hesitantly, on hers. She came out of her thoughts then, whatever they were, with a jerk and looked at me, blankly at first, then with surprise.

'Oh, you're here,' she said, moving her hands away from mine.

'I was upstairs. Where is the child?'

'Having her milk. I . . .' She paused and went on. 'She does not know her mother is dead. I have to tell her that.'

We looked at each other. Then she got up and went in. I followed her. Gracy had just finished her glass of milk. Some biscuits lay untouched on a plate. As soon as she saw us, she slid off her chair and came straight to Aru. 'I finished my milk. Can I go home now?'

Aru was trying to get back to her normal self as much as possible, but I could see that she was finding it hard to answer Gracy's questions.

'Gracy,' I asked, interrupting them, 'would you like to go out with me? Let's go to the park. Come on, wear your shoes.'

She seemed doubtful but Aru reassured her, saying, 'This is my Papa, Gracy,' (what a pleasure it was for me to hear her saying that!) and Gracy, thinking it over, finally said, 'Okay.'

I could see relief on Aru's face. Clearly, she needed some time to pull herself together. The child, though wary of me, trustingly put her hand in mine when we left. I wondered at the pleasure I got from the feel of her soft little hand in mine; it also made me understand Aru's fear at having to tell her the truth and shatter her world. How do you do such a thing to a child who has put her trust in you?

Gracy was with us for two days. We—Rohit, Aru and I—put everything aside and spent all our time with her. Even Aru and I seemed to recover a bit of our lost companionship as we shared the heavy load of the child's loss and tried to keep the knowledge of her mother's death from her. Despite all our precautions, I think she knew something was wrong; I'm sure she guessed it was about her mother. Children, like all dependents, are sharp, they are acutely conscious of the feelings of those who have power over them. Yes, she knew something had happened. I could see the weight of the loss we were trying to keep from her slowly settling on her shoulders; the sorrow she was yet to know seemed to have given her a certain dignity.

Having this child in our midst affected all of us. Rao came home for the first time the evening I brought her to my flat. He sat with us and entertained Gracy, creating shadow figures on the wall with his fingers, a talent, he told me later, he had almost forgotten he had. He was very skilful, creating swiftly changing pictures on the wall. I, like Gracy, was engrossed by the shadow play, by the way the pictures kept changing, the way a picture, for the brief moment it was on the wall, seemed entirely real and then disappeared as if it had never been. Gracy, sitting in a tall chair, her legs dangling, watched with grave attention. When Rao had finished, they smiled at each other like old friends who have shared a pleasure, her smile as adult as his.

I was Gracy's age, or maybe a little older, when my mother, no, when both my parents died. The enormity of what this meant took a long time to penetrate. Initially, I resented my routine being disrupted, and that our home was invaded by people who hugged me and wept and called me 'poor child'. I hated it. I wanted to be left alone, I wanted to get away from the constant talk and the weeping.

I often think that I have put my memories away, but occasionally, when I dredge them up, things which I did not know had been stored in my memory come back to me. A word, an image—it is like having the end of a string in my hands. I have only to tug and memories emerge, memories which are so vivid it is as if it all happened only yesterday. This child's mother's death has brought Sumi back. Both of them died in accidents. No, to call Tressa's death an accident is to wipe out the vileness, the culpability of the violent deed; it is to ignore the responsibility of those who planned this, of those who made the bombs and those who planted them with the intention of harming and killing. When I hear of such incidents, and there are so many, too many of them these days, I often wonder whether the men and women (yes, women are part of it too) have any regrets for the deaths they bring about. Or are they so blinded by the façade of courage, heroism and martyrdom that covers their actions that they believe they have done good, that the dead don't matter? Are they also trained to lose their humanity the way they are trained to make explosives? Can they retrieve this humanity when they go back to being fathers, sons, husbands and brothers? The whole thing is a mystery to me.

We pride ourselves that we are now more civilized and humane than we were before. In fact, history consists of the same story over and over again; the few letters of any alphabet are enough to contain the entire history of humankind. I sometimes have a fancy that human life is like a caravan, an unending caravan constantly on the move, never pausing, ever unchanged. There *is* nothing new in our story, not even the killing of innocents. But, yes, there is something new: women are part of the violence today. It seems to me that women go against their nature when they kill and destroy. I don't entirely agree with the theory that men and women are essentially alike; I think we are very different. I think women are meant to create, to nurture. I saw Sumi with her babies and I knew that however much I loved my babies, I could never be the same way with them. I see Aru pining for a baby now and though I am sure Rohit too feels the lack, it is not the same; it cannot destroy him as it may Aru.

Gracy has now gone back with her father. By the time he came, Aru, no shirker, had told her that her mother was dead. Rohit told me Gracy took the news stoically, silently. I was present when she met her father. She ran to him, but there was no joy in her face, only desperation, she clung to him with the same desperation.

Rohit took them home. When the car moved out of the gate, I turned to Aru. She looked so forlorn I wanted to be with her, to give her company, but it was not possible. We have moved apart. Oceans and continents divide Charu and me, but the real chasm is between Aru and me who live under the same roof. We were very close. After Charu's birth, I did everything for Aru. And because she liked to do things for herself, I taught her to dress herself, to buckle her sandals, to tie her shoelaces. She and I went shopping together, Aru walking as briskly as her little legs would allow, trying to accommodate her steps to mine, not letting me slow down for her sake. She was a curious child, constantly asking questions, waiting, unlike many children, for my answer and then considering it seriously. She stood before me when we went out on the scooter, letting me inhale the fragrance of her hair, her clean little-girl smell. And when Charu was old enough to accompany us, she sternly told her to hold me tight, not to let go. When we did things together she would hold her hand high as soon as it was done, waiting for me to strike my palm against hers, her face gleeful and jubilant. I saw her doing this with Pavan one day and wondered whether she remembered.

It's no use remembering. I destroyed our relationship. Aru will never trust me again. But even now when I enter a room, she looks up at me, her face eager and welcoming, then she remembers and turns away. Nevertheless, I live in hope. But I have to accept the fact that Aru is no longer the daughter who had loved her father. I hastened her out of her girlhood by what I did, as much as her mother's death did; she became an adult overnight. At times I imagine I can see two faint lines on her forehead, shadowy harbingers of future wrinkles, two lines which have been given to her by Sumi and me, Sumi by dying and I by leaving them. But I hope she will one day give me a place in her life, not as her father, maybe, but . . . as what? I don't know.

I wonder at times whether it is the special bond Aru had with me, whether her very love and admiration have turned her so much against me. Whether love can become bitter and rancid and admiration sour into contempt? The other day I saw two pictures in Aru's house. Unlike Charu, Aru has locked away the past, she has not put up any pictures of her early life in her house. But I saw these two pictures, one of the three sisters, and another of Sumi with her three daughters. I don't know who took the first one, Leo, perhaps. But I remember it was I who took the picture of Sumi and our daughters. Seeing it in Aru's house, I thought perhaps she has decided to go back to the period of her childhood. Perhaps she is learning to forget what happened later. And, perhaps, with these reminders of what our relationship was, she will learn to forgive me.

But when I look at Kasturi, my heart fails me. She too loved and admired her father; though she does not say so explicitly, something in the way she talks about him gives her away. She spoke to me once of how particular her father was about his clothes. He always wore a white dhoti and a white kurta, she said. 'And a . . . what do you call it? . . . Nehru jacket? Yes, a Nehru jacket on top. He had three of those: black, grey and cream. But his dhoti and kurta had to be perfectly white; if they were not, the dhobi had to take the clothes back.' Then she had added, 'He was a handsome man. He knew that, and he made full use of it.' She smiled as she said this, a smile which took away the criticism from the statement, which revealed her admiration.

It was he who gave her the pet name Sonu, she told me. She also told me that as a little girl she went with him on his election campaigns and his tours. But then she turned against him. I know now why that happened. Kasturi told me that it was because of a woman he got involved with, who used him, she said, to become powerful in the party. She alienated him from everyone, not only his family, but his companions, his advisers, people who had worked with him for years. He lost touch with people, he became insensitive. She destroyed him, Kasturi said baldly. And their family. She spoke of her mother to me, she told me how much she regretted not being fair to her, that she had thought her dull and had been impatient and irritated with her; she had given her mother neither love nor loyalty. Even when her mother died, Kasturi was so involved with her own life that she scarcely mourned her. In any case, her mother was such a joyless woman, she said, that it was hard to mourn her death. But, she told me, she learnt much later that her mother became a depressed woman after she learnt about the other woman, when she knew she had lost her place in her husband's life. She could vaguely remember a time when her mother was different; she was always silent, but not morose. 'Many times I think that it was her grief which hardened and became a fatal tumour in her brain. That woman killed my mother,' she said. 'She and my father.' Then she added, 'The two of them destroyed my life.'

'Destroyed?' I asked her, thinking, how long do we go on blaming our parents? How long before we take responsibility for our own lives?

'Yes, destroyed.'

'You don't look destroyed. You look all right. Very much all right.'

For a moment she looked blank, as if she had not expected this response. Then she laughed. 'Thank you,' she said in English.

'No, seriously, Kasturi, why do you give people so much power over your life that you think they can destroy you? Don't you have any power over your own life?'

'But some things, many things, are not in our control.'

'I know. But we do have *some* control.'

I asked her if she had ever played a game I had seen my sister's daughters playing, a game played with a loop of string. She looked blank, then said, 'I never played girls' games. I was a tomboy.'

I tried to explain the game to her. 'You loop a string over the fingers of your two hands, then make different designs with your middle finger moving in and out of the string. And then you transfer it—it's like a web—to another girl's hands and she . . .'

She suddenly interrupted me to say, 'Yes, yes, I remember, I think I've seen girls playing it.'

'I think our lives are like that. We are one of the two creators of the design of our lives. There's us and there's . . .'

'God?'

'I don't know, Kasturi, who or what the creator is, but there has to be a power, don't you think? A power greater than us, larger than life, not just human life, but all creation. We don't write the entire script of our own lives, do we?'

She was silent for a moment, then said doubtfully, 'Maybe you're right. Yes, you are right.' And added, 'Gopala, you are very good for me.'

She called me Gopala. It pleased me enormously.

Kasturi has gone out this week, she told me she was going out with the film unit for shooting. She rang me up today. I told her about Tressa and the child. She listened in silence and said nothing. When I was done she said, 'I am returning tomorrow.' As if she knew I was missing her.

My heart gave a youthful startled leap at that. I look forward to her coming, I look forward to our meeting, I look forward to talking to her. I don't ask myself why. It is enough to have this pleasure waiting for me.

There is nothing in the world as complete or as final as death. In an instant, the person ceases to have a place in the world, in an instant all ties are cut and the dead person becomes the past. Aru has known the helplessness that death compels, the utter hopelessness that follows it. Even when Sumi lay unconscious in the ICU and the doctor had told them there was little chance of her surviving, that she was just a brain-damaged body, they had hoped that she would come out of it, maybe there would be a miracle and she would survive. Death put an end to all their hopes and Sumi became the past.

But memories remain. With the passage of time, they can provide some solace, but in the first few days memories hurt, each one tears open the wound again and yet again. Tressa's empty chair, the telephone which is not picked up after three rings, the memory of her voice saying, 'Surekha madam's office,' these drive home her absence, the tragedy of her death. When her mother died, Aru had realized that it is the living who suffer the most. Once again she sees that Ramu and Gracy, their lives suddenly sagging without Tressa to hold them together, are the real victims. To think of them is to be aware of their pain, to feel the frustration of being unable to do anything for them. In a way it is a relief that they have gone to Ramus parents' home for the final ceremonies. Some of the weight of her grief for them lifts off her; she does not have to imagine them beginning their day without Tressa, of ending the day knowing that Tressa will never again be with them. It also helps that something comes to distract Aru from Tressa's death, something totally unexpected.

Seema's career has been a modest success, and if it seems impressive to the family, it is only because they had expected nothing from her. The fact that she has gone so far is itself a surprise to them. She was not ambitious, she was unwilling to push herself, or to network. And she was choosy: she would not run around with her portfolio looking for work, nor do ramp shows. She hated people looking at her, she said. She was more comfortable with the camera; in fact, she seemed to have a special affinity with it. Her greatest asset had been Leo, but even he could not push her into doing something she didn't want to do. Now, suddenly, her career takes an upward surge, the impetus coming from a most unlikely person—Kasturi. Aru would never have imagined that Kasturi could have any connection, however tenuous or distant, to the world of fashion and models. But she has a friend, whose sister, Delia, heads an advertising agency in Bombay. This agency has been searching for an Indian model to become the face of a large multinational cosmetics company that is poised to enter India. Kasturi had suggested Seema to Delia, and Delia asked Seema to get in touch with her daughter Maggie, who would be spearheading the campaign. Maggie had initially thought of Seema as a small-town model who wouldn't make the grade. But she could not say no to Kasturi.

Now the family gets the news that the agency has chosen Seema to be their model. It will be a two-year exclusive contract and the money will be more than Seema, or anyone in the family, has earned in a decade. Seema seems composed, but Aru knows she is nervous, perhaps even scared. Seema hates change and now changes will be forced on her. She will have to leave home, live in Bombay, travel extensively. Aru is also anxious about Seema entering a world, which, from what she has heard about it, is one of great struggle and fierce competition. Seema is not made for competition. Will it not affect the fragile poise she has achieved? Yet, how long can she live this swaddled and protected life?

Aru and Gopal wait anxiously for Seema to make her decision. Finally she decides to sign the contract with the agency. Aru and Nagma go through the contract and okay it. Yet Aru continues to worry. What if Seema can't cope? She talks to Leo about her anxieties and Leo reassures her. 'You haven't seen her at work, Aru. She's comfortable, she's really cool. And I'll be with her.'

He tells her he will be moving to Bombay with Seema. Aru is relieved, but she has to wonder again what kind of a relationship they have. She is almost sure it is not sexual. As yet. But how long will any man, however patient (and Leo has the immense patience of a good photographer) wait? In any case, the decision has been taken. Maggie comes down to meet Seema and they sign the contract in Seema's home, after which Maggie sits down to chat with the family. But she does not talk of Seema, or of her work. She speaks, instead, of her mother Delia who started the agency along with her father. 'But Dad died soon after and my mother had to cope with everything all on her own. She's done an amazing job.'

Before leaving, Maggie invites Aru and Rohit to a party she is throwing—for Seema, they guess, though she doesn't say so. 'We'll be totally out of place,' Aru tells Rohit. But they have to go for Seema's sake.

Maggie tries to make them comfortable. She takes them round, introducing them to people as 'Seema's sister and brother-in-law.' It's the first time Aru has been identified as Seema's sister; she finds it strange, but pleasing. Seema comes to them as soon as she sees them, but there are so many people who want her that Aru urges her to go. 'We'll be all right,' she says. Rohit, too, is immediately claimed by a college friend who is now in advertising. He comes up to them with happy cries, his drink slopping over with each step, thumps Rohit on the back and invites them to join his group. Aru refuses, but he drags Rohit away. In a moment, Rohit is part of the group. Aru admires the way Rohit can fit into any company, whether of masons, contractors, labourers, architects, lawyers or engineers; or, as now, the advertising world. He signals to Aru once to join them, but she shakes her head. She is happy to be left alone. Aru is incapable of small talk, she's not comfortable with total strangers, but she has a confidence that allows her to be alone, even in a crowd. She won't be left alone for long, of course, since she is an attractive woman. She would be surprised to know that she is attractive, for there is a kind of innocence about her that makes her unaware of her looks. Any male attention that she receives, she considers to be the usual male response to a young female. A bearded man (hoping, Aru thinks, to make up for his baldness by the lush growth of hair on his chin) now comes up to her, introduces himself and asks about her. When he hears that she is Seema's sister, he begins talking about Seema, about what a find she is and how she has exactly the face and the body the campaign needs.

Aru she has been forced to come to terms with Seema's profession, she has taught herself to tolerate it, though there are times when she finds it hard to do so. Like the time she saw a commercial for saris in which the models, wearing saris, played little girls' games (hopscotch, for god's sake, she had fumed to Nagma) giggling like schoolgirls, at the same time providing alluring glimpses of their slim waists, the curves of their breasts and hips. What was it about, she had thought angrily. Were they catering to the Lolita fantasies of males? Now, when she hears Seema being spoken of as a body and a face, the anger returns. She thinks of her as a baby in the cradle, crying, and she trying to soothe her, to amuse her in the way Gopal had told her to. 'Clap your hands,' he had said, 'and talk to her. Say something. Babies like people talking to them. And smile, show you're happy.' So each time the baby cried, she had gone to the cradle and clapped, she had talked to her and smiled at her. In a while Seema stopped crying, she looked at Aru intently. Then the tiny face had crinkled into a kind of smile, as if the baby recognized the face hanging over her and was pleased Aru was with her.

Meanwhile, the bearded man is still talking, speaking now of Seema's mysterious and inscrutable look, her almost Mona Lisa smile and enigmatic eyes, and how much she and Aru resemble each other. Suddenly Aru understands that praising Seema is just his way of getting to her, that the man is, in fact, coming on to her strongly. She wants to laugh and then sees Gopal at the door, peering anxiously round the room. She waves to him and he comes to her, looking suddenly happy. She feels a pang, knowing that she called him only to get away from the bearded man. But the man does not go away, he waits until she introduces Gopal to him. When he finally leaves them alone, she asks Gopal, 'Why didn't you tell us you were coming? We could have come together.'

'I wasn't going to come but Maggie insisted, and . . . Who was that man?'

'I don't know.' She has an impulse to tell him about Seema's 'Mona Lisa smile and enigmatic eyes'. She knows they would have laughed together at one time. But before she can speak, Maggie is with them. 'I'm so glad you're here, Gopal.'

Gopal? She knows him that well?

'Come on, Mira auntie and Ranjan are over there, Sonu auntie is with them. Come along, Aru.'

Aru has to go with her, to be introduced to Mira and Ranjan. Kasturi is with them and Aru understands that she is the 'Sonu auntie' Maggie had mentioned. 'Join us,' Kasturi says and Mira pats the seat by her invitingly. Gopal sits down with them, but Aru remains standing.

'It's okay. We won't be here long. We have to go soon. Papa, will you be here for some time?'

'I'll wait for Seema.'

'I'll drop them, Aru, don't worry,' Maggie says. 'But don't go as yet, stay for a while.'

That night, Aru rings up Charu. It had taken the sisters a while to get accustomed to making international calls so often and so easily. Used to their parents' and their grandparents' thrifty ways, long distance calls made them uneasy. But they realized after Charu went abroad how necessary it was for them to talk to each other, even if it was of inessentials. Now the weekly calls have become a part of their lives; they can't do without them. Much of the conversation is about Pavan, but tonight they also talk of Seema. Aru tells Charu about the party, about Maggie, Mira and Ranjan, they laugh together over the bearded man. Remembering how little Charu had sympathized with her anti-Kasturi prejudice in their last conversation, Aru does not mention Kasturi, though she is very much on her mind.

Charu still can't take in this huge change in Seema's life, she can't imagine her a part of such a glamorous profession. But she is enormously pleased that Seema is leaving home. Charu has often chided Aru for pampering and protecting her. Being Charu, she candidly admits that there is an element of jealousy in her strictures. Now she is excited that Seema may possibly be visiting her.

'Why don't Rohit and you come too?' she asks.

'Impossible.'

'Why?

'No money.'

'What's wrong? Has Rohit begun drinking? Or gambling?'

'Don't be stupid. You know that Rohit has cut down on his work because of his restoration project.'

'And what about Madam Arundhati, the busy and successful lawyer?'

'You know us. Surekha ma'am is called the Pro Bono Queen and Nagma and I are the Pro Bono Princesses. Lots of clients, but not lots of money. Like ma'am says, you can scarcely ask a client who's struggling for a tiny bit of maintenance from her husband to pay us a huge sum.'

Charu clicks her tongue. 'Shame on you. Go out and hustle for some rich clients.'

'We have those too. How else do you think we survive?'

'Try to get some more.'

'Yes, boss, will do.'

The problem is not money. The trouble is, as Aru herself has realized, she has been marked by the difficult days after Gopal's desertion. She remembers how Sumi had worried about money, how reluctant she had been to take money from anyone. Ramesh had been the most insistent. After being spurned by Sumi, he had come to Aru and told her that he was depositing some money in the bank for her and her sisters to take whenever they needed it. He had left some blank signed cheque slips with her, saying, 'Cash them when you need money, you don't have to tell me about it.'

It was extraordinarily generous of Ramesh, Aru had thought. She said so to him. 'Generous!' Ramesh had exclaimed angrily. 'Aru, Gopal may be my mother's brother, but he's been like my own brother. An older brother.' Yes, there was a strong bond between Gopal and Ramesh; nevertheless, it had been hard for Aru to think of taking money from him. She had sworn then that she would not touch the money, though perhaps she might have had to for Charu's various examination fees. Then Sumi and her father died and Aru, after she saw her grandfather's bank balance, realized she would no longer have to worry about money. But the fear of not having money, of becoming a dependent, remains. It makes Aru unwilling to spend money unless it is necessary.

'Anyway, Charu, I visited you, didn't I, when Pavan was born? That's not so long ago, is it?'

'That was different. We didn't do anything for you, we couldn't take you around. And what about Rohit? You must come together. Now that Seema is leaving, all you need to do is to make up your mind.'

Seema's leaving is the thought most on Aru's mind at the moment. But Seema looks pleased, almost serene when she is leaving. Aru sees her off with a light heart. I don't need to worry about her, she admonishes herself. Nevertheless, there is a sense of being bereft. Seema rings up every day, she seems all right, so there's no anxiety. And yet, Rohit notices, Aru looks a little lost. He says nothing but he decides they should go on a holiday.

'It's been a long time,' he says. 'We both need a break. Talk to Nagma and Surekha ma'am and tell me when we can go. But soon.'

When they are ready to leave, he warns her, 'No talk of clients, of divorcing couples, of brutal husbands and bashed women for the next few days.'

Aru laughs and says, 'I promise.'

But there are other hazards. They spend their mornings in the swimming pool and the shallow end is full of screaming splashing children. The paddling pool is even worse, crowded with toddlers, their tiny suits stretched over their tight little tummies. Aru watches one little fellow screaming his protest, clinging to his mother with the tenacity of a limpet as she tries to induce him to enter the pool. All the other children watch the struggle in intent silent curiosity. The next time Aru looks that way, as stealthily as a voyeur, he is paddling away, beating at the water with his palms with enormous enthusiasm, unconcerned, it seems, about his mother who is still watching him anxiously. Aru feels her heart turn within her. I must not come here, she thinks, I can't bear this.

That night Aru tells Rohit, 'Let's go out tomorrow morning instead of swimming.'

'Okay,' Rohit says after a moment.

He knows what it is about, he has seen her looking at the children furtively, as if she is ashamed of it. Once again the question clamours in his mind: why can't we adopt, he wants to ask.

Aru can read his thoughts. She knows he is unable to understand why she is against adoption. So, at times, is she. What am I afraid of, she asks herself. Am I afraid I won't know how to be a mother? Yes, to some extent, she is afraid. The nine months of waiting while the baby grows inside her prepare a woman both emotionally and physically for motherhood. Can I bond with a child overnight? So many do, why can't I? But what if I don't? She remembers the immediate, almost frightening bond between Charu and Pavan, she remembers the milk oozing from Charu's breasts, of her huge sigh of relief when he was put to her breast and began to suckle. Remembers too, Charu's total absorption in the process, the beatific look on Pavan's face, his tiny hands moving and beating at Cham's body as he drank. She remembers Pavan's yelp of protest when, in his eagerness, the nipple slipped out of his mouth, his greedy gulps when he got it back in his mouth again, Cham's happy laugh, her words, 'such a greedy little pig'.

After Sumi's death, Aru thought that she had seen the worst, that she was prepared for everything, armoured against everything. But there are always chinks in any armour and life gets back at you through the crevices; you can never be totally invulnerable. Aru has become aware that the desire for a child can be as strong as sexual desire, though more steadfast, never leaving you for a moment. Yes, I want a baby of my own, I want to carry my child within my body, I want to feel it kicking, moving, impatient to be born, I want my baby to come out of my body, I want to give birth to my child in blood and pain like Charu did. I want to play my allotted role in the world, to have my place in it, knotted into it, linked to the future by my child, as I am linked to the past through my mother.

'Aru?'

'Yes?'

'Can't sleep?'

'I'm trying to.'

'Try a little harder. And stop moving about so much.'

'Sorry.'

After a while she says, 'Rohit?'

'Yes, Am? What is it?'

'Nothing.'

Earlier he would have coaxed it out of her, he would have held her, caressed her, kissed her, they would have made love. But now . . .? What's wrong with me? Have I become hard and unloving? Intolerant? Kalyani had once spoken of a woman who had become rigid and unloving because she didn't have children. When you have children, Kalyani had said, you learn to put up with things, you become tolerant, you compromise, you understand the world is not made only for you, you become less selfish. Am I, then, becoming selfish and intolerant? Look at the way I snub Papa, the way I'm jealous of his and Kasturi's friendship! What's wrong with it, Charu had asked me. Let him have someone he feels good to be with, I'm sure he needs something more than his daughters, she said. Charu is generous, while I . . .?

The other day Kasturi said 'come and join us', but I didn't. She's a kind woman, she gets on with everyone, even Nagi. And Seema likes her. I looked down on her because she was free and easy with everyone, even with Lokesh, the car-wash boy and his assistant, Murali. But Rohit tells me she has managed to get Murali a chance to sing for a music director, only as part of a chorus, maybe, but the boy is ecstatic, he is overflowing with gratitude towards Kasturi. And Nagi tells me that the rickshaw driver I found her chatting with is a friend, that she had helped him once, (or was it the other way round?) and now he is like her brother. A kind woman, obviously.

And there's Nagma. Aru had met Nagma when she, an angry and passionate girl, had gone to see Surekha. At first, she had taken little note of Nagma who sat typing outside Surekha's office. But when Aru came out of the office, Nagma had looked up, smiled at Aru and, picking up her long plait, said, 'beautiful'. Surekha, who had followed Aru out, had smiled at the two young women and said, 'Rapunzel.'

After Aru joined Surekha's office, she realized that Nagma was not a typist, as she had thought, but a qualified lawyer. In the years since, they have become friends. They share a similar background. Nagma's mother is a university teacher like Gopal was, and her husband a professional like Rohit. Nagma helped Aru in the early days when Aru was baffled by the complexities of the legal language and procedures. They became friends and soon their friendship moved on to meeting outside the office as well; they went out for movies, shopping and to eat masala dosas for which both had a passion, one which their husbands did not share. But events from the world outside began impacting their friendship. They were on the same side about 9/11, about Bush and Iraq and Afghanistan. Then came Gujarat. Aru thought they were still on the same side, for how could anyone not feel horrified at what had happened there? But it seems that they were not, for one day Nagma came to work wearing a burqa. Aru did not take it seriously, she thought it was a gesture, a symbolic gesture maybe. But she soon realized Nagma was serious about it. Aru was aghast.

'But why, Nagma?'

To show that she was with the women killed in recent riots. To show that she wanted to be identified with them.

'But you're taking a step backwards. A woman like you shouldn't be doing this.'

It was exactly the idea that 'women like her' were superior to those who dressed the way she now did, the idea that women who dressed in a burqa were backward—it was this idea that she was trying to contest by what she was doing. 'If I am to protest against this custom I have to know what it is like to live this way.'

'Would you like Shabnam to live her life like this, gagged and blindfolded?'

'Don't bring Shabnam into this,' Nagma had said and suddenly laughed. 'Aru, you have absolutely no idea of how it is. Gagged? You don't know . . . No, the women are certainly not gagged, they have their voices. But never mind that. Just let it go, Aru. Let's not argue about these things.'

Aru would not stop arguing. 'Nagma,' she said, 'this is something imposed on women who have no choice. But you have a choice, you know that . . .'

'And this is my choice. Why can't you understand?'

Aru could not understand her. They went on arguing, often going round in circles, like dancers, then eventually coming back to their old position of comrades. Surekha had watched their tussle in silence and one day called Aru to her room. 'Aru, I want you to stop talking to Nagma about her burqa.'

'But, ma'am, what she's doing is not right.'

'Maybe for her it is the only thing to do.'

'But everyone knows . . .'

'I don't like this *everyone knows* argument, Aru. Who, exactly, is everyone?'

'Do you think it's right for any woman to cover herself up that way, ma'am?'

'No, I don't. I think women should be able to look at the world openly, I think men and women should be able to look at each other openly. But *I* can't decide what's right for Nagma. Tell me honestly, do you think you have the right to tell Nagma what she should do, how she should live?'

'No, ma'am.'

'Good. Otherwise what difference is there between you and those you think are brainwashing the women? Look, Aru, I've already told Nagma she can't go to court wearing her burqa. I don't want our clients to be affected by the judges' prejudices, if they have any. That's all we can do.'

'Yes, ma'am.'

'Try to understand Nagma. I think she is trying to find out something about herself, about her religion. You know the family have never been devout Muslims, they've never observed the rules. But now she wants to know what it is to be one of the women who were killed in Gujarat. It's like Gandhi wearing a loincloth to see what it was to be poor. Let Nagma go her way, let her find her answer. In the meantime, I don't want the office atmosphere spoilt.'

There was no danger of that. Their friendship was able to stand the stress of their differences, because Nagma knew that Aru was not fighting *against* her, that she was fighting *for* what both of them believed in. She was only sorry she could not make Aru understand that she was wearing the burqa exactly for those beliefs.

And then Tressa died. It put an end to all arguments. Nagma has begun introspecting, wondering whether she is, as Aru said, going about things the wrong way. Aru had said to her, 'Women wearing burqas give me a strange feeling, that they don't see me, that they don't *want* to see me, they make me feel I don't exist for them. I don't like that. I like to see recognition in a person's face, I like to see a spark in their eyes which tells me they see me, that they feel we have something in common, that we share something—our humanity, our gender. I get the feeling that these women are telling me, "We are different from all of you, we are the chosen."'

Nagma understood what Aru was saying. It had troubled her too, this sense of being apart from the world, linked only to others like her. And there was Shabnam. 'Would you like your daughter to grow up behind a veil?' Aru had asked. No, she thinks, no, I don't. I want my daughter to grow up free, unfettered. She wants to speak to Aru about these things, to agree that the burqa is a powerful barrier. That it seems to take away your connection with the world. She wants to say it was hard for her, harder perhaps because she had never lived with anyone who wore it, because it had never been a part of her childhood. And yet, how can anyone deny a woman the right to dress the way she wants? She had been waiting for the right time to say these things to Aru. Aru, too, sensed that Nagma wanted to speak to her. And then Aru got a sudden jolt. She came to know through Surekha that Nagma was pregnant for the second time. Nagma had not spoken to her about it.

'Why didn't you tell me, Nagma? Why did I have to hear about it from ma'am?'

'I was going to tell you

'Did you think that I would be jealous of you? That I would feel sorry for myself?'

'Aru, listen . . .'

'Let me confess—I *am* sorry for myself, I *am* jealous of you. But I'm also happy for you, for Shabnam, for Javed.'

'Forgive me, Aru, I am really sorry, I should have told you myself.'

And yet the fact remains that she didn't, that she thought it would hurt me to hear about her pregnancy. She thought I would be resentful . . .

Aru begins to cry soundlessly into her pillow, something she often does, careful to keep still so as not to disturb Rohit.

But Rohit knows she's crying, he knows that this happens often. He also knows that he has to leave Aru alone at such times, that he can, at this moment, do nothing for her.

'She doesn't like me,' Kasturi had said once about Aru. Mira had seen what Kasturi had meant when they met Aru at Maggie's party. Even from that brief interaction it had been clear that Kasturi was right.

' What have you done to her?' Mira asks Kasturi when they meet a few days later.

'Me? Nothing.'

'Then why is she hostile to you?'

'I told you, I don't know.'

'And her father, Gopal,' Mira goes on, 'I thought from what you said that he was a doddering old man.'

'What did I say about him?'

'You called him your landlady's father.'

'He is.'

'And you said he is a widower with three children. Now, don't say *he is.* He doesn't look old at all. In fact he looks,' Mira hesitates and finally says, 'distinguished.'

'Does he?'

'You know he does, don't pretend you don't. But, Sonu dear, he's dull, he's so dull. He had nothing to say for himself

'What could he say when you and I were talking all the time?'

Mira goes on, taking no note of Kasturi's interruption, 'He made it very clear he admires you. The way he looked at you

'What rubbish!'

'Don't be coy, Sonu. Why didn't you tell me about him?'

'What's there to tell?'

'Isn't there?'

'Well, we are friends . . . kind of. And only because he knows Jogipura. He too went to school in Shivpur.'

'Which school?'

'The government boys' school.'

'Dear dear! Those boys were such junglees.'

'You're a snob, Miri. I'm always surprised you became my friend; I was such a junglee myself. If only you had heard yourself speaking to Gopal that day—you made him so uncomfortable I'm not surprised he was silent.'

'What did I say?'

'And what do you do?' Kasturi imitates Mint's tone. 'You were like the General's lady talking to a jawan. That was so impertinent. If I was him, I'd have said I spend my time killing flies.'

'My goodness, she's angry, she's really angry! Sonu, are you smitten?' Only Belinda's daughter would have used the word *smitten.* 'Tell me everything, child.'

'There's nothing to tell.'

'Remember what you said after the last shenanigans?'

'Shen . . . what's that?'

'Okay, after the last imbroglio. And don't ask me what that means. Go and look up the words in the dictionary.'

'My three-new-words-a-day exercise?'

'Exactly. But don't try to change the subject. Let's go back to what you said after the last—okay, let's call it business with—whatshisname? The director? Whoever. You said, never again. It's over for me. No more men.'

'I've kept my word, haven't I?'

'Except for your old man.'

'He's not a man. Don't laugh, stupid, I mean he's not a man in *that* sense. And, anyway, he's too old. And so am I—for those things.'

'Men are never too old for *those things,* you know that better than I do, Sonu. And you old! You! I know how susceptible you are. And vulnerable. Listen, I'm warning you, you better not get involved with any man. I have plans for you.'

'Like what?'

'I want you to marry Ranjan when I'm gone.'

'What!'

'Don't laugh. I'm serious. I mean it.'

'I can't help laughing. You know how beautifully Ranjan and I get on together.'

'I remember how well you got on after my surgery.'

'At that time both of us were thinking only of you. That's the one subject we agree on.'

'Do the same again. And think how happy I'll be when I look down on you from wherever I am and see the two of you together.'

'You forget I'm not a Christian. I can't imagine anyone being *up there,* wherever that is. As a Hindu, I believe we'll all come back here eventually—sorry, I meant *down* here—living one more life. And what a selfish woman you are, Miri! I'll be happy, she says. What about Ranjan and me?'

'You can have your spats. That'll keep Ranjan occupied. He won't have time to mourn me.'

Kasturi realizes that Mira is not joking. 'You're mad,' she says.

'Ranjan is good husband material, you know that, you've seen him. Actually, that's why I'm afraid for him. He's so used to having a wife that when I'm gone, I'm sure he'll fall prey to any woman who sets her mind—no—her heart—on marrying him. And I know, I can feel it in my bones, it will be the most unsuitable woman. A fat, chattering, fish-eating, fish-smelling Bengali woman.'

'Are you talking of marriage or of shikar? I must say, Mira, you have a very high opinion of women.'

'Why deny the truth? The reality is that most women want husbands.'

'Not me, thanks.'

'Not even Gopal?'

'No.'

'That's good. That's a great relief. So think of Ranjan. Try him, Sonu.'

Thanks, Mira. But no, thanks.'

'Oh well,' Mira says, capitulating so suddenly Kasturi is taken aback. 'I just thought I'd try and see if you'd agree.'

After she leaves Mira, Kasturi thinks, surely Mira was not serious about Ranjan she couldn't possibly be; but she was probing into my feelings for Gopal. She spoke of the way he looks at me. I've seen the look, but it's not a lover's look, it's as if I remind him of someone and he's trying to remember who it is. Certainly not his wife, that airy-fairy woman. Who then? It doesn't really matter. I was lying to Mira, I know he likes me, but he's careful not to get too close, to get too intimate. Oh let it go. And Mira is right. That—what did she call it, *shen* what?. . . that something with Seshadri had been very bad. And entirely her own fault. She had sworn she would never get into that kind of relationship again. She is ashamed that she fell for that most banal ploy of my wife doesn't understand me. Once they began their affair, she realized that he was a weak man, she felt nothing for him. When she broke it off, he had been furious and humiliated. He had retaliated by spreading nasty rumours about Kasturi. It had hurt, it had been bad, but she had been relieved to be out of it; not again, no, never again, she had told herself.

Gopal is different. How could Mira speak of him in the same breath as that odious man, Seshadri? Gopal is clean and wholesome., I enjoy his companionship, I admire his conversation, the kind of things he talks about. I come from a family where the talk was of rain and crops, of cattle and fodder, of elections and votes and of which son of a bitch did what and how do we deal with him. But Gopal? The other day he spoke of a shloka in the Rig Veda which says that the world came first and then came the gods; so who knows how the world was created?

'Can you imagine, Kasturi,' he had said, 'such a sophisticated thought. . . so world-shaking, so original! And this was said ages ago.' His face as he spoke was eager and enthusiastic, like a young man's. Yes, Gopal is different. He likes me and so do I like him. More than any man I've met in years. I will leave it at that and not spoil what we have by imagining more. Yet, when she reaches home, pleasure spurts out of her when she sees him with Rao. The two men stop talking when she enters. They have been talking about me, she thinks; she wants to ask, but thinks it will sound vain and desists.

'Anyone wants a cup of tea? I'm having one.'

'This woman will drown herself in tea one day.'

'I'll join you,' Gopal says.

Kasturi is right, they have been talking about her. Rao has been telling Gopal how reluctant he had been to fall in with his daughter's plans for him in the months she and her husband were to spend in the United States. 'I didn't enjoy the thought of living alone in that huge house of theirs, even with two maids and a driver. I am happier here, comfortable with Kasturi. But I can't burden her for too long either. You know she's thinking of dabbling in—sorry, that's a wrong word—I mean, she's thinking of joining politics?'

'She spoke of it to me.'

'It won't work. A woman, unless she's connected to a powerful man, doesn't stand a chance today. But she knows that herself, I don't need to point it out to her. She knows a great deal about politics. In fact, she wanted to be a political reporter when she joined us. She didn't understand that in those days there was no way a woman would be allowed to report on political matters. She was impatient.'

That was the moment when Kasturi had entered. Now, listening to the sounds coming from the kitchen as she makes tea, Rao says, 'I like the sound of a woman moving about the house. I've been lonely since my wife died. I didn't think I would miss her as much as I did . . . as I still do. I didn't do her justice when she was alive.'

'None of us do our women justice.'

'You think so? Maybe you're right. Yes, none of us do our women justice. I suppose that's the sad story of humanity. But I'm ready to give Kasturi full credit for what she does for me. She keeps me from boredom. Do you know what the greatest enemy of old age is, Gopal? It's boredom. The biggest question in one's life becomes: how do you fill the twenty-four hours of a day, how do you occupy all the hours you have until it's time to go?'

'Isn't that what we are all doing—passing the time until it's time for us to go?'

'That's a very cynical thought. I didn't expect it of you, Gopal. Do you really believe that?'

There's a long pause before Gopal laughs, at himself, perhaps, and says 'No.'

'Nor do I. I'm sure nobody does. Life is good, especially when you're young. There's so much curiosity, so much excitement, so much hope. And what about all the mysteries we hope to solve, the questions we want to find the answers to? They keep us going. Even now, I may speak of going, but when I got close to dying, when I had my heart attack, I knew, as soon as I was able to think, that I didn't want to die. Strange, isn't it?'

'Not really. I think that unless there's extreme suffering, physical or emotional, all of us want to go on living. There doesn't have to be a purpose. Just to live is enough.'

Kasturi now returns with the tea and Rao immediately gets up, saying, 'If you will both excuse me, I must go.'

'Oh go on, you. We excuse you. I tell this man that after he's dead, when they reach the cemetery, he'll sit up and thank the men who carried him there.'

'I hope not, Kasturi. Dead should be dead. My dinner ready?'

'It's on the table.'

'Thank you, Kasturi.'

'No need to thank me. Dinner! Soup and a slice of toast. And you complain of constipation.'

'Aha! I'd forgotten that.' He raises a bony finger and announces, 'That's the second enemy of old age. Constipation.'

'What's the first?'

'Boredom.'

'Oh, that's the biggest enemy of children,' Gopal says. 'They're constantly complaining of boredom. I remember my daughters in the vacations. It was "Papa, I'm bored" all the time.'

'But that's only momentary. Their friends come and call them out to play and off they go, boredom forgotten. Think of how it is at my age, when there are no more mysteries left, everything has been charted and mapped out, the only unanswered question being the one of our grand exit . . .'

'What grand exit? We go out moaning and whining, most of us,' Kasturi says with asperity. 'And stop being morbid. I know you're hungry. Shall I make some chapattis for you? For you too, Gopal? We can have dinner together.'

'I'm off. If you stuff me with chapattis, I'll have to contend with the third enemy of old age.'

Rao walks off. Gopal looks inquiringly at Kasturi. Third enemy?

'Gas,' she says in a mock whisper and they laugh.

When they are left to themselves, Kasturi says, 'I didn't expect to see you here. You must be missing Seema.'

'Rao asked me to join him. He said you'd gone out.'

'I'd gone to visit Mira.'

'I thought so. Yes, Kasturi, I am missing Seema, but it's only for two weeks.'

'This is the beginning. After that. . .'

'I'm happy for her. And you made it all possible.'

'Oh, don't say that. I was only the instrument.'

'Nimittamatram bhava Savyasachin.'

'That's from the Gita?'

'You've read it?'

'No! I guessed. I know Savyasachi is Arjuna. But what does it mean?'

'Krishna tells Arjuna: stand up and fight, conquer your enemies, become victorious and enjoy your kingdom. As for your enemies, don't worry about them, they're already dead. I have killed them. You are—no, it's more positive than that, it's you *be* only the instrument. Nimitta matram bhava Savyasachin.'

'How nicely you explained it, Gopala!' she exclaims, using the intimate 'neenu' for the first time, taking a sudden, and to Gopal, a pleasing leap into intimacy. 'I wish someone would explain the whole Gita in this way. When you get old, you're supposed to suddenly start reading the Gita, or the Upanishads. When I get there, I'll make you my Guru and sit at your feet.'

'I'm an ignorant man, Kasturi.'

'You can't be ignorant. You understand Sanskrit.'

'What little I know of Sanskrit is because of my brother-in-law. He was a Sanskrit teacher, a true Pandit.'

'These things come easily to you Brahmins. Or so it seems to me.'

'Wrong. I've seen plenty of Brahmin duffers. And this, after centuries of monopolizing learning. Think of that!'

They laugh comfortably together, a laughter that suggests they have crossed many barriers. Kasturi thinks how he's used the English word 'duffer', one that her father had so often used in anger. Hastily she pushes the memory away and asks Gopal, 'But tell me, Gopala, it seems to me that you spoke as if you don't really believe what Krishna says.'

'Did I? Perhaps you're right. I don't believe that any of us can escape the consequences of our actions. Or words. I think Arjuna can't say I didn't kill those men, he can't say Krishna killed them, or that Time did. It sounds to me like a specious argument. Misleading. I may be missing something here, but I think to say you are not responsible for what you have done is to go against the basic law of the universe, of life itself—the law of connections. Words and actions are not floating free in the world, they are connected to someone, they have to be owned up to by someone. Nothing in this universe is unconnected. You can never escape the consequences of your words and actions.'

'You think so? That's frightening. Mira's mother was asking me about karma the other day. Is this what karma really is, then?'

'Maybe. Maybe karma is nothing but justice—justice on a larger, cosmic scale.'

Kasturi takes a deep breath—too deep to be a sigh—and says, 'Thank you, Guruji, for that wonderful exposition.'

He laughs, a little abashed. 'I'm sorry, I . . .'

'Why should you be sorry?'

'I don't deserve your praise. You don't know how badly I've messed up my own life.'

'Un-mess it, then,' she says sternly. 'To say you've done wrong and then to do nothing about it is just self-indulgence. Do something.'

'Yes, madam, I'll try my best,' he says with a grin. And suddenly changing the subject, he asks her, 'So you're going to Jogipura?'

'Yes.'

'You're looking forward to it?'

'Yes, I think I am. I never thought I would go back, I never imagined Vasant and Shalini would settle down in Jogipura. Shalini is a Delhi girl, she went to school and college there. Her father and mine were friends. Good friends—as much as two politicians can be. Now she has renovated the house and is having a big puja. She's inviting a lot of people, she wants people to take notice of their presence in Jogipura. She wants the family to become politically powerful once again. And she wants my help.'

'Why you?'

'She knows Vasant is of no use. A retired bureaucrat is good for nothing, she says. So it's either her or me. She thinks I have a better chance because I was on TV and my face is known.' She flashes him a smile. 'I don't think that's true, but . . .'

'I wish I had seen you on TV,' he says a little regretfully.

'You haven't missed a thing. It's a totally false presence. And a bubble. You're forgotten the next day. Shalini is fooling herself if she thinks people will remember me. Ibrahimkaka, my father's friend, he's got the most acute political sense, more than anyone else I've known, even more than my father, he's already told her very bluntly that women don't stand a chance unless they have husbands or fathers in politics.'

'What do *you* want to do?'

'I don't know, Gopal. I'm confused. Mira says don't go, her husband Ranjan says politics is a cesspool. Excuse me, I told him, I grew up in that cesspool. No, I don't know what I want to do. But I think I'd like to visit Jogipura once, to see how things are there.'

'You need the backing of a political party if you're serious about entering politics.'

'I know that. And I don't think I'd like to join any of the parties. Not that they will have me, except as a Jowly worker shouting slogans when women's issues crop up. But I've been thinking that I'd like to travel around, meet people, specially the women, then see what is possible.'

Gopal realizes that she is telling him something she has not spoken of to anyone; she is almost thinking aloud, sharing her thoughts with him. It pleases him. He senses that she has been, that she is, homesick for Jogipura; he says so to her, using the English word 'homesick'.

'Homesick? I don't know. Home is not always a place, is it, Gopala? It can be people, it can be a moment of time. Shalini tells me they have modernized the house, she says they now have running water in the bathrooms, gas in the kitchen, a solar heater. You'll love it, she tells me. But it won't be my home, the home I lived in as a child, will it? For me, home is what it was when we lived there together, my parents, my brothers and I, home is that time. Home is also Shivpur, it's Mira's family where I spent so much time in my school days.'

'If you go back to Jogipura,' he says, 'I'll miss you.'

It's the most direct thing he has said to her and she is confused for a moment. Then she says, 'Don't . . .' and stops.

What had she intended to say? 'Don't miss me?' Or, 'Don't say such things?' Or just, 'Don't be foolish?' She does not go on and Gopal leaves soon after that.

After he has gone, Kasturi thinks, this man has become important to me; but where do we go from here? She thinks of Mira's 'Are you smitten?' I don't know, Mira. I only know I like being with him, I enjoy talking to him, I am as comfortable with him as if I've known him for years. But anything more is impossible. There is no place for me in his life, nor does he have a place in mine. At our ages our lives, our pasts specially, are so crowded, it's hard to find space for someone new. It's too late for me to think of living with a man, of waking up with his head on the pillow next to mine. I'm done with all that. And yet, there's my body, it's still alive, it still wants its pleasures, it still makes its demands on me, it still longs for the act which make two people one. But love? I don't know. That madness is no longer possible. What we have is different, something cooler and calmer, something which can give greater pleasure, perhaps, than the tumult of feelings, part ecstasy and part pain, which I had with Neel.

Neel. Kasturi rarely thinks of him now. Their time together had been brief, yet she had crowded a lifetime of love and passion, of longing and joy in it.

***

She had met Neel in the tiny two-room flat Mira and Delia lived in. Since Mira had decided to go to Bombay for her post-graduation, (Delia was already working there) Kasturi had induced her father to let her go to Bombay, too, to study journalism, as well as work part-time in a magazine. Her father had agreed and he, or rather, Ibrahimkaka, who did all these things for him, got her a paying guest place not far from Mira's Bandra flat. But she was scarcely there; she was either working, or spending her time with Delia and Mira, whose place had become a hub for young people. There was Alan, who was engaged to Delia, and there were their many friends. It was the best time of our lives, Mira said later. It was true, it was a wonderful time. They were young and ambitious, they were working hard and were confident about their future. Mira and Delia, though they loved their mother, found that being away from her gave them a kind of heady freedom. With so many young people together, romance hovered in the: air like the aroma of fresh bread which came up to them from the bakery downstairs. But there was no physical intimacy. Delia was a kind of chaperone and Belinda's remote control was still powerful and impossible to ignore. Mira was unattached, Ranjan still a dot on the horizon, but Kasturi almost immediately found Neel.

'My name is Neil,' he told her, when he once saw that she had spelt it N-E-E-L. 'Haven't you heard of Neil Armstrong?'

But to her he was Neel. Blue, she said. Like Krishna, she told him and he was very pleased. He was Alan's cousin and was doing his post-graduation in surgery. They soon became a twosome. Then they started meeting on their own, away from Delia and Mira's flat, away from the others. They were together whenever Neel was free. They met in restaurants, on the beach, they had long rides in buses going nowhere, travelling up and down just so they could be together. Bombay, in spite of its crowds, makes room for lovers; privacy is always possible in the midst of a crowd. It was not long before they crossed the threshold and became lovers. They met in Neel's room in the hospital residents' quarters. When they were together, Neel put up a board on his door saying 'Disturb at your peril'. They spent long hours together and Kasturi was amazed at her body's response to him. When he kissed her, he seemed to suck all the breath out of her, so that she felt breathless, light, as if she was floating. He was not a silent lover, he constantly mumbled, saying things she could not understand, at times, she suspected, even medical terms. When she asked him, 'What are you saying?' he sternly hushed her, saying, 'Don't disturb me, I'm busy.' Which made her laugh, laughter she couldn't stop, until he stopped her mouth with his. For the first time she realized why love was connected to the heart; it was as if each beat of her heart pumped her love for him through her entire body, making it throb, come alive. Mira, ever the Puritan, was shocked when she learnt that Kasturi was sleeping with Neel; for the first time, there was a coldness, a rupture between them. But Kasturi had no regrets then, she has none now. If I hadn't slept with him, she thinks, I would never have known the miracle of becoming one with the man I loved, I'd never have known the joy of giving and receiving such intense pleasure in the act of sex. This made it much harder for her to go through what happened to her later; but she had the joy of knowing that she had once known what love was, what sex was really meant to be.

Passion that had been gathering, it seemed, through all the years of her life, had flooded her. Nothing could penetrate the world Neel and she were living in, everything was an intrusion. She came out of it when she got a message from her brother Vasant that her mother had been diagnosed with a brain tumour and that she would be undergoing surgery in a few days. She went back right away. Her mother died within two days of the surgery and they went to Jogipura for the ceremonies. 'I'll be back in Bombay as soon as it's all over,' she wrote to Neel.

She never did go back. Her father told her she was not going back, that he was going to get her married. She couldn't believe him; she argued with him, pleaded with Ibrahimkaka to intercede with her father on her behalf.

'Things have changed, Sonu,' he told her. 'Your father is not the same man.'

It was Ibrahimkaka who told her that the people she had been living with had carried tales to her father. They had told him that she was friendly with a Christian man. It was 'that woman', as Ibrahimkaka called her, who had put it into her father's head that Kasturi should be married.

'Your father only listens to her now. I don't matter. After forty years of friendship!'

Ibrahimkaka was right. This man was not her father. The woman had taken full control of his life, she had even begun to live in their house after her mother's death. It was her voice which spoke through her father now. 'Friendly with a Christian man!' Her father had never been narrow-minded. Ibrahimkaka, a Muslim, was not only his political adviser and his right-hand man, he was his closest friend, they were almost like brothers. They had studied together in Jogipura, they had been in the same class, they sat side by side on the same bench. 'Without your father, I would never have passed any exams,' Ibrahimkaka used to joke. Even later, they continued to be part of each others' lives. When her father entered politics, Ibrahimkaka was the one man he trusted with all his dealings, the man who did all the dirty things that had to be done so that her father could keep his hands clean. At home, Ibrahimkaka shared their meals, he was with them during festivals and on all family occasions. Her father, too, often had his meals in Ibrahimkaka's house, and his wife, Zubeidakaki, cooked a special vegetarian meal for everyone the day her father ate with them.

And there was Fitter. His real name was Peter. They discovered this after his death—but everyone called him Fitter. People thought that the name came to him because he looked after the machines and all the water pumping sets in Jogipura, specially the ones on her father's lands. He seemed to have a special affinity with these inanimate things, there was no pump he could not repair. He lived in a small room in their backyard where food was carried to him twice a day. He himself never cooked, in fact, he owned nothing. His loyalty to her father was absolute. And her father too, each time he came home, the first person he would ask for was Peter. None of them had any idea that he was a Christian until he died and her father sent for a Christian padre from Shivpur. He was buried on their lands as if he was a member of the family. Her father, silent and withdrawn, stayed on after everyone had gone. When he came- back, it was clear he had been crying. Later, he put up a stone with a cross on it on the grave. And now the same man was saying 'a Christian boy' with such contempt. Now he spoke of Mira and her family as 'those Anglo Indians', saying 'they have loose morals, they have corrupted you,' forgetting how fond he had been of Mira. He said that Kasturi was disgracing him, that it would harm his political reputation if people came to know his daughter was having an affair with a Christian man. He hoped to become the Chief Minister this time, he wanted nothing to spoil his chances. 'You are not going anywhere until you are married,' he said to her.

It's impossible, she had thought. He can't get me married, I'm not a dumb doll. But the impossible happened. She was betrayed by her father, by death, above all by time; she was deprived of all the time she should have had with Neel. Sometimes she thinks of the unused time as being still there, waiting in some dusty corner, a place she can never get to.

She wrote about her father's decision to Neel. 'Don't worry, I'm coming, I'll be there soon,' he wrote. She went to meet him in the guest house where he was staying. That evening, they went to the banks of the river to talk, they spent their time talking, making plans. She would go back with him, she would get a job and when he finished his M.S., they would have a home of their own. It was getting late and she had to go home, but she didn't care; she was with Neel, they were together, nothing else mattered. They made love there on the sands, a gentle and tender love-making, different from the earlier times. She had tears in her eyes and he kissed her eyes gently, he asked her, 'What is this now?' His last words. For then it happened. The river, which had been placid until then, suddenly came alive with a roar. She realized almost at once what had happened. It had been raining a great deal during the last few days, the gates of the dam must have been opened. How could she have forgotten that this could happen? But Neel knew nothing about it, he rushed to retrieve their clothes. And then, in an instant, he was gone. Even now she can see herself running up and down the bank of the river like a madwoman, calling out his name. The memory of her desperation, of looking for Neel, of imagining, of hoping that he would suddenly appear before her, alive and well, still haunts her. But he was gone, gone in a single minute which changed her life entirely.

That's all that remains to her of that terrible night, the memory of her madness and the fact of his death. There's nothing else left. Everything passes, nothing remains—neither love, nor passion, nor hate. Her hatred for her father, even for that woman, became in time a pale thin shadow. She can feel nothing for Neel either, except compassion for a man who died so young. She knew so little of him, theirs was such a brief encounter; she knows more about Gopal than she did about Neel. Yes, nothing remains forever except the ties of blood, the bond that the umbilical cord creates, the one bond that lasts.

The ties of blood are cruel, Belinda had said. It's true, even after all the years, the loss of her son hurts her more than it did in the early years, when she was engrossed with trying to survive. Even death is kinder, the hurt heals with time, we weep for a while, we mourn the dead, but we slowly recover and the tears flow easily, they are no longer so painful. But this loss of mine—the hurt never ceases, the wound remains open. 1 can feel the pain as much as I did when I left him. I can't bear it any longer, I want to see my son, my Krishna. I want him to know he has a mother, I want him to know that I am his mother. Is it too much to ask?

Tressa's death has complicated the working of the office enormously. In her years with them, Tressa had gradually taken most of the drudgery on herself. Suddenly they have to manage without her; grief is moving into regret, into a different sense of loss. Two substitutes for Tressa have come and gone. The third is now with them and, to their surprise, she has lasted a whole fortnight. She is a slow worker and a clock-watcher, but she seems willing to learn, likely to stay on and they are keeping their fingers crossed.

Ramu comes to the office one evening, bringing back the entire tragedy of Tressa's death. He looks like a lost soul. He is gaunt and his clothes, hanging on him, show how much weight he has lost. An air of neglect lies over him like the dust in an uninhabited house. Aru remembers how proud Tressa had been of him; he's the manager of a showroom, she would say, he has to dress very good. No longer; his clothes look shabby, his shirt is unironed. He says he wants to talk to Surekha ma'am. Aru hesitates, she wants to say she's only just gone home, but something in his face makes her ring Surekha. 'She'll be here in a few minutes,' she tells Ramu, 'she asked you to wait,' and begins to pack her bag.

'Don't go, Aru ma'am, I want to talk to you also.'

It has been a good day for Aru with a happy ending to a case she'd felt strongly about. Her client, a young woman, had sued a man who, she alleged, was the father of her unborn child, claiming maintenance for the child. According to her, they had had an affair, but when she got pregnant, he had reneged on his promise to marry her and had denied the affair and the child. A commonplace story; the unusual factor in this one was the girl. An ordinary working class girl, she had shown (extraordinary courage in deciding to have the child and claiming maintenance from the man. She made it clear that she herself wanted nothing; it was for the baby. 'It's his baby also, Akka, he must take the responsibility.'

The man had gotten married and in court denied both the affair and the child. He, or rather his lawyer, had tried to prove that the girl was promiscuous and trying to palm off someone else's child as his. Aru always wonders how the judges can entertain this much-used argument. But the court had agreed with the man. Aru had gone in appeal to the High Court, she fought for the right to have a DNA test done. It proved the man was the father. Aru is jubilant, she has grown very fond of this client of hers. Now Ramu drags her back into the reality of his shattered life, into Gracy's motherless fate.

Ramu tells Surekha and Aru that he has left Gracy with his parents. 'But she is crying all the time, Surekha ma'am, Aru ma'am. Every time I phone her, she says she wants to come home. I thought she will be all right in a little time, her cousins are there, my brother's children, but she is not adjusting.'

He tells them that his mother considers Gracy a spoilt child. 'But what is wrong with spoiling your own child, Surekha ma'am?'

Surekha makes a sudden flinching movement. Ramu, intent on what he is telling them, does not notice; the things he is speaking of have obviously been simmering in his mind for some time, he wants to speak of them to these two women who loved his Tressa.

'Really, Tressa was very strict. So many times I was telling her, don't scold Gracy, she's a small child, but Tressa . . . And now my mother says Tressa spoilt her. Tressa is dead, but they are killing her again and again, ma'am, they are killing her again and again.'

The women get a sense of his pain, a pain which has hardened and sharpened inside him and cuts him like a serrated knife.

'My mother wants to change Gracy's name. When Gracy was born, my mother wanted us to name her Geetha. But Tressa wanted Grace. So we named her Grace Geetha. Now my mother calls her Geetha and Gracy is angry, she says my name is Gracy, it is not Geetha.'

'Can't you make some arrangement for her here?'

'I want to, Surekha ma'am, I am trying all the time, but it will take a little time. Yesterday Gracy phoned me herself and said, I want to come home, Appa, I will do everything you tell me, I promise, I will stay in Amma's office until you finish your work.'

There it is, it has been said finally, the point he has been getting to all this while. Neither of the two women responds immediately. This is not something to be taken lightly.

Ramu goes on, not letting the silence between them last for too long, afraid of getting a negative answer. 'My mother was angry, because she says children should not make phone calls without asking older people, but Gracy wanted to talk to me. My mother has four children of her own, how can she not understand?'

Aru makes an involuntary sound and Ramu, thinking she is going to speak, quickly rushes in. 'My mother is not a bad woman, Aru ma'am. She looks after Gracy, her food, her clothes, everything. At her age it is not easy. And my father is not well, he has BP and sugar complaint, she has to look after him. But she does not understand that Gracy wants to be in her own home, she wants to be with me.'

And so the idea he has come to talk to them about. Can they keep Gracy for a few hours after school? He will pick her up before they close the office, she will be quiet, she will not give them any trouble.

The minds of the two women begin churning up their complicated, packed schedules. Yet, how can they disappoint this man who looks so anxiously at them, who's so desperate for them to agree? Finally Surekha says, 'I'll have to talk to Nagma and Mangala, all of us have to be involved in this. Then I'll let you know.'

The next day she tells him that they will do it, but, she warns him, this cannot be a permanent arrangement. 'You must find someone to be with her at home. We don't keep the office open during holidays. And what will you do during vacations, have you thought of that?'

He promises her that he will make these arrangements soon, he promises fervently that this will be only for a very short time. And so Gracy comes back to her home and into their lives. The child has changed. There is no more chatter, no longer a constant flow of questions. She is silent and subdued, no longer running about the place like the old Gracy. The first day she goes straight to Tressa's chair, sees Divya there, gives her a startled look and turns to Nagma, who has picked her up from her school, as if asking her a question. 'This is Divya auntie, Gracy, Nagma tells her gently and the girl turns away wordlessly.

She has obviously been told not to trouble them, 'otherwise,' she artlessly confesses to them, 'my father said he will send me back to my grandmother's house.' For which reason, she is scrupulously careful not to do anything that will annoy them.

One afternoon, Aru returns from the courts and finds Gracy in a large chair, bunched into a corner of it, fast asleep. She must have fallen asleep while she was eating, or trying to eat, for the lunch box on her lap seems untouched. She looks pathetic. Aru, unable to bear the sight, wakes her up. The child looks vaguely at Aru's face, then becomes aware of where she is and sits up so suddenly that the lunch box almost slides off her lap; Aru quickly retrieves it, places it on the table.

'I'm sorry, Aru ma'am, I am sorry, I was going to eat, I will eat everything, 1 won't leave anything, I promise, Aru ma'am . . .'

A huge rage fills Aru. No child should be humble, she thinks, no child should have to be humble. Children have a right to expect the world to have a place for them. Gracy had her place, a place she occupied with confidence. But Tressa died and that world was destroyed.

Aru stays with Gracy that evening until Ramu arrives. He rings up to tell Gracy he will be a little late, so Aru gives Mangala permission to leave. 'I'll lock up,' she tells her. She shows Gracy no trace of her feelings; instead, she tells her to forget about her lunch box and takes her out, gets her a cake and ice cream to eat. And, knowing she's doing wrong, feeling guilty about her indulgence, (she knows how strict Tressa was about junk food) Aru buys Gracy a bag of chips, which Gracy puts carefully away, saying 'I will eat it afterwards,' as if storing up a great pleasure. When they get back to the office, Aru plays snakes and ladders with Gracy—the game Nagma has brought for her. Aru takes pleasure in seeing some flashes of the old Gracy in the child when they are on their own. She is hugely excited each time she gets to a ladder, groans loudly when she has to slide down a snake. Aru plays up to her, exclaiming like Gracy when she goes up a ladder, pretending despair when a snake takes her down. But when Gracy and Ramu have gone, Aru feels drained, completely exhausted. She knows she has to lock up and go home, but instead she sinks into a chair, telling herself, I must get up, I must go home. Her mobile rings. It is Rohit.

'Where are you?'

'I'm in the office.'

'Still there? You sound tired. Are you ready to come home? Shall I pick you up?'

She says, 'Yes'. It is so unusual a thing for her that Rohit gets there in a state of anxiety. She has locked up and is waiting outside, the keys in her hand, knowing she has to drop them off in Surekha's home, but unable to move. Rohit, seeing her sitting on the steps, is even more anxious. He asks no questions, though; he says, 'Come, let's go.'

'I have to take these keys to ma'am's house.'

'Give them to me.' He sees her car and says, 'Your car is here.'

'Oh god, I forgot.'

'Never mind. I'll park it in ma'am's house. Give me the keys. You go and wait in the car.'

She is sagging in her seat, head resting wearily on the headrest when he returns. He says nothing, merely asks, 'Okay?'

She nods. But he can see that she is not all right. In a while he realizes she's crying, such a rare thing that it gives him a pang.

'What is it, Aru?'

There's no reply. He does not ask her again, but drives silently home. Then, without getting out, he asks her again, 'Tell me, Aru, what is it?'

She has composed herself to some extent now and speaks to him of Gracy, of what has happened, of what is happening to the child. Then she falls silent. He does not speak either. The same thought is in both their minds. When they get into the house, he asks her, 'Shall we go for a music performance?' A friend of his, part of a group which organizes classical music programmes for students, has invited him to a performance at their old college. 'That's why I called you. He's a young singer, Shruti tells me, he's very good. Shall we go?'

'I need to have a bath and change.'

'Do that.'

When they get to the venue, the large hall is full of students, the overflow crowded on the carpet immediately below the dais. Aru and Rohit put away their footwear on the pile outside and tiptoe in, looking for a place they can squeeze into. Two girls make room for them and smile at them. 'Comfortable?' one of the girls asks when they settle down.

'Very,' Rohit replies. Aru leans against him. She seems to have fallen asleep while the singer is being introduced. The girl who had spoken earlier asks Rohit in a whisper, 'She's sleeping?' Rohit would be surprised to know that she finds him attractive, that she likes the way he is supporting the woman with him.

'Yes,' Rohit whispers back.

'No, I'm not, I'm awake,' Aru says clearly. The girls and Rohit smile at one another. To the girls, Aru, in her shift-like kameez and hair casually gathered at the nape of her neck, seems only a girl. And from the way Rohit holds her, it is clear that they are lovers. 'Aren't they cute?' the girls signal to each other.

After the usual testing of the tanpura strings, the singer begins. At the sound of the young man's voice, Aru sits up abruptly and Rohit and she look at each other. They know this voice; it is the young priest who had sung at their wedding. It is seven years since they heard him and he has changed; he is a stunningly handsome man now, but the voice is unmistakable. During the aalaap, they are struck by the beauty of his voice, now enhanced by his skill and control.

They had intended to go away after a while, but they stay on until the last bhajan, a Tukaram abhang, he tells the audience, which he sings with such devotion that the crowd, even without understanding Marathi, seems hypnotized. It takes Aru and Rohit back to their wedding day, to this same young man singing the mangalashtaka, bringing about the same silence among the wedding guests.

Obviously he has seen them and recognized them, for when the performance is over, he acknowledges their presence by putting his right hand on his chest and bowing slightly, a sketch of a greeting, accompanied by a smile. When they go to him, Rohit's friend tries to introduce them. 'I know them,' the young man says, smiling broadly at them. 'I always remember you,' he tells them. 'Your wedding . . . it changed my life also.'

His grandfather is dead, he tells them, but before he died, he induced the boy's father to let him have his way and take up music full time. 'My ajoba said that when he heard me singing at your wedding, he knew that music was my life.'

'There was, there is, magic in your voice,' Aru tells him.

'There was magic in your wedding also, Arundhatitai. I was very happy to be there.'

'You remember my name?' she asks him, surprised.

'It is a beautiful name. How could I forget? I remember everything about your wedding so clearly. I recognized both of you at once.'

'We saw that.'

'I was nervous, this is the first time I am singing before such a big crowd. But when I saw you both, I somehow knew it would be all right.'

'Your last bhajan, the abhang, was wonderful, you sang it very beautifully.'

'It's not me, it's my ajoba, he's still looking after me,' he says, putting his hands together in a devotional namaste and looking up. 'And my Guruji,' he says, touching both his ears.

Rohit feels a sharp nudge in his side. It is his friend, Shruti, who frowns at him and says, 'There are others waiting to talk to our performer, Rohit.'

'Sorry, sorry. All right, we'll take our leave of you. But we will meet again.' It's like a promise. Rohit is moving away, then suddenly turns back to ask, 'Do you have a card?'

The young man's hands, which have gone up in a farewell namaste, fall down helplessly by his sides. Rohit says, 'Never mind, I have mine.' And, ever the professional, he brings his card out of his wallet as swiftly as a conjuror brings out his cards. 'Keep in touch. And let us have your phone number.'

The man, like he had done when he first saw them, again puts his hand on his chest and bows very slightly to them. Aru looks back once, sees him still looking at them over the heads of the people around him and waves to him. He smiles.

When they get into the car, Aru says, 'What a marvelous coincidence!'

'Hmm. You know, Aru, I was thinking that maybe I should ask Jagdish to invite him for his young musicians' festival. He's on the lookout for good artistes.'

'But Rohit, will this boy come for such a small event? Jagdish started it only last year. Very few people know about it.'

'How else does an event become big, Aru, unless good performers participate? And,' Rohit goes on smoothly, 'if he sounds reluctant, I'll just have to tell him that Arundhatitai . . . .' Rohit emphasizes the name, 'wants to hear him. He'll come running.'

'What rubbish!'

'He thinks you're beautiful. He has never forgotten you since he saw you in our wedding.'

'What nonsense! He's only a bachcha.'

'Not so much of a bachcha that he can't feel the attraction of a beautiful woman.'

'Oh stop it, Rohit, you're making me uncomfortable.'

Rohit had been very amused to find that any words of praise about her looks made Aru shy and uncomfortable. 'Okay, okay,' he says. 'Let's talk of more important things. Are you hungry?'

'Ravenous.'

'Let's eat, I know a place we can go to.'

He takes her, not to a restaurant, but to a small street full of handcarts lit by hissing petromax lamps. Fresh food is being cooked on each one of them, the aroma of the food heavy and enticing. The street is crowded with hungry people. 'I used to come here when I was a student. I would study till late, then come and eat here.'

He takes her to a cart, saying, 'The best dosas are here.' They are wonderful, Aru agrees. 'Or maybe they taste so good because we're hungry.'

'Don't take credit away from the dosas, woman,' he says. He seems happy, lighthearted, as if he has gone back to his student days. And then suddenly he says, 'The first time I came here, it was because Amma sent me out of the house. My father came home drunk and I was furious. I said something to him, I don't remember what. He almost hit me. And Amma said, Rohit, go, just go away, leave him to me. I wandered around, I didn't know where I was going, until I suddenly found this place. I came here often after that.'

It gives Aru great pleasure to share a part of his early life. She had felt the same pleasure when he had taken her to see the old bungalow they were to renovate. He had put his arm round her shoulders and taken her from room to room, telling her what each room was for, how it must have been, and how they would bring it back to what it had been. She had listened to him in silence, hearing much more than what he was telling her. Then he spoke of a painting they had found with one of the owners, a painting which, perhaps, the owner had commissioned. It was a painting of horses just come on shore after their sea journey from Persia, for there was the sea behind them and in the background, at a far distance, a small craft. The horses, splendid creatures, seemed a little bewildered at finding themselves on firm land. One of them seemed to be turning its head this way and that, as if trying to get its bearings, and another, a little one, raising its legs, getting ready to gallop away . . .

'I keep thinking how it will look when it's hung up in its original place in the hall—or what we think was its original place. I want you to see the painting, Aru. We've given it for cleaning, but as soon as it's ready, I'll take you to see it.'

Aru, listening silently until then, suddenly stood on tiptoe and kissed him. On the lips. Such an unusual gesture from Aru who was not very demonstrative and almost never demonstrative in public!

'What was that for?' Rohit had asked in astonishment.

'Does a kiss have to be for a reason?'

'No. Always welcome, ma'am, always welcome.'

But she had thought—it was for showing me your real self. Why did you never reveal this self to me until now? She feels the same way now. She can see the unhappy and confused boy, angry with his father, hating him, grieving for his mother.

It suddenly turns windy, the plastic covers on the carts begin to flap, making crackling sounds. 'It's going to rain,' Rohit says and they run to the car, getting into it just in time. 'Cyclone, perhaps.'

It's been a magical evening, what with the music, the young singer and the food afterwards. But Gracy comes back to Aru when they go to bed. She *sees* her once again, the little body curled up in the chair, her mouth a little open, tiny flakes of rice at the corners of it. And then waking up, awareness in her eyes, the sudden fear. 'I'll eat it, Aru m'am, I'll eat everything . . .'

'Feeling cold?' Rohit asks her.

'A little. Shall I get the razais?'

'No, I'll get them. You lie down.'

He gets the razais and covers her with one of them. 'Will you tell me now what happened?'

She speaks to him then of Gracy, of the anger and pity that had filled her when she saw Gracy so humble and helpless. She confesses to him the fears she has not revealed to anyone, not even to Charu. 'I've begun coveting other people's children, Rohit. When Gracy was with us, I began to think—maybe she will live with us always, maybe we can keep her for always. And then I wondered—am I glad that Tressa died so that we can have Gracy? I hated myself, I began to be frightened of myself. I can't tell you how relieved I was when Gracy went away. At least I wouldn't have those terrible thoughts.'

She tells him she's afraid she will become one of those childless women who haunt hospitals, looking for newborns to steal, women who go to children's parks and playgrounds to kidnap children.

'Not you, Aru,' he says, 'never you.'

'But it's true, isn't it, Rohit, one never knows what one is capable of. I always thought, this is what I am, I won't change. But situations change us and we never know how and when it happens. I thought we are always in control of ourselves, our lives, but . . .' She stops for a moment, then goes on. She tells him about Nagma's pregnancy. 'She never told me about it. She was afraid I would be hurt, that I would envy her. And I do, Rohit, I do.'

'That's very natural.'

'But, Rohit, I don't want to be like this.'

She tells him about her client, that extraordinary girl with extraordinary courage who refused to give up her child. 'It's easy for film stars and celebrities to decide to be single mothers, but this girl has to live among ordinary people who judge her harshly. And the men—she told me that men think because she slept with someone without marriage once, she'll be willing to sleep with anyone, anytime. They chase her like dogs in heat, she said. Even now she has to constantly fend off men; she has endured everything for her child, only for her child. And the child's father is a man she hates! It's hard to understand. All her courage comes from her love for her baby. Will I never know that love? Why am I denied that?'

She is silent for a while; Rohit says nothing, he waits for her to go on. 'Rohit, is it possible to have that kind of love for a baby not born of your body? I thought of how my client fought against the idea of adoption—everyone kept telling her to give her baby up, but she didn't. And I thought, any baby we adopt will have been given up with enormous pain. How can I take advantage of another woman's pain and suffering:' But when I saw Gracy today. . .'

Everything she has kept to herself, her grief, her fears, her anger, pours out of her. She tells him she has realized that this is a grief that has no end. It will stay inside you, like a tumour, all your life, not killing you, but not letting you live as you should, either. And even when you are dying, it will hurt that you don't have your own flesh and blood to sit by you, to hold your hand and ease you into death. 'I often think of Amma, of how we were constantly with her at the end, how Goda never left her side, how much it comforted her to have us by her. And yet, she waited until Premimavshi came before she let go.'

Rohit realizes that she is baring her deepest self to him. When she finally stops, he puts his arms about her. 'Come to me, my darling,' he says, 'come to me.' He strokes her on the back over and over again until she stops crying. His hands then move to her breasts, his lips to her face, to her breasts, to her lips. Speech and silence, lover and beloved come together, each becoming the other in the final, the ecstatic moment of union. Aru falls asleep immediately after, plunging into a deep dreamless sleep. But Rohit lies awake thinking, we have to do something, we can't go on this way.

Aru wakes up in the morning still holding on to the thought which had been with her when she had fallen asleep, the same thought that had been with her in the early years of their marriage: surely, when we love like this, it must result in a child, surely such love, such passion, cannot be fruitless! She remembers talking to Kalyani about marriage, about the huge risk involved in marriage, in loving. 'When I think of my parents . . .' And Kalyani telling her, 'Silly girl, with a man like Rohit you don't have to worry, there is no risk.' It was true. True also that it was he who had taken a risk when he had married her, a risk she now admires him for taking.

But looking at her face, Kalyani had asked, 'What are you afraid of, Aru? Are you not sure about him?'

'No, Amma, I have no doubts about Rohit at all.'

'Then what is it, child?' she had asked, her voice so tender it was like a physical caress.

It was herself, it was something in her. She wished, oh how she wished that she could have Charu's certainty. Charu, when she was going to the U.S. for her exams, had told her that she would be staying with Hrishi.

'I hope you know what you are doing. Are you sure, Charu?'

'About Hrishi? Come on, Aru, you'll ask me next whether I'm sure of you?'

Why can't I have that kind of certainty, she had thought. But she had been conscious of some kind of a barrier within her, something that did not allow her feelings to get out. When you love someone, she had thought, you become a hostage to life, you are always afraid. But perhaps the only way to get rid of the barrier is to jump over it, she now thinks. To leave it behind.

She gets out of bed, washes and sits in the small veranda for a while, looking at the courtyard. Then she goes into the kitchen and makes tea. When she comes back, Rohit is awake. She puts the tea tray on their usual table on the veranda. He joins her, picks up his cup and then asks, 'What are you thinking of?'

'What do you want? Boy or girl?' she asks.

Without missing a beat, he says, 'Girl, of course. A daughter first.'

'All right. Agreed. A daughter, then.'

They laugh together. The euphoria lasts for a while. Then the fears begin. Aru's fears. Rohit is careful not to push things, not to speak about the adoption agency right away. He waits for Aru to say it. And then comes the first problem. Aru is reluctant to speak to anyone about their decision. It seems to her too much like speaking of conception immediately after love-making; this has to be just as private as the thought 'I've conceived' that comes after intense love-making. But they need two references, the agency tells them. Two couples. Jaisimha and Surekha, and Murthy and Devaki, they decide. And yet, how can they speak to them and not to the others? And so, they tell the family about their plans to adopt.

Premi is so delighted she comes down for the weekend. 'I had to see you,' she tells Aru, though Aru supposes that seeing Nikhil is equally her purpose. But Premi makes no attempt to contact Nikhil. She spends all her time with Aru, Seema, Rohit and Gopal. Premi has been with Aru all the way from the time of her hopes and her fears to her despair. Now she becomes nostalgic, she speaks of Aru as a baby.

'You know, Aru, we, I mean, Amma and I, had to sneak out to see you. Sumi and Gopal were still in disgrace with Baba. Though Baba melted when he saw you. You were such a beautiful baby. The loveliest in the family.'

'What! More than Nikhil?'

'Nikhil was a little monkey, all wrinkles. His skin was so dry it seemed to be peeling off

'I can't believe it, he's so handsome.'

'Handsome is as handsome does.'

'Premimavshi, is this you speaking? I can't believe it. What has Nikhil done now?'

'Nothing. Just being his usual self. If I meet him it'll be Hi, Aai and Bye, Aai. It's a mistake, Aru, to care for someone too much, even your own child. Don't do it. But, of course, it will be different for you.'

'Why? Because I won't be giving birth? Will that always make a difference?'

Premi is shocked. 'No, Aru, I didn't mean that. I meant you'll be having a daughter. Daughters are different. Look at the three of you!'

But Lalita, Rohit's mother, does not agree. Lalita has not had much of a place in this story of Aru and Rohit's, not because she does not matter, but because she keeps away from them. Having suffered from a termagant of a mother-in-law for a great part of her married life, a woman whose goal in life seemed to be to make Lalita's life miserable, Lalita had decided that the best thing she could do was to keep some distance between herself and Rohit and Aru. She gets on well with Aru, there's a mutual respect between them.

'Why a daughter?' she asks. 'Why not a son?'

Rohit and Aru look at her in surprise. They had not expected this of Lalita. 'I thought you'd have been disillusioned about sons by now, Amma.'

'What do my daughters do for me? One never bothers to ring up, she's forgotten us, she never thinks of her mother, only her husband and children matter to her. And the other is married to her work.'

'Are all your children a great disappointment to you, Amma?' Aru asks.

'I can't complain about Rohit, Aru.'

Except for his hostility to his father, which troubles her a great deal. Lalita is grateful to Aru that she has brought about some kind of a rapprochement between father and son.

'If Appa wronged anyone, he wronged me,' she said to Aru once. 'And I've put that time behind me. Poor man, he was so pampered by his mother, so dominated by her, what chance did he have? And do you know why he began drinking?'

Aru had heard the story from Rohit, who also told her that he didn't believe a word of it. His father started drinking because he was not allowed to marry the English girl he had fallen in love with when he was in England. They decoyed him back home saying his mother was very ill, and once he came, they got him married right away to Lalita. And the girl, who had followed him to India, was unceremoniously packed off with enough money for her return passage. 'Appa tells everyone that he started drinking only after this,' Rohit had said with some contempt.

'Now he's given up drinking, he desperately wants Rohit to recognize that, you can't imagine how much he wants Rohit to be good to him, but . . . Look at him, Aru,' she'd said. 'Is he worth hating and being angry with?'

Aru knew what she meant. Rohit's father had become a pathetic old man.

'If you have expectations, you're going to be disappointed,' Lalita says, answering Aru's question about whether she's disappointed in her children. 'Which parent does not have expectations? But babies, Aru, babies are wonderful. You must bring home a very little one. There's nothing in the world like babies. When Rohit was born, I felt I was Devaki and he was my Balakrishna. And I'll tell you why I want a grandson. I already have two granddaughters, not that I ever get to see them, I have to be satisfied with seeing their pictures and hearing their voices on the phone—sometimes. So now I'd like to have a grandson.'

'We'll give you a grandson, Amma, a little fellow who will be much better than your son.'

Aru and Lalita smile at each other. Rohit sees them exchanging smiles, he wonders what it's about, but he does not really care. These are the two women he loves most in the world, both of whom, he now knows, love him as much.

'We'll give you a grandson, Amma,' Aru repeats Rohit's words. 'We're not going to stop at one. What do you say, Rohit?'

'Yes, Amma, we'll give you your Balakrishna. I promise.'

Ramu's experiment with Gracy has failed—to no one's surprise, not even his own. For Ramu, too, it had been no more than a hope, a hope born of desperation. But the plan goes awry after just two weeks. Gracy wakes up with a temperature. Ramu leaves her sleeping, asking the maid to stay on until he returns, which he will do very soon, he assures the woman. But when Gracy wakes up, she is alone and locked in. Terrified, she rings up her father, who rushes back to find Gracy rigid and mute with fear and the maid swearing she had gone out for just five minutes. Gracy held on to her father with desperation, she would not let him leave her even for a minute that day. She had imagined herself abandoned, she had thought her father too had died.

Ramu appealed to his father. They had to come, both he and his mother, otherwise he would lose his job. They came at once, but Ramu is confronted by a fresh problem.

'He'll get married, mark my words, they'll get him married,' Nagma had prophesied. Which is exactly what his mother is now asking him to do. He comes to meet Aru and Rohit, apologising profusely for disturbing their Sunday morning, but obviously, badly needing to talk to them.

He himself, he says, has absolutely no thoughts of remarrying, not now or ever. He is still mourning his Tressa, struggling to make a life for Gracy without her mother, hoping to see her happy and smiling as she was earlier: this is his only goal at the moment. But his mother says he must marry for Gracy's sake. She must have a mother, you must have a wife, a woman in the house, she tells him. She has come prepared with photographs, which she produces like a conjuror fanning out cards for a gullible member of the audience to pick out. Parvathy and Revathy, Sujatha and Sukanya—they are all, his mother assures him, good girls from good families. Good Brahmin families. This one has done computers, this one works in a bank, this one has done Home Science—and so it goes on. A litany, singing the virtues of unknown girls, (girls! They are older than Tressa!) unknown women, any one of whom, his mother tells him, will make him a good wife. Better than Tressa it was implied. A good mother for Gracy.

'She makes me feel that I made a mistake in marrying Tressa. I feel that she is all the time asking me—when there are so many good girls of our caste, why did you marry a Christian girl? I want to tell her I married Tressa because . . . because . . .'

He falters, words fail him, perhaps the language itself fails him. If he could have spoken in Tamil, he might have said, 'I married Tressa because I loved her, I loved her bright eyes, her eager look, I loved her smooth soft skin, her soft lips, her slim body. I loved her because she laughed so much and she made me laugh also. Raamaa Krishnaa she called me sometimes, saying my full name, making it even longer, teasing me, as if she was chanting god's name.' At times, he has had wild thoughts of saying these things to his mother, of telling her, 'I loved Tressa because of the curve of her hips, the softness of her breasts, the sweet fragrance of her when she came to me after a bath.' But he knows that not only can he never say these things to his mother, he can't even bring back these memories, because to let in such thoughts is to invite madness.

'I told my mother I don't want to marry, I want to live for Gracy and see her laugh again, I don't want to give her a stepmother.'

At which point, he tells them, his mother threatened that they would go back, they would wash their hands off him. Ramu has begged his father to stay for some more time, he is making arrangements for a woman, a neighbour, to be with Gracy when she comes home from school.

So it is not to ask them to look after Gracy that he has come. He has come for quite a different reason. Tressa's brother, the priest, has been writing to him, reminding him that Gracy is a baptized Christian. He insists that she should be brought up in a Christian family, that she should be sent to church regularly, she should have her Holy Communion at the right time. If not, he will approach the court and take her away from her father.

'Can he do that, Aru ma'am? I am so frightened.'

Aru tries to reassure him that no one can take Gracy away from her father. He nods, but says he still wants to meet Surekha. There is another reason he wants to meet her. The government is giving him compensation for Tressa's death. 'As if that can make up for Tressa,' he says angrily. But he wants it for Gracy's sake, for her education. 'Tressa wanted her to be a lawyer, I will make her a lawyer.' He wants to make sure that the money will not be touched by anyone, not even by him, that it should be kept for Gracy alone. Can it be done?

Yes, Aru tells him, it can be done. Go and meet Surekha, she says, I will fix an appointment for you.

Before going, he speaks of the bomb attacks which have taken place in Bombay, attacks which are far more serious than what happened in their city. For the first time, he speaks in Kannada, a language which Aru realizes he can speak very well, albeit with a Tamil accent. 'I thought I was the only one in the world to suffer, I thought my Gracy was the only one to become almost an orphan. But now I know there are so many others, so many people who suffer like us.' Then he switches over to English and asks, 'But why, sir and Aru ma'am, why? What for they are doing such things? And they are also saying what they did here was practice. So, my Tressa died to make more people die afterwards? I will never understand this, Aru ma'am, for me it is the worst thing—that Tressa died to make more people die.'

After he has gone, Aru thinks that his grief over Tressa's death is already sliding into the past. It is inevitable. She remembers how impossible it had seemed at one time that they could ever stop mourning Sumi. But they did. And a time came when they could talk easily of Sumi. Even if the tears came, they were no longer painful; they came easily, they brought relief. Ramu is now agonizing not over Tressa, but over Gracy. She thinks of his desperate frenzied love for his daughter, she thinks of Tressa's mother agonizing over the possibility of her daughter being cremated, not because she wanted a Christian burial for her, but because her dead daughter was afraid of fire. She remembers Kalyani's mother, Manorama, who wanted a son and rejected her daughter Kalyani. And Kalyani herself, who had two daughters and was considered a failure because she lost her only son. Aru thinks of her own parents, Gopal and Sumi, who had surrounded their three daughters with love. It was Gopal, more than Sumi, who had been there for Aru, because Sumi was, at times, moody and temperamental. Gopal had been the rock on which Aru had stood, but suddenly the rock had turned to sand and she was left floundering. Aru thinks of the letter she had found among Kalyani's papers when they were clearing up the old house before its demolition. It was a letter to Manorama from her village teacher, Yamunabai. Manorama had obviously written about her unhappiness at not having a son. And Yamunabai had written:

> What we really want is that we should not be forgotten. That our lives should not be completely wiped out as if we have never been. Very few of us can do great deeds which will be remembered for all time. But most of us will live in our children. Does it make a difference whether it's a son or a daughter who remembers you, Manu? You will live in your daughter, as much as you would in a son. The family name

> is something we have created ourselves, it has no meaning. Look at me, I have no children, but all of you, my students, are like my daughters, no, you *are* my daughters . . .

What a wise letter, Aru thinks now. What a woman she must have been, this child widow, who lived in a village and taught girls to read and write and to know something of the world, about themselves and their bodies. This letter, like Kalyani's will, has become a magic mantra for Aru, giving her courage and strength when she needs them. Now, at this moment, she takes the words to heart. Girl or boy, adopted or natural child—what does it matter? The child will be mine, she will be ours, Rohit's and mine. She is suddenly impatient to have the child come to their home. To her own home. How do women wait nine long months, she wonders.

As soon as she returns from Jogipura, Kasturi gets to know from Nagi about Aru and Rohit's decision to adopt. Kasturi no longer considers talking about the family with Nagi as gossip; the two women are now friends. 'When I'm with you, it's like being with Kalyaniamma,' Nagi had said to her. 'Kalyaniamma would have liked you,' she had added and Kasturi knew that, as far as Nagi was concerned, there could be no higher praise. 'These children, they are good children and Premiakka is very generous, but no one has any time to talk. With Kalyaniamma, I could speak of all my problems, she always had time to listen to me.'

Nagi had spoken to her earlier of how unfair it was that a couple like Aru and Rohit should not have children. They would make such good parents, Akka. You should have seen Aru with her grandmother when Kalyaniamma was ill. Sometimes I think you must have been my mother in my last birth, Amma used to say to her. Yes, she looked after her grandmother like a mother.' But Aru was also like a son, Nagi had said; she had shocked everyone by cutting off her hair when Kalyani died. 'Such long beautiful hair, Kasturiakka, you won't believe it now. And she cut it off as if she was Kalyaniamma's son. And now she can't have a child of her own. But that's how it is. God has eyes, but he can't see. When I went to Tirupati and saw how god has covered his eyes, I thought—no wonder it is such a terrible world. Why can't he open his eyes and see what is happening?'

'Because he doesn't want to see what a terrible world he has created,' Kasturi wants to say, but she desists. You can't say such things to Nagi. But Nagi herself goes on. 'Lucky man, he shuts his eyes to the world, he makes his wife stay at the bottom of the hill, and he stays at the top, accepting all the worship that comes to him.'

'That's why he's a god, Nagakka. How many of us can make ourselves so comfortable?'

They had both laughed then, though Nagi had immediately tapped both her cheeks rapidly with her fingers, crossing and uncrossing her arms, begging god for forgiveness for laughing at him.

After she learns about Aru and Rohit's decision to adopt, Kasturi thinks Gopal will speak to her about it as well. But when he says nothing, Kasturi imagines that the information is supposed to be confidential. Perhaps it's like the early weeks of pregnancy, when no one was to be told except the pregnant girl's mother. She herself had had no one to tell, no one to cherish and cosset her, the way she had seen other women being pampered in their first pregnancy. Her mother was dead, her father hostile, her brother alienated from her. There was only that strange silent woman, her mother-in-law, Awa, who seemed to know, without being told, that Kasturi was pregnant. She must have spoken to her son about it, which was why he kept away from her. It was an unexpected boon, a blessing, that she was free of his sexual demands. Demands? No, they were nightly assaults on her body. Assaults that began with his questions:

> Ask your father to get me transferred from here.
> Ask your father to get me a promotion.
> Ask your father to give us a house.

'No, no, no' she said each time, she said it over and over again. And then he became violent, after which came sex, leaving her bruised, shamed and full of fury. Sometimes she thought it was the violence that he really needed, violence which, she now realized, aroused him. He seemed to deliberately whip up his anger, calling her a whore, a loose woman, saying he knew she had slept with a man earlier, did she think he didn't know she was not a virgin when he married her?

For a while, the baby saved her; he became her saviour, he was on her side even before he was born. He gave her the joy she thought she had lost forever in life. She could watch him endlessly, sleeping or awake, every little thing he did a new source of delight, as if no baby had done it before. If she allows herself to, she can still remember his struggles to turn over, something that went on through all his waking hours, one fat little leg crossed over the other, his toes scrabbling for a foothold, giving up at times with angry frustrated cries, but soon starting all over again. She can vividly recollect the day he finally managed it, the little body turning over and lying prone. After a moments startled silence the yells began, cries of hurt surprise at finding his arm trapped under his body, the cries muffled because his nose was pressed against the bed. When she had turned him over, he had given her a stare and then begun the same exercise all over again, ending once again in yells. 'Don't ask me to help you the next time,' she had said sternly, laughing at the same time, 'You can lie there until you learn to put yourself right side up.'

Yes, she had laughed. Even in that home of cruelty and anger, living as she did with fury and silence, the baby had made her laugh. Yet she had abandoned him, she had walked away from him. If I had not, I would have killed that man, or I would have killed myself, she often thinks. I did not want my baby to have one parent dead, another a murderer and so . . .

But that was not exactly the way it had happened, had it? There had been no such clear reasoning; she had just been desperate to escape. For, the violence began all over again, the baby the excuse now, the demands made on his behalf, demands that her father should give his grandson something—land, money, gold. He had wealth enough, didn't he? He had made so much money that he could provide for generations. But she had been firm. She would not ask her father for anything. She never would have, and after the way he had treated her when Neel died, there was no chance that she would even talk to him.

Kasturi, on the rare occasions when she allows herself to revisit the past, asks herself the question so many women do: why did I stand it for so long? Why did I put up with the cruelty and torture? The answer she gets is: at first I didn't know how to cope with it. When my baby was born, I put up with it because I could not leave him behind, nor could I take him with me. And, finally, because I had nowhere to go, nobody whom I could ask for refuge.

'Why didn't you come to me?' Mira had asked her angrily when they met years later and she heard the story. As much of it as Kasturi told her.

'I was afraid you and your family, Alan and Delia specially, would blame me for Neel's death. And you had just got engaged to Ranjan . . .'

'So what?'

But the truth was that ultimately she left because she could no longer go on. The decision was made the day he locked her into a room, refusing to let her feed the baby. She could hear the baby crying, she could hear the old woman trying to soothe him. There was the clink of a spoon against metal which told her that the woman was trying to feed him with a spoon. She could almost imagine him turning disdainfully away, his mouth tightly shut, the milk dribbling down his chin. In time, the indignant crying slowly faded into piteous cries of hunger. And then her torture began. She had enough milk for the baby—and more. After a while her breasts were gorged with milk and the pain began, pain that shot through her like a thousand stabbing needles, driving her almost crazy. She had sobbed, she had screamed, she had banged her head against the wall. Ultimately the woman had unlocked the door, come in with the baby and put him on her lap. With frantic haste she had unhooked her blouse and put the baby to her breast. But at the touch of his eager, demanding mouth on her nipple, she began to scream all over again. Her breasts were so tender that the slightest touch was torture. The baby too, unable to get at the milk, began to cry again. The woman then took the baby away from her, she gently kneaded her daughter-in-law's breasts, massaged them until, finally, she was able to express some milk from the nipples. Then she gave her the baby back. Kasturi remembered for years the relief of being free of pain, the ecstasy of the baby suckling. He drank so fast that he had to stop after a few moments because he was breathless, snuffling, his nose pressed against her engorged breast. He took a few breaths and went back to suckling again. She had begun to laugh at his greed then, laughter that turned to tears. She wept as if she would never stop, she wept at the tragedy of her life, she wept for love of her baby whom she knew she would have to abandon. She wept as she never had and never would again, not in this way, never for herself. The old woman watched them both, the feeding baby and the weeping mother, in stoic silence.

Her mother-in-law still remains an enigma to Kasturi. Silent spectator of the cruelty done to her, of the war that raged between her son and the woman he had married, was she an enemy? Or a friend? She has often asked herself: from where did I get the courage, the confidence in her, to leave my baby to her? How was I so sure she would look after him, that she would care for him? Or was it neither courage nor confidence, but desperation that made me leave him behind? After all, the woman never said a word of comfort, never showed any sympathy or support. How, then, was I so sure that the woman would be good to my son? Sometimes Kasturi even thinks that her mother-in-law had abetted her escape. How else could the door of her room, as well as the back door, have been open that night? Had she left them open every night, hoping that Kasturi would escape? Kasturi had become so mistrustful of everyone that she had suspected the woman had wanted her to escape so she could have the child to herself. Now she no longer thinks so. Even if she did not have the courage to oppose her son, she had wanted Kasturi to go away, to escape the torture. Truly, the human mind is unfathomable, it is the greatest mystery in the world, she thinks.

It was after that terrible day, the day when her baby had been kept from her, that Kasturi knew she had to get away. Finally, it was the sight of her own bruised face that decided her. Her forehead was a mass of bruises, there were bloodstains on her sari. She was aghast. When had this happened? How was it that she could not remember it happening? It could not have been the man's violence, he was careful never to touch her face. She must have done it to herself. And she could not remember. I must be going mad, she thought. I can't stay here any longer, I must get out.

She had walked out that night with nothing but the clothes she was wearing. She went to the railway station and waited for a train. Desperation had given her the courage to ask a stranger sitting next to her on a bench for money to buy a ticket. He had given her a long look, walked away, then come back with a ticket for her. 'Keep the change,' he had said, stuffing some money into her hand. Desperation had upheld her until the train reached its destination and disgorged its passengers. She had watched them get out, relieved to get to the end of their journey, walking out purposefully, knowing where they were going, she envied those who were met with happy welcoming cries.

And she? At that moment she had known the complete black despair that leads to suicide. There was nothing for her except blankness and darkness. But she did not die. She lived. She survived because Raju, the rickshaw driver who almost ran over her—she had intentionally stepped in his path—took her home to his family and kept her there until she came out of her stupor and silence. She survived because Chandru, the man who had bought her a ticket, had also given her his card, which told her he was a journalist. She went to him and asked for his help in finding a job. He helped her to get a job, he gave her shelter until she got her first pay and could rent a room of her own. The bruises slowly faded from her face, from her body, though the scars in her mind took longer. Slowly the fears receded, the nightmares left her alone. She came back to life. She realized that Chandru, who had become a friend, wanted her. She went to him herself, she slept with him. After which her body felt clean, purged of all the ugliness and the violence that had been inflicted on it, purified of the hatred with which it had been treated.

Chandru and she are still friends. He had never forced himself on her, even when she was helpless; once they stopped sleeping together, he never spoke of those days. She too has put it away the way she had put away her marriage. But some things remain. Like Chandru, Raju and his family continue to be part of her life. Her child, however, is as lost to her as if he had never been.

But he comes back to her every time she sees mothers and children together. Motherhood can be joyful and innocent, she thinks, not a weapon to be used against you. Her terror and sorrow still come back to her whenever she hears a baby cry. For years, she has been haunted by the baby's crying; the pathetic wail of a baby in the night can still bring back all the grief and anguish of the time.

For years she nursed her hatred; he cheated me of the joy of being a mother, she often thought, he deprived me of my son. But her anger and hatred dwindled in time, the past became a distant country she had once visited. And now nothing is left but a longing to know where her son is, to see him, to talk to him perhaps . . .

She had told herself that she was going to Jogipura to lay the ghosts to rest, but she had known that she had hoped for more, for some news of her son. Maybe Ibrahimkaka, who knew everything that happened in the district would have some knowledge about her son, or at least about the man. She *had laid* some ghosts to rest in the course of her visit. Her hatred for the woman who had made her father a stranger to his own family disappeared when she heard that she was living alone, ill and, after Vasant had won the family properties back from her, almost penniless. Even better, Kasturi had been reconciled to her brother Vasant, as Shalini had hoped. She had nursed her grudge, her resentment against him for a long time. It was he and Ibrahimkaka who had urged her into marriage, telling her that the man was a good man, a quiet man, that he had a government job and no dependents except a widowed mother. Vasant had added, with a cruelty he himself had not perhaps realized, for he was not cruel, only insensitive, 'It's going to be hard getting you married now, Sonu,' he had said. 'Everyone knows you were found on a river bank . . .' He didn't add, 'half-naked and crying out a man's name over and over again.'

She had never hated Ibrahimkaka, though, she had always known that what he had done had been on her father's instructions. But Vasant was her own, her only brother! How could he have done that to her! The thought had stayed with her for a long time. Worse, it was he who had persuaded her to give up all claims to her own child during the divorce. Yet, when she met him, she was surprised to find that her resentment had disappeared. Vasant, too, had been conciliatory, Shalini affectionate and, best of all, their children delighted with this aunt who had, she realized, become a legend in the family. Yes, many ghosts had been laid to rest. Then, on her journey home, a ghost from her past had suddenly sprung out of nowhere. The train had halted at a junction, it was a fairly long halt. She had been looking idly out of the window when she had seen the man. Gaunt, grey, his body skeletal and emaciated, he looked like a very old man; but she recognized him immediately. It had been a tremendous shock; her body had immediately reacted with an involuntary shudder. When she saw the boy with him, her heart began lurching in her breast. No, not a boy, a young man. She knew his age to the minute, she had often counted the years, knowing that they were piling up, yet unable to realize that they were turning him from an infant into a child and then a boy; for her, he had remained a baby. Now, here he was, a young man. They look like gods at that age: Belinda's words came into her mind. Like a god, like a god. He was smiling affectionately at the man, his father. When the whistle went, he put his hand on the man's shoulder, said something to him, then raced through the crowd with the easy grace of the young. She followed him with her eyes as long as she could see him. Even after she lost him, she could still see him in the man's face, in his eyes, his upraised hand. The father's hand finally came down and she knew he must have got into his compartment. The train began to move.

Thank god, she thought, it's not a corridor train; otherwise she would have walked through the entire train, calling out his name. And what then? What would she have done when she found him? Would she have said, I'm your mother, I'm the woman who abandoned you when you were not even a year old? What would he say to that? I don't know you? Or would he just turn away in disgust and contempt? What had he been told about her? She has been thinking of him almost constantly since then, questions thronging her mind. How could I have left him with those two—that silent helpless woman and her cruel son? Why didn't I take him with me? What was I thinking, abandoning my son? And why did I give him up so easily later, losing him as the price of my divorce? She often thinks: he is in this city, we are inhabiting the same space, I might meet him somewhere, we might pass each other in a street, or meet in a shop or in a coffee place. Wherever we meet, I will know him at once. What will I say then? Don't you know me, we met once? Perhaps that is better than saying I'm your mother. Yes, that's what I will say. Don't you remember, we met once? But where? When? It is hard to think of him as a young man. Hard to imagine that the baby she had left behind had metamorphosed into a young man who ran with such easy grace. A young god. She often goes back to that brief moment, goes to it over and over again, each time seeing him put his hand on his father's shoulder, then beginning to run, shrugging to keep his backpack securely in place. After years of trying to forget that she had a son, she now wants to talk about him, she wants to say his name over and over again. Krishna, Krishna. It was like the time she had been in love with Neel; she had had, she remembers, a constant desire to talk about him, to say his name. The brief glimpse she has had of her son has whetted her appetite, controlled so rigorously for years, and she wants to see him *now,* to be with him, to have him as part of her life.

Mira, she thinks, I will go to Mira and speak to her. But she remembers that Mira is having her annual check-up the next day. It is now five years since her surgery. If all goes well we can breathe easier, push fear a little further away. But can Mira ever do that? She told Kasturi once that she is afraid of rejoicing, of proclaiming happiness. For, if you do, Mira said, there's someone waiting to pounce on you, someone who will say, 'Aha! Got you. So you thought you were going to be happy, were you?'

No, she cannot talk to Mira. Yet she has to go to Mira's house tomorrow, to give Belinda company, Belinda who has come because she couldn't bear to be sitting by the phone in Bombay. She can't bear to stay alone in Mira's home, either, waiting for Ranjan to ring her up. Come and be with me, Sonu, she had asked, come and hold my hand. Kasturi had agreed. She has to go and be with Belinda, to see her suffer yet again for her daughter. She remembers being with Belinda during Mira's surgery. While Mira was being operated on, she had seen Belinda put her face in her hands, as if she was praying. Looking down at Belinda's thinning grey hair through which the scalp showed, Kasturi had been full of pity. How long would she go on suffering for her children? As long as she lived? Or until age pushed her into the twilight world of dementia? She had put her hand on Belinda's shoulder. Belinda had looked up.

'Praying?'

'I don't know whom to pray to, Sonu. Or how to speak to god. I don't have the words. If I had, I would have asked him to take me instead of my child. I've lived my life, I can go easily. But life is not something to bargain for, it's not something to barter in the market, is it, Sonu?'

A little later she had referred to the book on her lap, a biography of Jane Austen which Maggie had given her. 'Do you know her mother lived many years after her death? We women are terrible. Husbands die, children go away and we go on living. But to see your child go first, that is cruel, that is the cruelest thing.'

She had not argued with Belinda then. Even now, she will not argue about that. But there is another kind of cruelty, Belinda, that you know nothing about; it is to lose your son even when he is alive. She would not speak of this to Belinda, though. She would go to her the next day, she would hold Belinda's hand, and if she could not pray, she would say all the mantras she knew. Or, maybe, she could says god's name over and over again. Hare Ram, Hare Ram, Ram Ram Hare Hare, Hare Krishna, Hare Krishna, Krishna Krishna Hare Hare.

Krishna. I named him Krishna. I told the old woman I wanted him to be named Krishna. I had thought of Neel when I said that. I tried to fool myself that this was the baby Neel and I should have had. Would have had, if not for our amazing bad luck. I was surprised that they did name him Krishna. But after all, it is a god's name. And perhaps the old woman told her son that the name was her own idea. Krishna. She herself had loved Krishna's different names, such sweet names she had thought them, all of them—Ghanshyam, Govind, Goverdhan, Mukund, Achyut, Gopal . . . Gopal . . .

Gopal, yes, I can talk to Gopal. I will talk to him, I will talk to him of my son. But not now, not at this time.

Gopal

When Aru told me that Rohit and she had decided to adopt a child, I rejoiced for them. My joy was greater because Aru gave me the news herself, something I would never have expected. I lost her trust long back. I lost it in a moment. I don't know how long it will take me to regain it, or if I can ever regain it at all. Charu has given me back her trust, though at times I sense some withholding. But she conceals it, she conceals it well; Charu was always better at hiding her feelings than Aru. And she was closer to her mother, which is why I hurt her less. Sumi mattered more to her. I think of her holding Sumi round the waist, looking at me belligerently, challengingly, saying, '*My* Sumi.' And Aru watching, silent, knowing she and I were partners, never threatened by Charu's declaration of an alliance with her mother.

Perhaps, in telling me about their decision, Aru was taking the first step towards me. I should have responded; but I was so overcome that I failed to tell her how glad I was. I think I was too curt and dry in my response. I could have spoken more, I should have asked her—boy or girl? I could have spoken of what the news meant to me, of how glad I was for them. And when words fail, there is the miraculous communication of touch which Kalyani was so good at. I remember her in the hospital, trying to convey something to a nurse in her inadequate English, and the nurse, whose English did not extend beyond medical and nursing terms, looking baffled. Kalyani had then taken both the girl's hands in hers and patted them, smiling at her, and the girl had immediately smiled too, a radiant smile; she had understood that Kalyani was praising her. The miracle of touch, indeed. Yes, I could have hugged Aru, at least put my hand on her back, on her head. I could even have gone back to her childhood and held my palm high for her to clap with hers. Hi fi, Aru used to call it. Let's do hi fi, she used to say. I did none of these things.

After Sumi's death, I had agonized over whether I should have told Aru what really happened, why I got to the stage where I had to get away from my family. But I did not speak, it seemed the wrong time to try and explain, to exculpate myself. And so the moment passed; no, in truth, I let it pass. The huge dark cloud of Sumi's death darkened our lives, nothing could make things better. Later, too, it never seemed to be the right time. How could I speak to her after so long and tell her that I left not only because I had been beaten up by the goons sent to attack me, but because I had so abjectly given in to the demands made of me. Withdraw your article, they said. Make a public apology, they demanded. Confess that you were wrong. I did all these things. In fact, when they asked me to bend, I crawled. Sumi pleaded with me, she thought I was wrong, she thought I should have stood up against the men. But I was adamant. If you believe in what you have written, Sumi said, don't give in. I *had* believed in it. I remember how excited I had been about my discovery of an amazing similarity between some anonymous erotic poems and the devotional poetry of a saint poet who belonged to the same period. I thought it fascinating that a man who had written such sensual poetry had been able to transform the love of women so seamlessly into love of god. He praised god in almost the same words, in the same way that he had praised a woman, he submitted himself as completely to the love of a woman, as he did to the love of god.

My article appeared in a very obscure journal of history. I thought no one would read it, though I hoped some scholars would take note of it. I had forgotten something—that the saint-poet who had fought against the caste system and had dreamt of a democratic religion, had himself, ironically, become the founder of a new caste. One that is now politically powerful. And so I was attacked. How dared I say that the saint had written erotic poetry? They had not only beaten me, they had threatened my family. We know you have a wife and three daughters, they had warned me. Remember that.

I did all that they wanted me to; I even resigned from my post in the university. I still think I did right. I had no right to sacrifice my family for any principles. I did not want to speak of these things to Sumi—or to anyone else. I did not want to argue, to be told that I should not give in. I wanted my family to be safe. And yet, at times, I asked myself—what did I achieve? I lost my family anyway. Sumi died, that has been my greatest grief. But there is a finality about death, we can do no more than accept that finality. But Aru—yes I regret my alienation from Aru. For the first time, I am hopeful that some day Aru and I will no longer have this wall of hostility between us. She is changing. Yes, changes are coming. Seema will soon be leaving home. I will miss her greatly. I still find it amazing that Seema has become what she is today. I wish Sumi was here to see what Seema has made of herself. We had worried about her, often wondered what would happen to her. I can remember the day Seema came to me in the room I had been staying in since I had walked out of my home. She came alone. Or so I thought, until she told me that Sumi was waiting for her downstairs. Seema had not come to see me until then. When I saw her, I felt a pang. She looked such a child, so defenceless. The first thing she told me was that she had 'grown up'. She was—how old? thirteen?—so it should not have been a surprise. But it was; I could never think of Seema as anything but a child, a helpless vulnerable child at that. At that moment, when she told me what had happened to her, I felt that suddenly a curtain had come between me and her, the veil of her femaleness. I suppose it happens to all fathers.

But she had come not only to tell me about her 'growing up', she had come to ask the question all of them had asked me: why had I gone away from them? She asked me bluntly, directly and somehow it was possible for me to answer her simply and in a straightforward manner. I held her hands and spoke to her as I had not been able to speak to any of the others—Sumi, Kalyani, Aru, Ramesh. I told her that I did not know why I had to go away. That it was a kind of illness and I felt I could do them no good by being with them. I could do no one any good until I was able to heal myself.

'So you will come back?' she had asked.

I had hesitated and said, 'Yes, if you need me. When you need me.'

I had no idea then that this would happen so soon, that Sumi would die leaving our daughters motherless. But I did not go back then. I returned only when Kalyani knew she was dying and asked me to return. I have been living with Seema since then. I have often told myself that I am waiting for the time when she no longer needs me, so that I can go back to the place in the mountains which had become home to me in the years I was there. Has that time come? No, I think I have to be here for some more time for Seema, so that she does not chink she has lost her home. And there is Aru, I want to see her baby, I want to see her as a mother, see her and Rohit as parents.

Are these excuses? Am I afraid that when I go back, I will not find what I had once found, am I afraid I will be (disappointed, disenchanted? And if I lose my dream, what then? Kasturi, when I once asked her whether she was homesick for Jogipura, had said—words I have never forgotten—'Home is not always a place, is it? It can be a time, it can be people.' Kasturi. Yes, Kasturi. Is it also because of Kasturi that I am reluctant to go away from here?

Kasturi and I have been meeting almost every day, I have got used to sharing my thoughts with her. I missed her enormously when she went to Jogipura, I was eager for her return, eager to see her, to hear from her about her visit. It was to have been a reconciliatory visit, she was getting back with her brother and his family. But when we met, she spoke very little of her visit, or of her family; she was withdrawn, listless, she answered my questions almost with disinterest. When she spoke, it was of Jogipura, of how much it had changed, of how easily people now went out of the place, of how the world had entered it through TV, so that people were much more knowing, much less ignorant of the world than they had been earlier. Listening to her was like reading a report by a journalist, or hearing a commentator on TV. Only my questions about the political scene roused her a little from her own thoughts, whatever they were. She said Ibrahimkaka had thrown cold water on Shalini's plans of Kasturi entering politics and becoming to the place what her father had been.

'Who will vote for you, Sonu?' he had asked.

'Other women.'

'You're fooling yourself. Men have cleverly turned women against other women. They will vote for whomever their husbands tell them to vote for.'

Kasturi told me that she had thought it over and realized that perhaps he was right. But that did not mean they should give in. On the contrary, 'I told Shalini we should give up her petty dream of reviving the family glory, that instead we should do something about what Ibrahimkaka said. Wake up the women.'

Shalini, reluctant at first to give up her plans, had finally agreed and they had decided they would start meetings of small groups of women. 'Go slowly,' Ibrahimkaka, the wily politician had warned them. 'Otherwise you might scare the women away, you might make the men feel threatened.'

Kasturi told me they had held one meeting when she was there.

'How did it go?'

'Oh, very well. I enjoyed it very much.' She hesitated, then confessed, a little shamefacedly, that being in a crowd, communicating with them, gives her a high. It excites her, she said. I laughed. 'Then perhaps politics is the right line for you.'

Kasturi seemed like her old self when she told me these things and I was somewhat relieved. Perhaps there was nothing wrong, just the turmoil that came from revisiting the home she had left years back. Before we parted she told me that she was to spend the next day with her friend Mira's mother while Mira went for her annual check-up.

I had given up hope of meeting her, but I see her as soon as I get out of my house after dinner. She has just come out of her door, like I have. We smile at each other.

'All well?' I ask.

'Yes, thank god, all well. I was just coming to see you.'

'Come in, then.'

'No, let's go out of the house. I need to go out, I have been sitting indoors all day.'

I take her to the seat by the old well, a stone seat that has been there since the house was first constructed. Both Sumi and Premi had made this place their own. I often saw Sumi sitting here, reading, her legs drawn up under her, wholly absorbed in the book. And Premi, doing nothing, looking as if she was hiding from someone. The place is always cool, shaded as it is by the mango tree. Today there is a breeze and Kasturi pulls her sari about her shoulders as if she is feeling chilly.

Suddenly, on an impulse, I tell her about Aru and Rohit's adoption plan. 'I know,' she says. 'Nagi told me. I am very glad for them.' And immediately after she says, 'I want to talk to you, Gopala, I want to tell you about my son.'

She has spoken to me of her parents, of her brother and his family. But a son? I look at her and she adds, as if replying to the question she *sees* on my face, 'I was married.'

She tells me of her disastrous marriage, which she had been hustled into by her father and brother after her mother's death. She does not tell me why she, her father's daughter, an educated and independent-minded young woman, had to marry a man she did not know and had never met. But she said they promised her he was a 'good man'—as all prospective grooms in an arranged marriage invariably are. He was an engineer working for the government in the irrigation department. He had no dependents, they said, except a widowed mother. That was all. And they somehow persuaded her (or forced her?) into the marriage.

'I was in no state to think then, I was in a bad state. But I knew this marriage was wrong. Though I never knew it would be such a terrible mistake. A terrible mistake,' she repeats.

I listen to her, not interrupting her, not even to ask her why she put up with the violence as long as she did. It seems incredible, seeing the kind of person she is, but I am sure she had her own reasons, compelling reasons. I listen in total silence, trying not to show any reaction. But the entire horror of her marriage, of its cruelty, hits me when she says, 'He never used any weapon on me, no, he never used a stick or a belt; he liked to use his hands on me. I think it gave him pleasure to feel my body under his hands, he liked to feel it cringe, to feel it suffer the pain.'

I am amazed that she can speak of it in such a detached manner. 'I've travelled a long way since it happened, Gopal,' she says in reply to my question. 'I may not have gone to the Himalayas on a yatra,' she smiles at me when she says this, as if telling me she is not disparaging what I had done, 'but mine has been an equally long and hard journey.' Listening to her, I know that she is talking of something that has become the distant past to her, that the man no longer matters to her. 'I want to talk to you about my son,' she said to me. It is her son who matters.

They were divorced some time after she left the man, she tells me. Her brother, who negotiated the divorce, told her that she had to agree to give the father custody of the child; the man had threatened them that if she didn't agree, he would make trouble for them, that he would bring up some ugly facts that would hurt her family, specially her father.

'It was election year, they told me it would harm my father's election chances, slim enough because of the Emergency. So I gave up my son, I lost him forever. Ultimately it was of no use, because my father lost the elections, he lost not only the seat he had held for years, he lost his party post, he lost everything. He died soon after. And I lost all the years I could have had with my son.'

She pauses, then tells me that she saw her son by chance on her way back from Jogipura. She now knows, Ibrahimkaka has found this out for her, that he is a software engineer working in this city, that his father is very ill, he has cancer.

'I keep thinking, Gopala, my Krishna is here, in this city, we are living in the same place. So what if it is a big city, there's always a chance that I might meet him somewhere. I want my son, Gopala,' she exclaims passionately. 'They say you need a son to take you to the other world. I don't want him to take me to the other world, I don't want him to light my pyre; I want him now. Here. I want him to be part of my life, I want to take him for granted like mothers do their children, I want to scold him, to pamper him, to laugh with him, to comfort him when he is unhappy. I want him, Gopala, I want him.'

I say nothing for a moment. Then I ask, 'Does he know about you?'

'I don't know. I don't know what that man told him about me, whether he told him anything at all. But I want to tell him I am his mother, I want him to know why I left his father.'

'His father is the only parent he knows, Kasturi, his father is dying. Perhaps, he loves his father.'

Kasturi reluctantly admits that the brief glimpse she had of the two of them on the railway platform showed that he did love his father. 'I was so afraid he would take out his anger against me on my child, but I think it did not happen.'

'There you are then. If you take away his father from him, you will have left your son with nothing. He may never forgive you.'

'He will have me, his mother.'

'Children can be very unforgiving, Kasturi, they can be very cruel, they judge you harshly.'

I know, even as I say this, that I am speaking of Aru and that I am being unfair to her. Aru is not cruel. And if she is unforgiving, it is only because she loved me, she expected too much of me, she didn't realize that I was, after all, just another flawed human.

'Don't I know that? I did it to my father,' Kasturi says. 'And my mother—I was so uncaring of her sufferings. But I will take my chance, Gopala. I have to try to get him back in my life, I can't stay this way any more.'

At this she begins to sob, the harsh staccato sobs of one who does not cry very easily. I let her cry for some time. When she has wiped her tears with her sari, I put my finger, as I have often wanted to do, as I have often imagined myself doing, in the pit in her cheek. She looks at me, startled, and I think she is offended. But, after a moment, she smiles. When I take my hand away, she holds it in both of hers for a moment before letting it go. She says, 'It is late, let us go in.'

We part at our respective doors. She goes in without a word. I wonder if I had said, 'Don't go, come into my house with me,' would she have come? It is so long since I held a woman's body in my arms. Today, I felt a response in her to my touch and I know we can find that joy in each other. But not today, not now. We have to wait. At this moment she is thinking of her son, she can think of nothing but her son. Besides, the blood no longer races in our bodies, pushing us into an instant and impetuous mating. Nor do I want a mechanical coupling with her. No, not now. Some day, some time, perhaps. We have much to resolve within ourselves, with each other, with our children, my daughters and her son, before that happens.

Yet, when I go to bed, I think that by speaking to me of her son, she has deliberately and knowingly crossed a line in our relationship. I feel comforted, after years I feel I am not alone.

Kalyani had her own calendar, one in which time was divided by the seasons, marked by the festivals, each festival linked to a season, to the flowers and fruits that grew at the time. Aru, who had thought this merely one more of Kalyani's idiosyncrasies, now finds it a fascinating tapestry of Time, providing another story, an entirely different concept of Time. So unlike her own humdrum monotonous succession of days, each day like another, nothing marking it out as different. Recently, she has begun watching a different measurement of time in Nagma's body, in the way the contours of her body change as the baby grows within her. She notices how Nagma delicately balances her body, guarding the baby from any impact. Nine months of this, finally arriving at ripeness, at fruition. There is a fierce pang of regret in Aru that she will never know this, that she has been denied it. Without her body participating in the rites of passage, it seems hard to grasp the fact that Time will bring her and Rohit the gift of a baby, *their* baby, hard for her to believe in the reality of the baby.

It is a time of confusion for Aru altogether. Seema's departure is looming over them. Seema herself seems to have suddenly realized that she will be leaving home and it has affected her poise. After a long time, she has become irritable, often on the edge of anger for no discernible reason. Leo comes to Aru in distress, telling her that Seema and he have had a spat. Aru has noticed that Leo is much less with Seema these days. In fact, Nikhil and she are more often together. And, to Aru's surprise, Nikhil, very unusually for him, goes straight to Seema, bypassing

Aru, greeting her with a very casual 'Hi, Arutai,' whenever he sees her. She is puzzled, but she decides not to ask him or Seema any questions. Leo, however, tells her about his quarrel with Seema in great detail. When he had asked her why she was avoiding him, Seema had accused him of being jealous—not only of her spending time with others, but also of her success.

'Me! Jealous of Seema! Tell me, Aru, you know me so well, do you think I would be jealous? And of Seema? I have worked more for her than she ever did for herself, I have always been more ambitious for her. When she signed this contract nobody could have been happier than me.'

Aru and Leo are old friends, she has known him almost as long as Seema has. His association with the family began when he took pictures of Seema for Devaki's calendar; it was strengthened when he became the unofficial photographer for Charu's wedding. When she saw his wedding pictures, Aru learnt to respect him and his work. Fashion photographer though he was, his pictures were never flat; there was always a different vision, something a perceptive viewer could never escape. One of her favourites is a picture of the three of them taken by Leo during Charu's wedding, in which Leo has somehow captured the individuality of each one of them, as well as their togetherness. Yes, Leo is a good friend. But now she has a sudden desire to snap at him, to say, 'Oh, sort it out yourself, why do you involve me in your spats? I'm not in charge of everyone's life!'

However, she restrains herself, she soothes Leo's feelings, telling him that surely he should understand that Seema is tense about the coming changes in her life. Which is true. Seema has been spending more time with Aru as if needing reassurance.

'Can I sleep here tonight?' she asks Aru at night.

'Of course.'

Aru sits with her for a while before going to bed. They ring up Charu and Seema chats with Charu, something she rarely does. Just as Aru gets up to switch off the light, Seema suddenly says, 'I don't want to go on with modeling for too long. I want to save money and start a place—not exactly a gym or a salon, but something which combines these things.' Even as Aru takes in this astonishing statement, Seema turns on her side and says, 'Switch off the light, Aru. And good night,' making it clear that the conversation is over. Aru goes to her room thinking, I've been anxious about Seema, concerned about her future. And here she is, sure of what she wants, her plans already made. Have we, have I, been needlessly worrying about Seema?

She thinks, for some reason, of Yamunabai, Kalyani's mother's teacher, the child widow who started a class for girls in a cowshed, trying to stimulate their minds, to give them some understanding of their bodies. And now there is Seema, who has learnt to understand her body and has used it to enter the world of money and glamour. Indeed, women have travelled a long way. She wonders whether she should tell Seema about Yamunabai, but Seema, like Charu, is not interested in the past. Perhaps they are wiser, my sisters, she thinks, better to leave the past behind.

As if she has come to know of Aru's anxieties, Kasturi speaks to her and tries to reassure her. She tells her that Delia, Maggie's mother, has promised to keep an eye on Seema. 'Delia is a very kind woman, I've known her since I was a child.'

Aru accepts her reassurance a little awkwardly, thinking Kasturi herself is a kind woman, why did I never realize that? She tries to put her anxieties about Seema away, to get back to her work. She is grateful that work is being piled on her. Apart from her own cases, Surekha has asked her to prepare for an important constitutional case that is to come up soon. Normally Nagma would have worked up the case, but now, because of her pregnancy, Surekha is careful not to overburden her. Surekha seems to be in a great hurry about this case, hustling Aru as she rarely does.

In the midst of all the toil and turmoil, Surekha's annual party comes as a welcome diversion. Nagma and Aru always receive a formal invitation for the Big Bash, as they call it, from Jaisimha. ('If I leave it to my wife, she'll say, come if you are free and she will forget to tell you the date and the time.') Jaisimha is very precise—the day, date, time, everything is given to them, as also a reminder that the invitation is for their spouses as well. As if, they laugh, they had thought the invitation was only for them!

It's almost the same crowd every year: some lawyers, a few bureaucrat colleagues of Jaisimha's, a smattering of personal friends. Jaisimha is an excellent host, refreshing people's drinks, making sure no one feels left out. Although Surekha's office and home are in the same compound, they are generally kept scrupulously apart. None of them ever enter her home, except Mangala, who goes to collect the keys in the morning and to return them in the evening. Aru had been there once, long back, when she had gone to Surekha for advice and help. She remembers how surprised she had been to see the house. She had imagined rich people (she had thought, naively, that people who had two cars had to be rich!) lived differently. Not like this! The curtains and cushions were faded and dull, the furniture old and a little shabby. Now, years later, the house looks exactly the same, as if it had, at some time, achieved a kind of poise. But Aru no longer finds the house shabby. She sees how comfortable it is, how unpretentious and how well it echoes the personalities of the two people who live in it—there are books everywhere, stacked in piles, a music system, a large rack of music CDs. But, unlike in most homes, there are no pictures, no family photos, no individual pictures, no, not a single one.

It has, unusually for the time, drizzled earlier and the doors of the living room have been kept open to catch the cool breeze, mosquito repellants plugged in as safety measures. The guests wander in and out of the room, many preferring to be out on the patio. Conversation moves along the usual lines: the changing climate of the city, the paucity of rains, the greater heat, the frenzied building activity, the traffic, the number of cars. The words, 'I remember a time when . . .' are frequently repeated, almost like a refrain, by people who are above fifty. Aru and Rohit smile at each other when they hear the remark, smiling at the predictability of humans. Inevitably the talk moves to development and conservation and, since Jaisimha, like Rohit, is passionate about the preservation of old buildings, he brings Rohit's project into the conversation. Aru listens to Rohit telling them about the old bungalow, noticing how different he is here, carefully keeping out the ardour which had infused his talk when he had spoken to her about it. He tells them about the stables. 'The man so loved horses, they say the stables were as good, if not better than the house,' he says and everyone laughs.

'We must have a look at them,' someone says.

'They're no longer there. Destroyed, unfortunately.'

'Like so many beautiful things. I always think it's a great pity Aru's family home was demolished. It was a wonderful specimen of its time.'

'Not guilty, sir. I had nothing to do with it. It was Aru's grandmother's decision.'

'But I'm glad it's gone. It was so inconvenient. All those huge doors and windows, the high walls. How do you clean them? And the kitchen—I don't know how my poor grandmother managed to work in it for so many years. You had to walk miles to cook a meal.'

'All for modernisation, eh, Aru?'

'No, sir, I'm all for making women's lives easier.'

'No argument about that. What do you say, Rohit?'

'None at all, sir.' Surekha now calls out to Aru. 'Come and meet Raghavan.'

Aru has heard of Raghavan, a rising star at the bar. She had imagined him to be a young man, he was spoken of as one. Instead, there's this portly man in his late forties, looking older because of his grey hair. His heavy features and thatch of thick wavy hair give him the look of a Roman senator.

'Glad to meet you,' he says to Aru. 'I was just telling Mrs Nagma *(Mrs* Nagma?) that I was looking forward to meeting the two of you. Good to know that we have two fine young women lawyers among us.'

The two women look at each other now. Women lawyers? Nagma signals to Aru with her raised eyebrows. What does he mean?

Aru's eyes, in turn, ask: Is he patronizing us?

Surekha catches their silent exchange and glances at them reprovingly, with a frown so small that it is just a ripple.

'And this is Hema,' she says to Aru.

'My wife,' Raghavan adds.

'I'm not a lawyer, I'm only a housewife,' the woman says with a nervous laugh, a sentence she obviously says very often. Why only a housewife Aru thinks, irritated, as she always is, by the phrase.

As if he has caught her thought, Raghavan says, 'We have two sons, twelve and fourteen. You can imagine how much work being *only a housewife* involves.'

'And how many children do you have?' the woman immediately asks, her question wavering between Nagma and Aru.

'One,' Nagma quickly replies.

'And one more soon?'

'Yes, ma'am.'

'And you?' She turns to Aru.

It is Surekha who fields the question. 'She's also going to have a baby very soon.'

The woman looks at Aru's figure with slight bewilderment.

'I've been talking to Raghavan about Ramu's problems,' Surekha says, getting away from the fraught topic of Aru's baby.

'Poor girl. I used to hear her voice on the phone. Such a happy voice.'

Aru is surprised by his perspicacity, she hadn't expected it.

'And now I hear the child's uncle is threatening to take the child away. I am glad the three of you are with the father.'

'He's terrified by the threat.'

'Obviously. It's his child. If anyone threatened to take my child away from me, I know I would be terrified. But I would fight back,' he says pugnaciously.

'A plague on both their houses,' Surekha suddenly exclaims.

'Plague?' Hema looks at her, confused, slightly alarmed.

'Hema, ma'am is quoting. Shakespeare, if I'm not mistaken? Am I right, ma'am? *Romeo and Juliet?*'

'On the spot, Raghavan,' Surekha says with her rare large grin. Why is she so pleased, Aru wonders. But his gentleness with his wife and his knowledge of Shakespeare have made Aru like him better. What difference does it make anyway, she asks herself.

The next day she realizes it does. Aru and Nagma are ready to leave Surekha's office at the end of a meeting when she says, 'One more thing. What did you both think of Raghavan?'

They are taken aback and look at each other. What do they think of Raghavan? *Why* should they think of Raghavan?

'That was stupid of me,' Surekha says, in response to their silence. 'What can you say after meeting him for a few minutes? But I must tell you I am thinking of asking him to work with us, to share some of my cases.' She senses their doubts. 'Don't worry, it won't make any difference to you. It's only that I have to be prepared for the fact that both of you will be taking leave some time now. And, I most sincerely hope, not at the same time.'

'We'll try our level best, ma'am,' Nagma says, with a bordering-on-the-cheeky smile.

'Ha! As if it is in your hands. Any news from the adoption agency, Aru?'

'No, ma'am, not as yet.'

'All the preliminaries over?'

'Yes, ma am.'

'Would you like me to talk to them?'

'No, ma'am, it's all right. I'm sure they'll get back to us when there's any news.'

'All right. Anyway, about Raghavan—he will work with me on some of the constitutional cases. He's good at his work, he's easy to get on with—a little too anxious about money, he's ambitious for his sons, I expect. But he knows me, he won't push too hard here. I hope the two of you will get on with him.'

'Yes, ma'am.'

'There's still time, I wanted you to get used to the idea.'

'Yes, ma'am.'

'And no smiles, please, if he calls you *Mrs* Aru or *Mrs* Nagma. That's just his style. Trying to show you respect.'

'We promise, ma'am.'

Surekha hesitates, she looks as if she has something more to say. They wait for it. After a moment, she says, 'That's all.' And then, suddenly, she calls Aru back. 'I have something to say to you, Aru. It's about Ramu.'

He is thinking about looking for a job in the Middle East. 'He wants to earn more money, he says, so that he can send Gracy to a boarding school. But that can only happen when she is a little older. In the meantime, he's also been thinking about the compensation he's getting for Tressa's death. He wants it to be kept exclusively for Gracy and asked me how to do it. I've given him some options. He now says he wants you and me to be in control of the money until she is twenty-one. Just the two of us, even he can't touch the money. He thinks this is the safest way. I said I have no problem, except that I'd have been happier if he'd had someone younger, someone who'll be around when Gracy is twenty-one. Anyway, we can do something about that. Add Nagma's name, perhaps. Okay with you, Aru?'

'Yes, ma'am, I have no problems, I'm okay with it.'

'Good, I'll tell him that. But have a talk with our accountant first, will you? And then I want you to draw up the papers. Oh yes, there's another thing. If he goes out of the country for a job, he wants you to become Gracy's local guardian.'

'Me? Why me, ma'am?'

'I think his idea is that Tressa's family won't try to tangle with a lawyer. And perhaps he hopes Gracy can come to you during vacations.'

'What about his mother?'

'Surprisingly, she has agreed. I think she too wants to keep Tressa's family away. But these are far-off contingencies. Ramu may never go abroad, right now his mother seems to have settled down here. I have a suspicion he's placated her with a promise to get married in a while. So who knows? He may get married.'

'Did you tell him, ma'am, about our plans?'

'That you are adopting a baby? Yes, I have.'

When she goes back to her table, Aru thinks of Gracy. Of Ramu, Tressa and Gracy. Man, woman and child. The basic unit of life. How simple and clear the future must have seemed to them. It was not an easy life, both Ramu and Tressa working hard, struggling to educate their child, planning for the child to come. ('Gracy wants a brother, she will get a brother') But a good life, nevertheless, the three of them a self-contained unit, sufficient for themselves. And now Ramu needs his parents, he needs Surekha and me, he needs paid help as well to do what Tressa and he had so effortlessly and lovingly done. What about us? How will we manage, Rohit and I? We are lucky, we have Rohit's mother, there's Premimavshi and Devimavshi and yes, Papa. Nevertheless . . .

She picks up the phone and rings up the adoption agency. Rohit had told her a few days back that he had called them and they had said there was no news as yet. But no harm in ringing again.

'Hello . . .'

When the conversation is over, she puts down the phone slowly and sits still for a long time. Then she brings out her mobile to call Rohit, but decides not to. I will wait until evening, she thinks, I will wait for him to get home. When Rohit returns, the house is in darkness. He calls out tentatively for Aru, switching on the lights as he walks through the house. He finally finds her in the enclosed veranda outside their bedroom. He is startled.

'Aru, why are you sitting in the dark?'

'Why did you reject a baby?'

After a moment's pause he asks, 'You know?' She is silent. 'It was stupid of me, I should have told you.'

'You should have *asked* me before rejecting a baby.'

'I did this for a reason, Aru.'

'I don't care what your reasons are. How could you . . .?'

'You must listen to me.'

But she is in no mood to listen. She tells him what the woman at the agency said. 'She said we are not fit to be parents if we reject a child who's a little sick.'

'A little sick? She's a very sick baby, Aru. She's not going to survive.'

'How can you be so sure?'

'I had her examined.'

'You showed her to a doctor? All this and without a word to me? I can't believe you could have done such a thing.'

'What if we brought her home and she died? We're adopting a baby to live with us, not to die on us.'

'The woman, Ratna, she said we would have had time to decide until the legal process was complete.'

'And do you think that because the adoption process was not complete, it would have been easy for us to watch her die? Could you have borne that, Aru? Could you?'

She refuses to accept what he's saying. He's insulted her, she says, by taking a decision without consulting her. He can shake her for being so obtuse. 'I admit I was wrong. But I knew you would find the decision hard. I wanted to spare you that. And how could that stupid woman say we are not fit to be parents? I'm going to complain about that, about her.'

'She also told me we go lower down on the list because of this refusal.'

'Just let her try to do that.'

'But she's right.'

'No, she's not. If she's so insensitive, she shouldn't be working in an adoption agency.'

'And if we are so selfish, we shouldn't be adopting.'

'Okay, tell me, Aru, what do you want me to do? Do you want me to grovel at her feet, say I'm sorry, beg for another chance?'

'It's too late.'

There's a long silence. Rohit is the first to break it. 'Aru, you have to accept the fact that you will always matter more to me than anyone else. Even more than our child. When we have one. If we have one. Just as I have accepted that I don't come first in your life. Your sisters mean more to you than I do.'

That's not true,' she retorts, stung by the accusation.

'Ask yourself how much time we've spent together in the last month.'

'We're both too busy

'No, we are not. You may not know or care, but 1 do. I grudge every moment, every single minute I don't get with you. But I don't hold it against you. I knew when I married you what my place in your life was. I will live with it. But I want you to accept that I did what I did because I care about you. Because I don't want you to suffer.'

He walks away, as he always does after a quarrel. But this is not like their other quarrels. Both of them are too sore to think of a reconciliation. The next morning Rohit leaves home early, even before she wakes up. There's a stab of fear in her when she sees his bed so neatly made, as if he hasn't slept in it at all, as if he has been away all night. It reminds her of her parents' bed the day Gopal left them, of her sudden panic when she went into their room and found both of them not there, the bed clearly not slept in. Rohit will call me, she comforts herself, knowing that he never lets the day end without talking to her. But there's no call. She tries to get involved in her work, though part of her keeps waiting for his call. When she gets home in the evening, he's still not home. Now she begins to panic. For the first time she thinks of his words, 'You will always matter more to me than anyone else.'

Though he had tried hard at first to control his feelings, presenting her with a bland pleasant self, she's always been aware of the strength of his feelings for her. Soon after marriage they had lived in a small rented house, the front room becoming his office, the rest of the place their home. One day he had said to her, 'I can't work when you're so near, I can't bear not to be with you when I know you're so near. I have to hold tight to my chair to prevent myself from rushing to you.'

An unusually extravagant statement from Rohit, which had taken her by surprise, making her a little ashamed, because she knew it was not like that for her. She remembers talking to Kalyani about Rohit, about her inability to make up her mind about marrying him. Kalyani had asked, 'Is there anyone else, Aru?'

No, there was not. But she had often thought of the man who had suddenly materialized out of the rain like a phantom when she was lost and had led her to an area she was familiar with. The young man had become a figure of romance for the girl she was then. Time now, she thinks, to put away that phantom lover, time to think of what Rohit means to me, of what Rohit has become to me in the years since we married, how my life has become richer and fuller because of Rohit. Without him, she seems to be surrounded by a vast emptiness. She remembers Kalyani's words of reassurance to her on her wedding day. 'Go,' she said. 'Goda is with me.' Goda, her talisman, her shield, her lucky amulet. She was saying, as long as Goda is with me, I'm all right. All of us need our own talismans, our shields and if we are lucky we find them. I wanted to prove I'm strong, I wanted to stand alone; I fought, not against love but against becoming dependent on anyone. But does love have to mean dependency? And what if Rohit does not come back to me? He will, of course, he will, Rohit is not the kind of a man who will walk out on his wife. But Gopal left us, Gopal, who loved us so dearly. He shrugged us off as if we were something he was wearing, something loose and easy to take off.

Aru knows—who better?—how easily couples divorce and for what seem to be the flimsiest of excuses, often, for no more reason than that the couple can no longer live together. They realize they are incapable of living with each other for an entire lifetime as they had hoped, because they have come to know that they cannot give each other what they need, that, in fact, they have no idea of what the other needs and expects. Rohit's brother Rajiv and Uma lived together for less than six months. It had seemed like any other marriage, there was nothing to prepare the family for such an abrupt and complete break. Though Lalita had had her doubts, she had always thought Uma unattractive. Uma was painfully thin—an anoxeric, Aru had suspected, until she saw her eating four idlis straight off!—her collar bones standing out, the salt cellars painfully deep. But when they separated, Aru knew that their parting had nothing to do with her looks, or, as Rohit's parents secretly thought, with her different caste, or with Rajiv's own vacillatory nature. It was just that they found they could not live together as husband and wife. In truth, it's a miracle that so many marriages survive at all. Most of the time it's children, habit, and, to some extent, sex that holds couples together. And Rohit and I don't have that greatest adhesive, children.

The categories of cruelty are not closed. The words come back to her. Has she been cruel? She thinks of his eager expectant look when she comes to the bedroom, her work done. 'Come to bed, Aru,' he says.

'In a moment.' But then Seema comes in, or there's a call from Charu, or Premimavshi rings her. By the time she gets to bed, he's sleeping. Or seems to be.

She sits watching the hands of the clock move. She remembers Gopal saying to her and Charu when, as children, they had put off doing some task he had set them. 'We'll do it afterwards, Papa,' they would plead. 'Kelu,' he would say to that, his voice and face solemn, almost portentous, one finger raised in warning, 'Kelu, taasu baarisuttide.' It made them feel something frightening was coming and they would scamper away with scared faces to do what they had left undone.

'Why are you frightening my poor little babies?' Sumi had said once, laughing at them. 'Purandara Dasa meant it for sinners, not for these little innocents.'

Sumi was wrong. It's meant for all of us. Listen, the hour strikes. Time is passing. Ask yourself what you have done with your hours on earth. Ask yourself what you have not done.

She thinks of herself struggling with time, trying to cut it into slices, allotting so much to different people in her life. But that's not how it should be, not with Rohit. I have not been fair to Rohit, she thinks. I thought we had a sensible relationship, no problems, except this one of a child. But I left out the most important thing, I left out Rohit's expectations, I left out what he expected from me. I thought that whatever I was, whatever I gave him, was enough for him. How could I have been so smug, so satisfied with myself? She thinks of Surekha and Jaisimha, who seemed to her, who seem even now, almost an ideal couple. And yet Surekha had told her that when their only daughter died in an accident, they had been on the point of splitting. But that was so much more terrible, they lost their child. While I—I haven't even seen the baby who has come between us. Why was I so harsh with Rohit? Why did I never show him what I feel for him? I never told him, no, not once, that I love him. I never could say the words 'I love you'; they are said so often that they've become banal, emptied of meaning, of real feelings. And yet, perhaps, Rohit needed, perhaps he needs to hear them.

On a sudden impulse, Aru rings up Rohit. 'Rohit, where are you?'

'In Jimmy's house. We were working, it got late, so I thought I'd stay over tonight.'

'Rohit, come home. Please come home, Rohit.'

There is a long silence after which he says, 'I'll be home in half an hour,' and disconnects.

When he comes, she can't keep up a pose of composure, she does not want to. 'I'm sorry, Rohit, I'm very sorry, I overreacted.'

'Maybe I did too.' His tone is as weary as his face.

'I was frightened, Rohit, I thought you wouldn't come back.'

'Where would I go? Where would I go, Aru? I tried going away once, remember? But I came back, remember?'

He goes in to have a wash. 'Have you had dinner?' she asks. 'No? I'll get something for us.'

She forages in the fridge, finds some eggs, makes a large omelette, takes the food to the table and then calls him. He comes and sits at the table, waiting, for the first time in their life together, for her to serve him. They eat in silence, not a hostile silence, but a tired one. As if all has been said and there is nothing left to say. There is a kind of fragile peace between them. When she clears up and goes to bed, she sees he is lying awake. He does not look at her, but abruptly asks, repeating his earlier question. 'You remember I once tried to go away from you?'

'Yes.'

'Do you know why I decided to return?' He does not wait for her reply but goes on to tell her himself.

He had decided to forget her, he had tried to lose himself in what he was there for, what he was learning. He had gone through the winter, warmed and sustained by what he was learning, by the sights of the noble old buildings he had visited. But that too was over and there was nothing left for him. He knew he had to go back home, but he was finding it hard to take the decision. Weekends were the worst, everyone seemed to be relaxing, having fun, being with families, with lovers, while he . . . On one of those days, when a faint sun peeped through, promising the end of winter, he had gone out for a walk on the common. There were not too many people about, it was still cold, but a man briskly walking his dog had said to him, seeing him, perhaps, cowering miserably in his coat, 'Missing your warm country, are you?' And then he had added, 'It's almost spring. You'll enjoy the spring. It's even better than summer, I think.'

Rohit had looked about him. Yes, spring was on the way. Little green shoots were already showing their heads, ready to emerge. And suddenly the words of a poem he had learnt in school came to him.

'In the spring a young man's fancy lightly turns to thoughts of love.'

'And I thought of you Aru, I thought of the moment I had seen you and how you had got hold of my thoughts after that. Not light thoughts, no, not light at all. But I was not in your thoughts, no, not at all. And so I went away. Yet you were always with me, there was not a moment when you were not with me.'

And then, he goes on, he sat down on a bench, cheered by the man's smile and his words and saw a couple walking together, obviously in the midst of a heated argument. Suddenly the girl had begun running away from the boy. He pursued her, caught up with her, put his arm about her, while she resisted. She was struggling when an older woman came to them and said something sharply to the boy. Perhaps the way he was holding her and the girl's tears made her suspect the boy was being harsh with her. She put her arm round the girl and the two of them walked away. The boy ran after them, Rohit saw him speaking energetically, animatedly to the two women. Finally the older woman let go of the girl, stood for a moment between them and walked off. The boy and the girl had looked at each other, then came together and kissed.

'I knew then that I had to come back, I had to try for you again, because I could never get away from you. It was impossible. I wanted you. And so I came.'

Is this a declaration of love? Is he reiterating his love for her? Why, then, is his tone so puzzled, as if he is asking himself why things are the way they are, why he has to love her? But there is no doubt that his words of love are truly meant; she has to be content with that.

Aru is surprised when she gets a call from Swati. She has not seen her for a long time. Nikhil himself had brushed away Aru's questions about her so cursorily that Aru had thought their relationship, whatever it was, was over, like that of so many young people. Why, then, does she want to see Aru?

'I want to see you,' Swati says, her tone demanding, urgent.

'Come,' Aru says, wondering what the reason can be.

Within moments of her arrival, Aru realizes that whatever Nikhil's feelings are, Swati is still in thrall to Nikhil and she's come to talk about him. The girl tries to keep up a pretence of all being well, but clearly something is wrong. And yet she dithers. Finally, Aru has to prod her. 'Is there something you want to talk to me about?' she asks.

Then it pours out of her. It *is* about Nikhil, of course. He's broken up with Swati ever since she warned him against some students he's been getting friendly with. 'They're much older, they don't have a good reputation, Arutai, everyone knows about them.'

But Nikhil was furious with her. 'Don't try to tell me what I should do or not do,' he said to her. And when she persisted, he stopped talking to her. Now, when she tries to meet him, he evades her, when she sees him, he walks away from her. 'And,' she is sobbing now, her misery out in the open, 'he doesn't even come to classes these days. He tells me he doesn't want to see me, he says, stop chasing me, aren't you ashamed to come after me when I don't want to see you?'

She stops speaking and gives herself up to sobbing. Looking at her, a sodden mass of misery, Aru thinks of the glittering metallic carapace this girl presents to the world—T-shirts with shiny, cheeky messages, rough thick jeans and belts with large metal buckles, steel bracelets and long black metal earrings. And inside there's this soft vulnerable hurting human.

Aru listens to her as patiently as she can, she tries to tell her, when she is in a state to listen, to be patient, that Nikhil in such moods is best left alone; he hates being crowded, and when he is, he becomes as slithery as a snake. When what she really wants to say is, 'Stop loving him so much, stop caring for him. He'll only hurt you like he hurts his mother.'

She doesn't say this, of course. It's futile telling anyone not to love, as futile as it is to ask someone to love; Aru has learnt that both these are impossible. Why we love and why we can't love are both mysteries we will never be able to fathom.

'I love him, Arutai,' the girl says through her sobs. 'I don't want anything from him, I don't ask him for anything. I just want to be with him, I want him to let me be with him.'

Aru, who has begun feeling sorry for the girl, loses her patience with her. 'Have some pride, Swati,' she says.

'I don't have any pride. I only want Nikhil. Please talk to him. I know he will listen to you, he likes you. I used to be jealous of you,' she says, after blowing her nose, 'but I don't mind now. Please help me, Arutai, tell him I was speaking for his own good, I was not interfering. Last weekend he went out with those guys, everyone knows they take girls with them, they drink and . . . But I won't speak of them, I will never say anything about them, if only he talks to me.'

Aru wants to shake her, but controls herself, knowing that the girl is beyond reasoning. 'I'll try, Swati. I'll talk to him when he comes home. I won't ring him up, he doesn't like being pestered, you know how he cuts you off on the phone.'

The girl has to be satisfied with this. Nevertheless, Aru does ring up Nikhil; there's something in Swati's story that makes her uneasy. His phone is switched off. She thinks of calling Premi, but decides against it. If I tell her what Swati said, Premi will come here right away. And I may be alarming her needlessly. After all, it is only Swati's word, and she is a jealous and unhappy girl.

Premi does come, anyway, on a morning when neither Aru nor Rohit are at home. She rings up Aru to say she's just arrived, and is going out, that she will see them in the evening. When Aru gets home, Premi has not yet returned. She comes a little later, looking exhausted and spent. Aru gets her a cup of tea. After she has drunk it and had a wash, Aru asks, 'What is it, Premimavshi?'

It's Nikhil. But something very different from what Aru has imagined. Nikhil has withdrawn a large sum of money from his account. Premi came to know about this because she's a joint account holder. She had to come because she could not get Nikhil on the phone. She went to his room in the morning, he wasn't there. She left a message and hopes he will come.

'Aru, have you met him recently? Has he spoken to you?'

Aru tells her about Swati's visit, about what Swati had told her.

'Why didn't you let me know this, Aru?'

'I wanted to talk to him first. I don't want him to think I'm carrying tales; he will never talk to me if he thinks I discuss him with you.'

Premi waits for him, tense and silent. Aru has no hopes that he will come, but surprisingly he turns up. He's aggressive and defiant, trying to put his mother in the wrong.

'Have I no right to use the money from my own account? If I don't, just put me on the dole and send me what *you* think I should have every month.'

Aru, sensing a serious quarrel, tries to leave, but both of them stop her. 'Don't go, Aru,' Premi says. 'There's nothing you don't know. And I'm used to his insults, I'm immune now, I don't mind you hearing them.'

'Yes, stay, Arutai, stay here and see how I'm treated. They never think any good of me. They distrust me, they spy on me.'

'Spy?'

'What else is it? You keep checking my bank account, you keep a constant watch on me.'

'I'm a joint holder, you forget that.'

'Exactly! I can't have an account of my own. I'm over eighteen, but to them I'm still a child. You see, Arutai, how they try to control me? When they say sit, I have to sit and when they throw a ball and say fetch, I have to get it back for them. Then they'll pat me on the head and say, *good boy, good boy.'*

The last words are said in such a savagely mocking tone that Aru flinches.

'If you want money, you can always ask me. But . . .'

'I don't want your charity.'

'. . . but we—I—must know what you need it for.'

'Drink, drugs, women—what else? And, oh yes, gambling. How did I forget that?'

'Nikhil, I'm serious, I need to know why you had to withdraw so much money from your account. Are you in some kind of trouble?'

Aru, listening to them, is amazed at the number of grudges and grievances that spew out of Nikhil. To accumulate so much in barely two decades of living! For that light-hearted surface to conceal so much molten lava! Nikhil brings up Premi's refusal to have a flat in the new house. 'I know you didn't want it because you thought it would allow me to be independent. Now I have to stay with Arutai, with Gopalkaka, so you can keep tabs on me and you can work your remote through them.'

'This is my mother's property. You have no right to tell me what I should have done with it.'

'Ha! That sucks, that really sucks. Look at me, I can't even speak of *my* mother's property.'

Aru wants to cry out, 'Stop, stop it both of you, stop tearing each other into pieces.' But she can say nothing. They are locked in a combat in which love has become a knife, a weapon to hurt, to draw blood. It is an unequal battle; Premi is the obvious loser, she has more to lose, she is more afraid of hurting Nikhil. When Aru, unable to bear it, tries to speak once, Nikhil turns on her. 'Don't you get into this, Arutai. And anyway I know you are on my mother's side.'

'I'm not on anyone's side, for god's sake, Nikhil.'

'Don't blame Aru. She hasn't done anything wrong.'

'No, I won't blame Arutai. I can't blame you and Baba either. I can only blame myself.'

'Nikhil . . .'

They're off again. Listening to them, Aru feels a huge question poised over her, an avalanche threatening to roll down and engulf her. She is asking herself: is this how it is? Is this what having children means? Many years back, when Charu and she had visited Premi in Bombay, she remembers how Nikhil, after going to bed, would call out persistently and monotonously for Premi, until she came to him, asking, 'What is it, raja?'

'Aai, come and sit with me.'

'We're having dinner, Niku, I'll come when we're finished.'

'No, I want you now. Don't go.'

And Premi sat by him until he fell sleep. What happened to them that they had to come to this? Is this how it always is? Would it have been this way with Sumi and me if Sumi had lived? Is it her death which makes our relationship seem so perfect? Do we need death to perfect a relationship? And then the question: is this what motherhood brings you to, finally?

Aru is surprised that Premi does not break down, as she had expected she would. Something more than anger, something greater than grief is driving her on; she does not let Nikhil evade her questions. The truth is Premi is not fighting *against* Nikhil, she is fighting *for* him. But how is he to know that? And so he goes on arguing, accusing, until finally, worn down by Premi's persistence, he admits that he had taken the money to give a friend.

'You gave two lakhs to a friend?'

'It's a loan. And don't worry, he'll give it back.'

'What did he want it for?'

'That's none of your business. Not mine, either.'

'Okay, who is this friend?'

'Again, that's none of your business. It's between him and me. And the money will be back in your account soon.'

'You must tell me your friend's name. Your father . . .'

'Aha! I knew we'd come to this. He's sent you here, hasn't he? Hands off, I say, hands off.' He speaks as if he is being manhandled.

'Don't exaggerate. We don't need your dramatics. And your father knows nothing. I haven't told him. I'll keep it that way. But you have to tell me your friend's name.'

'I'm sorry, I won't.'

'Nikhil, you're driving me to the edge. I think I'll have to let your father deal with this.'

'And what will he do? He'll lecture me about his position, he'll say, how can a High Court judge's son do this and so on and on. That's all he cares about, his position. He doesn't give a damn about me.'

'That's not true.'

Finally Nikhil puts a stop to it by walking out. Premi, who has held herself together by a superhuman effort, collapses, she seems to shrink, her face looks blank, her eyes equally empty. She'll look like this when she's dead, Aru thinks with a stab of fear and puts her arms round her, saying, 'Premimavshi, it'll be all right, he'll be okay.'

Premi straightens herself and looks at Aru, as if she's aware of her presence for the first time.

'Anil was right, Aru. When I bought Nikhil a car, he was furious, let him rough it like the others, he said. I always went about in buses and trains, he said. I haven't told Anil about this bank account, either. Nikhil complained about how humiliating it was for him to ask Anil for money, to explain each time why he needed it, so I thought . . . It's my fault, Aru, all my fault. I wanted Nikhil to love me, I wanted to be indispensable to him.'

'Don't do this to yourself, Premimavshi. Go and lie down for a while, I'll start dinner.'

Aru had heard Rohit come in, she had seen him peep into the room and seeing what was going on, walk quietly away with a small wave of his hand at Aru. Now she goes to Rohit and tells him what has happened, conscious that she is being apologetic, knowing that once again Rohit has found her involved with her family. But Rohit looks concerned, he suggests that they ask Gopal to join them for dinner, 'maybe he'll make Premi feel better,' he says.

However, Premi, when she joins them, has got hold of herself. She does not speak of Nikhil during dinner. She goes back instead to her childhood days, she speaks of how Sumi and she were deprived of so many things, 'not necessities, of course, but if we wanted something extra—like going for a school picnic, or a birthday party, or getting a new dress for a concert— it was always *no.* I know now it was not Amma's fault, Baba didn't give her enough money. But at that time, I used to get very angry with Amma.' After a while she suddenly says, 'Sumi used to steal books.'

'What?' Aru exclaims. Gopal makes a sudden exclamation as well. Or is he laughing? Yes, he is laughing. Aru looks at him in surprise.

'Oh yes, she did. She would borrow a book, keep it for a long time until she was sure the owner had forgotten about it. Then she would write her own name in the book. Sometimes she would tear off the first page if the owner's name was written on it. I remember watching her do it once—she cut out the page so carefully that nothing showed. I asked her what she was doing and she said, shut up, none of your business.'

Gopal is laughing openly now. Premi gives him a sour look and goes on, 'I knew what she was doing, but I never told anyone.'

'The loyal little sister.'

'Loyal little nothing. I knew no one would believe me if I spoke against Sumi.'

Aru says, 'Oh, Premimavshi,' and joins Gopal in laughing. Premi looks angrily at them and asks, 'What's so funny?'

'Nothing. But thank you, Premi, for not exposing Sumi.'

Premi refuses to respond to Gopal's light-heartedness and subsides into gloom after this brief outburst. Once, only once, she speaks of Nikhil. 'I swore when Nikhil was born, no, even before that, that I would never let a child of mine feel deprived, whether of love, or of material things. I swore I would let him have every single thing he wants.'

'He's a good boy, Premi. This is only a phase.'

'Easy for you to talk, Gopal. You don't have to worry, you have daughters. Daughters are different.'

Aru and Gopal look at each other and then just as quickly look away. 'My father,' Aru had once said to Rohit, 'is the original stithaprajna—detached from everyone and everything. Nobody, nothing matters to him.'

'That's not fair, Aru. Why would he have come back if he didn't care about the three of you?'

'To atone. I heard him say this to Amma once.'

'That too comes out of love. Be fair, Aru, don't wrong your father. You know him much better than I do.'

She had thought she knew him. She thinks of him teaching her to ride the bicycle, walking along with her, holding it steady for her, and when she found her balance, letting her go, quickly holding the cycle again when she wobbled, running along with her when she became a little more confident, finally letting her go and waiting for her to return to him, holding her as she fell off, exultantly crying, 'I did it, Papa, I did it.' The two of them grinning at each other with equal joy. It was this same man who abandoned them, his wife and children. It was still hard for her to put the two men together, to make sense of the puzzle. She remembers now what she had once said to Rohit, 'Maybe he cares, but he seems to be struggling against it.'

'At his age, why not?'

Yes, she thinks now, as she sees Premi tearing herself into pieces over Nikhil, why not?

After dinner, Rohit and Aru go into the kitchen to clear up, leaving Premi with Gopal. They work in tandem out of habit, but they are wordless most of the time. They are very careful with each other, treading warily, as if the territory between them is strewn with egg shells. Aru is so humble it hurts Rohit. I don't like you to be humble, Aru, he thinks. Our lives are so entangled that if you are hurting, I hurt too. Please, Aru, stop hurting, he wants to tell her, stop being humble. But when Aru knows herself to have been in the wrong, she can't go far enough to expiate. They have not spoken of the adoption after that day, except once, when Rohit told her he has got in touch with the agency and that there would be no repercussions from his earlier refusal. Aru knows that Surekha has spoken to the agency as well, that she has been sharp with them about the woman's words to Aru. Surekha agreed with Rohit, they have no right to be judgemental, she said. Now they are back to square one. 'They'll keep in touch,' Rohit had told Aru after his talk with them. Aru does get a call one day, it's a different woman, a different voice, sounding young and enthusiastic, speaking of the baby with excitement, as if it is an adventure. 'Be sure, Arundhati, you will have your baby soon. I have an instinct, you know,' she says.

But Aru has told herself she will not think about it, she won't be impatient, it will happen when the time comes. What troubles her is that Rohit remains aloof, behaving as if he's just going through the motions of living with her. It's our child, Rohit, she wants to cry out, I can't do this without you, I don't want to do this without you. We have to do this together, really together. But she can't reach him. She wants to cross the space between them, but is afraid of rejection, she is not sure she can bear the rejection. Who was it who said, (was it Rohit? Or is it her own thought?) that love which is not accepted becomes a burden? Was that how Rohit had felt?

Their work done, Aru is so weary she wants to lean against Rohit as she has often done. But he switches off the light and goes out. Aru finds the living room empty. Premi must have gone to bed, she thinks. But she is sitting on the edge of her bed, still in her sari.

'Not ready to sleep?' Aru asks.

Premi rouses herself out of her abstraction and says, 'I think I better go to bed.'

'Have you got everything? Oh, I forgot the water. I'll get a bottle.'

She returns to find Premi still immersed in her thoughts.

'Premimavshi, go to sleep now. Don't think of Nikhil. Leave it for tomorrow morning.'

'I'm not thinking of Nikhil, Aru. I'm thinking of my father. You know, when Nikhil was born, I felt full of power, I thought I could do anything. I would be the best mother, I would never let him feel the way I had often done—unwanted. Unloved.'

'You can't have been unwanted. Amma loved you.'

Premi disregards Aru's statement and goes on with her own thoughts. 'After Baba's death, when I was going through his papers, I found a document, a gift deed of a house to someone called Janakiamma. At first I was furious. How could he keep us short of money and then gift a house to a stranger? Then I began wondering who this Janakiamma could be. It didn't take me long to realize that she must have been his mistress, that she must have died before him—he'd drawn a red line through the deed and written "No longer valid" on it.'

Aru and Premi look at each other. 'Mistress? You think she was his mistress?'

'Makes sense, Aru. He had nothing to do with Amma for years. But he was a man, wasn't he? And why would a man gift a house to a woman if she didn't mean something to him? You know, Aru, I found a lot of unexpected stuff among Baba's papers—theatre tickets and playbills of Marathi plays. He must have been a great theatregoer in Bombay. Obviously he had to put it all away when he came here to become a husband and father. Husband and father!'

'Did Amma know?'

'At first I thought she didn't. Now I think she did know. When she decided to build this house, I offered to contribute some money, but she refused to take it. I told her that it would cost a great deal, I thought she had no idea about the money required. But Amma told me there was enough. She had sold some property, she said, through that man, that agent who used to visit her with his two little girls, what's his name . . .?'

'Nagaraj.'

'Yes, Nagaraj had sold it for her and she had got a very good price, she said. I remember her telling me that the property had suddenly become very valuable, because the locality had become commercial. Yes, I'm sure she sold Janakiamma's house.'

She tells Aru that curiosity had driven her to look for the house some time after Kalyani's death. But it wasn't there. The entire locality had undergone a sea change. At one time, perhaps, it had been the kind of place where a man could discreetly visit his mistress and not be noticed or talked about. Now, there were rows of multistoried buildings with office complexes and coffee shops; clearly the area had gone up in the world since the time her father had come on furtive visits to his mistress.

'I thought *you* had given Amma the money,' Aru says.

They look at each other, both of them thinking of the intricacy of human relationships, of Kalyani protecting the reputation (or perhaps not, but possibly, who knows? yes) of the man who refused to acknowledge her as his wife. Selling the house he had bought for his mistress with such secrecy that none of them got even a whiff of the entire business.

Suddenly Aru begins to laugh. 'So this house has been built with the money from Janakiamma's house.'

Premi looks a little shocked at first, then begins to laugh as well. 'Poetic justice, isn't it, Premimavshi?' Aru asks.

'Absolutely. But you know what, Aru, when I came to know about Janakiamma, I was pleased, a cheap kind of pleasure, I now think, because I realized that Baba was only a man like any other, that he had his "needs", like Godamavshi used to say in a peculiar tone. And I thought—why had I been so afraid of him?'

'Never mind all that now, Premimavshi. It doesn't matter any more.'

'Oh, but it does. Your parents never leave you. I found it hard to get away from the frightened girl I had been, even when I became a doctor, yes, even when I became a mother. It was as if I could never get away from my father's hold on me.' She pauses and adds, reflectively, 'I wonder what Nikhil will think of me when I'm gone—a failure as a mother, for sure. A mother who never understood him.'

'That's nonsense, Premimavshi. I won't let you say or think such things. Go to bed. Haven't you brought a nightie? Shall I give you one of mine?'

'Yes, do, Aru. Maybe when I wear it, I'll get some of your courage.'

'Don't say such things, you shame me. I'm such a stupid coward. I'm so fearful for all of you, always frightened that something will happen to Rohit, Charu, to Seema, to you, Nikhil. . .'

'That's. . .' Premi's phone rings. Aru knows from Premi's responses that it is Anil. 'No, I didn't, I'm sorry, Anil, I should have, I know, I'm sorry. . .'

What are you apologizing for, Aru thinks in irritation as she goes out with a wave of her hand to Premi.

The next day Premi's eyes give away the fact that she has not slept, that she had been crying. But she is determinedly matter of fact, talking to Aru and Rohit about the adoption. 'I know it's hard waiting, but waiting and patience, that's what motherhood—parenthood—is all about.' Suddenly she shakes her head and says, 'Look at me talking. I'm the last person to speak of parenthood, the last person to advise anyone about it.'

When Premi has gone, Gopal asks Aru, 'Did you speak to her about Nikhil and Seema going out regularly?'

'No. Did you?'

He shakes his head. They look at each other, the same thought in their minds. Then Gopal says, as if to reassure himself, 'It's only for a few days more. Seema will be leaving soon.'

Gopal

Premi was only a child when I first met her, an awkward girl, disappearing swiftly and silently whenever she saw me. But in spite of knowing her for so long, I have no idea why Anil and she had no children after Nikhil; I have no idea whether they did not want any more children, or whether they could not have any more. Whatever the reason, the fact remains that Nikhil is the only child of his parents, the only grandson for both the families, indulged and pampered by everyone. The worst thing for him, however, has been Premi's obsessive love. To have someone put her entire life, her whole heart and soul into you, is a burden too heavy for any human to bear. Even more so for Nikhil who wants to travel light; I can see that he chafes at the burden of his mother's love. Mother and son were very close when he was a child, but like all children, he moved away from her in adolescence, leaving his mother confused and distressed. It surprises me that Premi, who knows him so well, has been unaware of the depths and extent of Nikhil's feelings, of his anger and confusion. All that she can see is his desire to inflict hurt on her.

'I've lost my son, Gopal,' she cried out to me when we were alone.

It's only a phase, I told her. He'll grow out of it, it's a part of growing up, part of the human desire for freedom to rebel against parents, against authority. Give him time, he'll come out of it, he'll be okay. Don't worry, his anger won't last long.

The usual banalities, the same worn-out cliches. But Premi needed these words at the time; she wanted someone to say these comforting words to her. I don't know whether she even took in what I was saying, perhaps my talk was no more than a soothing murmur which flowed over her. But she seemed a little calmer when we parted.

'So your sister-in-law has gone?' Kasturi asks me when we meet in the evening, as we do so often now. I visit her the evenings Seema is not at home. And when Seema is home, I tell her where I am. I leave the door of Kasturi's flat open so I can keep an eye on our front door. I don't know why I am so nervous about Seema. Kasturi laughs at me, you must be the only father who needs his daughter's permission to go out, she says.

'So your sister-in-law has gone?'

'Yes, it was a short visit. She came to see her son.'

I had no intention of telling Kasturi about Premi's problems with Nikhil, but the way she looks at me, with an unconcealed curiosity, almost a child's 'what happened next?' look on her face, coaxes it out of me. She listens in silence and then says, 'Maybe I have been spared much.'

I realize then I should not have spoken of Premi and her son to her. I open my mouth to make some remark, but she stops me, saying, 'But I don't want to be spared. I envy her even her suffering.' Then she adds, 'But I envy you most of all, Gopala. You have such a wonderful relationship with your children. You are lucky you have your daughters.'

I have to laugh. She gives me a surprised look 'Why is it funny?' she asks.

'You're the second person to say this to me.'

'What?'

'That I am lucky to have daughters. I don't need to be told that.'

'Yes, but why did you laugh?'

On a sudden impulse I tell her about how I had walked out of my home, walked out on Sumi and my daughters. Once I have said this, it is like a dam has burst, and I go on to tell her of that terrible year, of the attack on me and of my giving up my job. I go on to Sumi's and her father's death and of my own wanderings after that. I tell her about the family who initiated my pilgrimage by taking me along with them, I speak of my accident, of Bahadur and Kunti and their children, of my good friend, the doctor, with whom I lived for a while. She listens in such rapt silence that I feel I have to go on and I tell her of the joy I had in setting forth each day, knowing everything would be new, of going back eagerly at night to my room, which felt familiar and comfortable, as if it was a home I had lived in for years.

When I fall silent, Kasturi asks me the question I had been asked again and again. 'Why did you abandon your family?'

I am silent for a while, then I say slowly, 'When people asked me that question—and almost everyone did, except Sumi and Charu—I had no answer, except that I could no longer go on living the same life any more. But I know what started the whole thing.' I tell her about the threat to my family and the way I gave in. She makes a sudden exclamation as if she wants to say something, then stops herself.

'It was not what they did to me, it was what I did to myself. I despised myself. I could not look Sumi and my children in the face. I could not live with them, I thought I would hurt them more by being with them. It's so hard to explain, Kasturi, it was a kind of madness, I suppose. It had happened to me once before, I had walked away from my sister.' I hesitate, but leave it there. 'I knew even then that I had hurt my sister terribly, but I could not help myself, I stayed away from her. Then I met Sumi and I was distracted by Sumi, by our children. Such a beautiful distraction! But after what happened, I felt I had to try and make sense of things before I could go on living. And then Sumi died and I had to go away, there was no choice left.'

There is a long pause. Kasturi looks at me intently as if willing me to go on. When I don't, she asks, 'And did you?'

'What?'

'Make sense of things?'

'You must have studied English poetry in school?' I ask abruptly.

'Yes, oh yes. But I found it difficult. Mira's mother tried to help, she wanted me to enjoy the poetry, but I never could.'

'We had to study some English poetry in the higher classes. Actually, I thought I had forgotten whatever I had learnt. But for some reason, some lines of a poem accompanied me through my travels. Surprising, I never knew that I remembered those lines. But there they were, waiting in my mind, through all the years.'

'What are the lines?'

I have to think for a moment before I remember them.

I am a part of all that I have met;
Yet all experience is an arch wherethro'
Gleams that untravell'd world, whose margin fades
For ever and for ever when I move.

'I don't know how much I had understood the poem when I studied it in school, but during my travels I felt as if the poet had written the poem, the first line specially, only for me. It's strange, isn't it, that he says *he* is a part of all that he has met, not, as you expect it will be, that all he has met has become a part of him? Such an Upanishad-like idea, I thought. You know the shloka Purnam idam, purnam adah . . .?'

Kasturi shakes her head. 'I told you I'm a duffer.'

'It's about the wholeness of the world, it's about connections. That we are complete in ourselves, yet we are also a part of something else, of everything else. Nothing in the world stands separate, alone. Do you understand what I'm trying to say, Kasturi?'

'Yes. No. Oh, let it go, what does it matter? I understand one thing about you: you must have answers, but I can live without them. Anyway, who wrote that poem?'

'Tennyson. Ulysses.'

'Ah! Alfred, Lord Tennyson,' she says, as if replying to a question in a classroom. And then she laughs. 'We had a poem of his called "Break break break". And I wondered why someone had to write a poem on breaking things. Belinda, Mira's mother, was in despair. She said, my god, Sonu, I've been breaking my head teaching you poetry and look at you! The thing is, Gopala, for me poetry is the language of the heart. It has to be in my own language. I am not much of a poetry person myself, but when I read poetry in Kannada—Bendre's or Adiga's, for example—the words go straight into me. Here.' She puts her hand on her heart. 'The only line I can remember of all the English poetry we studied is "I will arise and go now, And go to Innisfree".'

'Yeats.'

'My god, Gopala, you impress me.'

'I'm hoping to. I'm trying hard to impress you. Am I succeeding?'

'Let's see. You're still on probation.'

I have to laugh. Kasturi is the first woman to so engage my mind since Sumi. This companionship is a bonus, something I never expected to find at this time of life. She laughs at me, she treats me like no one else does, she has brought out a part of me that I thought I had lost forever, but which I now realize had gone into cold storage after Sumi's death. She keeps reminding me of Sumi, though they have nothing in common except the total lack of artifice. I had thought of Sumi when I went with Kasturi to the dentist. I accompanied her because I could see, to my great surprise, that Kasturi was terrified of going by herself. When she came out of the dentist's room, her mouth was stuffed with a bloodstained wad of cotton, her face a little askew because of the anaesthesia which had numbed one side of her face; but, her ordeal behind her, she seemed euphoric. She said something to me while we were waiting for a rickshaw, something I couldn't understand at first. She repeated it. 'Dentists are sadists,' she said in English and I laughed. She smiled back, a smile that came out crooked, lopsided. I thought it was so courageous a smile, and she, unaware of how she looked, unaware of how little like a smile it was. Suddenly, she seemed so innocent to me that I was filled with tenderness for her. And I thought of Sumi, of the day I had walked her and Kalyani home after a concert in which Sumi had taken part. Sumi's make-up had been hastily and clumsily removed, there were patches of white on her face, smudges of kajal on her cheeks, a streak of lipstick still remained on her lips. And there she was, walking by my side, unaware of how she looked, completely ignorant of her clown face; I was overwhelmed with the same tenderness for her then. Sumi looked, like Kasturi did, innocent and vulnerable. Both the women, totally devoid of artifice, offering me the selves they would not let the world into.

Sumi's death had blocked out all other women for me. The last time we met, Sumi and I, she had come to set me free. I knew from her words that she was saying, I let you go, you are now free. She had been absolutely clear in her mind, as clear as I was confused. She had grown in stature since I left her. At our last meeting, when she came to bid me farewell, she dwarfed me completely. It had been a farewell in another, in the final sense as well, since we never met after that. The pain of our parting held me in its clutches for a long time. The final image of Sumi made it impossible for me to think of any other woman. My body could still respond to a woman's presence, to her face, her laughter, her gestures; but that was all. I resisted not only the act, but the idea itself. The one time I succumbed to my urge was a bad day for me and I was engulfed by guilt. I envied my doctor friend, Gandhi, who looked upon sex as a natural and necessary activity. Good for both the mind and the body, he said. As long as it is mutual and both partners equally willing, what place does guilt have in the picture? In fact, there's only joy. He practised what he preached. It had surprised me at first that women succumbed to him; he was a short man, plump, almost cherubic, with a bushy moustache which somehow looked incongruous on his boyish face. Not the kind of man to arouse romantic feelings in a woman, I had thought. But I often heard women's voices in his room, many times there was laughter. Yes, there was never any doubt that he had willing partners. Kasturi will be a willing partner, I know that. She makes me laugh, laughter which has made an easy intimacy between us possible. She laughs at me, as well, which no one else does now.

'How old are you, Gopala?' she asked me.

'Nearing sixty. Old.'

'Age is a comparative thing. Why are you rushing towards old age? Let it come to you on its own. Belinda, Mira's mother, says that when people refer to her as an old lady, she is astonished, she thinks, old lady? What old lady?'

I laughed. 'I'm sure you'll be the same.'

The other day she suddenly took my hand in both of hers—her hands are large, the fingers shapely, tapering, slightly flattened at the tips—and after a very slight caress she let it go. It was an act of such artless intimacy that my body responded with a sudden arousal. But neither of us speaks of any relationship between us. We have our own reasons for that. I am prepared to wait. Strange, when I was young and had most of my life before me, I was impatient, I wanted Sumi at once, I thought I could not wait, I would not wait. Now, when I know my time is limited, I am prepared to wait, I have no desire to rush into intimacy. Both of us know our association will continue, our relationship will take a different shape one day.

'Some time I want you to come to Jogipura with me,[1] she said to me.

'Yes, I would like to come.'

By asking me to go to Jogipura with her she has taken a long stride in our relationship. To go there with her is to make our commitment public. Before that, I have my children to think of. For Kasturi, there is her great desire to meet her son, to make him part of her life. It's different for me. I think of Seema leaving home soon,, of Aru adopting a child, making her family complete. Slowly, the strands are loosening, their need of me is gradually coming to an end And then perhaps we will talk, Kasturi and I, of us. Till then I am content to wait, to leave it to Time. And so, I think, is she.

Thoughts of Nikhil have been weighing heavily on Aru's mind for some time. She realizes that he has neither come home, nor called her for quite a while. It's possible that he's still angry with her, but she does not want him to think that she has distanced herself from him. She rings him up and to her surprise, he takes her call, but is cool, noncommittal.

'We haven't seen you for a long time. Busy?'

'Somewhat.'

'Are you going home for Christmas?'

'You know we don't have holidays. Just the one day.'

'But it's a Saturday. Why don't you go for the weekend?'

'Too much trouble.'

'It will make your mother happy.'

'Thanks, Arutai, for the advice. But making my mother happy is not my priority right now.' He adds, 'In any case, nothing I do will make her happy. Both you and I know that.' And he rings off.

Knowing that when he is in this mood he is best left alone, she lets him be. She has a half-hearted idea of inviting a few people, including Nikhil, for new year, a kind of farewell for Seema. But Seema says 'no need'. And Rohit? They seem to have got back to their normal selves, to be as they were, but there is a sense of something between them, like grit in the eye, an irritating presence making itself felt. In earlier years they had invited family and friends for the new year. Aru remembers a year when the party was for Rajiv and Uma who were just married and wholly wrapped up in each other. Rohit's architect friend

Jimmy had been there, paying her extravagant compliments. He'd been a little drunk by then and Rohit had laughed at Aru when later she had complained. He had asked her, 'Why do you hate compliments, most women love them.'

'I don't know what to do with them,' she had confessed and Rohit had laughed again.

Why not just us this year, Aru thinks and invites Gopal and Seema to join them for dinner. But Seema has her own plans, so has Gopal; he is spending the evening with Rao and Kasturi. Rao will be going back to his daughter's place soon, Gopal tells her. Endings, farewells everywhere, Aru thinks, with a little tremor of fear. And yet there's also the possibility of a beginning. Rohit and she are waiting for the baby, though they don't speak of it to each other. The eager enthusiastic voice has told her, 'Remember, there's always nine months of waiting.' But this is different, Aru thinks; yet she does not have the heart to snub the woman who seems to be brimming with excitement on their behalf.

Lalita rings them up the day before New Year's Eve. Come and have dinner with Appa and me tomorrow, she says. We're alone, we need company. Which is true, for Rajiv has gone to Delhi, he's got himself a job with a national weekly. He's known for changing jobs and never seems to be able to work in one place for more than a year or two. But now, for the first time he's going out of the city. 'Amma wants to talk about Rajiv,' Rohit said and he has guessed right. Lalita is worried. Just when she thought Uma and he were coming back together, he has gone away. Does this mean they've given up on their relationship, that they will not get back together? Is Rajiv free now, or is he still involved with Uma? Lalita is confused.

'Stop worrying, Amma, Rajiv is no longer your baby. He's a grown man, he can decide for himself.'

'But if they don't want to get back together, they should get a divorce. At: least, he will be free. And she too,' Lalita adds hurriedly, trying to be fair. 'What do you think, Aru? Why don't you talk to Rajiv about it?'

'About divorce? No, Amma, I don't want to be a divorce lawyer for the family. That's one job I don't want. Let them decide.'

But Lalita can't give up. Rohit is the child who has given her the least trouble, except for his continued hostility to his father. Yet, Rajiv, who has given her most pain, is still the child of her heart. Aru thinks of Lalita's marriage, of her endurance of her husband's infidelities, his alcoholism. Now that her own marriage has reached a stage of mutual tolerance, she is agonizing over Rajiv's bad marriage, about her daughter not marrying. Does it never end? She knows Lalita has been deeply hurt by Rajiv's decision to take up a job in Delhi. 'It's terrible, just the two of us at home,' she told Aru. 'It's like a ghost house.' The house has changed with Rajiv's departure, the smell of old age is already seeping into it, as if the presence of even just one young person had brought in some fresh air.

Rohit's father is making an attempt to converse with him, trying to please Rohit. There have been no drinks, in spite of it being New Year's Eve; Lalita must have put her foot down, Aru thinks. One year Rohit's father had insisted on having 'just one drink, after all it's a special day', and then he had got drunk. But today he is quiet, he brings up Rohit's restoration project, knowing how close it is to his son's heart. He says, 'If I had known my son would be interested in old houses, I wouldn't have allowed my mother to sell our house.'

An unfortunate remark, because it was sold to pay off his own huge debts. Rohit, who can be so gentle with his mother, finds it hard to respond to his father's overtures. Aru is saddened. Why can't Rohit take the hand his father is holding out? But what about Papa and I? Is there an inherent flaw in the parent-child relationship? And yet we need one another, we continue to need one another, we can't give up easily on something that is so natural, something that will and can work if we try to make it work.

Rohit and Aru are silent during the drive home. Aru yawns again and again until her jaws ache. 'Stop it, Aru,' Rohit says, 'you're making me yawn.'

'Sorry,' she says and yawns again. Both of them laugh. It's a long time since they laughed together and they are heartened by it. And, though they don't know it, it will be a long time before they will be able to share a moment of laughter again. The nightmare begins as soon as they get home. Aru is, as usual, opening the gate for Rohit to drive the car in when she hears an exclamation from him. She looks towards the house and sees a man, caught in the headlights of the car, running towards them waving both his arms as if to say 'stop'. An extravagant gesture, like someone trying to stop a speeding train and save it from disaster. It takes Aru a moment to recognize that it is a frantic Gopal running towards them.

'What is it, Papa?'

Rohit has got out of the car and come to them.

'Rohit, leave the car outside. We have to take Seema to the hospital.'

'Seema? What is it? What's happ. . .'

'Rohit, turn the car round at once.'

'Papa, why don't you tell us what has happened? What is it?'

But Gopal is already moving toward the house. Aru runs after him, she catches up with him at the door, where Kasturi is waiting.

'What is it, Papa? Why don't you tell me?'

It's Kasturi who answers. 'Aru, we found Seema lying near the gate. She's unconscious, she's not responding to anything.'

Aru feels her legs giving way. She leans against the wall, looking at Kasturi blankly.

'Listen, Gopal, we can't take her to the hospital.'

'What do you mean?'

Rohit has driven the car in, as close to the house as possible. He gets out and joins them. 'Shall we . . .?'

'Come in, all of you. Before you decide to go to the hospital, I have to tell you something.' They look at Kasturi blankly. 'Come inside first.'

When they are in the house, she locks the door after them and says, 'Seema has been raped.'

Aru hears the words, but they don't register on her mind, they mean nothing. Somewhere, lurking in a corner of her mind, there's a thought, this is not real, I'll wake up and know this is only a dream, a nightmare.

'If you go to the hospital, it becomes a police case. Aru, you're a lawyer, you know about these things.'

'Where is she?'

'In the guest room,' Gopal speaks for the first time.

Aru rushes in. Seema is lying in a foetal posture, her knees brought up almost to her chest.

'Seema, Seema . . .' She touches Seema's face, it's not cold, thank god, she's alive. 'Seema, Seema, I'm here.'

'I think she's in shock.' Kasturi has come into the room. 'She needs a doctor.' Aru looks at her expectantly. 'Can Rohit get a doctor to come home?'

'Ask him.'

She goes out and Aru sits by Seema, holding her hand, trying to put her arms about her, saying over and over again I'm here, Seema, I'm here. As if those are the only words that can help Seema at this moment, the only words that can bring her out of the state she is in.

'Rohit has gone,' Kasturi whispers to her. 'Aru, are you all right? Aru? Aru?' She gets a glass of water. 'Here, Aru, drink this.'

Aru tries to, but her teeth begin to chatter, she is shivering violently as if she is freezing. Kasturi puts the glass down, she puts her arms about Aru, she rubs her arms, her back and holds her close. Finally Aru comes out of her shivering fit.

'I'm all right, oh please, please don't worry about me. But Seema . . . you said she's been raped. How do you know?'

'She's hurt, she's bleeding.'

'Oh my god, oh my god. How could it happen, how could

anyone . . .' She tries to straighten Seema's legs, but can't. 'Can we give her some water?'

'I tried. It was no use. We can try again.'

But the water dribbles out of her mouth. 'Papa, look at her, how did this happen, Papa, how could this happen?' Aru cries out to Gopal who has just entered.

He tries to speak, he can't say anything. Aru looks at Kasturi. 'What happened?'

'We don't know. But Aru, you have to take a decision for Seema, Gopal and you.'

'What decision? We have to take her to the hospital, we have to make a police complaint

'I think you should wait until the doctor sees her.'

Kasturi and Gopal go out of the room, Aru can hear them speaking in whispers. The thought keeps beating in Aru's mind—I was afraid, I was always afraid for Seema. But this . . .!

They wait in silence until Rohit returns with the doctor, an old friend of his. Aru has met her too, but now she is blank, she shows no sign of recognition. The doctor, with professional authority, asks them all to leave so that she can examine Seema. 'One of you stay back, I might need help.'

Gopal looks at Kasturi who nods and says, 'I'll stay.'

They can hear a murmur of voices from the room, they hear Kasturi making soothing sounds. When the doctor comes out, all of them turn to her. 'She's been raped,' the doctor says bluntly. None of them speak. 'What do you want me to do, Rohit? Aru? Do you want to register a complaint? I've examined her, I can confirm that there has been a sexual assault.'

Still silence.

'Rohit?' she says sharply.

'It's not my decision, it's for Seema's father and Aru to decide.'

'Well?'

'Is she badly hurt?'

'Bruises, mostly. Yes, there has been violence. And I think there was more than one person. Someone held her down with force, her arms are badly bruised.'

Aru looks at the doctor with anguished eyes. 'Does she know? Is she conscious?'

'She's in a state of shock, but it's wearing off. Yes, of course, she knows. I'd have preferred to sedate her, but if you want to file a FIR . . .' There is a sudden movement from Gopal. 'No, you don't have to do it right now, you can do it in the morning. But if you want to do it now, I won't sedate her.'

Silence again.

'All right, make up your minds. I've taken some vaginal swabs. They'll be with me in case the police need them. Okay?'

She goes back in and comes out in a few moments, ready to leave. But before she does, she says, 'I think you should file a complaint. Don't let the men get away with it. They must be punished.'

She said men, not man, Aru thinks. How many of them? It does not bear thinking of, if she thinks of it she will go crazy.

'Aru . . .' Kasturi calls out urgently.

Aru rushes into the bedroom. Seema is awake, she is struggling to sit up, she looks vaguely at the two women as if she can't recognize them. She is rocking herself, saying in a voice so high-pitched Aru can't recognize it as Seema's, saying over and over again, 'I want to die, I want to die.'

The two women look at each other helplessly, then Aru sits by her and tries to hold her, she tries to hold her hands which are flailing at the bed and at her own body, but Seema goes on and on until finally, she stops out of sheer exhaustion. Now the tears begin to pour out of her eyes, a steady stream, as if there is a bottomless well of pain within her.

Kasturi gently helps her to lie down, she goes back to applying a salve to Seema's arms. 'I'll get some ice,' she says and goes out. When she returns Seema is quieter.

'I don't want the ice, it burns,' she says.

'All right, no ice, only the ointment.'

Aru looks at the bruises—large contusions—and thinks, how could they, how could they? She is burning with anger. 'Try to sleep, I'm here, I'll be right here.'

Aru holds her hand and thinks of Seema showing her the hoarding, she remembers Seema's pleasure in surprising Aru, her own amazement at seeing Seema in so public a place, Seema as a beautiful, shy bride. How can we make this public? How can we expose this terrible thing to the world? But how can we let them get away?

In a while Seema's restless movements cease. Her hand in Aru's becomes heavy and unresponsive. The sedation is having effect. Kasturi comes to her and whispers, 'Rohit is back, Gopal wants to talk to both of you.'

Talk? What about?'

'I don't know. You go, I'll stay here.'

She goes out. Rohit has just returned. 'Rohit, I think I'll ring Surekha ma'am. No, I'll speak to Jaisimha sir. He can contact a police officer, someone he knows

'Aru, wait.' She looks at Gopal, waiting, her finger poised above her mobile. 'Don't do anything. Wait.'

'Why, Papa?'

'Seema went out with Nikhil.'

'What?'

'They went out together. And I've been thinking—whoever brought her here knew where she lives

'Papa, what are you saying?'

'Seema went out with Nikhil,' Gopal repeats, speaking clearly and emphatically.

'But. . . but. . .' She looks blankly at him for a moment, then swiftly rings up Nikhil's number.

'The customer you are trying to reach has switched off the phone. Kindly try a little later.' She rings again and gets the same message. Again and again she hears the message until it keeps running through her mind like something she has learned by heart. Like a mantra. 'The customer you are trying to reach . . .'

'I don't understand, I can't understand,' she cries out despairingly, putting the mobile away. 'Nikhil, Nikhil and Seema! I don't understand. Papa, are you sure she went with Nikhil?'

'I saw them off myself, Nikhil told me they wouldn't be very late, he said he would spend the night with us.'

Aru remembers the evening before Charu's wedding when they were all together. Someone had put on a wedding song from a movie and Nikhil had suddenly got up and held out a hand to Seema. 'Come, Seema, let's dance,' he had said.

Surprisingly, Seema had immediately got up and joined him. They had watched them dance, amazed by the unconscious beauty of Nikhil's movements, uninhibited, but not wild, and Seema, controlled and graceful. The two of them had danced in such harmony it was as if they had rehearsed this earlier. Two beautiful young people, Seema with her elegant, stately grace and Nikhil, vivacious and joyful.

'Let's try Premi,' Gopal says. Aru does not move. Rohit brings out his mobile and rings Premi's number. He nods when he hears the rings and holds it out to Aru, but she shakes her head. Rohit gives the phone to Gopal.

'Premi? No, it's not Rohit, Gopal here. Is Nikhil with you? No. No, no, it's not that. No, Premi, it's . . . will you let me talk?' Gopal's voice is sharp and angry, Aru has not heard this voice for years. 'Just tell me if you know where he is. Listen, Premi . . . No, I can't. Here, talk to Rohit.'

In a few words Rohit tells her what has happened, he listens to Premi for a while, nods and ends the call. 'She's coming . . .'

'When?'

'She's leaving right away, she thinks she may get one of the night flights. She'll be here before morning. And she says don't do anything until she gets here.'

Church bells begin to ring, firecrackers go off, there are jubilant cries from somewhere—the distant sounds come to them clear and loud in the silence of the night. They look at each other blankly. It is the new year being rung in.

The night is seared into their memories, a night which stays with them for a very long time. For Aru, the pictures are vague and disjointed. She remembers Kasturi going away, saying, 'Call me if you need me.' She remembers Rohit trying to induce her to go to bed and failing. He comes to her twice in the night. Once she is sitting on the floor, her head on Seema's bed, her arms covering her face. She seems asleep, but when Rohit enters, she looks up at him. 'Go to bed, Aru, I'll sit with Seema.'

'No, you go,' she says blearily and goes back to her earlier pose, to her thoughts.

Later, she remembers Gopal coming in many times—how often?—to look in on Seema. There is some sporadic conversation between them, but she has no idea what they talked about, except that they seem to be sharing unspoken anxieties about Seema, as they had done when she was a child. Nothing seems real. But the reality of the silent sleeper on the bed never leaves her or Gopal, it remains the centrepiece of all her memories of that night. For Aru, it is a night of agonized questions that she asks herself: Why did I not stop Seema from going into this profession? Why did I let her get into it? And yet, how could I have prevented her from doing what comes to her so naturally and easily? Her work is what has made her a whole person, her work has brought her out of that shadowy world she had been inhabiting since Sumi's death. How could I stop her from doing it? But I should have known. She remembers the way men looked at Seema when they went out. She herself had learnt, very early, to cope with men's stares, she had learnt to deal with their pathetic groping. But men looked at Seema proprietorially, as if, because she was a public face, they owned her. There was a man in a restaurant once who had stared steadily at her through their meal. Aru had been furious, but Seema had been unperturbed. Forget about him, Aru, Seema had said. She was used to it, she said. But the man's look had made Aru's flesh crawl, he had looked as if. . . as if.. .

Among all her disordered thoughts, there is the thought of the morning to come. Premi has asked them to wait for her. What do we do then? What if Nikhil is . . .? No, he can't be, it's impossible. But what if he did this, what if he was part of it? Do we remain silent? Or do we go to the police and file a complaint? And can we expose Seema to the world, make her a target of people's curiosity, of their talk? And Nikhil?

At some time she falls asleep. When Gopal comes in just before dawn, he gently covers her with a shawl. Gopal has been walking up and down most of the time. He knows Seema will sleep for quite some more time. She needs this blanking out of her ordeal, these hours when she can remain unconscious of what was done to her. Gopal remembers Kasturi's words to him, 'Gopal, don't let them get away. Let Seema show her bruises to the world, don't hide them, take photographs of them, let the world see what they have done. If I had done it, who knows, maybe my child would have been with me.'

But, Gopal thinks, Kasturi does not know Seema. And if Nikhil has been with her when this was done . . . A savage anger floods Gopal when he thinks of it. No, it can't be, Nikhil would never do such a vile thing. He loves his sisters. But where is he? Gopal is not looking forward to meeting Premi, he knows she will defend her son, he knows how fiercely she will defend her son.

***

Rohit opens the door wordlessly to Premi when she comes early in the morning. She puts her bag down on the ground and looks about as if expecting to see Nikhil.

'Nikhil?'

Rohit shakes his head.

'Seema?'

'She's sleeping, she's been sedated.'

'Gopal, are you sure Seema went out with Nikhil?'

'Do you want me to swear it in a court of law?'

Premi makes a warding-off gesture, like she's saying, don't hurt me. Gopal, in response to the gesture, speaks in a softer tone. 'I saw them going out together. Nikhil said they'd be back before midnight, he said he would stay the night with us.'

'Where is he, then? What's happened to him? Gopal, do you think they, whoever it was, did something to him . . .?'

Aru comes in with three cups of tea, puts the tray down and asks Premi in a cold voice, 'Premimavshi, have you come here only for Nikhil's sake? Only to defend him? Don't you care about Seema at all?'

Premi turns to Gopal, as if it is he who has asked her the question. 'Gopal, you know I love your daughters, you know your daughters, Sumi's daughters, are like my own. You know I would do anything for them. . .'

Her appeal to Gopal comes out of their long relationship, out of her strong bonds with Sumi's children, specially with Aru after Sumi's death. Premi had been only sixteen when she held Aru, a grave-eyed baby, in her arms. She had found a place in Premi's heart since then; they had become more friends than aunt and niece as Aru grew up. When Gopal left them and Sumi retreated into some place Aru could not follow, Premi had become the person to whom Aru confided all her thoughts. Premi had done everything a mother would during Aru's wedding, the two had been together during Kalyani's illness. Aru had wanted to share the task of preparing Kalyani for her final journey, but Premi had sternly refused to let her. 'No, Aru,' she had said, 'you are too young to have this experience, I won't let you.'

Now, neither Gopal nor Aru respond to Premi's appeal. But Gopal briefly touches the hand she has stretched out before she lets it fall. Aru gives her a cup of tea and asks, 'Does Anilkaka know?'

'I've told him.'

'Premimavshi, don't imagine that any of us believes that Nikhil would hurt Seema.'

'Thank you, Rohit, for saying that, thank you, Rohit.'

'But where is he? He must tell us what happened, otherwise. . . '

The door bell rings. Premi's face moves to hope, then back to fear again. But it is Kasturi, holding a large covered saucepan in her hands. Premi looks blankly at her.

'Premi, you know Kasturi. She and I—we found Seema at night. . .'

Kasturi nods at Premi and comes in, saying, 'I've brought you some breakfast. Uppittu.'

When she's gone, Premi exclaims, 'Breakfast? How can she think it's possible for us to eat!'

But Gopal understands. Kasturi comes from a village. Whatever happens, however large the disaster, life has to go on: animals have to be fed and watered, cows milked, cattle sent out to graze, babies and children to be bathed and given their food—yes, life has to go on.

Sure enough, when the uppittu is put on the table the aroma reminds them of hunger. Even if they can't eat much, the smell and taste of food drives out despair. They eat, they bathe, they change into fresh clothes. Meanwhile the milk boy calls out 'Haalu' as he drops the packets of milk in the bag hung on the gate, the paper boy flings the papers with a thump on the steps, Lokesh comes for the car keys. The day has begun. Like all humans who have gone through a night of pain and suffering, they find it hard to believe that life will go on as before, that they will resume their routine. But it is the only thing to do, there is nothing else they can do. Seema continues to sleep, Premi almost constantly by her side. By the time Seema wakes up, it's past noon. Anil had called and informed them that Nikhil was in Bombay. He arrived a short while back. Nikhil and he will come as soon as he can get away. Now there is a point of certainty, a time of the day towards which they can move.

Nikhil and his father arrive just as daylight is fading and the lights are switched on. The moment he enters, Nikhil goes straight to Aru as if she is the only person in the room. 'Arutai, I didn't do it, I promise you I didn't hurt Seema. I didn't know, I had no idea that they . . . Please don't hate me, Arutai, I swear to you I didn't do it.'

Are these the words of an innocent man? Anil's face indicates that he believes his son. But Aru does not respond to Nikhil's frantic pleas. She stares blankly at him, her eyes opaque, seeing, not him, but Seema lying in a foetal position, her body as rigid as a clenched fist. She can hear Seema keening in a shrill voice, her anguished cries, 'I want to die, I want to die.' Finally, she sighs and says, 'Nikhil, I don't know what to believe. I can only think of Seema. I will never forgive anyone who is part of what has been done to her.'

No, Aru is in no mood to forgive Nikhil, but she is too exhausted to rage at him. 'Go and see Seema,' she tells Nikhil wearily. He hesitates. 'Go to her. Talk to her, then we'll listen to you.'

They wait in silence for him to return. When he does, he is silent too, for such a long while that they think he will never speak.

Anil breaks the silence finally. 'Tell them, Nikhil, tell them what you told me.'

Nikhil looks around and for the first time seems to see that his mother is in the room. Mother and son look at each other and, surprisingly, Premi says nothing to him. Nikhil's flippancy is gone, revealing the frightened boy underneath. He takes some time to begin, and when he does speak, it is in a low and flat tone. He tells them about his friends, yes, they're the ones Swati had warned him against, he tells them that they had planned to go out for the new year. 'And bring your cousin along,' they said to Nikhil.

'It's my fault. I boasted about Seema being my cousin. One of them . . . he used to cut out Seema's pictures and put them up on the wall. I never thought he was—I mean, I didn't imagine— I thought it was like having a crush on a film star.'

The men flattered Nikhil until he agreed to bring Seema. They had booked a table, they told him, in a five-star hotel, they would meet in their place, and go on from there. He left Seema in the car when they got to their place. He knew how messily they lived, he didn't want Seema to see their home. But they said there was still some time before they had to leave, so 'why don't you ask your cousin to come in?' He was a little hesitant, he sensed that they had already had some drinks; but he had not found a good parking spot and he didn't want to leave Seema waiting in the car. He came back with Seema. They were very polite, they seemed awed by her, they treated her almost like visiting royalty. They told Nikhil to bring their car to the door 'while we get ready. We'll all go in our car,' they said. Nikhil thought it was sensible, after all, theirs was a much larger car. Nikhil walked up and down the street twice before he realized their car wasn't there. He was suddenly overcome by a sudden sense of uneasiness, anxiety flooded him and he almost ran back to the house. (As he speaks, they see the desperation and fear of that time on his face.) The door was locked. He rang the bell, but no one appeared. He rang again and again and began knocking on the door at the same time. At last, one of them opened the door. He was disheveled, sweating, he seemed to be in a hurry.

'Where's Seema?'

'Go, get your car.'

'Where's Seema?

The man shoved him aside, snatched the car keys from Nikhil's hand and went out. Nikhil, sure now that something was wrong, kept calling out loudly for Seema, he began knocking on the closed door of one of the rooms. The man who had gone to get the car returned, he almost pushed him out of the house and into the car. 'Seema, Seema. . .'

'Shut up, she's coming. Sit here and don't look back.'

When he tried to get out, the man held him in his place, so that he was unable to move. Nikhil heard the door bang, he heard the car door open, there were noises at the back. Once again he tried to turn, but the man in the back seat held him while the other drove. When they reached Seema's home, they told Nikhil to get out of the car. They forced him to walk away, one of them walked with him and put him in an auto.

'Go where you want, but don't come back here,' the man said. 'Your Seema will be safe, don't worry about her, just go. And don't talk to anyone, understand? If you do . . .'

'I didn't know what to do. Finally I went to the airport. I sat there all night and bought a ticket for an early morning Bombay flight.'

There is silence. He has nothing more to say, nor has anyone. Finally Aru says, 'How many of them?'

'What?'

'How many men?'

'Three.'

'My god! Oh my god! Go away, Nikhil, just go away.'

He makes the same warding-off gesture his mother had made, then obediently gets up. But Rohit, knowing that if the bitterness is not to go deeper they cannot end it this way, stops him.

'Have you made a police complaint?' Anil asks Gopal.

Gopal shakes his head.

'You can relax, Anilkaka, we won't do it, Nikhil is safe.'

'Don't be this way, Aru,' Premi pleads with her.

'What do you want me to say, Premimavshi? Look at Seema, just look at her. And we can't do anything, we have to sit with our hands folded in our laps and let them get away unscathed. Why did you do this, Nikhil, how could you do this to Seema?'

She puts her face in her hands. Nikhil rushes to her, he kneels at her feet, he tries to take her hands away from her face.

'Don't, Arutai, don't, you know I never meant for this to happen, I never dreamt they would do such a thing. How can you even think I would . . . But I'm ready to be punished. I should be punished. I'll go to the police, I'll tell them everything, I'll accept whatever they do to me

'Nikhil!' Premi's cry rings out.

'No, Aai, let me speak, don't interfere.' He looks at Aru, but she stubbornly refuses to uncover her face. Nikhil turns to Gopal. 'Gopalkaka, you tell me what to do, I'll do whatever you say.'

'It's not for me to say, Nikhil. It's Seema's decision.'

But Seema does not want them to do anything. She seems to have turned her back resolutely on the incident, she won't talk of it, she won't let anyone talk to her about it. Surprisingly, she bears no animus against Nikhil, she refuses to blame him.

Before leaving, Premi talks to Aru and Gopal, she begs for their forgiveness.

'Who am I to forgive, Premi? I have no right to judge anyone.'

'Don't say that, Gopal. You have to forgive Nikhil, both Aru and you. And I . . .' she turns to Aru, who has been silent so far, 'I have no one, but Gopal and you girls. My Sumi's daughters. If you don't forgive me, I'll be all alone, I will lose everything.'

'Premi, don't. We'll work it out somehow, but we need time, give us some time.'

'Aru?'

'I too need time, Premimavshi. Right now, I can't think of anything but Seema. Give me time.'

Premi has to be satisfied with that.

Anil comes to Gopal before they leave. The two men, though married to two sisters, have had very little to do with each other. Anil has stayed away from his wife's family for reasons of his own. Now he tells Gopal that he will see the men are prosecuted. 'Nikhil tells me they forged his signature on a cheque. When he found out, they said it was a mistake and they would give him the money back. But I'll see that they are prosecuted for that.'

Gopal knows that this is Anil's way of asking for forgiveness. A stiff-necked proud man, it is hard for him to say it more openly. In any case, Gopal thinks, forgiveness is all very well, to forgive is not hard, but what about Seema? What will happen to her now, how will she live with the knowledge of what was done to her?

Gopal and Aru watch Seema all the time. It's like they've gone back to the old days, to their old partnership, when they looked after the baby Seema because her mother was ill and couldn't care for her. This time, however, Kasturi is with them, she is with Seema when both Gopal and Aru have to be away. It seems to comfort Seema to have Kasturi with her and there are times when she talks to Kasturi. Otherwise, Seema, who always spoke little, has become almost mute. If only she would talk, Aru tells Charu on the phone. Seema goes mechanically through her day now, Aru says, her old routine completely forsaken. She seems to have given up on her body, the body which she had looked after with such devotion. Her cuts and bruises are slowly healing, the bruises changing colour day by day; they are like a message telling them how long it has been since that terrible night. But there is no clue to what is going on in her mind. Aru gently asks her if she would like to see someone professional. No, she says with such firmness that Aru desists.

'Can't you make Seema change her mind about going to the police?' Kasturi asks Aru. 'Gopal tells me you are the only one she may listen to.'

'I can't—exactly for that reason.'

'But they will get away.'

Aru shrugs helplessly. Kasturi seems about to say something, then moves away and Aru wonders why it matters so much to her.

Now Charu alerts them to another, a more hideous possibility. It is two weeks since it happened. 'Do you know the date of her periods?' Charu asks.

'You think she may. . .'

'It's possible.'

'My god!' It hits Aru like a blow on her face, the world goes dark for a. moment. Then, with a sudden leap, her mind grasps a thought—I can keep the baby. And she is horrified at herself. What's wrong with me? How can I be so selfish? Do I expect Seema to carry a child of rape in her body for nine months? It will kill her.

Fortunately, Seema gets her periods at the right time. Perhaps she too had thought of that dire possibility, because it is after this that she tells Kasturi she wants to speak to Maggie. Maggie comes down and takes Seema out, nobody knows where they have gone. When they return, hours later, Maggie tells Kasturi that Seema has told her all that happened to her. 'I've told her that it makes no difference to me at all.'

And so, in a few days, Seema goes back to her routine. When she appears at Aru's door one morning, ready for her run, Aru is startled, a little frightened, and then pleased. 'I have to get dressed, I'll be with you in a moment,' she says. She gets ready, swiftly pulling on her track suit, unused for so long. The sisters walk briskly and in silence for a while. Then, as usual, Seema takes off and begins to run. Aru finishes her two laps and waits for Seema, who, when she is done, sits in silence by Aru. She is sweating profusely. Aru gives her the towel and says, 'Don't push yourself too hard, Seema, take it easy.' Seema wipes her face, takes the water bottle, drinks from it and then makes a small movement of her head, which could be either 'yes' or 'no'. Or both. Then she says, 'Aru, I've told Maggie I'll be in Bombay next week—as we had planned.'

'I know. Kasturi told us.'

'And I've asked Leo to come with me. He's willing to come, we'll be living together. Having him with me will help.'

'I'm glad.'

'And, Aru, I'm sorry I couldn't—I'm sorry I let you down. I wish I could have . . .'

'It's okay, Seema, the decision was always yours.'

'I should have killed him—them,' Seema says in such a savage tone that Aru flinches. 'There was a knife on the table, I remembered it later. Every night I think, I should have used that knife, every night I see myself picking up the knife and then . . .' She makes a downwards thrusting gesture with a clenched fist, her gesture as fierce as her voice had been earlier and Aru's body goes cold. She feels as if she is at the edge of a precipice. They are both silent for a while.

'And don't hate Nikhil,' Seema goes on in a more normal tone. 'If he hadn't come and made such a noise, banging on the door and calling my name, they would have gone on. Don't hate Nikhil,' she says again.

'I'll try.'

'And look after Papa.'

'I will. If he lets me,' Aru says.

'And don't worry about me, Aru. I don't want you or Papa to worry about me.'

Seema has not spoken so much, not for a very long time. Now, having said what she wanted to say, she stands up, ready to go. 'Get up, Aru,' she says. Wondering a little, Aru stands up. The moment she does, Seema puts her arms around Aru and holds her in a close embrace. So very unusual a gesture for her, for she is never demonstrative, that Aru's eyes fill with tears. She knows Seema is bidding her farewell, she knows that she is saying, 'now let me go'.

Nothing more is said. By the time they get home, the light has changed with a miraculous swiftness as it always does; it is brighter, the day has begun. At home, they see Rao strolling as usual in the front yard, they find Rohit and Gopal obviously waiting for them, though neither of them says so. They look up when the sisters enter, Rohit neatly folds the newspaper he has been reading, or trying to, puts it down and says, 'I'll make the tea. Tea for everyone?'

Aru goes to see Gopal the evening after Seema has left. The house seems unchanged. Seema has taken little except some of her clothes. Is it to keep this place intact, or is it so that she can start a completely new life? They can only guess. But the house feels empty and Aru is saddened to think of Gopal living alone.

'Why don't you come and live with us, Papa?' she asks.

'No, Aru, I'm okay. I'm used to this place. And Seema would like me to be here, I think. Anyway, Aru, Rohit and you need all the space you have, once the baby comes.'

The baby! How could she have forgotten? She suddenly realizes how long it has been since they last heard from the agency; they seem to have been waiting forever. And then, like babies always do, she suddenly arrives. There's a call from the centre. 'Arundhati, your baby is here,' the eager voice tells her. 'Come and get her, she's waiting for you, come with Rohit.'

'Now?' she asks in sudden panic, her voice quavering. 'But we're not ready.'

'Never mind. You can have a look at her and come back for her tomorrow.'

There is no question of tomorrow. Rohit and Aru rush off instantly and find the woman (surprisingly, so much older than her voice) waiting for them, as impatient, it seems, as Aru and Rohit are. 'Here she is, your baby. All yours,' she says. And so their baby comes home. She is a dark baby with jet-black curly hair and large eyes that look at the world with immense curiosity and pleasure. A happy two-and-a-half-month-old baby who chortles contentedly to herself when she is well-fed and yells with outraged anger when she's hungry and the milk delayed. She is used to a plentiful and instant supply of milk, breastfed by her mother, a healthy girl of eighteen who, like so many girls, was happy until she got herself pregnant by the wrong man. A determined girl, she decided she would keep the baby with her for a month and then give her away. She did all this with great courage and fortitude. Thankfully, Aru knows nothing of this.

As soon as they get home, Rohit goes out with the list he has been given, a bewilderingly long list of things the baby will need. The baby, who has been sleeping all this while, wakes up and begins to cry at the strangeness of her surroundings, perhaps, or the lack of familiar faces. Aru is confused, she does not know what to do. She carries the baby from room to room, as if showing her her new home, wondering when they will get used to each other. Nagi follows her around, equally confused. She is happy that a baby has come home, regrets that it is not Aru's own, she thinks it is not right for Aru to be alone with the baby, but does not know how to help, or what to do. To her relief, Kasturi, hearing the baby crying, comes down. 'Give her a bath,' she suggests. 'Sometimes it quietens them.'

'I can't.' Aru confesses how terrified she is of handling her, how petrified of doing something wrong. What if I hurt her, what if I drop her, what if she slips out of my hands? Aru is learning fast how fearful parenthood can be, how vulnerable a parent can be. Kasturi laughs at her and says, 'Give her to me.' She puts the baby face down on her outstretched legs and after a little hesitation, murmuring, 'It's so long since I did this', (later Aru remembers her words and realizes she must have had a child) bathes her competently enough, uncaring of the baby's loud howls of protest. When she is bathed, they wrap her in a huge towel, only her little face showing. The sobs have dwindled to whimpers, but the woebegone little face looks so comical in that huge bundle that Kasturi bursts into laughter. The baby gives the three women an offended 'what have you done to me?' look and immediately starts crying again. 'Oh, don't,' Aru exclaims. Fortunately Rohit soon returns. Even better, he brings his mother Lalita with him to be part of the moment, to share their joy. And, to be honest, for support as well. Suddenly he, a grown man, who thought he knew how to deal with the world, is terrified of a tiny baby. So, he knows, is Aru. Lalita has come with some old baby clothes she has stored for years. The three women try to soothe

the baby, they dress her in the clothes Lalita has brought while the baby continues to howl in protest.

In the meanwhile, Rohit and Aru get a bottle ready for her. Aru's hands are trembling. 'Steady, Aru, steady,' Rohit says to her. 'This is going to be an everyday affair.' Finally, the baby begins drinking and there is blessed silence. She is very hungry, at first she takes huge gulps, scarcely stopping to breathe. But in a while she settles down to a steady rhythm of drinking, her eyes fixed unwaveringly on Aru's face, her tiny hands, clenched into fists, digging into Aru's body, her plump little legs in constant motion. Aru looks down at her, her heart turns over and she thinks jubilantly—so this is it, this is it.

***

They name her Kalyani Gauri. Gauri is Lalita's suggestion and Aru and Rohit, realizing that she wants to be part of the child's existence, accept the additional name without demur. In any case, the baby will ultimately become Gauri, it's so much easier a name to say.

On the day of the naming ceremony the house is full, buzzing with sound, alive with activity. Almost the entire family is there; even Jai and Deep, Ramesh's twin sons, are present. Genial giants, towering over everyone, they try to fit into the occasion while Ramesh and Chitra look on proudly. The twins have imbibed from their father a great respect for Aru, they have heard of and seen her struggle after Gopal left them and after her mother died. She is a hero to them, something which would embarrass Aru greatly if she suspected it. Thankfully she does not; but she is greatly pleased they happen to be home at this time, that they seem to be happy to be with the family. Rajiv has come from Delhi and so, surprisingly, has Radhika, Rohit's sister. She has come home after a long time. Rohit thinks she looks more relaxed and easier than she has been for years. She is now a recognized figure in the TV channel for which she is working, she is somebody who counts. Success suits her, Rohit thinks, it has taken away her restlessness. Looking at her cooing over the baby, Lalita's heart lifts for a moment, she thinks, maybe she will get married soon, have a baby. But then Radhika sets eyes on Seema—yes, Seema has come for a day, no, only half a day, she is already getting used to a furiously fast pace of life— she immediately goes to her and begins talking to her animatedly, about an interview, perhaps, and Lalita's face falls.

Surekha looks appreciatively at the vigorously kicking crowing baby and says with satisfaction, 'She won't put up with any nonsense.' Nagma and Aru, who know what Surekha means by 'nonsense', smile at each other. Ramu and Gracy are there, Gracy delighted to have become an 'akka'. Shabnam and she spend all their time near the cradle, talking to the baby, who seems equally delighted by their company. Ramu has brought his mother and Aru is amazed to see her, she's such a tiny birdlike woman. Ramu had painted her as an ogre, but this woman looks harmless, surely she can never frighten anyone!

'You don't know her, Aru ma'am,' Ramu mutters darkly, when she says this to him. But Ramu's mother becomes a saviour to Aru and Rohit, they are enormously grateful to her, for she gets them a young woman from her hometown, a woman who takes charge of the baby and who, thankfully, is able to get on with Nagi.

Kasturi is part of the celebration, she has come with Mira and Ranjan, who are present, both as Maggie's representatives and as Kasturi's friends. Mira watches Kasturi closely, specially when she is talking to Gopal, noticing how, even when she is not talking to him, they seem to be aware of each other. Premi and Devi are curious about Gopal and Kasturi, too, and so, to some extent, is Ramesh, all of them having come to know of Gopal's friendship with Kasturi. Premi and Devi notice that Kasturi seems comfortable, almost at home here, they see, to their surprise, that Kasturi seems as easy with Aru as she is with

Gopal. And they are left with doubts, they wonder, they think: after Sumi, how can Gopal . . .?

Premi and Anil have arrived that morning. Nikhil has not come. It will be a long time before he can face either Gopal or Aru. But Premi takes her old place by Aru's side, she and Devaki are with Aru and her baby, no longer trying to be substitutes for Sumi, but as themselves, as Aru's aunts. They wish, of course, that Sumi was there to see Aru, Aru who looks an entirely different person, not only because she is wearing a sari and has flowers in her hair, like on her wedding day, but because of a new tentativeness in her, a kind of tremulous happiness, which touches all of them. In the midst of the ceremonies, Charu rings up. From her home in that far-off continent, Charu hears the happy noises, the bustle and bursts into tears. 'Floods here, guys. As usual,' Hrishi says resignedly, taking the phone from Charu. Pavan, who has stubbornly refused to talk until then, suddenly shouts 'Kalyani' before Hrishi rings off. There is much laughter and some tears from the proud grandmother, Devaki.

Moments of happiness, moments never to be forgotten. Magic moments, which travel with us and stay with us all our lives, illuminating even our darkest days. The right time, perhaps, to leave the family to themselves at this ephemeral moment of celebration, of happiness and togetherness.

The Crystal Ball

'We bring our years to an end, as it were a tale that is told.'

The Book of Common Prayer

All novels, even the longest ones, have to come to an end. But the story goes on. Intrepid travellers in space and time, we are constantly moving on an endless road of which we know neither the beginning nor the end. Each one of us imagines that we are unique, that our journeys are like none other. Unaware, too, that we are hurtling towards an unknown future, we continue to live as if this moment, this little slice of time given to us, is forever. Perhaps we are fortunate that the future is unfathomable, that it remains dark. Astrologers, palmists, tarot card readers, soothsayers try to penetrate the darkness, they tell us they can see what is to come; but it is like holding a lighted match in the darkness of a moonless and starless night. Even the novelist's crystal ball, wayward and unreliable at the best of times, and smudged by much handling, yields very little, though the clouded and misty surface does allow some space for the imagination. That little space suffices to round off this story.

Aru, like Marianne Dashwood, a heroine she had never liked very much, has lived not, perhaps, to 'discover the falsehood of her own opinions', but certainly 'to counteract, by her conduct, her most favourite maxim'. She is much chastened, she has realized that justice, which had seemed to her such a simple, clear and incontrovertible matter, can get trapped in the sticky web of love and loyalty. It continues to haunt her, the thought that they let the men go unpunished, that the same men might, perhaps, attack another woman at another time. At times, looking at Seema, her feelings change, and she thinks, perhaps Seema did right. But she is no longer sure, she knows she has to live with the possibility that she failed in this matter. Her anger against Premi dissolves, the bond between them is too strong to let her hostility survive. It takes her much longer to be reconciled to Nikhil, though ultimately, remembering his sweetness as a child, she will give him a place in her life. Most of her hard feelings about Gopal have melted away and she is comfortable with Kasturi's place in his life. Her feelings about Kasturi change as well; she is ashamed of her earlier prejudices, of her hostility, she regrets she had so misjudged her, she is contrite, as only Aru can be.

Aru and Rohit were, as Nagi once said to Kasturi, born to be parents. And as parents, they move into another life, a family life built on the rock of their feelings for each other; they discover another world, one in which everything is subordinated to the needs of the children. Yes, children, for little Balakrishna joins the family soon. Just the two of us is not enough, Aru had thought. She knows now that it was not enough for *her*. In caring for their children together, Aru and Rohit find a greater certainty about themselves, they uncover a new face of love.

Life is not easy for Aru with her work and two children. It is a huge blow to her and Nagma when Surekha tells them she has been offered a judgeship of the High Court and that she has accepted. (And therefore Raghavan, they realize.) They are delighted for her, of course, they rejoice that there will be a woman—a woman like her—on the bench. But in the next instant comes the woeful thought: how will we manage? What will we do without her? In time they learn, they discover, that it is always possible to manage. Aru remembers the question she had once asked Premi, 'However did you manage, Premimavshi?' Now she knows the answer. By constant juggling. She feels like a juggler juggling many balls with her two hands, and somehow, miraculously, never dropping any of them.

Gopal learns that he can find peace, not in stillness, but in movement. He is constantly moving between his home in the mountains and the family home; he comes home whenever his daughters want him, or when he wants to see them, his grandchildren and Kasturi. Seema is the first of his children to visit him. He is amazed at the ease with which she fits into the spartan surroundings. Her tall elegant figure, striding as easily on the hill roads as if she has lived there all her life, soon becomes a familiar sight; people stop staring at her, she is accepted as Professor saab's daughter. Kasturi and Gopal live their separate lives, but when they meet, it is clear to everyone that they are together. Gopal has visited Jogipura, he has met Kasturi's family, he knows they look at him with some suspicion, with a little disapproval, he also knows he can take it. So can Kasturi. Kasturi and Gopal, too, are, like Aru and Rohit, discovering a new face of love.

Charu continues to yearn for home and Hrishi continues to talk of coming back 'soon, some time soon'. His parents live in hope. So do Anil and Premi. They have yielded to Nikhil's wishes and allowed him to take time off, to travel for a year, after which, he said to them, he will decide what to do. He wants to rough it, he told them, and added that he does not want them to worry about him. Premi has schooled herself not to ask questions, not to be anxious, but to wait for him to contact them. Which he does, though not as often as they would have liked; but they don't complain. And so they live in hope.

And Kasturi, after learning about her ex-husband's death, waits for the right time to approach her son. Perhaps I will be able to talk to him, perhaps he will accept me, she thinks. The hope of meeting him lights up her days, it comforts her nights. She too lives in hope.

The truth is that it is only hope, hope even more than love, which can lighten the burden of parentage, it is hope, much more than love, which makes it possible for us to live, to go on living.

Acknowledgements

A Matter of Time, an earlier novel of mine, contained some vague glimpses of the future. I left it there, but the characters didn't forget my promise to reveal their future and, years later, came knocking at my door. And so *Shadow Play,* which takes up their story about ten years later.

The line quoted on Page 116 is by Seamus Heaney and comes from *Voices from Lemnos.*

There are so many people who have unstintingly given me their time when I wanted some information, that it would be impossible for me to name them all. I will just say 'thank you' to all of them.